Velveteen

Velveteen

DANIEL MARKS

Delacorte Press

Text copyright © 2012 by Daniel Marks
Jacket photograph copyright © 2012 by Rustam Syunyakov

All rights reserved. Published in the United States by Delacorte Press,
an imprint of Random House Children's Books,
a division of Random House, Inc., New York.

Delacorte Press is a registered trademark and the colophon
is a trademark of Random House, Inc.

Visit us on the Web! randomhouse.com/teens

Educators and librarians, for a variety of teaching tools,
visit us at RHTeachersLibrarians.com

Library of Congress Cataloging-in-Publication Data is available upon request.

ISBN 978-0-385-74224-5 (hc)
ISBN 978-0-375-99051-9 (lib. bdg.)
ISBN 978-0-307-97432-7 (ebook)

The text of this book is set in 11-point Galliard.
Book design by Trish Parcell

Printed in the United States of America

10 9 8 7 6 5 4 3 2 1

First Edition

For Wayne Henry,
the original storyteller in the family

Velveteen

Chapter 1

When Velveteen Monroe pictured Bonesaw's house—
and she did, more often than could be considered healthy—
blood striped the paint a muddy reddish-brown, internal
organs floated in jars of formaldehyde, and great big taxidermy crows leered from branches that twisted from the
wall like palsied arms.

Velvet always did have a vivid imagination. It was part of
her charm.

But she'd never have guessed that the first thing to jump
out at her in the murderer's dank living room *wouldn't be* a
human-bone coffee table cluttered with the latest issues of
Sociopath Weekly and *Insanity Fair*, dog-eared and swollen
with scribbled Post-its like her mom's *Cooking Light* magazines, nor the killer himself, wild-eyed and clad in a blood-
spattered rubber apron, growling maniacally.

He wasn't there at all.

The first thing Velvet noticed was a dangerously normal Kleenex cozy with the words "Home Sweet Home" cross-stitched into its side. As if there were anyone sweet dwelling in that boxy, bland farmhouse.

Bonesaw had dropped the ball on macabre creativity. It's like he never got the text message. When a serial killer decorates his home, it's his duty to opt for, at the very least, a moderately freaky and off-kilter, if not deranged, design scheme.

Everybody knows that.

It's Psychopath 101.

The couch and chairs were as sandy brown as the paint job and plainly arranged rather than all backward or spotted with gore like you might expect of a properly insane decorator. The carpet was clearance-sale beige and just the slightest bit threadbare in a meandering path that led to the old-fashioned swinging kitchen door. The only thing remotely weird was an alabaster ashtray the size of a hubcap, with a half-eaten peanut butter and jelly sandwich stubbed-out in the middle instead of a cigarette butt.

Velvet's eyes lit on a giant TV—not one of those LCDs, but the other kind, with the big tube in the back—teetering atop a small chest. One of the stand's doors hung open just a crack, and something twinkled from its murky depths like a lonely star. She reached out and swung the door open on its squeaky hinges, half expecting to see a knife collection of the variety sold on home shopping networks.

"Look at all of you." Velvet cocked an eyebrow as she peered inside. "Lined up like toy soldiers."

Bonesaw collected salt and pepper shakers. Lots and lots of them.

Mexican guys in sombreros, turtles with top hats and canes, and even a pair of Oreos with bites taken out of them—though how delicious cookies were related to salt and pepper was beyond Velvet.

"Correction," she mumbled. "*Used to* collect them."

Velvet snatched a pair of hideous cacti, the pickle color having faded into a pale, sickly lime from age or, maybe, Bonesaw's relentless polishing. She launched them across the room, where one shattered into a hundred pieces and the other dug into the drywall, jutting from it like a diseased tooth. A couple of cockeyed chickens were next to get the fastball treatment, followed by the rest of the animal-shaped dispensers. They exploded against the back of the front door, salting and peppering the carpet with tiny shards of porcelain but no actual salt and pepper.

The cabinet emptied, Velvet clamped her fingers under the edge of the coffee table and heaved it forward onto its top, sending the magazines flapping across the room and the giant ashtray thudding to the floor. The peanut butter and jelly dropped away as the mammoth disk of alabaster rolled off on its side, ridges beating a rhythm across the thin pile of the carpet. It collided with the chest, and the TV rocked precariously before settling back onto its base.

Velvet cocked her head to the side; black waves of hair fell over her shoulder and cast a shadow across her face. She quickly tucked a lock behind her ear and assessed the situation for maximum destruction. A slow grin carved its way across her lips, as jagged as a jack-o'-lantern's.

"That won't do, will it?"

She spun, kicking the chest with her full weight, and watched with glee as the TV toppled to the floor with a bang. The screen exploded satisfyingly, spraying the carpet with tiny splinters of TV glass that twinkled like morning dew. The booming echoed through the small house exquisitely, the sound defiling every normal-as-white-bread corner.

If you overlooked the vandalism, the house was the kind of place where anyone could have lived.

Even the killer of four high school girls from New Brompfel Heights, New Jersey.

That crapload of crazy had all started the summer before Velvet's senior year, when Misha Kohl hadn't shown up at home after getting wasted at a kegger, but instead appeared eight days later in several different ziplock freezer bags down by the river. The town had gone shit-bag crazy over that. Curfews had been instated. Buddy-ups for the kids whose houses didn't warrant bus stops. Cameras pointed at the playgrounds like owls on the hunt for woodland scamperers.

Velvet had been pretty sure Bonesaw wasn't a scamperer.

Those cameras hadn't been about catching the serial killer anyway. They'd been about parents pretending their teenage girls were playing on swing sets rather than holing up in some sweaty basement, dodging boys' grabby hands.

Totally delusional.

Despite an obvious love of thick eyeliner, eighties Goth music, and giving her mother heart palpitations, Velvet hadn't been particularly interested in the Bonesaw case at the time. She would have, if pressed, admitted to a certain fascination with sociopaths, and she had spent more than a few "library enrichment" hours scouring the *Encyclopedia of Tragedy and Mayhem*, but a few missing girls didn't really thrill her as much as you'd think.

Sure, Ted Bundy was kind of hot if you squinted really hard, but he wasn't nearly as extraordinary-looking as his "survivors" always claimed on those History Channel psycho-killer shows. Velvet's interests didn't have anything to do with romanticizing psychotic personalities, anyway. What intrigued her was the whole disconnectedness-from-emotions "thing" that unites all true sociopaths, like they're part of a Moose lodge or a fantasy football league. She'd been accused of the same behavior on more than one occasion (the disconnectedness, not participating in a ridiculous pretend sports thing). Whether she was guilty of having the symptoms was debatable. Lord knows the counselors at her school were happy to discuss what they termed her "oppositional defiance" at *every* parent conference *ever*.

Velvet's thoughts on that had been consistent, clear, and resounding.

Two big middle fingers to everyone involved.

The counselors should have been more interested in the actual sociopaths in the neighborhood, rather than playing junior psychiatrists with her school records. Why couldn't they have been like everyone else in New Brompfel Heights and fixated on Bonesaw like he was a new fad diet? Because, seriously. People were obsessing over the case like it was the itchiest mosquito bite known to man.

Eventually Velvet was, too. But it turned out that someone

very close to her had to make Bonesaw's cut in order for him to grab her attention.

Very close.

Which brings us back to busting up houses.

And in particular the houses of serial killers.

No matter how exhilarating destruction can be—and to Velvet it had always been that rarest high—things have a tendency to become boring over time.

A little stale.

For example, today, when Velvet crept back in on what would be her twentieth breaking-and-entering charge, the furnishings were even more boring because she recognized each and every one, and Bonesaw never replaced anything she broke, which essentially stripped the fun out of fucking his shit up. No more salt and pepper shakers, no ashtrays, and even the TV had been replaced by a crappy clock radio. She could flip his coffee table only so many times before it just seemed futile. Luckily, she'd thought of a way around this little problem.

Velvet strode through the living room, past the only two flingable objects that she avoided—a leaden urn and a framed photograph of someone she assumed was Bonesaw's mother, the woman's wrinkles stretched smooth by a severe chignon. Velvet had opened the urn once and found ashes inside. Until then, she'd always thought cremation got rid of the whole body, but little pieces of bone stuck up from the gray powder like a tiny shadowed diorama of a graveyard, ivory tombstones pegging the ashen soil.

Best to leave that alone, she'd thought.

Bonesaw's kitchen was a sterile place, plain except for bright yellow café curtains hanging in the window above the steel sink and a stained coffee mug sitting on the counter. A bleach smell nearly overwhelmed the space, bringing to mind hospital wards and Laundromats, and the linoleum, a hideous tan with pink sparkles, was probably clean enough to eat off.

Velvet crossed the room, swung open the refrigerator door, and leaned in. As usual, row upon row of butcher paper packages lined the chilly shelves, each marked in Bonesaw's meticulously neat penmanship.

Ground beef. Porterhouse. Linguica.

There was never any milk or butter, and, worst of all, no cheese. Velvet missed cheese and just for a moment wondered whether the guy was lactose intolerant, before she remembered that she didn't give a crap about him or his dietary restrictions. What the refrigerator lacked in dairy it made up for in condiments. The door was full of steak sauces and catsup—not ketchup—mango chutney, and that disgusting green junk you're supposed to put on lamb, because who doesn't love neon crap on their food? The amount of meat the guy consumed was frightening.

Velvet had always hated meat and how it sat in your stomach like a brick, though she couldn't for the life of her turn down a taco.

Funny how things worked.

She jarred the refrigerator shelves loose, clanging them against the sparkling interior. The meat packages thudded to the floor, skidded across the linoleum like hockey pucks, and settled under the small bistro set in the corner. The ones nearby she stomped on, squishing the raw meat out through the tears in the paper. Ground beef smooshed onto the floor like a curl of bloody toothpaste.

"Have a nice supper, Ron," she said, and laughed.

Her eyes lit on the sink stopper—the reason she'd bothered to come in the first place. She dropped it into the drain and flipped on the faucet. Water gurgled and spat into the metal sink, slowly rising. He was going to be pissed, she thought. With any luck, he'd have an aneurysm and die when he saw the flood. After snatching a few hand towels, Velvet crouched and shoved them around the base of the back door, a makeshift sandbagging in reverse.

She lounged on one of the bistro chairs, crossed her arms, and appraised her work. The water coursed over the lip of the sink, spreading across the counters and waterfalling onto the linoleum. It was almost pretty.

Several minutes passed, and the water grew from a puddle to a nice destructive lake, spreading under the kitchen door to soak the dining room carpet in a big soppy half-moon.

Velvet wished she had a latte—it was definitely a latte moment.

Instead, she glanced out the window and gasped.

In the backyard sat a silver minivan, perfect for hauling groceries from the supermarket, grass-stained kids to and from soccer practice, and several teen girls to a shed in the back of an isolated farmhouse for some not-so-wholesome slicing and dicing.

Velvet's eyes snapped past it to a tin-roofed outbuilding sitting squat in the thin slice of pasture. A dense forest towered behind it like a castle battlement. She shook off the heavy weight of dread that always fell on her at the sight of the shed and replaced it with hate. If Velvet could count on anything, it was access to that particular emotion, especially when it came to Ron Simanski.

That was his real name.

As far as Velvet could tell, the guy seemed to lead a perfect existence—for a complete nut-job with a meat obsession. He worked all day at the local Round Up Grocery, packing away meats in white paper or those Styrofoam trays that pop and break like communion wafers. Clearly it was only training for the big leagues.

"What are you doin' home, Ron?" she muttered to herself.

Velvet bolted from her chair. It slid out behind her and banged against the wall as she passed into the backyard. Dewy weeds and grass, weeks overdue for a mowing, barely registered her movement. She peered through the van windows, which were clean, of course, just as spotless as the kitchen.

A glint of sunlight sparked off the shed's tin roof.

"Don't be back there," Velvet said aloud, the words swallowed up in the late-afternoon mist.

She tried to tell herself that there was a possibility that the killer had merely gone shopping—presumably for more meat . . . or condiments—and that he'd for some reason felt the need to circle around the front of the house and enter that way, despite the route being completely inconvenient and ridiculous. *It could happen,* she thought. *Right?*

As if in reply, curls of dead leaves from the autumn maple

skittered across the weedy yard like rats. They piled against the tiny outbuilding, rustling as though trying to speak. The sounds of metal grating against metal echoed across the yard. Without even looking in the smoky window in the back of the shed, she knew what the killer was doing—sharpening his tools, scraping his big thumb over the blades.

Knives. Cleavers. Those little curved paring instruments with loops on the end.

A shiver ran through her, and she nearly backed away, considered running.

What good will that do? she thought. *Bastard will just keep on doing it.*

Velvet stepped into the shed.

Bonesaw was resting against his workbench, relaxed and confident, his white uniform coat spattered with blood as dry as clay, and open to his bare chest. His tattoo was clearly visible, a heart with a ribbon coiled around it, inscribed with the words *And now for something completely different.*

The phrase crept up Velvet's spine like a freshly spawned brood of baby spiders. If Bonesaw had been able to see her, it would have appeared that she shimmered in the air like ice crystals in a fog. But he couldn't, of course.

The last time he'd seen her was the day he'd killed her.

A tallish guy and absolutely, positively too normal-looking, Ron wore his standard brown hair cropped close to his skull, and he had bland metal-framed glasses that cast only the slightest shadow across the apples of his cheeks. He was neither good-looking nor ugly, not tall or short. He was a little doughy around the waist, and his nose had a point to it that poked its way into Velvet's dreams some nights. But other than that, Ron Simanski was so average that you'd never even notice him until he was on you.

Velvet hadn't.

He coughed then, a phlegmy rattle that bounced off the walls, interrupting her trip down memory lane, just as she'd begun to relive the miserable day he'd abducted her. Velvet hoped the cough was a symptom of something incapacitating, the beginnings of tuberculosis or lung cancer. Ebola. A disease that'd knock Bonesaw on his ass.

When she glanced up at him again, a chill blew straight through her. His eyes bored into her, black with something—lust, she suspected—and the fear coursed through her veins like fever.

"Uh . . ." The sound escaped her mouth like air leaking from a tire.

A sinister grin played at the corners of his lips, twitched there like an electrocution. The smile was all too familiar to Velvet, and she felt the inevitable freak-out coming. A train ready to derail.

News at eleven.

He wasn't looking at her. How could he be? It's not like she was visible. Her heart sank, and her carefully cultivated anger disappeared, replaced by a quaking dread. Velvet knew what she was about to see before she spun to look at the old-fashioned school desk bolted into the floor in the corner.

A girl.

Younger than Velvet had been when Simanski had taken her, maybe fourteen or fifteen. She was tied to the desk with fishing line; the line ringed her, making her entire outfit (and skin) look like wide-wale corduroy. Her hair hung limply around her placid, pasty face.

"Holy shit, Ron! Another one?" The alarm was gone in an instant, replaced with comfortable fury. Velvet started to run the numbers.

Bonesaw never kept a girl longer than a week.

Misha Kohl. Sandra Barry. Hanna Johannsen.

Velveteen Monroe.

One week. Every time.

As dependable as a monthly period.

Velvet circled the girl, scanning her exposed skin for bruising, for marks. The only thing she could find was a milky crust dried at the corners of the girl's lips like a cold sore—the residue of whatever it was he drugged them with.

This one was new.

Brand-new. Fresh. Velvet was sure that was how Bonesaw saw her, just like the packs of hamburger floating in Lake Kitchen, complete with an expiration date. Just like the others Velvet had happened upon since her death. Over the next week there'd be no food, only a little water, and zero bathroom breaks. The abrading would start soon—Ron loved his cruel nutmeg grater.

Then the cutting.

Dammit!

Velvet paced the room, stabbing the killer with furious glares. If she'd only been able to haunt Simanski the day before, given him something to tweak out about other than his psychotic urges, maybe she could have stopped this one. She was sure she'd managed to derail a few of his abductions simply by providing him with vandalism to clean up. He certainly wouldn't have found the time to stalk and abduct the poor girl if he'd been busy bailing out his house like a sinking rowboat.

But that didn't matter now. She was on deadline.

Velvet crouched beside the girl and ran her fingers carefully over her hair, making sure not to displace any and freak her out or draw the attention of Bonesaw's obsessive gaze. "I'll take care of you, whoever you are," she whispered. "I'm going to get you out of here and away from this son of a bitch. Don't worry."

Those last words were ridiculous, she knew. How could the girl do anything but worry? Even now, as subdued as his victim was, her jaw was clenched, her knuckles white in their death grip on the edges of the old wooden school desk. Tensing up for the battle.

"That's good," she whispered into the girl's ear. "You're smart to prepare yourself for the worst."

And then, even though she was certain the girl couldn't hear her, Velvet murmured to herself, "Especially if I screw this up."

She turned and glowered into Ron's eyes. Madness floated there like stray lashes. The same evil she'd witnessed for one hellish week, all those months ago, still lingered there, fevered, septic. "And you!" she spat, her voice escalating to a scream. "I'll have you know I don't have time for this bullshit. I'll sort you out, Bonesaw. This is the last girl you get to bring to this pit, and I guarantee you, you won't get any satisfaction from her! None!"

Velvet's fingers curled into claws. She wanted to tear into

him, dig his eyes out, make him feel every ounce of pain he'd meted out on Hanna and Sandra and Misha Kohl. Make him hurt.

Make him know he hadn't won.

She knew it would be a battle. She'd tried to put an end to it all before, to end Bonesaw. To kill him. Make him kill himself. Those attempts had been a mixed bag of successes and failures. She'd saved his last one, the redheaded girl—Alexa, she believed her name was—and the blonde with the broken glasses, and the one who hummed constantly. But the closest Velvet had come to offing the monster himself had been a small fire she'd managed to set outside Ron Simanski's bedroom door. The man's overly efficient smoke detectors had alerted him to the danger almost immediately, leaving her sour and screaming obscenities.

Velvet gave one last glance toward this new girl and was satisfied that she had a little time left before the bad stuff happened. With the flood in his house, she'd done enough to keep the maniac busy for a while, enough to keep him off his victim.

It was time to go back.

"It might take a while," she said, turning back to the slumped figure. "Just a little bit. But I promise you. I promise . . ."

Her voice trailed off.

In Velvet's mind, there was no question she'd be able to save the girl's life. Help her escape, at the very least. She'd saved three now. If there was one thing she was better at than vandalism, it was extraction. Of course, living people were more difficult to deal with than their spirits. Trickier.

Things had gotten messy. But that wasn't the point. Bone-saw didn't get to play his games. Not while she was around.

She pushed back the memories of how quickly the cutting would start. The slow gouging that would leave tunnels in the girl's flesh. She wouldn't think about that.

She couldn't.

"There's a surprise waiting for you in the house, you sick fuck," she finally said. "And one of these days—" She drew a make-believe blade up her wrist to her elbow. "Local butcher commits suicide. Too bad. So sad."

Velvet passed through the shed wall and into the twilight, mumbling, "He was such a quiet man. Polite. We never suspected a thing."

Chapter 2

Velvet lingered in the burgeoning night long enough to watch Bonesaw complete his ritual padlocking of the shed. He pressed his body up against the metal door, as close as a lover. Listening—as if any abductee in their right mind would start maneuvering out of their bindings the *second* their abductor left the room. Then, glancing around suspiciously, he stomped back to the farmhouse. Once inside, he began to bellow. The sounds of plates clattered against walls, shattering, then splashing. All of it was muffled but oddly comforting.

He'd found her mess.

She wished she could manage a smile, but the weight of her duty to Ron's new victim really messed with her vandalism high. So she trudged across the pasture, past wooden fences and cows that shivered as she passed through their hulking bodies—far enough that she could no longer hear the killer's screams. Beyond the boundaries of Simanski's property, a dying giant towered over the rest of the forest, an oak tree, bark gray and branches bare, ribboned in dense tentacles of ivy. Velvet stood before it and huffed, ankles deep in spiky ferns with fronds like crooked emerald fingers. She braced herself against the tree, trying to compose herself, trying to shake off the anger and horror she'd picked up in the shed.

She needed to calm down.

Way down.

When Velvet passed from the daylight back into purgatory, there was more than a little finesse involved. She needed to concentrate and construct the image of the other side. The alley. From there, she'd need to move quickly, blend into the crowd before they noticed that she'd just appeared. She didn't want anyone to ask questions about where she'd come from. People asked too many questions. In fact, most of them never shut up.

Velvet had to play it cool.

If anyone had reason to accuse her of haunting, they'd do it without hesitation. Petty, nosy souls, the lot of them. If the travel did not benefit purgatory, it would be seen as frivolous, dangerous, and, worst of all, traitorous in the eyes of the powers that be.

Velvet couldn't have that.

A blackened crack ran up the length of the big oak, the scar of a lightning strike that had done more than kill the tree. In this case, it had torn straight through the veil between the world of the living and the dead. It had paved a road—a secret one, sure, but a road nonetheless—from the glen to a neighborhood in purgatory. A road, Velvet hoped, that would never be found by anyone else.

She gave her arms and legs a little shake, trying to work out the kinks from the tension foisted upon her by Bonesaw's addiction to awfulness. She needed to be calm, centered. Velvet sought out the imagery necessary to divine what was called a pull-focus—kind of like dropping a digital pin on a GPS—a triangulation of visuals from the other side. First, she imagined the tight gray walls of the alley. Then, the small box she kept there with its tattered sticker—the words worn to shadows, meaningless, yet for some reason intriguing—her wadded-up clothes blossoming from inside. The final image was distant but key: a thin sliver of the main street flickering in the gaslight.

Stretching her fingers toward the thin black crevice, Velvet felt the City of the Dead reach toward her with its familiar pull. It was as though she'd pressed her palm to the bathtub drain and was being sucked close. Her diaphanous fingers began to elongate, deteriorating into curling wisps of smoky thread that streamed into the crack. Her arms were next, the opaque flesh unraveling like yarn from a sweater.

Velvet clenched her eyes shut and ground her teeth.

No matter how many times she made the journey, she never got used to being torn apart. Disassembled. Even the word reminded her of what happened to Bonesaw's victims. Shaking off the thought, she fell forward, rushing through somewhere thin and windy. She pictured a vast pipeline, though she knew this was just her imagination. No one had any clue what lay between the daylight and purgatory . . . except maybe the flies. But it's way too early to gross you out with their story. Suffice it to say, those nasty black bugs seem to know their way around a crack in the universe.

The buzzing was maddening.

There were times when Velvet thought she caught glimpses of vast caverns, as black as soot. But the images came so briefly and never lingered longer than the several seconds it took to travel.

A moment later—or maybe it was an hour—Velvet was spat out into the dimly lit cobblestone alley. Where light filtered in from the street several yards away, she could barely make out shapes of souls rushing past, arms loaded with packages, chatting to their companions, moving on to somewhere very important, no doubt.

And most likely, not just returning from a prohibited jaunt into the daylight.

Velvet snatched her clothes from the wooden box she'd stashed in the darkest corner of the alley. She supposed there was a chance that one day she'd come back and find the box empty, as scarce as fashionable clothes were in the afterlife—stolen by some urchin scouring the alleys for castoffs or something. But so far it hadn't happened, and she hoped it never would. Nothing would give away a secret haunting like showing up in public naked.

One of the biggest sucks about going to purgatory instead of somewhere good like Hawaii or a college party was that most souls couldn't manage to bring anything but themselves through the cracks. Clothes included. Which was lame, because when Velvet was alive, she had the most amazing pair of Fluevog boots—toes as pointy as a pair of switchblades. Passage through the cracks stripped a soul of everything but its essence. It's like this: Souls are made up of memories, which don't look like anything in the daylight, but in purgatory, the memories are burning white coils, firework fuses. They thread through a soul so tightly and brilliantly that when a person first pops through a crack, sometimes they're so bright you have to look away. In purgatory, the ether of a soul is transformed into flesh. On that first day, they're given clothes by the station guides and taught to apply a thick coat of ash to pretty much everywhere that clothes don't touch.

Souls look a whole lot like their human selves. Dirty, but human.

Or human-*ish*.

All you really need to know is this: If you ever have the misfortune to end up in purgatory, you're going to arrive at the station naked. And yeah, it has the very real possibility of being embarrassing as hell.

Velvet had learned to keep a box handy for storing her clothing. There were no guides at this crack. And hopefully, there never would be.

She stabbed her feet and legs into her torn jeans, wrapped herself in the warm peacoat, and laced her feet into the combat boots. She grabbed a few handfuls of ash from the bottom of the box and rubbed it on her face and hands, and ran big clumps of it through her hair until she barely shone. She glanced at the thin sliver of black sky above her and watched as what looked like stars tore by with long trailing tails.

Velvet sneered. "Show-offs."

Eyes narrowing to slits, she crept toward the opening of the alley, watching as the souls scuttled down the steep, almost suicidal slant of the street. She clung to the deepest shadows—no sense drawing attention where it wasn't wanted. Two glowing eyes staring out of the darkness, while common in a city of dead people, can still be startling if you're not expecting it. But as she reached the mouth of the alley, the other souls simply trudged on down the hill, wrapped up in their early evening business and blissfully unaware of the delinquent in their midst.

The passage let out between two shops. On one side, an advisor's office was shuttered up, a Closed sign hung in its tiny window. Velvet never gave advisors much thought. She knew souls were interested in learning about themselves, growing, resolving their remainders, and all that. But she figured those people were just looking for a way out. An early release from prison, if that's what purgatory was.

She had too much on her mind for any of that. It seemed frivolous, too. Why not just do your job and leave well enough alone? You move on when you're meant to. At least, that's what Velvet believed.

She crouched and quickly backed into the crowd as though she'd been retrieving something from the ground. She nearly bumped into a very smartly dressed woman in a dark suit and pillbox hat. The woman's face undulating in the flickering gaslight that hung nearby.

"Excuse me. I was just—" Velvet stammered, figuring she'd need some excuse. But the woman merely rolled her glowing eyes and scuttled away on heels far too high for the uneven cobblestones of the Latin Quarter, her ankles popping.

A quick scan of the other passing faces revealed none of Velvet's acquaintances, thankfully, so she took a deep breath and turned the corner, only to have to fling herself back into the alley, falling onto her butt with an aching thud. That souls could still feel physical pain was a cruel joke.

A rush of souls muscled past her, waving banners and brandishing torches like angry townspeople chasing the Frankenstein monster. Black smoke ribboned from the flames, blending into the inky forever night. Their expressions were uniform, lots of glowering and sneering and hate.

"Down with the station agent!" they shouted venomously. "Depart! Depart!"

Velvet shook her head as one of the fanatics stopped short and plastered a flyer on the stone wall, crimson ink glaring and glue dribbling from it like tree sap.

"You ought to join us, you know." He nodded casually, eyes blazing in his head with the kind of fire only someone completely brainwashed could muster. "Our way is freedom."

"Dude!" Velvet bristled, readying for an argument. "Do you know who I am? What I do?"

The man shrugged and bolted back into the throng. Within a few seconds, their crazed numbers thinned and their shouts dwindled to distant whispers. The street's regular inhabitants were left shaken. They gathered in small groups to discuss the Departurists' intrusion—an otherwise pleasant purgatory evening ruined.

Velvet changed her mind about the advisors next door. If the alternative was joining a crazy cult, more power to those poor souls who want to simply talk it out.

She pushed herself off the ground and brushed the ash from her clothes before taking the corner again.

The building that made up the opposite wall from the advisor's office housed the Paper Aviary. Big picture windows clouded with age were crammed with the most amazing origami birds. Not mere cranes folded to resemble their counterparts in the daylight, the birds perching inside looked real—like for real, real. Velvet was particularly fascinated by the current display. Rows of crows lined up on thick black wire were glaring down at a lifelike diorama of a small schoolhouse and playground and a smartly dressed woman sitting on a bench. The folds were so tight in each of the little miracles, that they disappeared into the bodies, becoming feathers, beaks, even tiny talons; the creases hung perfectly from the schoolhouse like real clapboard; and she didn't even know how it was possible to make such a lifelike person in miniature. It was simply amazing.

She recognized the scene instantly.

Alfred Hitchcock's *The Birds.*

Velvet's mother was a movie freak—one of the few things they had in common. Almodóvar, Jarmusch, Kubrick, and, for sure, Hitchcock. While most of her friends had been out seeing the big Hollywood blowup piece-of-crap movie of the week, Regina Monroe had carted her grim little daughter off to the Orpheus for some "cultural enlightenment." She was fond of the word "Philistine" and mismatched terms such as "mass-market under-education," whatever those meant. And she often curled her lip as they'd drive straight past the multiplex to the tiny theater with busted seats and old popcorn. But she'd been right about the movies, and *The Birds* was one of Velvet's favorites.

When she looked past the scene and deep into the shop, Velvet jumped.

A pair of glowing eyes pierced the darkness. Velvet very nearly turned to run, before Mr. Fassbinder stepped from the depths of the back room and into the lantern light. He grinned pleasantly and crossed the room toward the door. It opened with a scrape, a wave of ashes roiling at its base.

"Good evening, Ms. Velvet. You like the new diorama?" A special glint glowed from under Werner Fassbinder's felt hat. Today he wore a fedora; on other days when she visited, he'd tip a porkpie in a funky little way. Like a beatnik, she thought they were called, or a hipster, maybe. He wore his wavy black hair a little long, just brushing the wool shoulders of his peacoat. His old-fashioned style gave a hint as to his true age—though he looked to be only in his late twenties. Velvet wasn't certain how old Mr. Fassbinder was, exactly, but she couldn't bring herself to call him Werner, despite his many requests.

Velvet grinned. "It's fantastic. I love that part of the movie, too. So creepy."

"Hitchcock had a way with tension," Mr. Fassbinder agreed.

She nodded, remembering the flocks of birds gathering behind Melanie Daniels, the snotty-ass main character, who totally deserved to get pecked in the head. Each time the camera panned, there'd be more and more, until she turned to see that they were everywhere.

Very Hitchcock.

"Is that why you chose this scene?" she asked. "Are you tense?"

Mr. Fassbinder shrugged and tucked a long lock of hair behind his ear with heavily bandaged fingers. "I don't know. Maybe. Or maybe it's a statement about all the hustle and bustle we've brought into our afterlife."

Velvet cocked her brow. "If you say so."

"But you are one to talk about being tense." Mr. Fassbinder's eyes crinkled sympathetically. "You look wound up tighter than a grandfather clock."

"Do I?" Velvet flinched. She hadn't meant to convey anything in her body language, but when she looked down, her fists were balled up tight. She spread her fingers quickly.

Mr. Fassbinder shook his head, wrapped his arm around her shoulders, and led her toward the door. "Come inside and take a closer look. I have some parakeets today. These actually chirp."

"Really?" Velvet stopped, and her eyes narrowed suspiciously.

"Would I lie?" he asked, a sinister but familiar grin twisting the corners of his mouth.

They had played this game before, she the unwitting victim to his creepy shopkeeper—sick, considering Velvet's history. But it was all in good fun. Mr. Fassbinder was the kindest man she'd ever met, and he always knew how to cheer her up. Better than anyone else, it seemed. He was definitely attractive—in that distinguished teacher sort of way—and when he was younger, was exactly the kind of boy Velvet would have sought if she'd lived to do so, but those thoughts were fleeting. He was, after all, super old, and thus thinking about him that way made her feel creepy.

Creepier than usual.

Velvet giggled, triggering wild guffaws from Mr. Fassbinder as they stepped inside.

He hadn't been kidding about the parakeets.

The display tables, normally lined up in rows and packed to overflowing with birds of every imaginable variety, were pushed to the edges of the main room to make room for Mr. Fassbinder's masterpiece. A huge globe made of densely gathered black spikes and needles hung from the ceiling, as though a giant sea urchin had made its way from the ocean and somehow invaded the place. Pocking the sphere were little round alcoves, each home to one or two green birds with yellow breasts. Hundreds of black eyes all seemed to stare in her direction.

"Wow, that's insane." Velvet felt her hands creeping up to clutch her shoulders. The structure of the thing was really bothersome. It looked like a planet or a fortress. And the birds didn't seem happy there.

They seemed imprisoned.

"But wait." Mr. Fassbinder reached out—the bandages on his fingers spoke volumes about how much work had gone into the project—and tapped one of the spikes, sending a little quake through the nest. The birds responded by chirping wildly, tiny paper beaks quivering with their ululations.

26

The sound rolled over her, giving her goose pimples. The birds sounded alive. Each of the parakeets rocked back and forth as it sang; some even ruffled their feathers. Despite her reservations about the nest, Velvet couldn't deny the awesomeness. She applauded.

"But what is it?" she asked. "I've never seen anything like it."

"They're a very specific type. They're called monk parakeets, and they live communally. South American birds. The spikes are to defend against predators. It's really quite genius."

"So that's like their dormitory or something?"

"Exactly."

Dorm. The thought pinged around her head and triggered a memory. *Crap!*

Velvet stomped her foot. "Just remembered, I told a friend we would sit together at salon tonight, and I'm totally going to be late."

"Maybe you can come back tomorrow, then. Come by and I'll make you a special bird." Mr. Fassbinder's smile and the offer of one of his magnificent paper birds stripped the horror from Velvet's day.

She rushed forward and hugged him. "Absolutely. And we'll talk." She turned to walk away, but stopped and added, "About movies."

"Perfect!" Mr. Fassbinder waved. The thin strips of cotton woven around his paper-cut fingers fluttered in the air like ribbons.

Chapter 3

If you ever find yourself walking down a street in purgatory, the first thing you'll notice—once you stop sobbing—is a distinct lack of style, or maybe it's an abundance of style.

Too much style.

The buildings are either ramshackle and slightly askew but made of the finest Corinthian marble, or majestic and perfectly constructed from dense packs of cardboard shipping boxes or rolled newspaper bricks. It's definitely a hodge-podge of architecture, and the only constant is the color gray. Ashy mind-numbing gray.

Or it used to be.

The Departurists' bloodred handbills scarred the walls like gory bread crumbs trailing in the angry mob's wake. Velvet could hear the crowd still, their shouts echoing down the narrow streets like crows' cawing.

Talk of the revolution had been around for a while, mostly

as bitter grumbling in district courtyards and as bad poetry and spoken-word performances at nightly salons. But whether the protests had become as visible in districts beyond the Latin Quarter was unknown—news traveled slowly between the boroughs, due in no small part to the large walls separating the districts. Velvet wasn't particularly interested in what was happening in other parts of purgatory anyway. What filled her with piss and vinegar—to use one of her mother's sayings—was that the disenfranchised and obviously bitter had started to gather, organize, make a huge ruckus, and vandalize *her* street.

"*I'm* the vandal around here," she mumbled. "If anyone is going to tag up the place, it'll be me."

Of course, it'd been months since she'd seen a spray paint can this side of the veil, so that kind of fun was totally out of the question.

The whole district clung to the side of a massive, nameless mountain looming on the horizon, as dark as night. At its top, a grand old station stood, stony and gray, where a snowy cap might have been. Hundreds of sets of rails trailed from openings around the circumference of the building, like the tentacles of a Portuguese man-of-war. Wooden cars rattled up and down the tracks at all hours of the darkness, filled to overflowing with souls, old and new. So Velvet wasn't surprised when an abrupt rattle and clang echoed off the buildings and interrupted her growing anger toward the Departurists.

She stepped away from the pair of quivering rails embedded in the cobblestone as one of the wooden railcars rumbled into view. The souls inside the car were new arrivals.

Frightened glowing eyes gave them away; so did the poorly smeared, amateurish ash application on their faces. Rays of internal light shone from patches of un-ashed flesh as though they'd been spotted with mirrored tiles.

She didn't have time to dwell on what the arriving souls might be feeling. And besides, she knew all too well. She'd been where they are now, and it wasn't so great. Sure, they should just be happy there's an afterlife at all, that they get to go on in some fashion. Even if they've moved on to a place known for an eternal night and constant reminders that they aren't good enough for heaven, at least they weren't made into human bacon frying in Satan's big nonstick skillet.

She shook her head. It didn't do any good to be so judgmental.

They'd all been held back, after all. Velvet included.

These new souls would be met by their dormitory supervisors soon enough. Most of the buildings in purgatory were dorms of some kind, each filled with people who shared the same kind of work, or experience, or interest—salespeople, constructionists, paper workers, and the like.

In her case, Velvet lived with the rest of the small Salvage team in the Retrieval dormitory, a massive building that had a courtyard in the middle and that also housed the Collector crew's dorm. Her team was in charge of the search and rescue of wayward souls, whether held back in the daylight by accident or, as so often happened, by nefarious circumstances. A great deal of notoriety came with being a member of the Salvage team, and a little glory, which didn't help pass the time any but was nice, Velvet had to admit.

The Collector's job was—there's no delicate way to put it—to steal from the daylight so that souls in the darkness could have clothes on their backs, to snatch the very stuff purgatory was made of: stones, some metal, paper of all sorts, and random other stuff. Velvet didn't know the specifics of Collecting, but she'd been told that the Collectors have access to the largest cracks in purgatory, large enough to pull tangible objects through. Where these cracks were located was a closely guarded secret.

One Velvet would love to know, if only to be able to cross through with her Fluevog boots. Of course, there was a talent involved. In purgatory and in Retrieval, whether Salvaging souls or Collecting stuff, it always seemed to boil down to skilled labor and not merely simple tricks.

Nothing was ever simple.

Velvet pressed on down the hill, past massive facades of stone and paper and past gaslight globes that hung over the bustling souls' heads like lightbulbs of ideas. She quickened her pace, feet gliding over the sometimes slick stones. As the street opened up onto a plaza of activity, a giant square that she'd have to cross to reach her dorm, Velvet caught the edge of a cobblestone and took a header into a magazine stand. The rack nailed her in the chest with a jarring thud, and a flock of tabloids took flight around her and landed noisily on the ground.

"Crap!" she yelled, and then she fell to her knees and started stacking the magazines. "I'm so sorry. I shouldn't be in such a hurry. So clumsy, it's ridiculous!"

An elderly soul with knitting needles stuck like antennae

from a charcoal hair bun knelt beside Velvet, shuffling the rest of the magazines into a tidy pile. "It's fine, dear. Falling on the ground doesn't make them any less used than they were when the Collectors brought them back, does it?"

"I guess not." Velvet gave the woman a polite smile.

A dull ache in her chest where she'd smacked the rack brought her attention back to her injury, and she pulled the neck of her shirt open, just in time to see a squiggle of memory slip from a tiny wound like a worm. It flared brightly for the tiniest moment and then burned to ash. The gray husk floated in between her and the magazine seller before drifting into the crowd of night shoppers visiting the many kiosks around the square.

"So hard to hold on to," the old woman whispered.

"What?" Velvet asked.

"The memories. At least the pain reminds us of what it was like to be alive."

Velvet guessed that was true. But it still hurt like crap. She rubbed her chest and nodded, then rushed through the throng of souls toward her dorm.

In keeping with the deranged construction of the city, the columns on the facade of the Retrieval dormitory were askew. She imagined the Collectors breaking them from some forgotten ruin far off the beaten path of civilization and smuggling them here a long time ago, or not so long, or last week, even. Time was a strange thing when you were living in the same city as people who'd died hundreds of years ago and yesterday. Like one of Dalí's melting clocks, it seemed to stretch beyond the limits of believability into forever.

Sections of the dorm were littered with graffiti in all different languages. Cyrillic mingled with English lettering. Thai battled with Sanskrit for tag supremacy. There were even some bright pink kanji characters, as though the column pieces had made an around-the-world trip before settling in to decorate and hold up four floors of balconies.

Smoky windows spotted the facade like hundreds of little eyes, though you couldn't see into a single one. Not that there weren't plenty of people trying. Gossips and town criers always haunted the square in front of the dorm, sitting behind newspapers with ridiculously obvious eyeholes cut into them, or wearing sunglasses even though the City of the Dead was never brighter than a swampy pool on a moonless night. They waited for the most famous of the Latin Quarter's citizens, the Salvagers and the Collectors, to go in or out or to screw up, have arguments, anything that they could report on at any of the hundreds of nightly salons taking place around purgatory.

When she climbed the stairs to the enormous front doors, she found another flyer plastered there. On it, in big crimson letters: THE DEPARTURE IS COMING! And underneath, something Velvet hadn't noticed before—small, spidery handwriting, a tiny *a* and a *c*. Initials, maybe. The sight of them triggered the edge of a faint memory that vaporized like a puff of dust from a fallen hollow acorn husk before she could get ahold of it.

She tore the flyer from the door and crammed it into the pocket of her jeans, intent on bringing up the Departurists' demonstration to the station agent the next chance she got.

A clamor of voices rushed out as Velvet pulled open the tall double doors into a darkened alcove that led to a bustling courtyard. The nightly salon was already in progress.

"Dammit," she sighed. Luisa was going to be pissed.

The courtyard was packed with souls all facing a small stage at the far end. Someone—Bethany Cloud, she thought, though it was hard to tell from where Velvet stood in the shadows—was bleating out "Pretty Vacant" along with the Sex Pistols. Ironic, considering the girl was as dumb as a stick. That Bethany could drown out Johnny Rotten's violent vocals was less a testament to her talent than to the fact that her voice sounded like a rusty funicular. Just behind her on the stage, a boy rode a bike connected by a system of rods and gears to an old-time gramophone.

No one could ever accuse purgatory's souls of a lack of ingenuity.

Without electricity, the Collectors had to focus on finding simple entertainments. They couldn't play CDs, obviously, so along with clothes and books, you'd often find stacks of vinyl record albums on the returning wagons. Their house was the proud archive of a library of some really great punk and Goth music from the seventies and eighties.

"We're vacant!" Bethany growled. The crowd nodded, agreeing that, at least, Bethany most certainly was as blond as they come. Some of them even danced, glowing eyes bobbing in the dim light like lighters and cell phones at a real concert.

"You ain't kiddin'," Velvet mumbled, clipping off a giggle too silly for her social status in the room. She'd already drawn nods from the few people who'd seen her apparently not so stealthy entry.

She scanned the crowd of faces until her eyes fell on her best friend, Luisa, a raven-haired girl of about twelve sitting on her hands at a table near the stairs to the Salvage wing and watching the entry door intently, her eyes afire. She sat as far from the Collector wing as possible, which was their way. Salvagers and Collectors mixed about as well as oil and water. Salvagers didn't go near the other set of stairs—not because it was off-limits but because the Collectors were really douchey.

Particularly Isadora Lawrence and her gang of professional judgers.

As Velvet sidestepped chairs and excused herself through the courtyard, she not so surprisingly caught the devil-eyed glare of Isadora herself. Even while applauding Bethany in slow lazy claps, Isadora managed her patented sneer. Like a dog protecting its bone, she curled her vermillion-smeared lips back from her teeth. She even rolled her eyes.

Multitasking. That Isadora could manage facial expressions and complex hand movements at the same time was miraculous; any more than that and the girl would probably short a circuit.

Not conventionally beautiful by any sense of the word, Isadora did have some exotic qualities, and they drew nearly every boy to her. Something to do with her long blond hair (white in purgatory) and the fact that she'd supposedly sleep with just about any guy who'd look at her.

Isadora leaned in toward Shandie Charles, a pretty black

girl with long curly hair tucked up inside a satin top hat, and whispered something, pointing at Velvet. Both girls laughed riotously. Whispered. Laughed again.

Velvet wanted to launch herself over the rows of tables and beat them both until their nerve endings spilled from the wounds like escaped goldfish flopping on the floor, but just as her fingernails were starting to bore holes into her palms, the music stopped and she felt a tug at her sleeve.

"Where the hell have you been?" Luisa's eyes were cinched into threatening slits.

"I'm so sorry. I was walking. I lost track of time." She glanced back at Isadora, in time to see the putrid girl blow a snarky kiss. Velvet groaned.

Luisa was far too embittered to notice. "Seriously? Walking where?"

She had to think quickly; Luisa could smell a lie like a dog smells a bone. "To the park."

"Cherry Tree or Stationside?" The girl's eyes narrowed even more with scrutiny.

"Cherry Tree." Velvet knew a simple answer wouldn't be enough to stop Luisa's interrogation and quickly added, "I got to thinking about my mother and all the movies we used to go see. Are you through nagging?"

Luisa sucked at her teeth. A tiny menacing squeak escaped. "No."

Velvet shrugged, puffed out her chest like she'd seen boys do when they were ready to fight. "Bring it."

Luisa slipped deeply into the chair, her legs dangling and her back straight with annoyance. She continued to glare at Velvet with those chiding, angry eyes. "You better quit it with that crap. I don't save seats for just anyone, you know."

"Sorry," Velvet replied, instantly sheepish. "I'm totally a dumb-ass."

Luisa smirked and nodded. "Well, you're not normally late, so I'll let it slide this once. Next time, I'm whoopin' your butt."

Anyone else might have tasted Velvet's fist with a comment like that, but Luisa was her closest friend and was probably smarter than the rest of her whole team combined. Despite the girl's brains, she and her brother acted as the crew's poltergeists, the muscle of the team. Badasses. And more than any possibility of being beaten senseless by the girl, Velvet just didn't want to disappoint her.

She pulled a chair from under the table and eased into it. "So what did I miss up in this den of iniquity?" she asked with a wink.

"The usual. Readings, gossip, and . . . singing, if you call it that." Luisa flipped her hand toward the stage nonchalantly. "That one girl—the one whose name I can never remember—was on before brainiac up there."

"Renata?"

"Yeah. Her. She sang 'The Star Spattered Banner.'"

"'Spangled'?" Velvet offered.

"Whatever." Luisa crinkled her nose in Renata's direction. "With that lisp, it's hard to tell." She brightened as though just remembering something awesome. "You also missed Kipper trying to get Quentin laid, and irritating the shit out of me in the process."

Luisa slouched back in her chair, and Velvet noticed the apple-cheeked boy with a smug smile that curled on his face so intensely that his nose flared out like a bull's. He was a thick kid with linebacker shoulders and a crazy mop of comb-resistant hair that he always had to blow out of his eyes. Gary Kipness—Kipper to his friends—part-time Salvage trainer, mercenary, and resident gay playboy, was also a smart-ass and a horn dog and about to be the lucky recipient of Luisa's famous "knuckler."

His smirk turned into a grimace as the little girl pounded her fist into his thigh. "Dayum!" Kipper sang, rubbing his leg and glaring at Luisa. "What was that for?"

A satisfied grin spread across the little girl's face.

Kipper had been busy poking Quentin in the ribs and stabbing his thumb in the direction of someone across the room.

Quentin, eyes shielded by a sleepy worn-down expression and a mop of straight hair that seemed to always fall in his face as well, nodded in Velvet's direction before wincing forlornly back across the room at whomever he was mooning over that week. Quentin was constantly crushing, which was odd, considering he was totally girl-phobic and would break into the most entertaining panic attacks at the mere mention that someone was looking at him.

"Glad you could join us, *Velv*." Kipper leaned around and winked lasciviously. Despite his faults, he could be great fun, he never seemed short of a smart-alecky comment, and he was Quentin's best friend, so Velvet decided she wouldn't kick him until he stopped moving.

She grunted a response instead.

"I'm just sayin'. We hate to miss your bright cheery personality."

"Yeah, yeah," Velvet said, and turned her attention to the lanky redheaded kid, who held his face in his palms. "Is he bugging you, Ginge?"

Velvet rarely teased people directly unless they were close friends. She never saw the point of making fun of strangers—how could you possibly know enough about them to hit below the belt? Quentin she knew, and she was always up for ribbing her favorite redhead. Though out of the daylight, his was, like so many, a head full of gray hair.

"I'm not ginger; I'm strawberry blond," Quentin mumbled, and peeked through his fingers, eyes wandering back across the room.

Kipper followed his gaze. So did Velvet.

And was surprised to see that the girl he was pining for was sitting next to the most horrible girl in Collections. And not just an ordinary lackey—no. Velvet resisted the urge to hurl. Quentin's crush was Shandie, Isadora's lapdog in a top hat.

Figures, she thought. *Guys always want what they can't have.*

Always.

Quentin was the undertaker on Velvet's Salvaging team. It was a crappy enough way to spend one's time—raising the dead could be quite messy—but worse than that, an undertaker didn't have a chance with a Collector. It was a matter of principle. Sure, you could argue it shouldn't be that way; the Salvagers (of which an undertaker was a unique and deified member) and Collectors did some of the same stuff, after all. The Collectors Collected things—clothes, junk, lo-fi appliances. The Salvagers Salvaged things—souls, spirits, banshees, problems. But one team (the Salvagers) did get more attention than the other, and that left the Collectors noticeably bitter.

So, so very bitter.

Throw into the mix that the undertaker in question was super shy. Quentin couldn't string together enough words for a sentence when he was around a girl he liked. As long as Velvet had known the guy, he'd been stricken. This one time, she'd witnessed Quentin go full-on panic attack when Mandy Murdock winked at him. Velvet had nearly had to talk him down from a ledge on that one. In the end, Kipper had simply snatched him back to reality like a rag doll.

"Dude!" Kipper prodded now. "Just go talk to her. What's she going to do, bite?"

Quentin's brow arched hopefully. "Maybe?"

Luisa chuckled. Velvet shook her head.

"Listen," Kipper continued. "If you don't get some release soon, those blue balls are gonna go nuclear. Kaboom!"

Quentin groaned, his head dropping to the table. "Shut up, man."

When he looked up, the glare from his embarrassment broke through the ash on his cheeks like otherworldly freckles.

Velvet watched as Kipper opened his mouth, preparing for another volley against the poor kid, and she decided she couldn't take it. She reached behind Luisa and flicked him on the ear. "Knock it off, Kipper."

The mop-topped boy leaned forward, chin resting on his steepled index fingers like some mob consigliere. "You know, you could use some, too, Velvet. A boyfriend, I mean."

Luisa gasped but smirked wildly in Velvet's direction.

Kipper went on, pouting sympathetically, she guessed. "You seem so lonely." He shrugged. "And maybe you wouldn't be such a bitch."

"Maybe it'd make me a bigger one." She launched over the table and slugged his arm. "Besides. You'll have room to talk when you snare your own man."

Kipper stiffened. His mouth dropped open and he spat out an incredulous laugh. "I get plenty," he said defensively. "Besides, you don't get to make those comparisons, Little Miss I-Don't-Wanna-Be-Tied-Down."

"Yeah," Quentin mumbled, not at all convincingly.

Velvet huffed, shook off their ridiculousness. "Shut up already. If I need your advice, I'm sure I can find it on a bathroom wall . . . along with your number."

"Are you callin' me a slut?" Kipper glanced back and forth among the group. "Is she calling me a slut?"

Nods. All the way around.

Velvet shrugged. "Like that's news."

"Oh," Kipper said, as though it had just occurred to him. "I really am a slut."

Luisa piped up, slamming her fist on the table. "Hey! I wanna be the slut!"

Quentin nodded. "Me too."

Velvet leaned into the table, eyes passing from each member of her team, except Logan—

Luisa's twin brother sat on the far side of Quentin, barely in the circle at all. His eyes shaded beneath a less than menacing golf visor, Logan shuffled a dull and dog-eared deck of cards like a Vegas shark. The little boy, smaller than his sister and wiry, wore his black hair short, and it fell forward to a widow's peak that made him look like the littlest vampire. Occasionally he would make gestures toward souls across the room, the kind that gave away his true age, his thumb crossing his throat in a slow slice like a mob enforcer.

He glanced in Velvet's direction and nodded politely.

Velvet winked back. A rougher version of his sister, Logan would find himself in some sort of brawl by the end of the night, she was certain, but she couldn't help liking him despite his violent tendencies, or possibly because of them.

"It's settled then," Velvet said, giving the group her most serious gaze. "We're all sluts."

They burst into the kind of laughter that friends manage when lost in a moment, the kind that draws stares and jealousy. When Velvet saw Isadora's group scowling in their direction, she was forced to flip the girl an abrupt and forceful middle finger.

She had no choice.

Kipper drummed his palms on the table, grinning, biting his lip and nodding to the music—Bart Penney had taken up a spot at the lectern, barely singing along to some Joy Division song. It didn't seem to matter to Kipper, who danced in his seat and pointed at the guy like he was a bona fide rock star, instead of the house paper stacker. "Bart! You freakin' rock!"

The boy on the stage winced, but kept mumbling into his toilet paper roll microphone.

Typical Kipper. Making everyone feel comfortable.

It's not like Velvet was a nun, by any stretch. She was interested in boys, probably just as much as Kipper was, or maybe a little less. It's just that they never seemed to stick around. She was dead certain she wasn't suited for relationships. Just couldn't keep up with them. Velvet got into too much trouble. It was a gift. If she weren't dead, she'd be in juvie.

She didn't need to look at Quentin again to know he was still gazing like a deer in the headlights at Shandie. And sure enough, the conversation hadn't wavered, either.

"She's not completely hideous," Luisa said, squinting as she assessed the object of Quentin's affection from their vantage.

"Yeah," Velvet said, taking a peek at the girl, too. Shandie was regaling Isadora and her group with some highly dramatic tale that involved flipping her sideways ponytail like she was having a seizure. "Too bad she's infected with Isadora's personality herpes."

"She's gorgeous." Quentin spoke so softly, Velvet almost thought she'd imagined it.

Normally she'd have had to continue to make fun of him for a while, just to maintain the balance of power, but the boy sounded so sincere, and he was, after all, her second in command. So Velvet let it slide.

"You want me to talk to her for you?" Velvet offered, and she would, too, despite exposing herself to the contagion of Isadora's lackey. That's what friends do, she guessed.

But instead of being thankful, Quentin's eyes went wide with horror. His hands shot out as though Velvet were coming at him with a knife. "No! No! Promise me you won't. Promise!"

"Fine," she said, shrugging. "I promise."

Kipper shook his head, kicked back in his chair, and made with a smoldering expression for the benefit of a cute boy standing against the far wall. The boy caught his glare and furrowed his brow, apparently confused. That was probably Kipper's hope anyway. Confused suited him, he'd once told Velvet. Kipper broke into a laugh that sounded a lot like a seal barking. When Quentin looked at him, Kipper snapped back to the action, pantomiming a nuclear explosion coming from his own crotch.

"I'm tellin' ya," he said. "Kaboom!"

Quentin's head hit the table.

Velvet had every intention of shaming Kipper in the harshest possible way, but just then a bell rang from the direction of the stage.

Bart Penney wrapped up his rendition of "Transmission," and the room quieted. Miss Antonia, the Salvage mother, shut down a conversation with her cohort from the Collectors, the pinch-faced and always eager to humiliate Mrs. Connie Lawrence. Looking at the woman's snide expression, Velvet couldn't help but see exactly where Isadora inherited her venom. What was the expression? Like mother, like daughter.

44

Miss Antonia strode across to the lectern, looking every bit the prison warden in a gray skirted suit, her hair in a tight bun revealing a neck so long that it reminded Velvet of one of those modern mannequins, the ones that sometimes don't have a head.

Miss Antonia had a head, of course.

And huge nearly white eyes that blazed like headlights into the dimly lit courtyard. She curled her long fingers around the top of the lectern and set her glowy gaze on Velvet.

Too intently.

She was staring, even.

Velvet nodded politely in return. It didn't bode well to get on the bad side of one of the dormitory mothers, especially the one that was supposed to be on the side of the Salvage team.

"Thank you! Your voices are improving. . . ." Miss Antonia's eyes narrowed as, from across the room, Bethany let out a squeal of delight, Renata beamed, and Bart roared and pumped his fists into the air. Then she added, "Marginally."

Renata's lips curled into a sneer while Bethany, as dumb as ever, continued to clap her petite hands together as though she'd been bestowed top marks. It's possible Bart hadn't heard the slur against his vocal prowess. He was busy choking his girlfriend, Courtney, with his tongue. He seriously looked like he was going to eat her.

So. Gross.

The Salvage mother cleared her throat. "It's time to choose your storyteller. Bring in"—she paused and then, with a sinister hiss, said—"the Box."

A cold dread fell over Velvet.

Sure she'd had to sing. Her favorite was "Candyman." It had that right blend of creepy and aggressive that Velvet didn't mind promoting. She even did her hair like Siouxsie Sioux when she had to perform, and she already had a black enough wardrobe to do any Goth proud. But since arriving in purgatory, through luck or some miracle, she'd somehow managed to avoid telling the tale of her death. Even she thought it was too weird that she hadn't yet had to tell anyone. What were the odds?

But she was happy to sing rather than tell her story.

Ecstatic, in fact.

Quentin had stuttered through a short version of his own tale once, a pathetic account of falling on a metal rake at a track meet. Logan seemed to enjoy telling all about the Halloween car accident that had taken out his sister and him in a squealing melee of metal and gore. And despite being the most outgoing person Velvet had ever met, Kipper had been mortified when he'd been forced to admit in front of everyone at salon that he'd died by choking to death at the Nathan's Famous hot-dog-eating championship.

The kicker: He hadn't even been a contestant.

But Velvet's tale was far more horrendous than any she'd ever heard, and she'd often wondered if, once called, she'd end up making up something completely false and possibly humorous just to avoid revealing her wounds. She'd much rather, especially since she'd spent so much time pretending she didn't remember.

It was just better that way.

Grant Cheever, an awkward Collector kid, shuffled across

the stage carrying the simple pine box with the lottery of names inside it. It reminded Velvet of the Shirley Jackson story about the town that picked a human sacrifice in much the same way. Not that she could compare her fear to being stoned to death. There was no comparison.

Velvet's was totally worse.

Anyone could die. That was natural.

There was nothing natural about recounting the specifics of your own brutal, ritualistic murder for entertainment purposes.

The scene played out on the stage in slow motion, Miss Antonia plunging her hand deep into the box, jiggling it around while seeming to leer in Velvet's direction—of course that last bit might have been a figment of Velvet's imagination. Miss Antonia snatched out a tiny folded slip of paper and toyed with it, her long fingers manipulating the folds until she was holding it out before her.

Miss Antonia snapped the paper tight and started to say, "This evening's distraction comes courtesy of Ms.—"

Velvet hung on the woman's words, her fingers aching from the grip she held on the wooden seat beneath her. But the Salvage mother didn't finish her statement. Her eyes were glued to something going on above them.

Several dozen heads turned skyward.

There, beyond the gas lanterns strung from their black rubber hoses, in that square of night where the passing souls—the lucky ones—moved on to better places, an inky tentacle of shadow curled over the inner stone wall like a greedy tongue.

Chapter 4

"Shadowquake!" someone screamed, or several someones—
it was hard for Velvet to tell over all the screaming. The
courtyard had erupted into chaos, and not because Velvet
had been granted another salon free from the dreaded
storytelling—though on any other night that would certainly have been cause for celebration.

Residents stumbled over toppled chairs and crawled across
tabletops. The earth shook beneath them, steady one moment and then suddenly as rough and purposeful as if someone had set the ground to vibrate. Furtive eyes blurred into
smears of light, like fox fire hanging in the humidity of a
swamp.

Above the crowd, a great bank of obsidian fog billowed
and roiled, blotting out the view of the forever night sky.
The fog swelled slowly, infiltrating the upper floors first, and
then expanding, pressing downward toward the courtyard.

Residents flooded from both stairwells into the throng. A single black tentacle took shape out of the curling inky shadows. It was joined by several more that slithered down each of the four walls of the courtyard, coiling around the gaslights, shading them so perfectly, it was as though the lights had been snuffed out. No one could ever recall witnessing the source of the wicked appendages, but Velvet imagined a mammoth black kraken unfolding itself from some yet unknown crack in the afterlife and looming over them.

Seeking.

As if the dark itself had taken shape to teach them a lesson about who was really in charge.

Miss Antonia cried out to the gathered residents, "Get to the strongholds!"

She snatched the box and scuttled off the edge of the stage, scything through the tumult of the crowd to reach Velvet and her team. She shouted over the din, "This is a bad one!" Her eyes skittered toward the approaching tentacles. "Get your team to the station! And you—" Miss Antonia stuck a finger into Kipper's chest. His fiery eyes extinguished, replaced by full-on sad puppy. "—are not going with them. Get these people to safety!"

The boy nodded, then bounded into the crowd, arms outstretched to corral loose souls. He herded them away from the walls and toward the open area before the stage, Collectors and Salvagers alike. They faced out, every eye glued to the approaching horde of tentacles and compacted against one another, a widening circular mass. Their screams were now terrified whispers.

Velvet noticed a straggler.

Bethany, frantically scrambling toward the center of the room, suddenly stopped dead in her tracks. The girl's face went slack, and Velvet knew instantly why. A shadow tentacle curled around her waist and drew her backward, knocking over chairs and upending tables with her limp form. It lifted her petite figure a few feet off the ground and then stopped still. Velvet's heart sank. The girl's feet were twitching, and her face took on a look so unambiguous, an advisor wasn't necessary to instruct onlookers of its meaning.

Horror.

The unseen owner of the shadow tentacles didn't eat the souls. It didn't take them away or bring them to some secret lair.

All of the tortures were quiet ones.

To project. To play out its victim's greatest fears on the screen in the back of their brain. Full-color 3-D horror, HD with Digital Surround. Or so Velvet had heard from the gossips in the square.

She had a strong stomach for lots of things. Violence. Gore. Sex. Even cruelty. But the look on Bethany's face was pure, undiluted terror. Velvet wondered what the thing was showing the girl. What it would show Velvet if it had the chance. The wave of emotion struck her like a fist to the throat. Her mind was back in Bonesaw's shed.

Her skin, shredded.

Grated.

Tendrils of gristle shook in the killer's teeth as he barked with laughter.

Velvet shook it off and glared into the darkness. A hollow

roar echoed through the courtyard, interrupted briefly by the clatter of tiles sloughing from the rooftop like dandruff. The unseen kraken on the move. She didn't need Miss Antonia to tell her twice. Her team was the best for a reason, and while they were usually tasked with routine reconnaissance, they lived for a chance to take down a bad guy. And every time they'd had a shadowquake—every single time— there'd always been a bad guy doing something awful in the daylight as well.

Witches, banshees, whatever—Velvet and her team were on it. Like black ops but ghosts. Ghosts with very specific abilities.

Velvet, besides being the team leader, was a body thief, which, when asked about it, she usually described like so:

"Remember that movie *The Exorcist*? Well, think of me as a demon . . . only hotter, obviously, and not evil. I can squeeze right into a body without them even noticing and work my mission without leaving a scratch on them."

Quentin pulled off a similar deal with dead bodies, but it's too soon to talk about the specifics, as it's completely disgusting. "The muscle" was really too simplistic a description for Luisa and Logan's duties as poltergeists. They were experts at causing trouble, getting into fights, and generally messing things—and people—up. Plus, their ability to create distractions *always* came in handy.

"Come on!" Velvet yelled for Quentin, Logan, and Luisa to follow her as she darted for the front door, cutting between toppled tables and hurdling chairs along the way. A tentacle crept toward the entry alcove from above, forcing

Velvet and the rest into a low scrabble as they barreled beneath and past its beseeching undulations.

Outside, the glass-shaded streetlights shattered and showered the cobblestone with shards as tiny as sleet, leaving the gaslights transformed into flaming torches whipping in the miasma of molten tar descending on them like an eternal night. There weren't many tentacles outside, but the few that Velvet's team witnessed had already found an audience for the horror show. Slack citizens hung in the air around the square like sad gray ornaments on a dying tree.

"Velvet!" a froggy voice called out from the darkness.

She didn't need to look up to know Quentin was making his shaky way toward her. Velvet pushed herself up into a crouch and reached out for his hands just as the boy stumbled and crashed onto his knees with a painful groan.

"Oh, crap!" she cried out. "Are you okay?"

The scrawny kid rubbed at his knees while bracing against Velvet's shoulder just to stay upright in the constant rumbling. Everything about the boy was thin, from his gangly limbs to his awkwardly narrow head and barely visible lips. He'd have looked like a pencil if it weren't for his chillingly lovely eyes, alive at that moment with terror. "This is the worst it's ever been," he said. "Somethin' real bad is happening!"

"No shit!" Velvet shouted.

He craned his head to glare in the opposite direction. "The twins were right behind me!"

Velvet glanced over his shoulder, and sure enough, Logan and Luisa emerged from the smoky haze of the shadowquake, grimaces of frustration plastered on their normally calm faces. They clung to the building's mortar lines spotlit by one of the few remaining streetlamps, like the twins had been mistakenly forced into a jailhouse lineup.

Fear was a temporary thing for the twins, who were the best poltergeists to come along in decades, or at least that's what the station agent said, and Velvet was totally in agreement. Logan and Luisa could scare the crap out of the worst kinds of villains and, as their months together had shown, took great pleasure in crushing skulls, when they had to . . . and even when they didn't.

"We gotta get to the station!" Luisa cried, her tone battened with dread.

"Now!" shouted Logan from over her shoulder, his eyes wild with excitement. It was looking like that brawl was definitely going to happen.

They were right, of course, and were voicing the obvious. The station housed the primary cracks between the world of the living and the dead. That Velvet had found another and hadn't reported it was, well, beside the point at the moment, but nonetheless bad. Even now, the station agent would be gathering intelligence about the source of the shadowquake. Her visions might not nail down what horrible event was occurring in the daylight, but she'd get a clear enough picture so that Velvet's team could focus on the journey.

Velvet watched the sky. The shadows struck and recoiled off each other, battling to be first to the mountain. She felt a surge of adrenaline roil through her, and the light within her glowed brightly through tiny cracks in the ash she wore, like magma peeking through fractured rocks.

She bolted for the funicular ramp.

The wooden carriage itself might turn out to be useless, with the ground rolling as it was, but they could always climb onto the tracks and use them to get up the hill to the massive station at its peak. She hoped it wouldn't come to that; it would take forever to hike the several miles to the top, especially with the ground convulsing like an epileptic. Velvet could barely see six feet in front of her now; the clouds of inky crap had descended into her line of sight. She vaulted over the rail and onto the raised funicular platform, the others moving like a wolf pack behind her, fluidly, in unison.

Despite the situation, she knew she was grinning. Maybe not in the same way that Logan was, in gleeful anticipation, but her excitement was there on her face.

It always was when there was a mission.

Nothing could keep her mind off her troubles with Bonesaw like a big giant commando operation–inducing catastrophe.

Dropping into the pit where the railcar traveled, Velvet closed her eyes and crouched to feel the bronze rails. The rocking and rolling was stronger there, and she had a difficult time distinguishing the feel of the ground's shaking from the vibration of metal against metal. It was subtle at first. An infinitesimal shudder ran through her grayed skin, just a hint of what was rolling toward them, cutting through the shadows like a knife.

"There it is," she said.

Quentin nodded hopefully.

There was a consistent tremor driving through the bronze.

The railcar was still functioning. She turned and looked down the track. Realizing it could be several feet away, barreling toward her, and she wouldn't even know it through the curtain of darkness, Velvet jumped up and scrambled back onto the platform.

"Is it comin'?" Logan searched her face for the answer. Sometimes he was so dense.

"Well, duh!" Velvet snapped. "I just jumped out of the way, didn't I?"

He planted his hands on his hips and looked from her to the thick gray mist and back to her, then back to where the railcar should be, a sneer spreading. "Yeah. Like you were about to get splattered, then . . . uh. Nothing."

Velvet waited a moment, wishing for the wooden train to appear, and then acquiesced. "Sorry! I meant to say, 'Yeah, it's coming.'"

A squeal pierced the night as the heavy bronze plow of the railcar cut through the shadows and into the station. The contraption was packed with souls. Gray powdered arms thrust from glassless windows set in the doors—each row of seats had its own—and behind those, faces twisted into masks of terror floated in the dark depths of the carriage. The shouts began almost instantly.

"We got no room!"

"Don't even try to get on!"

Velvet stepped forward and yanked the nearest door open. A small woman in a pillbox hat, nose pinched and upturned, held the soul of a plump baby in her lap. She hadn't bothered to make it gray with ash, and it glowed eye-achingly bright. Velvet raised her hand to shield against the glare of its firing synapses. Clearly she couldn't ask this woman to vacate her spot—that would be terrible. Not to mention rude. She leaned inside the cab and assessed the other passengers; most couldn't look away fast enough. Velvet spotted a pair of young men in ratty baseball caps pulled down over their eyes, one fidgeting with his bill.

"You two!" she shouted, and when neither glanced her way, Velvet motioned for an elderly woman sitting in the row beside them to get their attention.

One peered up from his spot, his shoulders wilted, shamed, and rightly so.

"Salvage business!" Velvet yelled menacingly. "Make room or suffer the consequences, dingleberry!"

She ducked out of the cab and slammed the door. Then she stomped to their section, tore open their door, and jerked them out by their worn hoodies. They fell into the benches on the platform and scowled.

"No worries, gentleman," Luisa said as she strutted past. "I'm sure there'll be another car along in no time."

As if to punctuate the joke, a wooden roof tile from a nearby building shook loose and slapped one of the guys in the back of the head.

"Yeah!" Logan chuckled. "You'll be perfectly safe here. What are you worried about? Dyin'?"

"Dying!" Quentin howled with laughter as he slunk past the pair. "That's a good one, Logan. 'Cause they're already—"

"Yep." Logan stopped him with a hand on his chest. "That's why it's funny."

Quentin clammed up and slid in after an old woman. Logan followed. Velvet followed Luisa into the row vacated by the two boys and slammed the door behind them.

She thought about the faces in the crowd—so many her age, some younger and some a bit older. It seemed that purgatory was built for the young, those who died far before their time and with so much left to learn. They'd be there forever. But youth is resilient, as the station agent was so fond of saying. That's why Velvet had been enlisted—and Logan, Luisa, and Quentin—to track down souls that should have made it here but didn't for whatever reason. She just wished there were more accidental causes and fewer nefarious ones.

She reached for the cord that ran down the center of the ceiling in limp droopy scallops and yanked it. A series of bells started to chime, and moments later the railcar jerked into motion. Swift movement caught Velvet's eye. Outside, the extricated slacker boys were already hanging limply at the ends of a pair of plump shadowy tentacles that were pulsating and tightening around the boys' waists. Another, larger appendage slapped against the side of the car with a wet *thwap*. It coiled around the frame of a nearby door before striking, snakelike, at a frail-looking gentleman with a bag on his lap. At the slightest touch, the man went soft in his seat, slipping away from danger and onto the floorboard, loose enough that he could have been deboned. The tentacle reared back, ready to attack again.

Screams rolled through the cabin like a wave.

At that moment, the railcar jerked forward and the tentacle was torn free, and it disappeared into the charcoal night. The screaming calmed into hushed discussion, though the passengers were noticeably compressed into the center of the bench seats and as far from the glassless window frames as possible.

Velvet leaned over the back of her seat and helped the older soul, now conscious, into his proper place.

"Are you all right?" she asked, patting his shoulder.

He shook his head, glancing back and forth, confused, and then his eyes went wide with memory. "Oh, God."

"What?"

"It showed me . . ." His voice trailed away and his face, crinkled with ash, dropped into his palms. "It showed me horrible things."

She patted his shoulder again. She knew she should say something. Something comforting—but the words wouldn't come. Velvet turned and faced forward as they traveled the hundred or so remaining yards to a track interchange.

A pair of gruff-looking souls in coveralls chained the funicular cars to a massive wedge and then backed away as the car shook violently and began its long trudge farther up the steepening hill. The wedge acted like a stair and kept the train as level as could be expected during a shadowquake. Normally it ran quite smoothly, but now it rocked and the train rattled and squeaked as the entire wedge began to roll underneath them.

Velvet scanned the faces in their car, half expecting their fear to be dissuaded simply by the presence of the Salvage team, but the tendrils of mist were dark, and the shadows still crept in through the arched openings in the doors, reminders of the black tentacles and their dark work. It dawned on her then, it wasn't enough that her team would eventually do something about the shadowquake. The fact was, they weren't doing anything about it currently.

She decided to remedy that and climbed atop the wooden seat, bracing her hands against the ceiling for support.

"Nothing to worry about!" she announced, arms outstretched in what she hoped was a show of strength. She'd seen Madonna do it in some movie about South America or something, also Nixon, though throwing up peace signs didn't seem to fit the moment. "Your Salvage team is here to protect your afterlife."

She looked toward Luisa for approval and was met with a grimace and a finger slice across the little girl's neck, the international symbol for shutting the hell up.

There were some nods among the passengers, and some murmurs of dissent, or encouragement; it was hard to tell amid the grinding of the gears and the moaning of the ropes that pulled the railcar up the steep and treacherous incline. Her money was on the prior, though.

"Smooth," Luisa pointed out when Velvet sat down. "Really empowering."

"You think they bought it?" Velvet whispered.

"Absolutely."

She brightened but noted a smirk at work on Luisa's lips; they were even quivering. "Really?"

"Not a chance."

Velvet sank back into the seat and groaned.

Outside, the blurry shadows of rocks and precipices fell away to a solid wall of obsidian as the tram entered the shaft into the lower depths of the station. The sounds of souls screaming in the distance fell away, and the passengers grew eerily quiet.

Velvet considered the cause of all this, steeling herself for the job at hand, whatever that might be.

Witches, mediums, fortune-tellers.

The blackest kind of magic.

Sure, most of them were harmless, flipping cards, pointing out the obvious, telling people what they wanted to hear. It was almost noble. They actually kind of helped people, like counselors or something. Velvet never gave them much credit, but there were others, the ones that were a bit *too* accurate in their predictions, *too* powerful. In daylight, that magic was seen as a special gift, but the effect it had in purgatory was dangerous. A simple incantation could cause a quiver beneath the cobblestone streets, but shadowquakes rippled from an epicenter of dark intent, black magic stabbing like a sword from the daylight straight through to purgatory, the shredded fabric of the veil transmogrified into tentacles of pure horror.

That was the trouble with the living. They didn't recognize that actions had consequences. And that was the real issue. It pissed Velvet off, royally. Almost as much as Ron Simanski. He certainly acted without concern for the costs of his behavior.

If only the asshole were dead, she thought. If only she could manage to do it.

Make him cut his own throat.

She'd never have to worry about another girl, or seeing his

ass again. He wasn't likely to have an ambiguous afterlife. His path was certain.

Straight to hell.

Luisa's hand nudging her thigh shook her from thoughts of homicide. "What are you thinking about?"

"Nothin'." Velvet shrugged.

"I thought you were going to invite me the next time you took a walk?"

She cringed.

Luisa's eyebrow raised, and Velvet saw a tinge of suspicion spreading over the girl's normally placid face. This wasn't the first time this confrontation had played out, and she suspected that her poltergeist friend might be on to her escapades, but Luisa never uttered the words in Velvet's presence, never made any actual allegation. And she wouldn't, of course, for the very reason that they were best friends.

To say it aloud . . .

Haunt.

To speak that most horrible of syllables was to call the wrath of the station agent and the Council of Station Agents.

No. Luisa would never say it. And that's why they never discussed it. Velvet lied to protect her friend and herself, of course, no matter how difficult it was to keep the secret, and no matter how much she wanted to confide in Luisa. She wouldn't place that kind of burden on Luisa's shoulders. Ever.

"It was just a walk," she mumbled. "It's not like I was out committing crimes or anything."

"What?" Luisa shook her head.

"Nothing. Forget it. Just a walk."

In the sea of blackness, it was impossible to tell how far into the tunnel the railcar had carried them. The shadow-quake's black fog swirled around them and the rails still shook, but they hadn't seen another tentacle since the old man had been attacked, so the train fell quiet. Her shoulders hunched with exhaustion, and she could swear she heard Logan's grumbled snores over the clatter of metal on metal.

The dark mist hung inside the car like oil floating atop a hot cup of coffee. It dotted the air like specks of ink. She held up her finger to poke one, and the droplet seemed to react, skittering away toward the opening in the door as though alive.

Velvet shuddered at the thought and then jumped, ridiculously, as the wedge jolted over the hump into the station proper, a thin stretch of tunnel that ran for at least a mile upward toward the center of the massive structure.

A few feet into the tunnel, the dense mist loosened its grasp and dissipated from the door hinges and the ropes that hung from the ceiling for passengers to steady themselves. It fell away as though the inky tendrils themselves were traveling to the station, though Velvet knew the idea was insane. Mist didn't think. Neither did shadow.

Ridiculous.

The shadowquake was the strongest yet, and while it shook the Latin Quarter of purgatory like a rag doll, its influence could not penetrate the stoic power of the station. The railcar began to travel smoothly. Gone were the bumps and shimmies, and soon the aura from the globes of gaslight in the tunnel wall broke through the gloom.

Velvet nodded toward the elderly woman in the seat in front of them and smiled at the baby she was holding. "So bright, that one," Velvet said, leaning over the bench.

"Yes," the woman responded, her voice crackling like a wood fire. She dropped her chin toward the glowing bundle and smiled. "This soul is so strong. I won't have him but a moment. He'll be movin' on faster than you can jump a live one, I suspect."

Velvet made a forced attempt to chuckle. The woman had certainly been around long enough to know the cycle. Babies always moved on the quickest. They'd had a few infants in the Retrieval dorms, and they'd passed them around between people for a couple of days before they'd start to fade.

Dimming, they called it.

Their light goes out, flickers and dies, and all that's left is a dusty husk that crumbles and blows away like the powder in a packet of Sweet'N Low. *Of course, it's much weirder with adults,* Velvet thought. *And there was way more Sweet'N Low.*

Way more.

Chapter 5

The amber glow of gaslight trickled into the train from the tunnel's mouth, not in steady streams but jagged rivulets, mixing with the dust until the air around the passengers was streaked a muddy sepia. The gruff railmen bolted from the lead car and tossed off the heavy chains that bound the railcar to the giant wedge beneath them. The metal screamed back with a loud echoing clatter. Then the car was lurching forward, rattling across the connecting tracks into the station itself.

The left side of the railcar opened to a vast platform filled with huddled groups of people, haggard and wrapped in blankets or quivering under propped parasols as tiny bits of debris showered from the ceiling. When she was alive, Velvet had done a paper on the immigration of the Irish into New York, and the image of these souls, these refugees, looked almost exactly like those encyclopedia pictures of Ellis Island, downtrodden people exhausted from their travels and gathering together to hold themselves up. Among them, station guides roamed with handheld signs indicating a stall in departures.

"No departures for the duration of the incident!" they shouted.

The passengers spilled from the railcar doors and onto a gently rumbling cobblestone floor, the clops of their shoes echoing in the hushed space. Then a quiet fell over them. The disembarked stood, faces stunned and staring into the crowd, as though waiting for someone to tell them what to do, where to stand.

Velvet wasn't that person.

I guess you should have taken my efforts to calm the situation seriously, huh? she thought smugly.

She, Quentin, and the twins darted past them, weaving through the throng of people, through clouds of dust and ash wafting from their soiled clothing. There was something else in the air, too, a thin striation of the gas that fed the lanterns and globes. Velvet's eyes darted toward Logan and caught him inhaling deep mouthfuls before noticing her gaze and then shrugging dismissively.

Once an addict, always an addict, she thought, shaking her head.

"There!" she shouted, pointing toward a towering arch topped with a stained-glass transom—in its beveled shards were the silhouettes of four heroes, a Salvage team from some long ago and certainly harrowing event. She wasn't aware of the story, and just then, with her nerves firing like a machine gun, she didn't really care. Her team had their own story to carve out.

Beyond the arch, a stair led up into the vast hub of the station. Single file, they took the risers two at a time, barreling through souls making use of the stairs for seating. They shouted warnings of "Salvage team passing! Make way!" And stepped on only a few hands.

At the top they were met with a daunting vista. Fresh unashed souls poured into the station from the primary crack. Their memories burned as though God had dropped a star into the station. Station guides pummeled them with fistfuls of ash and pointed them toward long meandering lines that led to a bank of a hundred or so lecterns. Intake officers bellowed orders and sorted souls as fast as they could, despite the continued quaking beneath them.

A glass dome towered above them all, though the panels themselves seemed made of a shiny boiling tar. The mist of the shadowquake blocked out everything even at that height.

Velvet wondered how far the quake had spread.

Had it passed into Little Cairo? Into Kerouac? Certainly not as far as Vermillion. That would mean the magic they'd be facing was monstrous. Were there at this very moment other Salvage teams speeding to their stations, crossing into the daylight to converge on the source?

It was hard for her to imagine a disturbance so vast.

The last shadowquake hadn't been nearly this large, and as they had traveled to get to the station, they'd broken free from its clutches about halfway up the mountain. They had been piled on top of each other in the rear seat of the railcar, and looking behind them, they could make out the shape of the thing, round, or roundish, with flares of darkness exploding from it. The shadowquake was like a reverse image of the sun, and stripping away the heat from everything it touched.

Velvet remembered looking upon the shape, terrified . . . and that had been at a distance.

It squicked her out to think they were still inside the center of the dark blob, like being in the belly of some gigantic ink-fueled octopus monster or something equally disturbing—Velvet wasn't really into descriptive metaphor at the moment. She had much more pressing matters to tend to.

Luisa nudged her. "This is a big one. Something really terrible must be happening out there."

"Thoughts on what it is?" Velvet shouted to her team.

"A sacrifice!" Logan's hands curled into the claws of some imaginary monster. "A witch or something. Warlock!"

"Knock it off, dork!" Luisa swatted him in the back of his head, and a puff of ashen powder exploded from his dark hair. "It's not a sacrifice."

"It could be." Logan's mouth scrunched up hatefully. "You don't know."

"I do know," she said. "This isn't the Dark Ages. There aren't any magicians performing weird rituals out there. Don't you remember last time?"

He shrugged. When it came to his sister, Logan did a lot of shrugging.

Everyone remembered the last one. Dr. Hazel Perkins.

A self-described medium and the host of her own moderately successful cable-access TV talk show, Hazel had chanced upon a cell—an orb filled with a stolen soul. They still didn't know how that had happened. She'd planned to use it to conjure up images of people's loved ones and "give their tortured minds some relief." Unfortunately for them, on the night her show featured the act, their relief was purgatory's torture. They lost three whole buildings that day, disintegrated down to rubble and spirals of twisted metal—not that the buildings in the City of the Dead were all that well constructed. After all, the people that threw them up weren't necessarily builders or carpenters. They were more likely accountants, prostitutes, and children, which was probably why some of the buildings looked more like patchwork quilts than actual domiciles.

"Over here!" a breathy voice called.

Manny, their station agent, broke through a ragged group of refugees, waving cheerily. Platinum-haired and busty, Manny had been a film actress before a tragic car accident had left her with an even more tragic severed head to deal with. Though none of the Salvagers could remember her from the movies, the boys were nonetheless mesmerized by her every movement.

Like that was a surprise.

She was slick and graceful, with slender fingers and a shrewd strength flickering in her eyes that belied her bombshell exterior.

The group followed as Manny turned and stalked off toward a tall gate, her heels clicking as she widened the gap between them. Beyond the black wrought iron lay a darkened cavern.

The Shattered Hall.

"Your crew has its work cut out for it on this one," Manny said.

"Looks like it!" Velvet jogged to keep up.

"I've isolated the epicenter of the disturbance to a fortune-teller's shop in Philadelphia. The details I've conjured will place each of you within a few blocks. Though this insertion will be a little different, you'll be scattered where you need to be. The cemetery is not reasonably close, so I'm opting for a morgue."

"Tricky." Velvet glanced behind her to find the twins straggling and Quentin walking backward, still gawking at the mass of souls in the hub.

Manny and Velvet came up to the tall gates, and the rest of the group crowded in behind them. Velvet cringed. She hated this part. Manny waved her hands in front of a huge spiral locking mechanism embedded in a solid block of metal, and then stepped away. The coil retracted like a screw pulling out of cork, scraping against the insides of the block. The sound was nails dragging across a chalkboard, or rather, a big metal lawn rake dragging across a chalkboard.

Screeeeeeeeeeeeee!

The crowds of people behind them in the hub turned en masse toward the squelch, clapping their hands over their ears and grimacing, a wail of general complaint issuing from their gaping mouths. Velvet was right there with them, keeping out as much of the sound as she could before it got a chance to crawl up under her skin and start a different kind of quaking up her spine.

The sharp end of the coil slid from the block, and Velvet watched with amazement as the metal sealed itself, healing, as though it had never been pierced to begin with.

"No matter how many times I see that, I think the same thing. Genius, doll!" Logan's mouth lolled, and his tongue protruded from his lips. He always tried to figure out the process, to see if it were a trick of light or some magical illusion the station agent was pulling. It was as if he were convinced it was an earthly sort of magic, one he could learn. He was determined to dissect her movements. But after the process was complete and there was nothing else to examine other than the gates swinging into the darkened passage, he exhaled heavily and shrugged it off.

Velvet admired perseverance and recognized it immediately in the kid. He'd never give up. Never stop wondering about the mechanism, and never veer from completing his poltergeisting. They were alike, the two of them, though she hoped her face never twisted up the way his did while he was concentrating.

Super crazy-looking.

They followed the click of Manny's high heels into the darkness, and stopped before a barely visible stone wall, itself the color of coal.

Manny drew a matchstick from her sleeve and struck it against the wall. It spit to life and cast a living glow on the facade, revealing the appropriateness of the hall's name. Fissures lined the wall; some split into the rock from floor to ceiling while others were mere scratches. The largest crack ran straight up the center, a foot wide and so deep that Velvet imagined it running straight through to the center of the planet—if purgatory was even *on* the planet. A library ladder clung to a rail that ran the full length of the hall, however long that was. Velvet couldn't remember ever seeing where it ended.

"And so it begins," the station agent said.

She ran her slender finger along the sharp edges of the crack. It reacted to her flame, shimmering deep inside as though some treasure were sheltered in its depths, a thread of mother-of-pearl, opal. Something. No one was sure exactly how long ago the station's foundation had been poured or how it had been done. Some speculated that the foundation was here before the first soul arrived, but that the station itself was constructed over time, as souls with the skills to construct it passed through. The final phase appeared to be turn-of-the-century work, but these halls, these walls and fractures, were old.

Ancient, even.

Not likely the work of human souls.

"Now," Manny said, and gestured for Quentin to stand beside her. "One at a time. Like I said, this isn't a routine extraction. And the location is not exactly conducive to plopping you down all in the same place." She nodded in Velvet's direction. "You'll also have the late hour to deal with. It's past two in the morning."

Velvet sank. That would make things much more difficult.

"Remember," Manny said in a stern voice. "Follow protocol, and everyone makes it back. Got it?"

"Yes, ma'am!" Velvet barked, and glanced around at her team.

"Yes, ma'am!" the other Salvagers shouted in unison.

Manny narrowed in on Velvet, a hint of playfulness in her eye. "I've been waiting to tick off your fifty-seventh soul for some time now, Velvet. I hope you won't disappoint me."

"No, ma'am." Velvet suspected Manny had a bet going with some of the other station agents—nothing she could prove, but the thought kind of lingered like a bad headache. Regardless, the woman reminded her that she was staring down the elusive number fifty-seven.

A benchmark moment . . . like a centennial or a sweet sixteen.

"Did you get a clear view of the involved?" Velvet asked.

The station agent's mouth tightened with distaste. "A medium. Madame Despot is her name."

Velvet nodded.

With that, Manny leaned into Quentin and whispered. The boy nodded and moved to stand by the crack. She moved on to Logan and then Luisa and finally clutched Velvet around the shoulders and spoke softly into her ear.

"Where you're going, there's a blue car with a flat tire. The police have labeled it for towing with bright orange wax lettering, an *L* and a seven. A cat with one blue eye and one brown scratches itself beneath a lamppost; a tiny bell jingles around its neck from a red necklace of yarn. A stack of newspaper has turned into a mound of rotting pulp, but still visible in its center is the image of a fireman carrying a crying baby wrapped in a tartan."

The pull-focus. Three details worked best.

The car. The cat. The newspaper.

Manny shook the flame off the long match, thrusting

them into dusky shadows. Then she stomped back toward the hub without another word.

Velvet spun around to inspect the faces of her Salvagers, which was much more difficult now in the absence of a flame. Logan's lip curled in a sneer. He gnashed his teeth and pumped his fist in the air. Ready. Luisa had the steely eyes of a hawk that was prepared to hunt. Quentin . . . well, he was busy scraping a pebble from the sole of his shoe with a thin rod of metal. On the upside, he was very focused on it, and Velvet figured that was a good thing.

"Nice focus, Q," she said.

"Tha-thanks, Velvet," he stuttered.

She gave him a nod, and he mirrored her and gave her a thumbs-up, as though they shared some secret she wasn't aware of. Velvet returned the gesture furtively.

"You're welcome." She turned toward the crack and began to strip off her clothes. "Pass me a box, will ya?"

One skittered across the floor and crashed into her leg.

"Ow!" she yelped.

"Sorry," Quentin responded quickly. "Can't see all that well in here, since there's no light and all."

She was sure he meant that he couldn't see her, though she knew for a fact he could, but she merely turned her back, stripped out of her clothes, and stuffed them into the box. She pressed herself close to the wall so the others could have their privacy.

"Ready for number fifty-seven, Salvagers?" she asked, her voice echoing down the hall.

"Yeah!"

"Totally!"

Velvet led the charge, pressing the tips of her fingers against the crack's sharp edges, digging her nails in as far as she could. She felt for the energy there, the familiar suction, and was off.

Chapter 6

Moonlight flooded the deserted street in an eerie purple glow, casting bruised shadows on the rows of buildings. In the distance, Velvet could hear the low rumble of car engines but nearby, quiet had settled in for the night, until the sound of a tiny bell jingled and Manny's tabby sprang up and pranced across the hood of the abandoned car—blue, of course. The cat stared at her, one blue eye and one brown, and hissed. Velvet backed away, sidestepping a soppy mound of newspapers, and darted down the street.

She peered in darkened windows as she hurried from shadow to shadow, frantically searching for a body to possess. Her mind reeled, recounting the events of her day. It seemed she'd been running from the minute she'd left Bonesaw's shed. If one more thing went wrong, she swore she'd have an aneurysm or whatever the ghost equivalent was.

At the very least she'd scream.

The poltergeists would already be scouting out the source of the shadowquake, or hunkering down in the walls, or making ghost chains, or whatever it was they did to prep for their part in a mission. She kind of left it up to them. Logan and Luisa were damn good at their jobs, and if Velvet were the one to hold up the show, they'd never let her hear the end of it. She'd be witness to a near constant floor show of ridicule, and that was *not* something she was about to let happen.

Man, she thought, searching frantically for a host body. *At this rate I'll be lucky to beat Quentin to the perp.*

Fog crossed the next intersection looking exactly like a big fluffy semitrailer, but Velvet trudged through barely noticing, a rarity for her, as she loved nothing more than afternoon cloud identification . . . except for finding a body that worked well.

As she came out the back of the thick mist, she spotted the most likely candidate of the evening. Well . . . "likely" might have been an overstatement.

Smoke curled from the nurse's wrinkled lips in greasy gray ribbons. It snaked around her sunken eyes and creased forehead before drifting up toward the glare of the streetlights in fluffy tufts. She slouched against the brick wall behind her, scraping her rubber clogs against the sidewalk and primping her silver hair, which was pinned back in an insane imitation of a pompadour. With each pat, a log of ash dropped from her cigarette, banked off her crisp teal scrubs, and exploded into tiny mushroom clouds as it struck the concrete.

A miserable sour-faced woman—probably in the last hours of a double shift at the hospital, muscles lagging with fatigue—not the best choice for the job at hand. But she was all Velvet had to work with, the street being as quiet as it was on that cold October night.

Velvet grumbled.

What I wouldn't do for a healthy street kid, she thought.

But she'd seen only two other people on the entire walk there.

The first was a total waste of her time, a gangly homeless man with a scraggly beard spotted with the remnants of several meals. He wore a puffy floor-length woman's parka, stuffing falling out where the rats had been at it. The minute she'd jumped into the guy, she'd understood what pickles must go through in their vinegary brine. He was pirate drunk, which, everyone knows, is the drunkest you can get. Velvet couldn't even begin to figure out what to do with his boozy frame. It wobbled and stumbled as she grappled for control. To make matters worse, when she finally dispossessed the guy, she felt a little tipsy herself. Took a few minutes just to shake off the contact buzz.

The second target was only slightly more amenable.

A small boy pulled a squat pug down the sidewalk, pleading for the dog to do its business and shut up its yipping. Velvet kept pace with the kid for half a block, drifting in and out of the dark places, noting that he had the same scrunched-up face as his dog and a nose running like a summer fire hydrant. But it was the dog that Velvet was worried about.

What would she have done with it? Tied it to a fence? Let it bark the neighbors awake and alert the kid's parents to his absence? Nope. She had to move on.

"Why me?" Velvet lingered at the corner, just another wisp of fog, a stray curl of shadow with jet-black nails and a scowl.

She scanned the sidewalks and alleys for other options. The street was, of course, deathly quiet, and the fall chill hung in the air like smog. Not that she could feel it; she was just remembering is all. *It would be nice to feel.* Tendrils of night mist topped the streetlights in halos, and very few things moved behind the closed curtains or peered out from behind the many storefront Closed signs.

Quiet.

Except for the nurse, who had started hacking up a lung.

That's the trouble with the living. When one needs a little peace and quiet, they're buzzing about like flies over a dead cow, but when, like Velvet, you're in need of a quick body for thieving, there are so few about, or they have issues, painful sciatica, meddlesome tumors, or worse, a prosthetic leg.

No worms, though. Thankfully.

She was damn happy not to be an undertaker like Quentin.

Velvet trailed her finger along a mortar line in the building as she strode toward the woman, steeling herself—thievery required preparation, after all, especially when one's target was a human body. But with Velvet's second step, the woman jumped and fanned away the cloud of smoke, glaring into the night.

"Who's there?" the nurse spat.

Velvet stopped dead in her tracks. She supposed it were possible the woman had heard her, that she'd somehow, through some phantom exertion, forced a pebble to scuttle across the sidewalk. Highly unlikely, but possible. Thankfully, very few living people honed the skills necessary to detect the dead among them—maybe a couple hundred on the whole planet. She eyed the awning of Madame Despot's Fortunes and Favors not a block away and shook off the possibility that two such people would inhabit the same short distance.

Velvet was so sure, she even spoke, "Just your run-of-the-mill wandering spirit, lady. Nothing to see here."

The woman continued to stare, looking past Velvet into the darkness, and then shook off the moment. She hadn't heard or seen a thing. Déjà vu, she would be thinking, perhaps a rat scurrying from the back of the nearby Jewel of Marrakech restaurant, anything but the thing that was actually approaching.

Velvet noted the time on a clock hanging above a jewelry shop—2:20 a.m. She had to hurry. Quentin would be well on his way to securing his own body, disgusting as it might be, and Madame Despot wasn't getting any less evil the longer it took to get their mission underway.

Velvet sprinted the last few yards and threw herself at the nurse, crossing the clammy chasm of air between them and slamming into the skin of her torso, slipping straight through the flesh, and wrapping her fingers around the woman's spinal cord as though she were swinging around a pole in the schoolyard. She steadied herself, filling into the woman's frame and forming the link. These were subtle manipulations. Velvet's thoughts played across the nurse's nerve endings like fingers on piano keys. She imagined them coiling and sparking, the woman's control being turned over, her mind shutting itself away in a tiny little box.

Safe and quiet and relaxed.

Velvet repeated those words in her mind like a mantra. It slowed her machinations, helped her to focus on the woman's nervous system, made her be extra careful and do no harm.

To the woman, the whole thing felt like a soft breeze chilling her flesh, right before the lights went out and she fell into slumber. The headache afterward would be a bitch, but that was none of Velvet's concern. The body was doing a public service, as far as she saw it.

Velvet peered from the nurse's eyes, glanced at the cigarette between her slender fingers, looked both ways down the street, and then took a quick drag. The smoke went down hot and ashy, and she coughed an unexpected phlegm globber onto the back of the nurse's teeth.

"Nasty!" She spat it out and tossed the butt to the ground, grinding the filter into a twisted ball. "I can't believe I did that."

And did it she had, more than once, but that was beside the point.

The door squeaked open behind her. "Antoinette?"

Velvet startled and spun around. "Ye-yeah?" she stuttered.

Another woman, eyes as dark and saggy as a pair of wet

tea bags, peeked out. "Delores wants you on the floor in five minutes," she said through a pinched nose, so the words sounded like the squelch of air escaping a balloon. "You know how she is, Antoinette."

Velvet didn't, of course, but she nodded anyway.

Chapter 7

Velvet heard the shuffling of calloused feet against concrete moments before the corpse stumbled into the column of streetlight, withered and muddy, its clothes tattered and hanging off the front of its body like an untied hospital gown. As if sensing her presence, it lurched in her direction, reaching for her with twisted fingers worn down to the dusty ivory of exposed bone. Its jaw creaked open, and a low groan escaped its shriveled mouth, a whisper at first, the last hiss of air bellowing from the dead thing's dry lungs. But as it shambled forward, the sound grew in volume and malevolence, beseeching.

Hungry.

Velvet stepped out onto the sidewalk and planted a hand on her hip. "What are you doing? You want to call attention to yourself? You better not screw this up, Quentin."

The moan turned into a chuckle, and the zombie shrugged its shoulders. "I was just messin' with you, Velvet."

The corpse's lip clung to its desiccated gums in an Elvis sneer, hideous and rotten. Velvet smiled at the creature, ran up, and gave it a careful punch.

"I know you were. And it was scary. Really. Quite frightening," she said sarcastically.

He cocked the thing's eyebrow.

Velvet scanned the windows across the street. Most were dark, but others fluxed with the movement of tenants, employees, and other nosy parkers, as her grandfather used to say. She pushed the corpse inside the small entry alcove of the next shop, pressing him deep into the shadows.

A glint of moonlight caught on his bare teeth, and for a moment Velvet felt the familiar tinges of a freak-out creeping into her skull. She realized her hands were lingering on his torso, and the imagery of the old woman and the zombie standing in the secluded spot caused a raucous shudder to roll through her. She jerked her hands away.

"Just stay put," she barked.

Quentin continued to grin. It was unfortunate that his fear of girls didn't seem to include her—not that she thought he was interested in her, at least in *that* way—as fear was an important part of any manager-employee relationship. It kept up the status quo.

She'd have to work on that.

Velvet glanced up and down the street. In the distance, she could see the mist swirling around the light above the clinic door. She turned back to Madame Despot's, rapped three times, and waited. When she didn't hear a sound from behind the tall door—she'd never been accused of being a quitter—she hammered at it some more and harder, until she did hear something. Humming and the soft whisper of slippers against floor. She had to hand it to the nurse; despite her age, her ears worked great.

She glanced to her left. Quentin had lost a good chunk of his body's forearm, and he was busily trying to pack the squishy flesh back around the exposed bone. He grinned nervously. Then again, corpses always look like they're grinning—it's the lips; they have a tendency to shrivel back from the gums.

It's never pretty.

"Gross," Velvet said. "Can you just stay out of sight for a sec?"

His eyes were mournful.

Quentin shuffled backward, and when he did, his left ear slid down his head. It tumbled off his shoulder with a wet plopping sound. He fumbled it between his fingers, popping it into the air like a hot potato and then missing it as it fell with a splat between his feet.

"Really?" Velvet rolled her eyes.

"Sooooorrrryyyyyy," he moaned, as zombies have a tendency to do. It's not nearly as endearing as you might expect. Or funny.

A series of metal clicks sounded from the door. Velvet shushed and waved frantically for Quentin to shut up and quit flapping about, making squishy noises. He pressed himself flat against the wall. Velvet reminded herself to squint as best she could to keep her glow from spilling out of the nurse's eyes—difficult, as she'd still need to be able to see. She found it was reasonable to let a crack of glow show. Anyone who saw it would immediately rationalize it away as a simple reflection off a tearful eye, for instance. Anyone human, that is.

The latch on the door clicked, and it squeaked open, with such obvious creepiness that Velvet rolled her eyes again—Madame Despot probably wet the hinges every night to get the effect.

Silhouetted by the hall light, the shop's namesake cast a big lumpy shadow that swept out onto the sidewalk and over Velvet. Velvet had to squint to make out the woman's massive nose and the odd, bulky turban coiled atop her head like a dollop of whipped cream. The woman wore sunglasses at the tip of her nose, not unlike a pair of reading glasses, but so large and dark that her eyes remained completely hidden.

Blind? Velvet wondered. *Hungover?*

Either seemed a possible explanation for wearing sunglasses at night, or possibly a nod to crappy eighties songs. Velvet sensed a tinge of something sinister about the woman at that very moment—something evil, like when she saw people wearing fur or gushing over the excruciatingly awesome talents of *American Idol* winners. It was more than just a possibility that the fortune-teller was in possession of a little dark magic.

Or a lot.

But Madame Despot stilled Velvet's suspicion with a curt jab from the wet end of a fat brown cigar. "Well-come, then,

Doctor. Get on in here." Her voice was higher than Velvet had expected, whiny, and it bore an accent steeped in the Deep South. "It's terrible cold tonight. Just terrible."

The woman sounded kind of nice. She even pronounced the word "terrible" in such a way that the first syllable rhymed with "purr."

Turrible. Just turrible.

"Thank you. I'm not a doctor, though." Velvet forced the corners of the nurse's mouth into a smile and slipped past into the warm parlor, her hand brushing against the rough and staticky polyester of the woman's muumuu, picking up the charge.

She cringed.

Velvet hated being shocked almost as much as being surprised. Her brothers used to chase her around the living room, shuffling their feet against the carpet and reaching their grubby little sausage fingers for her earlobes. She'd tried to make sense of this incessant behavior by believing she'd been secretly adopted, or transversely, by believing that her parents had won her brothers at some supermarket contest, or perhaps they'd come free with a new bank account. Both had mops of sandy hair, while Velvet's was jet-black. Also, she could string words together into actual sentences and not just grunt like a couple of cavemen. Adopted cavemen. Regardless, a decade of surprise jolts to her ears had been more than enough to create a nasty little phobia. One that you'd think would be promptly cured upon the occasion of her death.

No such luck.

She drummed her fingers against the scrubs, hoping to discharge the static naturally, quickly.

Madame Despot shut the door behind them—between them and Quentin—and, to Velvet's dismay, slid every one of the nine bolts into place loudly. She spun and began to sweep past Velvet into the main room of the house. Velvet threw herself against the wall in hopes of avoiding the horrifying arc of electricity that was sure to discharge if the woman touched her again. Velvet sighed with relief as the woman passed and left her unscathed.

Velvet looked around quickly for signs of Logan and Luisa. A smear in the air. A shimmer. Something. The poltergeists needed to be made aware of the locked door situation—if they weren't already. Someone was going to have to get those locks open if Quentin and his corpse were expected to provide any sort of backup.

"I hope y'all don't mind the mess," the woman said in her welcoming drawl. "I haven't dusted in a good bit."

Velvet stepped into the room, eyes zooming to grim corners, to spiders building cities of death, plaster gargoyles leering from shelves of dark candles and books with leather spines, and black velvet curtains drawn up in shiny obsidian rope, dripping tassels like wax. A dense cloud of patchouli hung in the air like a concert hangover—thankfully covering up the cigar smoke to a small extent—while monks chanted quietly from a little stereo at Madame Despot's feet.

Goth heaven.

Velvet had nothing but respect for the decorator, though her choice of music was a tad dramatic. Benedictines were definitely at the esoteric end of the spectrum. She might have chosen some Sisters of Mercy or Lacuna Coil, but that's beside the point.

Luisa and Logan weren't anywhere to be seen.

Where are those ingrates? she thought. *And why is it I can't possibly lead a dependable team?*

She contemplated a quick jump from the nurse, just long enough to scream for the poltergeists beyond Madame Despot's auditory range, and then a dive right back in. Unfortunately, some people were really quick to recover, and those few seconds could blow the whole operation. You just could never tell. Velvet had to trust that they'd show up eventually. Also, if Luisa could be counted on for anything, it was to make it known when Velvet was being impolite. And shouting was definitely outside of Miss Manners's rule book.

"Have a seat, my dear, and tell me what you've come to see Madame Despot for." She puffed away and pointed to a chair on the opposite side of the table as she sank into her own.

Velvet looked at the chair and scowled.

Metal, of course. A scrolled filigree *metal*-backed chair. Tucked in neatly under the table, too, so she'd have to grab it and pull it back to be able to sit down.

Velvet bit her lip and inched her hand toward the chair, dreading the zap. Then, sure enough, it happened. She swore she could see the blue fiery arc cross the gap and shock the crap out of her fingers. She yelped like one of those yippy little purse dogs, jerked her hand away, and rubbed it against her leg.

"Woohoo. Static got ya, dinnit?" the fortune-teller said, and cackled.

But there was another laughing.

Quiet, childlike giggling echoed from just behind the walls. Luisa and Logan were either amusing themselves while they waited or had peeked into the room at just the right time to see her humiliate herself.

Velvet relaxed a little. Now if they'd just do something about the locks on the door, they could get this show on the road.

"Yeah," Velvet grumbled in response as she took a seat, then launched into the prepared speech. "I've come because I lost my brother recently. A horrible—"

"Had he been sick a long time?" the woman asked, interrupting, brow furrowed in concern.

Velvet recovered from the invasion into her memorized speech. Poorly. "Car crash. Car. A car. I was going to say 'car crash.' There was a crash."

"Oh, my," Madame Despot said, tilting her body awkwardly and fumbling for something under the table. "That is terrible." She retrieved an intricately carved wooden box, set it gently to her left, and dusted the top carefully.

It was *turrible. Or would have been,* Velvet thought. *Had it been true.*

She was, at that moment, completely mesmerized by the fortune-teller's actions, waiting for the magic to reveal itself. Velvet had already dismissed the idea that a spell was at play; there simply weren't any signs. No smudges marring the air, no glowing auras blistering from Madame Despot's hands like gunpowder residue. No. The shadowquakes were the result of something much more foul, anyway, and Velvet wondered if the magic would reveal itself from inside the box. Would the woman put the power of an imprisoned soul into play so soon? With the door still locked and everything? She chewed at the nurse's lip.

Madame Despot drew a wood match from a porcelain dish and sparked it to life at the end of her cigar. "And you want to know that he's okay? In the afterworld, I mean." She lit a squat crimson candle—the flame's reflection danced on the lenses of her sunglasses—and waited.

"Um . . . yeah," Velvet managed. "You think you can help?"

The woman said nothing, just continued to stare, or, Velvet supposed, she could have been taking a nap, for all Velvet would be able to tell with the fortune-teller's eyes hidden like that. She'd dismissed the possibility that the fortune-teller was blind. That would have been another matter entirely. Blind seers were nearly always authentic, at least in her experience, and wouldn't need a captured soul or something to prestidigitate. Their magic was pure. For the most part, it didn't send waves of hate into purgatory.

Meaning either of two things.

One, Manny's visions had been skewed and Velvet's team was barking up the wrong tree, and the epicenter of the most recent shadowquake was actually someplace else, somewhere hidden. Or two, this woman was a serious threat and could easily banish Velvet, Quentin, Luisa, Logan, and the yet to appear fifty-seventh soul with no more effort than you'd use to swat a fly.

So not cool.

Velvet shook off the discouraging thoughts—their intel couldn't have been that far off. Manny was very precise. And besides, if the fortune-teller was a real threat, she wouldn't need Velvet's fifty-seventh soul. Velvet glanced at the box. *Is it a cell?* she wondered. *Is this where Madame Despot keeps her magic?*

The woman unlatched the lid and opened it, creaking back the rusty hinges (more cheap effect). She reached inside and retrieved a package wrapped in a floral scarf and set it on the table. The scarf was knotted, and Madame Despot proceeded to loosen it and spread the silky fabric out like a tablecloth.

Inside was a deck of cards.

Tricky, Velvet thought. The woman was holding back. A soul couldn't be trapped inside a card. A proper cell required a hollow, a talisman, or a juju bag, something fit for a soul. Tight with magic.

"Um." Velvet held up one of the nurse's fingers. "Tarot cards?"

Madame Despot's hands stopped midshuffle. "Would you prefer something else?" Her words went from casually comforting to crisp and short. "My tarot are *very* accurate, dear."

"Something different, I mean," Velvet said. She had to tread lightly here. If Madame Despot did in fact possess a soul, then she'd be suspicious of anyone who might request that she use it. She thought quickly and responded, "I don't really believe in tarot."

The fortune-teller guffawed. "Don't believe in it! Why, it's the cornerstone of modern divination, and has been proven reliable by lesser readers than yours truly." She stopped and glowered across the top of her glasses; a glimmer played in the whites of her eyes. One that Velvet hoped was a reflection of the candlelight and not the other thing.

It couldn't be.

Velvet quickly shook off the possibility that she'd seen another of her kind staring out from behind the woman's eyes. It just didn't make sense. Plus, they'd have known before now. *Wouldn't they?* Manny would have sensed the presence of a possession at play in this shadowquake, surely.

The woman huffed and then wrapped up the deck quickly and set it and the box aside. She swiveled around and began to reach her short stubby fingers toward a porcelain cup with rose vines wound about it like chain link.

Tea leaves?

Velvet felt the irritability creeping through her nerves and stopped short of blurting out, *"Where the hell do you have the soul, witch?"* She opted, rather, for the ultimately more subdued. "Uh. Do you have anything more dramatic? Something . . . showy? I have money, you know. I'd like a little entertainment—"

Madame Despot spun on Velvet, her sunglasses reflecting the nurse's grizzled face.

Velvet wished she could eat her words back out of the air, but no such luck.

"Entertainment?" the woman spat. "I thought you were interested in making contact with your brother, were concerned about his welfare."

"Oh, I am," Velvet backpedaled. "I just—"

"Well, if it's entertainment you want, it'll cost you." The fortune-teller slammed her hand down on the table, bringing her face so close to the nurse's that Velvet could barely breathe from the cloud of cigar smoke billowing from the woman's mouth like a chimney. "And I don't have a credit card machine."

"I have cash," Velvet lied quickly. "Plenty."

"You'd better." Madame Despot tore the cigar from between her lips and tamped it out in the match bowl, sparking a few to life in the process and leaving them to flare and flicker. She launched from her seat and disappeared behind a thick curtain. Her grumbling muffled but audible, she banged around in the hidden room.

Velvet, not seeing even a hair of either Luisa's or Logan's lousy head, took the opportunity to scramble for the locked door. She jerked around to make sure the woman was still midsearch before slipping into the vestibule. Then she slid open the bolts slowly, one by one, wishing she had some oil to stop the tiny squeaks that crept out—sounding way louder than they actually were, she hoped. The next to last one screeched like an owl. Velvet cringed and had to force a quick cough to cover up the racket.

"It's here somewhere!" Madame Despot called out. "Just be a second."

Velvet straightened and waited for a sign that the woman had continued her search. Clang and clatter echoed through the space, and the woman cursed and spat in response. Velvet went back to work on the door, unlocking the last bolt before rushing back through the hall and into the room.

She'd nearly made it to her chair when Madame Despot whipped the curtain open with a grinding hiss from the bronze rings holding it to the rod.

Velvet froze midstep.

"Oh. Were you leaving?" the woman asked, her mouth crimping into a tight line.

"Nah—no. Nope. Of course not."

"Thought you might skip out before I'd issued your bill? Make a run for it? Dine and dash?" Madame Despot's lips had completely disappeared by this point.

"I'm not sure how that last one is appropriate, since you haven't offered any food. And you haven't given me a reading, yet, so . . ."

A grin flickered on the woman's lips.

Velvet continued, "But no. I was just admiring . . ." Her eyes scanned the bookcase by the front hall, eyes lighting on a ratty-looking stuffed crow. "Your lovely taxidermy."

"Oh?" The fortune-teller wasn't convinced.

"Um . . . yes. I love stuffed animals, and this is a particularly nice crow specimen."

Madame Despot tilted her head to the side, glancing in the direction of the bird, her shoulders loosening along with her suspicion. "It's a raven."

"Well, then, it's a fantastic piece. Where on earth did you get it?"

"Oh, dear, I don't know. Target, probably. You want this reading or not?" She pointed toward the empty chair, disappeared behind the curtain briefly, and then reappeared carrying a crystal ball on a footed stand.

Velvet inadvertently caused the nurse's abdomen to tighten.

A cell.

The *actual* cause of the shadowquakes. Killing a person wasn't nearly enough to create such a disturbance. The real evil was in the spell that imprisoned a soul inside the crystal ball. It had to be shattered to stop the destruction in purgatory.

Velvet sat back down in her chair, eyes never leaving the cloudy depths of the glass orb. "Yes," Velvet said, trying to contain her desire to leap over the table and snatch the ball immediately. "Very much."

"What was your brother's name?" Madame Despot asked.

"Spencer. Spencer Pratt." She took the name from a television show she hadn't thought of in years. If she recalled, Spencer was a bit of a douche. Much like her real brothers, only, to be fair, much older and worse.

"Spencer Pratt," the woman repeated. "And your name?"

She almost responded "Heidi," then thought it might be a jinx and recalled the nurse's actual name. "Antoinette."

"Of course." She pointed at Velvet's chest. "Silly me; it says so right on your badge. I'm going to call for your brother now, see if he'll come in search of your essence."

That'll make two of us, Velvet thought, and glanced toward an antique mirror, dark and smoky where it met the ornate frame that held it. Sticking straight out of the center was Grover, fresh from Sesame Street and nodding wildly. The costume, the one Logan had been wearing the Halloween night when he'd died, never failed to surprise her when it popped up, wild eyed and tongue protruding from the fuzzy blue mask's wide mouth. She thanked God she hadn't been wearing her ratty bunny slippers the day she'd died, or she'd be stuck in them every time she crossed into the daylight. Why wearing slippers to school was ever a fashion trend would remain a mystery—an eternity of *cute* was enough to send chills spiking through her, right to the bone, or whatever it was that kept her frame up these days, so hard to tell. But Logan didn't seem to mind his costume. He was like that, good-natured, easy. Until it was time to fight. Then watch out.

Their eyes met, and Velvet motioned with a nod of her head toward the crystal ball. Grover nodded and ducked back inside the mirror, presumably to collect Luisa and get ready for the attack.

Madame Despot caged the ball between her stubby fingers, running the tips over the glass and moaning annoyingly. "Spencer Pratt!" she bellowed.

Velvet rolled her eyes.

Logan must have alerted Luisa and they'd met up with Quentin, because the next thing Velvet knew, amid Madame Despot's loud orchestrations and ball rubbing, Velvet heard the soft click of the front door latch and the sloshy footsteps of what could only be the bare rotten feet of a corpse.

And if she could hear him, it wouldn't be long before Madame Despot would.

Velvet forced out a violent cough and joined the fortune-teller in yelling, "Spencer!"

Madame Despot's eyes snapped open and glowered. "Please! Let me do my job."

Velvet made like she was locking her lips closed with a key, and the woman went back to her show. It didn't matter what kind of drama she employed; the soul inside the cell would be implored to respond no matter what. Even now, the cloudy imperfections in the glass turned inky and swirled inside.

Luisa appeared through the curtain hiding the back of the shop and waited.

So did Velvet. She sensed Quentin's readiness to her left, and after Logan appeared in the mirror again, Velvet nodded to each of them to begin.

Luisa and Logan disappeared and immediately began making a racket in the back room. Pots and pans clanged, chains rattled—it was amazing how those two always managed to find kitchen stuff to bang together, not to mention chains.

Where do you even find chains when you're alive?

Velvet expected Madame Despot to scream, to jump from her chair on cue and spin toward the clatter.

But she didn't. She did turn her head a bit, glancing suspiciously in the direction of the curtain.

Seeing the smallest opportunity, Velvet dove across the table for the glass ball, and so did the fortune-teller, her hands twisting into gnarled claws, her face recast into a tortured grimace. Velvet looped her finger around one of the stand's knobby feet and pulled the base out from under the orb. Madame Despot's hands slammed against the bare table, and both watched as the orb rolled across the table-cloth toward the edge.

"Nooooo!" the fortune-teller cried.

"Yesss!" Velvet hissed, hoping that the thing would just shatter when it hit the floor.

But by some trick of fate—and frankly the fates hadn't been so kind as of late—instead of busting into a thousand pieces, the crystal ball bounced off the soft fringe of the Oriental carpet beneath them and rolled across the maple floors toward the entry hall. Madame Despot dropped to her hands and knees and scrambled after it. Velvet launched herself from her chair, sending it crashing somewhere behind her as she cursed herself for picking such a slow body for a job as important as this one.

"My cell!" the woman yelled. She tore at the floor with loud scrapes of her nails as she scuttled toward their rolling target. If the fortune-teller could have acted guiltier in that moment, Velvet was pretty sure she would have won an award.

Velvet darted up next to the woman and felt a thick arm slam into her shins, clothesline style. She lost control, and the nurse's body dropped forward onto knees that screamed with pain as they banged against the solid surface.

"Oh, crap." Velvet winced. That was definitely going to leave a pair of bruises.

The fortune-teller swiped at the ball, nearly grasping it, but her fingertips clipped it and sent it rolling off toward the door. "Dammit!" she shouted, and sprang up from the floor, sneering at what she saw waiting for her in the hall.

Velvet stood up slowly, favoring the nurse's sore knees, brushing the dust from the scrubs. She saw the dull glow of Quentin's spirit in the dead thing's eyes. "You don't mind zombies, do you, Madame Despot—or whoever's in there?"

The woman's sunglasses fell from her face. She turned a pair of scornful glowing eyes on Velvet. "Shut up, girl. Don't think I don't know who you are."

Velvet wasn't prepared to fight another body thief, but the way this one was talking to her, she was kind of looking forward to it. It wouldn't hurt to burn off some of her aggression after the afternoon's run-in at Bonesaw's shed. Plus, she had a pair of the best tackles in the business in Logan and Luisa. Velvet glanced over her shoulder at the twins, Logan as Grover the happy-go-lucky Muppet, blue hands balled into tight fists, snarling and ready to rumble, and Luisa, a pretty little girl in pigtails and a Catholic-school uniform. She stood in a crouch, her fingers clawing at the air dramatically. The ghost in Madame Despot didn't have a clue what was coming at her.

Not a clue.

"I'm probably not going to shut up," Velvet said as she strode into the hall and accepted the crystal ball from Quentin's bony grip. "What I am going to do is shatter your evil plans, right about now."

"You can't stop the departure. It's coming. It'll be glorious. Angels will sing."

Velvet hesitated, the words scurrying over her like bugs. But she couldn't let the evil spirit win; she lifted the crystal ball high above her head, just as the fortune-teller turned.

"Oh, why be so hasty?" Madame Despot held her hands out in supplication. "Surely we can strike some sort of bargain."

Velvet feigned considering the bitch's offer, then brightened. "Maybe so. How about, right after I bust the crap out of this . . ." She tossed the cell into the air.

The woman cried out, and then relaxed a bit as Velvet caught it.

Velvet loved having the upper hand in negotiations.

"Let's agree that you'll be going back to whatever borough in purgatory you stole out of, and I won't imprison you inside a Tylenol and feed it to this guy." She stabbed her thumb in the direction of Quentin's zombie suit. The corpse's mouth hung open with the kind of disgusted expression that screams, "I need to be consulted about that kind of thing." Velvet rolled her eyes. Sure a trip through someone's bowels wasn't exactly effective in expelling a possession, but it sure would be gross.

Madame Despot stood with her hands planted on her hips, sucking her teeth. "I don't suppose we will be making any deal, then."

"Smart." Velvet turned toward the main room and raised the ball over her head.

The woman screamed and bolted forward, arms outstretched and hands balled into fists. Quentin stumbled toward her, as fast as he could move the corpse's decaying muscles.

Velvet slammed the cell onto the floor with all the nurse's strength.

Instead of a loud bang or the crash of glass shattering,

the second the crystal ball made contact with the floor, the room fell into an eerie silence. Nothing happened at first, but Velvet knew enough to jerk the nurse's hands away from the cell and step back as quickly as she could. Even Madame Despot's struggle with Quentin had diminished to a stand-still.

A spark ignited deep inside the crystal ball, twitching there like a fleck of gold caught in the current of a souvenir snow globe. The more Velvet watched, the brighter it grew, until a brilliant flare of light exploded out of it, filling every corner of the murky room. The force of it hit Velvet and tossed her backward against the wall, and she slid down until her butt connected with her ankles. Across the room, Quentin and Madame Despot were a tangle of flowy robes and rotten flesh. Logan and Luisa were still in the process of tumbling toward the curtained doorway.

Light spiked and shimmered from the cell through a web of tiny fissures that spread across the surface of the crystal. Then, as the magic holding the little prison together truly fell apart, the ball glowed as hot as an ember, pulsing so brightly that they had to shield their eyes to follow the rest of its transformation.

The cracks disappeared entirely and the glass took on a molten gelatinous quality. It ballooned and twisted upward until it resembled a glowing blob of soft-serve and then abruptly fell over onto its side with a wet thud and throbbed against the floor. The thinnest end of the oblong shape split into two long appendages, and the upper melted into the shape of a head, torso, and arms.

The rest happened so quickly, it was hard to track through

human eyes. The glass crystallized and cracked. Velvet covered the nurse's face with her hands. A sharp pop echoed through the room, and shards of glass rained down on them with an oddly musical tinkling.

When Velvet gaped at the spot where the soul had taken form, it was gone.

A little sigh of relief escaped her.

The dark magic was broken. Even now the dark mists would be receding from the Latin Quarter, the tentacled beast releasing its imprisoned audience, the ground stilling.

Her eyes darted toward Luisa. The girl was chewing on her lip and gawking in the direction of the black curtain. Velvet craned her neck to peer around the fallen table beside her. There, amid a carpet of broken glass twinkling like fallen snow, was the ghost of a boy, his head lolling against his shoulder, his long legs tangled up in the dark fabric.

Handsome, with one of those sharp angular jaws and the kind of comfortably disheveled dark blond hair that belonged on a surfer, but this kid wasn't. He was lanky, more than six feet tall, and he had a body for basketball and trouble.

Luckily for Velvet, he was also totally unconscious.

Chapter 8

"Deal with him!" Velvet shouted to Luisa, stabbing one of the nurse's spindly fingers toward the boy. The girl rushed across the room. Velvet spun back toward a howling Madame Despot. The possessed woman had wriggled free of Quentin and was sneaking toward the curtained room with more speed than the body's weight suggested was possible, and with an inexplicable expression of glee.

Velvet followed the woman's course to its ultimate conclusion and saw a surprise waiting for the fortune-teller, of the Jim Henson variety. Deep inside the hidden room stood Logan—Grover mask on but blue paws dangling from his bare wrists like sweaty winter mittens. He mashed his fist into his palm, polishing. Velvet couldn't help but giggle as he leapt up and pounded not the turbaned woman, but the ghost lingering inside. Logan, small for his age, but lithe, clung to the front of Madame Despot's muumuu with one hand, his knees pressed into her gut for leverage. With each punch, the back of the possessing ghost's head broke past the confines of the turban, a glowing bulbous tumor in need of excision.

"Release that body, ghost!" Velvet shouted. "I can see you bouncing around in there like a lotto ball!"

A ghostly arm sprang from Madame Despot's chest like an alien, connecting with Logan's hip and knocking the little Muppet into the air and through the wall of the back room. The woman jerked her head toward Velvet and spat, "Never, body thief! She's mine, and I'll take her to the grave if I like."

Behind Velvet rose the not so gentle stirrings of her fifty-seventh soul extraction.

"What the hell?" the boy shouted. "What's happening?"

And then Luisa was on him, whispering into his ear, doing her best to calm him, or at the very least keep him busy while they finished the work at hand. Velvet couldn't help sneaking a peek in their direction; the boy was on his feet now, towering over the younger girl. His eyes were as big as saucers, and his fingers were clawing at his basketball tank.

Freak-out in three, two . . .

A scrabbling drew Velvet's attention back to the possessed woman. Madame Despot lurched forward and snatched a letter opener from a nearby bureau and held it to her own throat, even as Logan reappeared, his face scrunched in anger. A phantasm of chain dangled from his fist and trailed off behind him into the wall. Madame Despot's eyes widened at the sight.

"Hold your poltergeist back, girl!" the fortune-teller yelled. Her voice had gone deep and gravelly, and her possessor's eyes blazed fury from her skull. "Or I'll banish the girl and the little furball to the cold depths of a jelly jar!"

Velvet was taken aback. Not by the threat, which was just that—Velvet knew of only one way to cram a soul into a jar, and that was by force . . . lots of it—but by the instantaneous desire for a peanut butter and jelly sandwich, strawberry, preferably.

Damn food cravings.

"It'll be hard to do your . . . banishing spell with a clammy corpse hand against your mouth, won't it?" Velvet glanced over her shoulder and barked, "Quentin, get over here and muffle this thief. I'm tired of listening to it blather."

"I'll cut it," Madame Despot said, and pressed the dull blade of the letter opener deep enough into the body's neck that it disappeared in its folds. "I swear it."

"Yeah, yeah." Velvet yawned.

The corpse shambled forward to the strains of the new soul's screams of "Zombie! Zombie!" And then, "This isn't happening. This isn't happening. This isn't happening." The boy had found a mantra.

Quentin clamped a rotten hand across the fortune-teller's mouth. It settled there with a sickening sucking sound, and the woman's eyes swelled. Velvet was certain Madame Despot had just taken a mouthful of pus, or something likewise as gross.

"This isn't happening. This isn't happening. This isn't happening."

Okay, Velvet thought. *That's getting a tiny bit annoying.*

"We'll be with you in a second, got it?" she growled, glancing quickly away as Quentin dragged the fortune-teller, kicking, screams muffled, into a shadowy corner of the room.

"I guh-guess so," the boy stammered, and stood, confused, the fear visibly quaking in his legs.

It wasn't that Velvet didn't have any sympathy for the kid—of course she did—but she had a job to do. Besides, this was the fun part.

As Madame Despot jerked and struggled, Quentin's borrowed arms creaked and popped like knuckles, as though one jerk away from dislodging and flopping onto the floor. The woman cursed and growled like a dog protecting a bone.

"You're not coming out, then?" Velvet asked.

More growling.

"All right, this shit is getting old." Velvet sighed and nodded to the poltergeists. "Bring on the bear traps."

Logan tore off his mask. It hung off his shoulders like a furry hood. Luisa ordered the new boy to stay put and shoved her hand into the nearest wall, tongue thrusting as she searched and then found the end of another chain. Glowing links, as blue as ice, emerged one by one, clinking and clattering until a ghostly trap slid from the wall, already set, its sharp teeth glistening and sparking.

Velvet crouched down as, on the opposite side of the room,

Logan whipped the chain around his head like a lasso. His trap swung dangerously in a broad loop, cutting through the walls soundlessly.

"No!" the ghost inside Despot screamed.

Luisa slid her trap into the center of the room as Quentin pitched the fortune-teller forward onto it. The body thief stumbled directly onto the trigger and howled as the teeth snapped through Madame Despot's legs and bit into its hijacking spirit. Logan shouted, "Punk rock!" and launched his trap forward. It caught the woman's chest with a sharp snap. The human body fell away, taking a few awkward steps before collapsing into a mound of robes and flesh with a thud and a groan.

What remained upright was gray, nebulous, and totally pissed off, its form slipping from human into something sluglike and splotchy with dark oily smudges. The old guard Salvagers called the affliction "going banshee," since the longer a ghost tread in dark magic, the more deformed it became.

And the louder it could scream.

The sound reverberated through the room. Free from its human shell, the ghost's voice carried an unfettered violence that quaked every surface. The dust on the floor clouded around their ankles. The chandelier above the seer's table swung.

The banshee began to twist and struggle with the bear traps, its form wringing and spasming even as it continued to wail. Chains whipped and jumped in Logan's and Luisa's hands, forcing them to anchor their feet ankle-deep into the hardwood floor. Dimples pocked where the pair of traps gnashed and continued to clamp tighter into the ghost's flesh. Fat globs of ectoplasm plopped onto the floor and snaked their way back to the creature's feet, where they were reabsorbed.

"Gross." Luisa crinkled her nose, even as she tightened her grip on the chain.

"Seriously," Velvet agreed. "You got it, though, right?"

Luisa nodded. Logan's sneer and cocked brow more than implied he'd taken offense. "Obviously!" he shouted.

Velvet turned to Quentin and gestured back at the boy crouched by the curtains. His chanting done, her fifty-seventh soul had jammed his palms ineffectually over his ears to close off the sound of the banshee's nearly constant scream—as if that were possible. "Let me get this guy out of here and then, well, you know what to do."

She didn't have to tell him twice.

He forced the corpse to hunch over and right a chair. The zombie took a seat, wriggled its shoulders, and closed its eyes, face turning slack and placidly calm. Undertaking took the most concentration of any Salvage position, but it was also the dirtiest.

Better him than her, Velvet thought, knowing all too well the teeming process underway beneath the dead body's skin. She ducked under the bucking chains and crossed the room to meet the freed soul.

He was taller than she'd first thought, probably older too—seventeen or eighteen—and he was likely a hot guy when his face wasn't twisted up in a mask of horror. He wore his sandy hair closely cropped to his skull, but messy, tussled in an unintentionally sexy way. Like he'd just finished making out with someone and didn't care who knew it.

Not Velvet's type at all.

Though—she cocked her head to the side and squinted—with the right scars, tattoos, and piercings, he wouldn't be so terrible to objectify on a regular basis . . . given he kept his mouth shut and didn't annoy her.

She didn't have to worry about any of that anyway. The guy was only along for the ride until they got him through to purgatory. After that, she didn't care what happened to him. Didn't have the time to care. Or the energy.

But he was pretty freaked out, and Velvet wasn't completely heartless. She supposed there was a tiny ghost of the organ still beating inside her, shrunken and dark and cold, a last line of defense against the encroaching apathy.

Still.

She squatted beside him and rested her hand on his shoulder—Manny always stressed the importance of empathy, real or feigned, in guiding new souls out of dangerous situations. It made them placid, like sheep or something.

But the boy didn't react. Zero eye contact. He rocked in place, and there was a low murmur that she could barely detect except when she saw that his lips were moving.

Velvet gave the boy a quick slap on the cheek.

Empathy only went so far . . . and they were, after all, on a timeline.

Startled, he fell back on his butt and glared at her, panting. Confusion clouded his eyes. "The girl said I'm a ghost, like her," he whispered. "She's crazy, right? Tell me I'm right."

Velvet glanced back at Luisa. "The girl" had wrapped her

end of the chain around her wrist and was grinning, tugging at the bear trap ferociously. With each pull, the banshee's wail changed pitch a little, until Velvet could make out just the hint of a song in its cry.

Was that?

Yes.

"London Bridge."

Velvet returned her attentions to the boy. She nodded. "Most definitely. Luisa's clearly insane. Nothing to worry about."

His shoulders sagged a bit at that, and she thought she heard a gentle sigh escape him. Her gaze lingered on his mouth, on the gentle bow of his lips, parted and perfect. She had the odd urge to kiss them, and recoiled immediately.

What the hell was wrong with her?

Her job was to protect. To deliver.

To extract.

And certainly not to terrorize this kid with the crinkled lips of her old lady suit.

"Listen," she said, probably a bit too harshly. "Get up and follow me. Those crazy kids over there are going to be doing something you don't want to see."

His eyes grew large, and he shot a glance at the struggling banshee, the ghostly twins, and the corpse rotting in the corner. "But, what's—"

"No questions." Velvet noticed Quentin's skin was already starting to pock and vibrate. Beneath the banshee's scream, an almost undetectable hum filled the room. "We've got to move!"

The boy scuttled to his feet, and Velvet motioned for him to fall in behind her. When he lingered, she snapped her fingers in front of his face and screamed, "Now!"

She herded him past Luisa and into the entry hall, turning to catch the girl's attention. "Get out as soon as Quentin makes the transformation. Don't risk it. You know how that could end up."

Luisa quivered.

Once outside, the boy seemed to calm down a little, though he was intently focused on her—apparently it was easier to connect with an old nurse than the ghost of a twelve-year-old girl in a Catholic-school uniform. Velvet could see how that would be a little weird. Souls don't even know they're dead when they come out of the cells, let alone know to identify a kinship with other spirits immediately. That'd be too easy.

She figured she'd better take advantage of his temporary serenity, before things got crazy. "What's your name, new guy?"

"Na-Nick," he stuttered meekly. "Nick Atherton Russell."

Velvet narrowed her eyes. "What's that, one of those hyphenated names? The kind rich people have?"

He shook his head, the hint of a smile at play on those amazing lips. "No. Far from it. My mom's a cocktail waitress in SoHo."

"Was," Velvet mumbled, correcting him as she glanced toward the curtains in the front window of Madame Despot's shop. The thick fabric had opened a crack during the struggle, and deep against the far wall, beyond the horrific mutation of a spirit, Quentin's corpse had nearly doubled in size. The surface of its flesh bubbled and throbbed with such intensity that, from where they stood, Quentin's zombie began to look like a smear on the windowpane.

"What'd you say?" the boy asked, stepping between her and the window.

Velvet shrugged, absently peering over his shoulder. "Well, technically, I guess you're right. I'm incorrect. Your mom could very well *still* be a cocktail waitress. The 'was' applies to you, mostly."

"Okay. Now you're talking like that nut-job kid in there."

She ignored the boy. Luisa and Logan stretched the banshee sideways, both pulling like quarter horses. Luisa was almost to the window, the petite oval of her face twisted with effort, ready to drop the chain and slip through the wall as soon as the undertaking was complete.

And from the looks of things, it wouldn't be long.

Quentin was about to pop.

"Now, you're going to hear something a little weird, Nick," she said. "That's your name, right?"

He nodded.

"Like I said, it's gonna get weird."

"So just now? Like in a minute?" The sarcasm dripped from his words. " 'Cause all that stuff from before? Perfectly normal."

Velvet glanced back at the boy. She was certain he thought he was being cute, and that may have been true, but the truth was, he was her responsibility only until they crossed into purgatory. "Yep. Whatever you do, don't turn around."

"Why not?" he asked, and turned toward the crack in the drapes.

She reached out and grabbed his cheek, turning him to face her. "Because it might freak you out. And I'm not really in the mood to chase you down the streets of Philadelphia in the middle of the night. It's been a really taxing day already."

"Oh! *You've* had a bad day!" Nick shouted. He threw up his hands and started to pace back and forth in front of the window, gesturing wildly. "I'm sorry, lady. Did you just recently wake up in the middle of a horror movie and realize you were the ghost?"

Nick's outburst couldn't have come at a better time. The low hum from before had turned into an angry buzzing, so loud that it began to drown out the piercing scream from inside. Velvet watched as the body in the chair exploded into a swarm of flies.

"So you realize it, then?" she asked, keeping the distraction going. "That'll make things a ton easier."

"Is that supposed to be a joke?" Nick asked incredulously.

But Velvet didn't need to answer. Luisa darted through to the sidewalk a second before the flies rained sideways against the window, tapping and fluttering and getting stuck between the curtain and the glass. Nick turned to see where the girl had come from and recoiled at the sight of the flies. He stumbled back into the street at the very second a car sped by, zipping quite unaffected through his ghost.

"Really?" he shouted after the speeding car, and then louder, "Really?"

Velvet peered back into the shop.

Flies swarmed about the raucously undulating spirit, carpeting its gray flesh in a teeming, chomping mass. The banshee let out a final scream, clogged quickly to silence as the black army of insects marched past its lips, stuffing phantom entrails. The occasional disfigured limb sprang from the throng, dense with spasms and pain, and was bitten free and dropped to the floor.

While the new guy continued to make an ass out of himself ranting and raving about reckless driving, Velvet walked quietly back to the shop door and opened it. She stood back and felt an infinitesimal pressure on her arm as Luisa slipped her hand through the crook of Velvet's elbow, huddling up.

"Do you suppose we should warn him?" the girl asked.

Velvet glanced in the direction of Nick; the boy was pacing, shouting, making fists, and throwing pretend punches. From the look of Logan, who'd made a stealthy appearance, he was egging the ridiculous boy on. Free from the rotting corpse he was engineering, Quentin merely leaned against the wall, squinting with his chin trapped in the cage of his thumb and index finger.

Waiting.

"Nah," Velvet grunted. "Why bother? He's busy distracting himself from the inevitable."

Luisa nodded.

With a whoosh, a solid entity of flies punched from Madame Despot's vestibule like a fist, black and howling. Victorious. The doorframe creaked and splintered from the weight and bulk of their exodus, showering the sidewalk with toothpick shards of wood and sheared-off nailheads. The swarm slammed into the window of the building across the street, a rubber stamp store called Inkies, before banking upward into the sky. The force of the impact left the glass as pocked as a road trip windshield.

Nick, staggered to a stunned silence, wandered back over to Velvet, scuffing the gravelly concrete like a child as his gaze followed the insects' dramatic exit.

"That was . . . ," he began, mouth hanging open. Still staring.

"Awesome?" Logan offered.

"Skillful. And/or brilliant?" Quentin shined his fist against his chest.

Luisa clucked her tongue and began to wander off toward the stamp shop.

Nick shook his head like a dog shaking off water. "Wait. What was that?" he shouted. "What the hell was all that?"

"Oh, Christ," Velvet said. "You act like you've never seen flies dispatch a ghost before."

She peeked back into the shop and, hearing the stirrings of Madame Despot's recovery—mostly grunts and gurgles and moans—shut the door as quietly as she could into its buckled, broken frame.

Chapter 9

Velvet took in the street with a dull interest. It was even more abandoned than when they'd crossed over, deader than a skinhead at a 50 Cent show. No cabs in sight, no bums snoring off cheap wine, and thankfully no more banshees swiping souls.

It was a good night in that respect.

Nick trudged along behind her, nearly clipping her heels, yammering and looking unreasonably hot, which should have been much more annoying. But Velvet was tired and more than a little high from the beating they'd delivered to the villain du jour to worry about the hint of attraction creeping through her brain.

"Wow," he said, his tone far less broody and angst-filled than a newly dead kid had any right to be. "That was mad crazy."

"Right?" Luisa nodded, grinning.

"That, son," Quentin bragged, slapping the new guy on the back, "is what separates the undertakers from the regular run-of-the-mill body thieves." He winked at Velvet.

"Yeah, yeah," Velvet turned and strode off ahead of the group.

"Mad crazy," Nick mumbled again. "Where we headed?"

"Home, I guess," Velvet said. "After a while."

"Home?" Nick seemed to think about that. "Like the place you're all haunting or something?"

Velvet stopped dead and spun on him. "Don't you ever say that!" She pressed her hand to the very edge of the borrowed body's skin. The nurse's hand would pass right through Nick, but hers wouldn't. She gave him a forceful shove, and he toppled over onto his ass, astonished.

"I wouldn't do something like that ever," she continued. The lie fell so easily off her tongue, it surprised her, but she had to make her point. "None of us would. That's station rule. No haunting ever."

"Well, what were you just doing in there?" He jabbed a thumb in the direction of the shop. "That in there with Madame Despot?"

"*That!*" She got up in his face. "*That* was our assignment. *That* was an operation. *That* . . . was us saving your lousy butt." She pivoted and stomped off.

She heard a defeated sigh, but before long the boy was scrambling up behind her again.

"Hey. How could I know?"

Velvet shot him a cruel glowering stare, before realizing

he was absolutely right. She hated to admit it, but she was being a bitch again . . . unintentionally. She must have been tired. Exhausted, even.

"I mean, I'm sorry," he said finally, those sad eyes doing the puppy dog thing.

She slowed down, her face softening a bit. "Fine. You're new. It's okay. It can't have been easy being trapped in that crystal ball for however long you've been in there. I'm the one who should be sorry for yelling at you." She gave him a reassuring smile and patted him on the shoulder . . . or right about where his shoulder would have been had he not been see-through, you understand.

"So why . . . ," he began another question.

Maybe the guy just had a naturally curious personality—those could keep a person talking long after they'd found out something really horrible—or maybe he just liked to hear himself speak. There were certainly plenty of boys who wouldn't shut up, despite being told directly to do so. The boy's eyes were still saucers, wild and darting from one image to the next and then back to the nurse's face as though she were the only real thing. Shock. Had to be.

Whatever. It was getting on her nerves.

"No more questions," she snapped.

The clinic loomed ahead of them, two stories of stark white brick, with windows as glassy-eyed as her fifty-seventh soul extraction. An ambulance idled on the curb, its back doors open and its tailpipe blowing smoke rings that clung to the chilly air like fat sticky doughnuts. A young woman in scrubs hugged herself, outside the swinging doors, rubbing heat into her arms and peering out into the silent night. As they approached, she squinted.

"Is that you, Antoinette?" the girl ventured.

"Sure is, hon!" Velvet waved at the girl and spun back toward Nick to hiss, "Stay put."

She jogged the short distance, clogs clopping on the concrete, and snatched the nurse's pack of cigarettes from her uniform's front pocket. Velvet shook a cigarette up through the opening and fished it out with her lips. Then she lit it and inhaled deeply. Despite never having picked up a cigarette while she was alive—the very thought of it had grossed her out—when it was someone else's lungs, and in particular someone who smoked, Velvet couldn't resist taking a drag. She supposed it was like eating. Souls were deprived of that, too.

She tilted her head back and exhaled.

"You don't have time for a smoke, Toni!" An accusation worked its way into the girl's expression. "Delores . . ." The girl's eyes skittered toward the crack between the doors as though an ogre were about to burst through and devour them at any moment. "Delores is pissed. Seriously. She's about to crap crepe-soled shoes or something. I'd get back in there if I were you. And I'd have a good excuse when I did."

Velvet raised the nurse's eyebrow at the girl and took another drag. She couldn't contain a slight giggle when the young nurse spun on her heels and marched back inside — probably to alert the aforementioned ogre, Delores, of Nurse Antoinette's clear disdain for clinic politics.

"Enough of this bullshit," Velvet muttered.

Across the street, four ghosts waited not so patiently, two expressing a pretty clear annoyance. Logan wore a sneer, shaking his hand as though throwing dice . . . or, rather, Velvet hoped that's what he was indicating. Knowing him, he was late for some late-night alley gambling. Luisa, meanwhile, was likely ready to get back to her reading. She tapped her foot so brutally that Velvet could actually hear the blatant accusation in the tip-tapping of her shoes, the sound echoing across the street like exclamation marks. Quentin stood apart from the others, aloofly staring at the moon, likely deep in impure thoughts about Shandie and her Afro Puffs of Wonderment. But it was Nick who commanded Velvet's attention.

He stood halfway across the street, stone-still and staring at her intently, a glowing statue of Adonis in a basketball tank and long satiny shorts as though he were just coming from a game. There was something about his face, intense and open at the same time, his eyes focused on her every movement.

She felt the unwelcome niggling of attraction rise, and she became instantly furious.

Nick undoubtedly had the same effect on all the girls in his life.

Velvet wasn't having it. She didn't have time for anything more than a casual admiration. She could look, but she wouldn't touch. Distractions were the enemy.

Nick was the enemy.

Besides, she was busy unloading a body. Dispossessing without getting the person into too much trouble wasn't the easiest thing in the world. Antoinette had played such an invaluable role in saving purgatory tonight, and she didn't even know it.

So selfless. So innocent.

A tickle traveled up the back of the body's throat, followed by a terrible niggling thought.

So possibly cancerous.

Velvet's borrowed lungs heaved just then, sputtering phlegm up into the woman's mouth. She spat and tamped out the cigarette on the white wall, leaving a slash of black and a shower of glowing embers. She crushed the nearly full pack in her fist as another cough rattled through the body with such force, Velvet felt herself slipping out, her head nodding past the mask of the nurse's face. When it did, she saw Nick approaching, head tilted to the side and a look of redundant confusion on his face. Trying to figure out what exactly he was looking at.

He'd know soon enough, she thought.

The swinging clinic doors banged open, and a very sturdy nurse emerged, her hands planted on her hips and more hair on her upper lip than on her thinning scalp. Her eyes were ringed red. Her cracked lips twisted in a grimace. Delores, undoubtedly.

"Antoinette!" she hollered.

Velvet eased the woman's body backward toward the wall, sinking into a squat. Uncoiling her thoughts from around the mental box containing Antoinette's consciousness, she stepped away from the possession. As she did, the nurse slid down the wall and onto her butt with a thud. The woman groaned and sputtered little saliva bubbles, her limbs slack and askew. Generally and obviously incapacitated.

"Toni!" Delores swept in beside the prone form of her employee and snatched up her wrist, trying for a pulse. She patted the woman on the cheek rapidly, but Antoinette was, as so often was the case, completely unconscious.

A medical emergency was like a get-out-of-jail-free card. And Delores, despite her villainous, dramatic entrance, had crumbled into maternal fear for her worker.

Well done, Velvet thought.

She crossed to the center of the road, Nick's eyes following her every movement. And she realized he was truly seeing her for the first time. He shook his head, the realization parsing itself in small bits rather than all at once—

Velvet was a body thief like the spirit who had been inside Madame Despot . . . only cuter, obviously—how could she *not* be, in the black retro dress she wore as a ghost, shredded satin skirt floating in tatters around her favorite pair of Fluevogs.

"You're a—you're a . . . ," he stuttered.

"Yep. You got it."

He sucked back the ridiculous question and thrust out his hand.

Velvet glanced down and, finally, gripped his hand with her much more petite fingers.

"Big mitts," she said as they shook.

"I'm Nick," he said. "Nick Russell."

"Yeah. I know." She raised an eyebrow suspiciously and strode past him. "We've met. I was just engineering the nurse over there when we did." She pointed back toward the commotion in front of the clinic and began to walk away.

He trotted up behind her, matched her pace. "Engineered? Between what I just saw and seeing those flies take out that smoke thing, I'm thinking that's kinda like a possession. Emily Rose or some shit?"

She shook her head. "Totally. I'm your friendly neighborhood demon, Nick. Except I don't think anyone would call me friendly, and if my head spins around and the green spew starts, you should be scared."

"No doubt." He chuckled nervously. "But I figure you wouldn't have come to save me if you meant to mess me up."

She looked at him and laughed, a sweet chirping sound she didn't expect to come from her own mouth. It was mildly embarrassing. It probably would have caused her to blush, if Velvet didn't thoroughly expect to dump this guy off at the station and never see him again. "No. I guess not. But there's still time for me to change my mind."

The boy grimaced.

"Settle down there, Nick. I'm just kidding. I'm not going to go all Regan on you. I'm just an average everyday body thief. Well . . ." She reconsidered, glancing toward Quentin. His smirk was back. "Above average."

"Body thief, huh? So what's that make the ghost kids? Luisa?"

"She's an old soul," Velvet cut in. The girl was stomping off ahead of them, just turning the corner toward the blue car, the cat, and the mound of sodden newspaper. "Older than either of us, just not . . . grown up. Souls get kind of stuck, so she still looks like a kid. Watch how you talk to her; she'll cut you."

He nodded stoically. "Got it. Watch out for the little one. She's stabby."

Velvet couldn't conceal her smile. "Riiight," she said. "We got a lot to cover tonight before we can get home."

"So you've said before. And I'm really hoping it means you're getting me back to midtown."

Midtown? Manhattan? The banshee had wrangled Nick a long way from New York. Velvet wondered if there was something special about the boy. Why had he been chosen? Or had his imprisonment been merely a convenience?

"Manhattan?" she asked.

"Yeah," he said, suddenly excited and talking with his hands. "Me and my mom got this boxy midtown apartment. Rackety radiator, too hot in the summer, not hot enough in the winter, and the pipes groan like a submarine in those World War II movies, like any minute, the walls are gonna explode and drown us in rusty water. My mom insists it's full of 'vitamins.' Or used to . . ." His voice trailed off, eyes darting to the transparency of his fingers.

"Yeah, about that?" Velvet reached out and pushed his hand back down to his side. "Home is a little more complicated now. Where we're going is a million miles away from here, or just over there." She pointed at a bench bolted into a foundation of cement.

Nick shook his head.

Velvet tossed her hair over her shoulder. "It's really hard to explain. It's just easier to show you."

Nick planted his feet and refused to move another inch. "Maybe I don't want to go! Maybe I want to get back to New York and be done with all this weird shit!"

Velvet didn't turn back to look at him. Just stood there, glaring, waiting for him to finish with his tantrum.

"We all want to go home, Nick. Each and every one of us." She glanced back over her shoulder, attempting to look sympathetic—and for all she knew, maybe she'd nailed it. "But we're not going to. There's no point."

She drifted toward him. Her face softened, her posture slouched, aggressiveness melting away. "You're not going home, either," she said. "Even if you did, your mom wouldn't be able to see you."

"What are you talking about?"

"You know."

He shook his head.

She shrugged and threw up her hands. "You're dead."

"Yeah, right," he said, and turned to leave.

"I'm not kidding, Nick," she shouted after him. "I'm totally for real here. Welcome to the afterlife. How else do you explain being see-through? This doesn't happen because you sweat too much or lose too much weight or something. This shit is permanent."

He stopped still, and she watched as his gaze dropped away and down to his hands, past them. Through them. The flesh of his fingers and palms were reduced to a translucent glaze thinner than the sugary shimmer on a doughnut.

"Wait. Wait. Wait," he repeated, backing away from her, from the moment, from everything.

Velvet folded her arms across her chest. It was bound to happen. "Freak-out in three, two . . ."

She couldn't even hear her own voice finish the phrase. Nick was too busy freaking out.

He panted and mumbled. Velvet wasn't even sure he meant her to hear it. She reached out and took his hand, dragging him around the corner while he continued to deny the obvious.

"Is this it?" Luisa called from where she stood next to the blue car, her finger pointing down at a crack in the sidewalk.

Velvet nodded and twisted to watch Nick deteriorate into the inevitable mass of quivering boy tears. It was never pretty, but when crying started, Velvet felt the curious need to suppress it, to tamp down his pain. Maybe it was *her* having a nervous breakdown, she thought.

Nick shook with such ferocity, he'd begun to blur, and Velvet sensed the very real possibility that he was going to bolt down the street and away from them, try to get back to his mother.

She had to put a stop to that. Her team had done their job. She wasn't going to subject them to another manhunt, not at that late hour.

That would just be cruel.

She reached out and grabbed him by the arm, pushing him backward toward a bench. He pinwheeled a moment as his expectation that he'd land in the seat, rather than move through it and onto the ground, slipped away and landed with a thud.

He peered up from the ground, his expression pained.

Velvet flopped onto the wooden slats of the bench, expertly, crossing her legs and fixing the boy with a cold gaze.

"Let's make this quick," she said.

"Wha-what?"

"This!" She waved her arms about her, flailing. "The big crazy! We've got things to do and places to go. So you're going to have to run through your grief stages pretty quick. Have you managed to burn through denial? That's a tough one."

Nick stared back at her blankly.

"Listen. You have every reason to be feeling all those weird emotions about dying, but really, we can cut to the chase. Grief is for the survivors, the family. What you need to accept is, you've just learned a very valuable truth. You're the only one you know who's clued in to the secret."

"What are you talking about?" Nick lifted himself up onto his elbows.

"It's real, obviously. There's life after death."

Nick shook his head, as thought trying to shake the words out of his skull. "You say it like you just told me aliens exist, like it makes it any better."

"Yeah, but wait; it does. Because it's just like aliens. Like what if a flying saucer landed right over there and no one saw it but us? You'd know it was real. You'd accept it."

"Yeah."

"Well, you have to accept this. Check it out. You know how when someone dies, people are all sad and stuff?"

"Yeah?"

"Well, why are they sad?"

His face scrunched up quizzically and then brightened. "Because they won't be able to see their loved ones again. They'll miss them."

"No!" she shouted, suddenly standing and pacing like a detective delivering the evidence to a room full of suspects. "It's because they have to rely on faith that they will see that person again in heaven or . . ." Her eyes drifted toward the sky. "Wherever. When someone close to you dies, your faith is at its shakiest. Even if you're an atheist."

He cocked his head to the side, "How do you figure?"

"It just happens. Death causes people to reevaluate their beliefs. It brings up questions you don't want to ask; it creates anxiety."

"Well, I'm sure as shit anxious about it."

"What I'm saying is . . ." Velvet knelt down beside him and covered his hand with hers. She didn't expect the action to be as comfortable as it was. Her hand tingled at the touch. She tried to ignore it and continued, "You never have to be anxious again. Because you *know* what's up. The ones you've left behind don't."

She stood and started to walk away, then stopped and added, "Sure, you'll still feel sad, but it's not going to be about death."

He rolled onto his feet and bounded after her. "You're pretty blasé about all this."

"Yep."

Nick opened his mouth and shut it, as though he couldn't think of what to say next. Instead he just studied her as she backed away, toward the crack, toward Quentin and the twins.

Velvet pulled Logan and Luisa close and whispered, "I'm going to do something—something probably shocking, but whatever. After, right after I've slipped through the crack, you push Nick through."

"But he needs direction. He needs the details." Louisa's voice was filled with concern. She liked order, routine, and Velvet was clearly making this up on the fly.

Velvet glanced up at the boy. His eyes were narrowing suspiciously as he loped around the bench to join them.

"Oh, he'll get details."

He came up to them, listing to one side, a broken boy. Even his voice sounded like the cracking of bone. "Velvet?" he asked. "That's your name, right?"

"Yep."

"Why can't I remember it? I mean, I can remember the stuff around it, but not actually dying."

She sucked in her breath. "I'm not gonna lie to you. Something nasty happened to you. Had to have for a banshee to get a hold of your soul."

"But shouldn't I remember? I mean, it must not have happened all that long ago."

She had no answer for him.

"Velvet?"

She turned around then, serious. "Don't question a lot of this stuff, Nick. You're not remembering it for a reason. The moment of death is traumatic, especially for people like us."

"Like us?"

"Well, yeah." She shrugged, sighed. It was difficult enough to get someone to buy into their own death, but it was close to impossible to walk them through the fact that they hadn't gone to heaven or hell. Limbo was a tough sell. "If you weren't like us, you'd have seen a nice big bright light and felt compelled to drift into it and stuff. But you didn't. You got trapped in that crystal ball by a mean-ass banshee, and we're going to figure out why. For now let's just get you oriented. Get you feeling safe."

Without even considering it, Velvet reached out and pressed her hand to his cheek and held it there.

"That feels good." His head lolled against his shoulders.

It was hard to explain, but a soft vibration seemed to pass between them, and he was looking at her again, gawping.

She withdrew with a snap.

"Thanks," he said quickly. "Thanks for saving me, but I really do need to get back home."

Velvet raised an eyebrow. It was time to put her plan into action. He may not have wanted to go with them, but he was definitely going to. She slunk into him, closing the gap and slipping her arms around his waist. He pulled back, startled, and then relaxed as she rested her head against his chest.

"Uh . . . ," he muttered. "Are you okay?"

She tilted her head back and straightened onto her toes, her lips nearing his. "I am. If you're going to leave, then I want to give you something to remember me by."

"Uh . . ." Nick's eyes widened.

She pressed her mouth to his, and felt a soft whimper escape him. Velvet parted her lips and sank into the kiss. The boy was clutching her now, buoyed by her actions, and groaning. He'd remember that particular detail vividly, and just one more. Enough for the pull focus, she hoped.

Velvet pulled away, leaned upward toward his ear, and whispered, "Where I'll be, there are shattered walls. Cracks everywhere. It's dark, but I'll be a light." She nibbled on his earlobe for good measure, pushed away, and then crouched to slip into the crack that split the sidewalk between them.

Chapter 10

Velvet tumbled forward into the murkiness of the Shattered Hall.

The gravelly floor grated against her hip as she skidded to a stop. She winced with pain but didn't stop moving. She couldn't. Nick would be right behind her. The last thing she needed was the boy to see her vulnerable and, worse, naked.

Nothing usurps authority like full-frontal nudity.

After scrambling over to the crate on her hands and knees, Velvet snatched her clothes out and wrangled her sore legs into the safety of her panties and jeans. But when she thrust her hand back in for her bra and shirt, all she felt was the slick leather of the combat boots, and beneath them, worn splintery pine.

"Dammit!" she shouted, and arced her hands back and forth along the cave floor. *So stupid*. She must have mistakenly tossed her bra and shirt out of the box when she'd grabbed the jeans. The Shattered Hall could really use some decent lighting.

How the hell did millennia pass without someone stringing up a freakin' gas line?

A thin whisper and an even fainter glow called Velvet's attention back to the crack. By the time she craned her neck toward it, a soul was already spilling out, a small bioluminescent fog, tendrils as fine and fragile as paper doilies. She draped her arm across her chest.

The cloud began to solidify into a pale boy curled up onto his knees, shivering violently. Nick. And he looked terrible—incapacitated—his gray-blond hair plastered to his scalp and his flesh pulsing with luminous memory. He flickered like a candle and cast the shadows into the far reaches of the hall, just illuminating a mound of fabric bunched up next to the boy's clawing fingers. Velvet snatched up her shirt and pulled it on quickly. At least that bit of crisis could be averted without too much drama.

If only Nick's would wind itself up so easily.

He was at once bigger and smaller than she'd expected. Vulnerable. She admired the flesh of his back. It was smooth and delicate, porcelain. He twisted his face toward her, and she nearly expected a crooked smile. She hoped for that. What greeted her instead was a tortured rictus of horror. Nick's lips curled away from his teeth, which shined inside his mouth like dull diamonds. And then he screamed.

Velvet winced and clamped her hands to her ears, wishing that Luisa, Logan, and Quentin were there to help him. Luisa especially would know how to comfort him.

The sound echoed about the hall and pierced her brain,

jarring not a feeling of compassion but a memory she kept jailed deep, behind great stone ramparts of pain.

She had wandered the pasture surrounding Bonesaw's shack for what seemed like hours—and had stood over the monster as he'd lain shirtless and breathless in the weedy grass, the full lamp of the moon turning great splashes of blood into inky sarcomas on his chest. That ignorant tattoo of his blessedly obscured except for a single word.

"Now."

Yes, she'd wondered. *What now?* What was this dull ache that followed her every movement? And what had happened in that darkened outbuilding? When could she go home, fall into her mother's arms, and sleep?

The shed sat amid the knee-high dandelions, as still and quiet as a mausoleum.

Beneath her, he dozed, blissfully unaware of her presence. *How could that be?*

Bonesaw had tortured her. She remembered that much.

Grated. Gored. Slit.

Her suspicions told her that every hurt he'd committed to her flesh lay inside the awful shed, balled up and red and perfectly still.

When could she go home?

She'd backed away from her killer and from that other Velvet—the one who had a chance to love and live and not hate—and wandered over the grassy knolls and hills.

It was merely by chance that she'd come upon the glen and the lightning-blasted oak, a faint glow tinkling within its blistered bark. It had called to her, and she had wondered if the famed "light" those near-death people went on about was just vastly exaggerated.

Then she'd touched it and shut her tearless eyes.

And was tossed out into the station from the primary crack amid a star-white orgy of fear and revulsion.

Screams.

Nails dragging across stone floors.

Nick scratched at the gravel, his long slender fingers quivering, catching, and slipping. Tracks carved into the grit like evidence. Velvet hovered over him, her thick wool peacoat in her hands and the breadth of the boy's muscled back beneath that. She was hugging him.

Shielding him.

Luisa stood nearby, Logan and Quentin blinking silently behind her outstretched arms. Already clothed, both of the boys had faces with masks of confusion. Luisa's head was cocked to the side, assessing not the boy—they had all seen plenty of terrible reactions to the crossing—but Velvet.

Velvet shrugged. "What?"

Luisa shook her head. "Nothing. It suits you."

Velvet recoiled, left the coat dangling atop the naked boy. She glanced down at Nick and saw herself that day so long ago now. And with her team watching, she fell atop him and held him tight.

"You'll be all right," she whispered over and over. "You'll be all right."

Eventually he stopped shaking.

"Thanks." Nick's voice was minuscule but there.

She shifted herself until she was beside him. Hunching there, close, she reached out to touch his cheek, and tilted his face to hers and said, in her most stoic tone, "You'll be all right. Because you have to."

He nodded, his eyes becoming less downcast.

"Because you're strong."

He nodded.

Luisa was smiling at her. On any other day, Velvet would have taken offense. Perhaps she should have, but something was pinching inside her.

Empathy is a memory, she figured.

She'd need to jot that down.

Luisa stepped forward, her patent leather shoes scraping away the melancholy. "Quentin, help Nick get into some clothes and meet us outside."

Luisa looped her arm through Velvet's and tugged her toward the gates that led out of the Shattered Hall. "Wow," she said. "There are sides to you, girl, I've never seen."

"Shut up."

"No," Luisa assured her. "I'm being serious."

"Yeah?"

"Yeah." Luisa nodded.

"Yeah," Velvet agreed, then added quickly, "shut up."

Behind them, Nick shouted—a welcome change to the maudlin emotionality, Velvet thought—his voice frantic and garbled, "I think I'm gonna hurl!"

The two girls turned back just in time to see him hunch over and heave an angry gush of sparks from his gaping mouth. They danced across the floor like firecrackers, snapping and popping amid a slurry of white liquid that evaporated before their eyes.

He fell back on his butt and groaned, rubbing at his temples. "I think I have a migraine. I'm seeing things."

"No, you don't," Quentin snipped. "You just puked up about six months' worth of memories."

"Yeah," Logan said, and guffawed. "You'll be wishing you had some of those to spare next time you get into a fight!"

Nick looked up at the boys, squinty-eyed and blinking, shading his brow with his hand like a visor.

"Are you two glowing?" he asked.

Logan and Quentin broke out in booming laughter. It echoed through the cavern and infected Luisa, and shortly after, Velvet joined in, doubled over and barely able to breathe.

"What's so funny?" Nick shouted. "I fail to see the humor."

Luisa fell into Velvet, riotously cackling.

"It's your sparkling personality," she shouted back to the boy.

Freshly outfitted in brown woolen trousers, dusty wing-tipped shoes, and a gray button-down shirt, Nick trotted up to meet them, the other boys hot on his heels. "Be serious!"

"You ever hear of phantom limbs?" Velvet asked.

His eyes drifted to his arms and the thin threads of light struggling just beneath the surface. She reached out and gripped his wrist until he winced. His eyes snapped back to her.

"Sure," she said. "You've heard of it. Shark attack victims complaining about pains in a leg that isn't there anymore because a great white ate it and pooped it out a long time ago?"

Nick nodded, the hint of a smile breaking through the confusion.

"Well, this right here . . ." Velvet lifted up her arm and unfastened her cuff. She noted that his eyes narrowed as her fingers manipulated the button and hook. His jaw twisted a bit, his tongue splitting his lips slightly. It amazed her how boys worked. One minute vomiting, the next thinking about, well, things they shouldn't be.

She pulled back her sleeve to reveal the same thin threads of light pulsing beneath her skin. "This is the reason why. When our bodies die, or even a part of our body dies, our spirits retain the memories in our nerves or whatever these sparky wires are. And so if we don't die from the trauma, we continue to *feel* like the part is still there. It itches. Aches. All that. Well, down here we just happen to have the whole body, not just a chewed-off arm."

"B-but we're not ghosts anymore," he stuttered.

Luisa strutted between them, clearly becoming annoyed with all the exposition. "Of course we're not ghosts. We're people; we just look a little different. Ghosting's like our day job. A uniform, if you'd like. Now can we get this show on the road?"

Velvet nodded and the Shattered Hall's gates swung open as they approached.

"Welcome to purgatory, Nick."

His mouth dropped open and he stared into the Great Station in wonderment.

If nothing else, purgatory was perpetually resilient. It was a mere hour after one of the worst shadowquakes to hit the Latin Quarter ever, and recovery was well under way. Gone were the downtrodden refugees, replaced by a new consignment of souls flooding in, their blister-hot memories shining like a sun from the cordoned-off area around the primary crack. The crack itself, a vertical chasm running a hundred feet up the far wall of the station, hummed with energy. Impossibly deep, and wide enough at its base that souls shambled out of their own accord, ether-light, onto the station floor, the Primary pulsed with activity today.

An influx. Velvet wondered if there'd been a plane crash in the daylight or something likewise terrible to explain souls thrust through in such volume. As the souls shuffled from the corral, guides tossed ash into the air, shouting, "Welcome! Rub it in! Welcome! Faces, too!"

Others shouted directions frantically, as the perpetually long lines of new souls heading for processing had begun to coil around each other like a great swirling nautilus shell. The new souls moaned and screamed and pawed at Velvet and her team occasionally.

"What is this place?" they cried.

"Heaven? It's heaven?"

No such luck, dude.

Velvet watched Nick as they trudged around the intake lines, avoiding the jarring of elbows passing in the opposite direction, toward the tunnels and the funiculars. His eyes were cast skyward and his lips parted. Above them, souls shimmied and hung from ropes and black rubber gas lines.

They glowed nearly as brilliantly as the globes of light, all the better to perform the intricate work of replacing broken panels of the glass dome that covered the atrium.

Velvet couldn't imagine passing into purgatory on this night. If there was one thing worse than waking up dead, it was molasses-slow intake workers at the far curve of the stadium of commotion. Luckily for them, and Nick, being on the Salvage crew afforded them a certain level of VIP treatment.

Not much.

But at least a smidgen of preference to set them apart from the rest of the dead. Velvet wove through the lines, meandering and nodding politely at the frightened ash-covered mass of humanity. They stared back, likely wondering why they glowed so brightly, expecting her to say something, provide some guidance.

Velvet merely shrugged occasionally and stayed her course.

She turned back to find Nick, Quentin, and the twins silhouetted by the harsh glare of the primary crack, their faces faint yellow blurs, making them appear invisible except for the dark clothing they wore, characters from the golden age of cinematic horror.

Nick faced a massive pair of iron doors, intricately laced by the same filigreed locking mechanism as the path to the Shattered Hall. Behind it, she knew, were the Collectors' access points.

"Keep up!" Luisa called out to him over the wail of the crowd.

At the head of the lines, the intake lecterns lined up twenty

wide, and behind each one, as you might expect, stood a disgruntled social worker. There seemed to be an endless sup-
ply of burned-out federal and state employees in purgatory.
Word was that declining economies and layoffs had turned
some already disgruntled folks into machine-gun-wielding
psycho killers.

Velvet couldn't blame them.

She dreaded this part of her job, because without fail, no
matter how many intake workers were away on break, if there
was one thing Velvet could count on, it was that Mrs. Sylvia Allerdice wasn't among them. Velvet used to think that
there'd come a day when she'd get lucky and the crotchety
old woman would be in the employee cafeteria, complaining
about policy or how rude new souls were in that shrill, bitter, and unquestionably monotone voice, instead of on the
frontline of intake.

Today was not to be that day.

"Next victim!" the woman called out, beckoning with
curt, crooked fingers.

The sound of her voice climbed up Velvet's spine with
grappling hooks. Velvet stabbed her hand between Logan
and Quentin—both shook in silent laughter.

"It's like fate," Logan muttered, and both of them broke
up chuckling.

"Bastards," she hissed, and she stomped the little boy's
foot and elbowed the taller one in his skinny chest.

She gripped Nick and yanked him forward, pulling him
close to her side as they strode the several yards to Mrs.
Allerdice's lectern. "Okay," she whispered. "Be totally

honest with her. Don't ask any questions. Oh! And don't piss her off!"

"What?" he asked, shaking his head nervously as she pushed him ahead of her toward the crinkled, ash-covered skeleton of a woman.

"And whatever you do," Velvet warned, "don't cross the yellow line! Go!"

He shuffled forward, placing the points of his wing tips on the urine-colored line drawn in crooked chalk in front of the lectern. She watched as he craned his neck to examine the other lecterns. None of them had what Nick was looking for; Velvet could have told him. Mrs. Allerdice liked her work space just so.

Velvet fell in behind him, but not quick enough to avoid the eagle eyes of the decrepit wench.

"Velveteen," Mrs. Allerdice rattled, using Velvet's full name as though she owned a permit to do so.

"Velveteen?" Nick asked softly.

"Never mind." She prodded him.

"So this is your number fifty-seven." The woman set her scrutiny on Nick, giving him the old up-and-down look. "Interesting. I never thought I'd see it."

Velvet jerked her head around Nick's shoulder. "Thank you?" she queried.

Mrs. Allerdice shrugged, the shoulders of her stiffly pressed blouse rising and lowering like cardboard shelves. She turned her beady eyes back on Nick, her lids crinkling like wadded newsprint. Velvet sighed, relieved to be out of the woman's sights.

"I suppose we should sort you out."

"Yes, ma'am?" he said.

"Is that a question?"

Velvet poked the boy in the back. He startled a little but rebounded quickly. "No, I don't have any questions."

"That's good. Let's keep it that way."

She vigorously shuffled paper in front of her. Velvet could swear she heard the woman's bones creaking like ancient floorboards as she worked, her joints twisting on nails rusty enough to give everyone who passed through a stiff case of tetanus. That she was making with the busywork at all was purely for aggravation. There was only one real purpose for the social workers—or in Mrs. Allerdice's case, antisocial workers—and that was to figure out where new souls would fit in purgatory's cogs and gears.

Sufficiently satisfied that all her edges lined up, Mrs. Allerdice picked up what looked like a large aluminum knitting needle. She balanced it point down on the edge of the lectern, where it stood perilously on its end, twisting slow pirouettes on the oak top of its own volition, and so intently that a curl of freshly carved wood trailed behind its sharp point.

"Name?" the woman bellowed.

"Nicholas Russell." His words rushed out in a clipped staccato.

"Place of birth?"

"New York City."

"Place of death?" A smile creased her lips at the question, and her eyes rolled slowly up his body to his face. Velvet placed a hand on Nick's shoulder to still him, felt his back tense.

"She knows you don't remember," Velvet whispered into his ear. "She can tell it without you answering. Just ignore her."

"What's that, dear?" Mrs. Allerdice skittered to the side of her lectern to stare holes into Velvet. "Are you being smart?"

"No, ma'am," Velvet said, and both her eyes and the old woman's flicked to the metallic instrument teetering atop the wood stand.

"I was going to say . . ." Mrs. Allerdice's attention drifted off as she went back to rummaging through the papers, straightening them, rummaging again. Finally she retrieved a folded brochure, which she tossed at Nick. It pegged his shin and dropped onto the floor between his shoes. "Here's a pamphlet."

Nick bent to pick it up, revealing Velvet nearly entirely.

Mrs. Allerdice tsked. "Why? Why? Why?" she asked. "Why do you insist on being the one to deliver your extractions, girl? Must you *always* take the credit?"

Velvet felt her fists balling up hard, her stomach twisting in her gut like the timer on a secret bomb. Behind her, she thought she heard Luisa's gentle urgings to rein it back. But she couldn't.

"No. That isn't it, ma'am. With all due respect. A respect you've never repaid me, I might add. . . ."

The woman's brittle fingers started for the gently twisting rod. Its metal glinted, calling for violence.

Velvet took a breath, steadied herself. Beneath her, Nick started to rise up, and she pressed him back, swallowed, debated, and then continued, shouting, "I wouldn't dare subject my team to your horribleness!"

"Ah, Christ," Luisa sighed behind them, clearly addressing Logan and Quentin. "Now she's done it."

Mrs. Allerdice snatched the needle from the lectern and, with a rapidity far too unreasonable for her fragile frame, bounded not around the wooden stand but over the top of it. She brought the rod up and slashed the air between them swiftly.

For a second, Velvet didn't think anything had happened. She hadn't felt a thing.

But when Mrs. Allerdice stepped back and smiled warmly, almost maternally, Velvet knew the old witch had hit her mark. Something trickled down her face. Without taking her eyes off her attacker, she reached up and found the memory. It slithered atop her index finger before catching fire in the ether and floating away like one of the ashes from Nurse Antoinette's cigarette.

"You cut her!" Nick yelled, his posture changing, ready to charge.

Velvet rolled her eyes. The last thing she needed was a champion in her way. The rest of her team knew better than to jump in and rescue her. The repercussions would be massive . . . or, rather, she wouldn't speak to them for a week. She clamped her hand around his shoulder and held him to the floor. His struggles were minimal, unnecessary, and altogether unrealistic.

"Don't," Velvet insisted. "Not a word." And then, turning her eyes back to the woman, she said, "Point taken."

As much as it pained her to admit defeat, she knew better than to react in any other way.

"Well, then," Mrs. Allerdice said, absolutely beaming

with delight. "Let's get on with this. Time to sort you out, number fifty-seven!"

"Is that my new name or something?" he asked out of the corner of his mouth as the woman returned to her spot behind the lectern.

Velvet shook her head. "No. It's nothing. You're the fifty-seventh soul we've extracted. It doesn't mean anything."

"That's exactly right!" Mrs. Allerdice spat, wiping the tip of the needle on the hem of her blouse. "Nothing. Now tell your boy to be good for the assessment, Velveteen. You know how it *spooks* some." She paused, her lip quivering in anticipation. "Makes 'em run."

A shiver ran up Velvet's spine. She quickly shook it off and straightened. "You can get up now, Nick. Just do what she says and we'll be done here."

The sooner, the better, she thought. This extraction had been nothing but trouble from start to finish. Velvet just wanted to get back to the Retrieval dorms, to nestle herself in her bed and sleep like Rip Van Winkle.

And that was exactly her plan.

She nudged him again, and he took to his feet.

"All right, then, Nicholas Russell," Mrs. Allerdice said. "Give me your palm and do try not to pull away." She grinned wickedly. "This is going to hurt some."

Nick stretched his hand between them, across the yellow chalk line, almost to Mrs. Allerdice's lectern, before turning it over and exposing the flesh of his palm. To his credit, Velvet noticed, the boy shook very little. He merely stared straight into his assessor's eyes as she pinched the end of the needle and held it aloft, where it sparkled in the gaslight. The woman glared at him. "Are you a brave one, then?"

"We'll see," he said.

"Good answer." She brought the needle down like a praying mantis, skewering Nick's palm at its center.

"What the hell?" he cried.

"Was that a question?" Mrs. Allerdice asked, twisting the needle deeper.

He sucked in a deep breath and clenched his teeth.

"I didn't think so." She withdrew the needle slowly.

Velvet watched intently as the woman drew the wriggling memories close to her eyes, as if to evaluate the ferocity of their struggle, before unhinging her jaw and slipping the nerve endings still firing with life off the tip of the needle and into her mouth.

The rumblings of the station fell away, replaced by an eerie silence. Velvet could sense Quentin and the twins creeping up behind her to get a better look at the spectacle of the assessment in action. Nick stood beside Velvet, cradling his quickly healing hand.

Mrs. Allerdice's eyes rolled into the back of her head as she savored her mouthful, rolling the memories back and forth across her tongue as though critiquing a fine vintage. There were *mmm-hmm*s and *ah*s. Note jotting on the many papers before her.

And then, as quickly as it had started, it was over.

The sound rushed back in and the woman gasped, once, twice.

Three times, before settling her eyes, not on Nick to

deliver his sentence, the occupation he'd be fulfilling until, well, whenever, but on Velvet.

"Well, isn't this interesting?" she asked, delight at play in every bit of her expression.

Velvet knew better than to ask the woman what the hell she was talking about. She bit her tongue instead and waited.

"He'll be going home with . . ." She paused. "You."

"Excuse me." Velvet was sure she'd misheard. "I thought you just said that Nick would be coming back with me."

"Oh, yes. That's exactly what I said. He has Salvage crew written all through his cellular levels. So he's yours—and, more important—not my problem."

Mrs. Allerdice laughed thinly and long, her assessment apparently twofold. While she'd been divining Nick's aptitude, she'd also been pegging Velvet as wanting to get rid of the guy. She cocked her head glibly at Velvet's plight, enjoying her petty torments.

"I'm sure you're aware of protocol in these matters." She winked at Velvet before slapping a table tent atop the lectern and clopping away. Velvet gawped after her, stunned, before turning her eyes back to the little sign.

Sorry about your afterlife.
I'm on break.
Please take a pamphlet.

Chapter 11

As the rest of her team rushed in to congratulate Nick—peppering him with premature praise and backslapping—Velvet stood aside to take another look at the boy. Had she underestimated him? If she had, it was clearly understandable, considering Nick's less than stalwart first impression. But Allerdice had seen something in him. And had Velvet felt something, too? Some strange connection that forced her to reevaluate herself and those feelings she barely ever accessed?

Her shoulders sank from the weight of the endless day. Velvet couldn't even remember the last time she'd slept. Serial killers, shadowquakes, banshees, and new boys, even seriously hot ones, were so freaking tiring. Thinking about Nick straggling along in her wake like a lost puppy for even another hour was exhausting, let alone days or weeks. But what choice did she have? Purgatory's evilest intake worker was right. Protocol insisted that Salvage-approved souls be assessed by qualified individuals. The honor of the who, what, and where fell to the Salvage mother.

And anyone who's held a job knows the old adage, "Shit rolls downhill." Velvet knew all too well who was at the bottom of that hill—her team—and things were about to get really brown.

"Well," she sighed. "I guess you better come with us."

Nick's face lit up, and she noticed he still favored his lanced hand, despite the fact that it had long since healed itself.

"What does all this even mean?" he asked.

"It means you're going to be annoying me for a little longer. Now shut up, quit cradling that hand like a Dumpster baby, and follow us. We've got an appointment to keep with the station agent."

She didn't wait for him to answer—or, more likely, ask more questions. She simply pivoted toward the stairs to Manny's office in the distance. She could just see them, over the heads of all the new souls, a thin crooked line drawn around the curved walls of the atrium. While Nick had been undergoing his assessment, hundreds of people had added to the logjam, cramming together so tightly that child souls were being hoisted onto adult shoulders so that their memories wouldn't be crushed out of them like toothpaste from a tube.

"Stay close," Velvet shouted behind her.

The nervous energy made people chatter on endlessly, and when you multiplied that by the thousand or so people in the station, you got a metric ton of noise pollution. Despite all the shouting and cries of confusion, as Velvet and her team crossed to the stairs, Velvet was able to pick up on snippets of conversations going on behind her. One in particular caught her attention.

"So what do you think of Velvet?" The voice was Logan's, clearly in the mood for starting stuff.

"She's, well . . . ," Nick said. "She definitely makes an impression."

"Yeah," the other boy said, and sniffed. "But what kind?"

"She's got that whole bitch thing down, but instead of making me want to turn the other way and run—I don't know—for some reason, it's kinda hot."

Velvet resisted the urge to turn and rail on him, her attention already drifting to a tight corral of well-ashed souls on the near horizon. They were shouting, and from the right, something—more colorful and flexible than a soul should be—was being hoisted aloft. It was crowd-surfing across upraised hands to the music of enraged voices. And then it was gone and the yelling mixed back in with the regular din.

"Yeah, that is true." Logan's speech slowed to a crawl, as though seriously considering her. Velvet began to feel a twinge of discomfort. "She walks a tightrope between psycho and smokin'."

"It's so wrong that that should be hot, right?"

Yeah, she thought. *It is.* And it seemed a berating was called for, but before Velvet had a chance to turn and give the two boys a piece of her mind, Luisa shouted, "How about the two of you shut up. Whether Velvet's *hot*"—she lingered on the word ridiculously—"or whatever is beside the point. She could whip both of your butts anytime, so don't act like you've got a chance here. You just don't measure up."

"That's a penis slur," Logan said, deadpan.

"Definitely," Quentin agreed from somewhere nearby.

"Jesus," Luisa muttered, and slid up next to Velvet. "Don't listen to them. They're clearly infants."

"I wasn't," she said. Though if her cheeks weren't blazing white with embarrassment, it would be a miracle. If they were, Luisa, thankfully, didn't comment.

They broke into a brief opening in the crowd, past the intake lines now and onto the general traveler portion of the station's bizarre show. Velvet could see the pod of souls she'd seen before and could hear the upraised voices.

"Look at that up there," she said, pointing it out to Luisa.

The crowd of people was gathering, and as Velvet and Luisa fell in behind them, another row of people crowded at their backs. They were lumped around one of twelve columns supporting the glass roof, the stairs to the station agent's office just behind them.

A plume of smoke coiled from the center of the crowd.

A fire. Velvet felt a stitch of fear ignite in her belly.

"They're at it again!" shouted one man, as tall as a park statue and scowling fiercely.

"They won't stop until purgatory is destroyed!" This one, a woman in a hideous flowery sweatshirt, waved her arms about as though the end of the world were upon them.

Another, and perhaps the most ominous, shout came from a disembodied voice somewhere behind them. "You can't stop the revolution. It's only a matter of time!" The voice was as sour and malignant as Velvet had ever heard. "Burn the station agent!"

Furious shouts sprang up, and there was a rush in the crowd toward the unseen figures. Velvet twisted around to see the men in the group pouncing on someone beyond her field of vision. They pounded at the owner of the wretched voice. Luisa pulled at her arm and began to drag her away from the struggle.

"Come on. We don't want to be anywhere near *that*."

"But what *exactly* is that?" Velvet cried out, shaking Luisa off. "Get Nick over to the stairs, I've got to find out what's happening here!"

Velvet stood stiffly before the column where the mob had centered. Nearby, where the souls thinned, Velvet could just make out the figure of a woman kneeling in supplication. She was familiar, horribly so. It was Manny.

Velvet felt a scream catch in the back of her throat as flames licked from the station agent's bare flesh, charring away skin in big curls like birch bark. She rushed forward to the gap between the crowd and the horrifying spectacle. A man nearby grabbed her arm and held her at bay.

"But," she screamed, "we can't let it—"

"Look," he said. "Closely."

The ashes detached and floated away with the smoke. The fire climbed the station agent's raised arms and sparked from her fingertips like a morbid candelabra. Velvet almost looked away as flames burst from her eye sockets and mouth, set wide in a silent scream.

It took a moment for her to realize that the figure wasn't Manny at all. It wasn't even a woman. The figure wasn't screaming because she wasn't real.

It was made of paper.

The mannequin, or whatever it was, began to cave in on itself, in odd sinking depressions. Folds were exposed, loosening and unfurling like the opening of an accordion.

"It's all about that mess!" Logan shouted, suddenly beside her and stabbing his small finger at a flyer plastered onto the stone surface of the column.

She didn't even need to read it to know what it said, but she turned her eyes to its bold crimson lettering anyway:

A REAL Departure Is Coming!

Velvet pushed Logan behind her as she backed away, rejoining the rest.

"What does it mean?" Nick asked, staring at the flyer.

Logan stepped forward, face as serious as a heart attack. "You don't want to know. It's bad, though. Real bad."

"It's the revolutionaries," Luisa whispered. "They're here in the station now, those people."

As if to prove Luisa's statement accurate, a new ruckus sprang up, and in the distance a brawl was storming like a mosh pit, swirling around some epicenter. It seemed that whoever had posted the incendiary flyer, whoever had staged the burning of the effigy and then run away like the coward they were, was getting their ass beat times a hundred.

The horror of the event still clung to Velvet, but she pushed it down.

Things were happening so fast, so brutally fast. They needed advice.

"We don't have time for all this," Velvet admonished. "We've got to meet with Manny, like forever ago." She spun and marched off toward a broad stone staircase that circled the walls of the round space like a corkscrew, ending near the rafters of the domed hub.

From behind her she heard Nick ask, "Who's Shandie?"

She twisted around in time to watch Quentin darting back down the stairs. Just before he disappeared into the crowd, Velvet thought she caught a glimpse of the Collector girl, massive puffs of hair bobbing through clumps of souls like a cartoon character.

Velvet, so tired of rolling her eyes, tried to ignore the fact that her undertaker had turned into an official honest-to-God stalker.

As they rushed up the stairs, the brawl on the floor began to look like satellite images of hurricanes. Everyone seemed to want to get a lick in on this guy and his crew. And Velvet did, too. The revolutionists were dangerous and possibly deadly. For constantly putting up flyers in the Latin Quarter, they deserved imprisonment in the Cellar. But burning paper mannequins in the perfect image of Manny, when paper was at such a premium?

That was just plain wrong.

Sure, the woman could get bitchy, but what had she done to piss these people off?

The guys were talking again as they ascended, hitting on everything from Nick tripping balls over this whole afterlife thing to Manny's generous endowments to Quentin's girl problems to, if she'd heard correctly, the decidedly heart-shaped quality of her butt, which was flattering in that let-it-slide-until-the-objectification-gets-gross kind of way.

Plus. She'd certainly done her share of ogling this evening.

Velvet tried very hard not to glance over her shoulder . . . and failed.

Nick lagged behind, Logan dancing around him as they plodded up the stairs, chirping away happily about his favorite topic—breasts—complete with the accompanying hands cupped in front of his own chest.

Velvet almost laughed. Boys were so predictable, but when she glanced at Nick's face, expecting to see him salivating lasciviously, she was actually surprised—something that didn't happen too often. Her fifty-seventh acquisition wasn't focused on Logan's pantomime of a bullet bra but on *her*. He was grinning, of all things. And it was a devilish one at that, like he knew something about her.

Like he knew.

Nick doesn't know anything about anything, she thought.

She spun back toward the station agent's offices, fists in tight little balls. *I'm not looking at him again, until I absolutely have to.*

Manny's doors towered before them, as dark as coal and carved with scenes of a battle. When Velvet had first seen the monstrous things, she'd guessed that upon closer examination she'd find angels and devils fighting, or something else as obviously religious, but no such imagery hid within the doors' intricate detail. Shapeless forms, as worn away as the faces on temple ruins, warred with their own kind, and in the distance a domed mountain rose from the landscape like a blister.

She'd wondered what it meant. Was it a piece of their collective history, a metaphor or a detail from a premonition? The only time she'd ventured to ask Manny, she'd been answered with a dismissive shrug, as though the door was of little significance. A decoration.

"You like him, huh?" Luisa asked.

Velvet jumped, spun in the girl's direction, and then relaxed as she registered what she was actually being accused of. A slow smile spread across the little girl's glowing face.

"Who? Jockstrap back there? You gotta be kidding." Velvet huffed and stabbed her hands into a copper pot filled with finely ground ash beside the threshold to the station agent's office.

"Yeah. I must be, huh?" Luisa leaned against the wall, watching the boys nearing. "'Cause he's not hot or anything."

"Shut up," Velvet hissed. Her eyes darted toward the approaching boy even as she spread some of the ash under them. "He'll hear."

Luisa nodded, the grin still plastered on like a wicked little mask. "Wouldn't want that. Better to keep these kinds of things a secret so you won't have to interact with anyone on a real level."

"If I need advice, I'll go see Miss Antonia."

Luisa threw her head back and laughed. "Oh, good idea. Perfectly reasonable solution. I'm sure she'll be receptive, too. In that she won't be at all."

It was ridiculous, of course. The woman in question had

never been a people person. Probably ever. And if there was anyone Velvet would accept advice from, it would be Luisa. But not this advice.

A scattering of pebbles nearby announced the boys' approach.

"Never mind," Velvet spat, hoping to put an end to the conversation.

"Hey, Nick!" Luisa called the boy over. "You're about to have yourself a rite of passage."

"Another one? I think I've hit my quota." Nick shoved his hands into the pockets of the wool pants and bounced on the balls of his feet, watching Velvet with an odd quizzical expression as she coated her skin with the ash. "Is that what people have all over their faces and stuff?"

"Yeah. She's ashing," Luisa said. "The *why* is self-explanatory, I think."

"Otherwise everybody's eyes would hurt all the time, right?" He cocked an eyebrow and returned his gaze to Velvet, lingering on her delicate fingers smudging the ash across her pale luminescent flesh.

"It dulls down the nerve endings," Luisa said.

Velvet narrowed her eyes as Nick's gaze lifted.

Luisa continued, "Despite us looking bright right now, we get brighter."

Velvet nodded, but refused to look. "Also meaner."

The little girl waved Velvet off, grabbed Nick's wrist, and twisted it so that he could look at the underside. Hundreds of phosphorous threads throbbed beneath its surface. With her other hand, she pressed his fingers into a fist, and the boy's eyes widened as the threads began to spark and glow brighter than the filament in a lightbulb.

"Whoa." Nick squinted.

"That's why we ash. Brings down the glare, so it doesn't hurt other people's eyes."

"Plus," Velvet said, breaking her visual embargo and looking directly into Nick's eyes. "Manny doesn't like to look at sparking. It bugs her. And no one likes her when she's irritated. No one."

"That's the truth," Logan agreed, dunking his own hands into the pot and gesturing for Nick to do the same. "Rub it all over, man. Even your eyelids."

The older boy scooped the gray powder from the bowl and pressed it between his fingers. "Just regular ash?"

Logan nodded. "More or less."

"Just," Luisa interjected, "regular ash."

Velvet watched as the girl scowled at her brother, chastising him with no more than a glance and a promise that he'd get more later if he continued. Nick didn't let on that he'd caught the exchange at all, busy as he was coating the backs of his hands and wrists with the gray smudge. He crouched and mirrored the other boy, rubbing the ash into his ears, over the thick cording of his neck, his sturdy jaw.

Sufficiently proud of the job, Nick mugged for Luisa and Velvet.

He looked good.

More than good, the voice in her head responded. *Frickin' gorgeous.*

Velvet cursed her conscience. It could shut up at any time.

Nick, somehow, even made the muted coloring look natural.

And he seemed so calm. Gone was the shuddering mound of boy emotions she'd held in the Shattered Hall. His resilience was impressive. It hadn't been longer than an hour since he'd learned of his fate, and he hadn't even broken down all that hard, in the scheme of things. No more tears, no sign of the agonized mourning that went so well with the gray motif. It was as though he was taking the whole death thing in stride. Velvet had seen the type one time before.

Number thirty-three, Rachel Snable.

She'd died in a car wreck, and her soul had somehow gotten trapped within the twisted wheel well of a Dodge Charger. The car was a complete mess and in a wrecking yard when Velvet found it. A group of misdirected kids in black robes were worshipping it as a prophet. Something about the construction of that particular make and model had a tendency to capture souls more than others. No one knew why, exactly. Rachel held it together pretty well, stiff and businesslike all the way through her debriefing with Manny, but then, on the way to the dorms, she broke down into great buffoonish sobs. Velvet had almost been embarrassed for the woman. She'd never, herself, been a fan of emotional displays, and Rachel's had been so loud. So. Loud.

Nearly everyone had been watching her, gawking.

But then the oddest thing happened. Rachel's light went out and she turned to dust.

Just like that.

Manny hypothesized that Ms. Snable's remainder, her leftover import, that thing that keeps souls in purgatory

160

until it's resolved, whatever you wanted to call it, had been the ability to express emotion.

And boy had she ever. You could hear her wailing all through the Latin Quarter, sobbing and heaving her shoulders one minute, and then, poof, they were all standing there alone, picking ash off their tongues. The fact that she'd broken down on the railcar meant that Velvet and her team had been responsible for cleaning and collecting the ash and delivering it to the local ash pot.

Yes. Those ashes.

The greatest form of respect was to wear them. It might have been disgusting, but it was tradition. Try having hot dogs at Thanksgiving and see how that goes over. People don't like change, and neither, it turns out, do souls.

She was pretty sure that expressing emotions wasn't Nick's remainder, though she wasn't great at prediction. *Maybe,* she thought. *Maybe I just hope it isn't.* Either way, he was bound to have another breakdown soon. It was inevitable. A teenage mind processes things so quickly that they get bored and start to remember why they're here, and then . . . boom!

Another meltdown.

She shook away the idea and focused on the door. This meeting had very little to do with Nick anyway. She'd be explaining to Manny the banshee they'd collected, or the all-out brawl with the revolutionary downstairs—but probably not the effigy. That would really hurt the station agent's feelings. There was lots of business that didn't have to do with hot boys. She didn't have time to worry about someone who probably wouldn't be around long anyway.

Velvet pressed her shoulder to the doors and shoved. They

shuddered and split in a crooked zigzag instead of a straight line, as though an earthquake had cracked the carved mountain at its center in two. The hinges screeched loud enough to cause a hush to fall over the crowd below. Luisa and the boys rushed over to the rail, and Velvet saw them framed in the aura of the angry mob's emotive glow.

A whoosh of warm wind spilled from the gap, flooding the air with powdery notes of jasmine and orange blossom, tussling Velvet's hair and making her nose crinkle.

Disgusting, she thought. *Where the heck does she find that perfume?*

"It's Arpège by Lanvin." Manny swept out, seemingly alive with pink powdered skin and a tight-fitting sweater and skirt to match. She tapped across the stone floor on dangerously high heels. "Don't you love it?"

"Something like that," Velvet lied, wondering if the station agent had added mind reading to her varied and substantial talents. The question didn't hang in the air long, as Manny sped around the balcony misting from a small brown atomizer.

Velvet choked back a gag.

"It was my favorite. My signature scent. Thank the good Lord for the Collectors."

"It's *really* something." Velvet didn't care to thank anyone for Isadora, Connie, Isadora's mother, or their team of Collectors. Their job was to steal castoffs and lost things and bring them across the veil between purgatory and the daylight. Their taste level was suspect. Half the crap they brought through was complete butt.

Velvet followed the woman into her office, a vast and lavishly appointed Hollywood set of a room lit by the same glowing orbs of gaslight that filled the station hub with columns of light. She flopped down into the armchair next to the davenport, which is what Manny insisted on calling the couch.

"So, what happened out there?" Manny asked in her breathy old-fashioned way. She swished around the settee and settled into it. She crossed her legs elegantly and popped her ankle like a signal flare. "I heard a ruckus."

Velvet hesitated and looked over her shoulder. Sure enough, the others had wandered in, Logan's mouth gaping, as usual. Thankfully he'd gained some control over his normally lolling tongue. The station agent definitely had Nick's attention too, but not all of it. His eyes darted in Velvet's direction.

And before she could stop herself, a small smile escaped.

"Oh!" Manny shot up and skittered across the room. "This must be your fifty-seventh soul! Congratulations!"

She gripped Nick by his biceps and let out a sharp, "Ooh! Strong, this one."

Velvet grimaced.

"I'm Nick, ma'am." His cheeks glowed dimly through the ash.

"Oh, my. So formal and polite." She raised her index finger to his chin and tapped it playfully. "You can call me Manny, doll."

Nick jittered a bit, grinning nervously. "Um, okay . . . Manny."

"Good boy." She pivoted and sauntered back to the gray

knobby davenport, and flopped down near Velvet. "How are you adjusting there, Nick? You don't seem at all bothered by your . . ." She paused as though pondering her words. "Change of circumstance."

"You know, doing my best to stay calm. Soldier on. That kind of thing. Coach would say—"

"Coach?" she interjected. "A sporting man? Athlete?"

"I play basketball."

She clapped deliriously—everything Manny did was peppered with a flair for drama. The actress in her never died, just the body, she'd told Velvet once.

"He's assessed as Salvage." Velvet watched Manny carefully.

"Well, then, kid." She beamed at the boy. "You're in luck, because Velvet and her team are the absolute best. And you'll want to watch them very carefully. Learn everything you can for when a spot is found for you on another team."

"Oh," Nick said, sounding suddenly morose. "I thought . . ."

"You thought what, darling?"

He glanced from the twins slowly to Velvet, then tilted his head downward.

"Are you sulking?" Velvet prodded.

"No!" he snapped. "I just thought I'd be on this team. It just feels right."

"Really?" Luisa's smile spoke uncomfortable volumes. Her stare all but poked Velvet in the forehead.

"Really," Nick replied.

"Oh. Well. That's not likely. . . ." The words falling away along with her smile, Manny turned toward Velvet, suddenly stony and serious. "What caused such a severe shadow-quake? I suspected a collection of souls. I am surprised that Nick was the only save from this operation."

Velvet glanced at Nick, who looked as though he weren't sure how to take the comment, an expression between hurt and curiosity at play on his face. Though he could have been confused by Manny's schizophrenic change in direction—God knew Velvet was.

Manny noticed, too. "Oh, dear. No offense, young man. You are certainly both large and strapping."

"Uh . . . none taken." He puffed out his chest.

"There *were* two spirits," Velvet said.

"Oh, my. I was afraid of that." Manny slipped out of her shoes and curled her legs up under her, getting comfortable to hear the rest of the tale. "Go on. Go on."

"Nick was imprisoned in a glass cell. A crystal ball. That was no surprise, but when we tangled with his captor, we found her to be possessed."

"Yeah!" shouted Logan. "Tell her what it was!"

Velvet shot him a glare and continued, "It was no ordinary soul engineering the woman. It was a deformed one, all bansheed out and screaming and stuff. Logan and Luisa were quite valiant in their battle with the beast. Quentin's timing was spot-on."

The little girl pushed Velvet's leg to the side and scooted in next to her, balancing on the edge of the chair. She beamed at the acknowledgment.

Logan was more demonstrative. "It grew to, like, seven feet tall, Manny!" He stretched up onto his tiptoes to indicate the size discrepancy and his own fearlessness. "I tore—"

"We!" Luisa interjected.

Logan nodded. "*We* tore that thing right out of this old fortune-teller woman. Bear traps!" He brought his hands together like the jaws of the phantom machines and shouted, "Snap! And it was real pissed, Manny."

"Mind your language," Manny scolded.

"It was very angry," he corrected quickly. "Twisting and turning like a tornado." He reenacted the struggle with the banshee, rolling on the floor and grunting like a pro wrestler.

"Heroic!" Manny clapped her hands and grinned at Logan's display.

Luisa rolled her eyes.

Nick chuckled.

Velvet took over. "The flies took it."

She pivoted toward Nick, and stifled a giggle. He quivered uncontrollably, and completely on purpose, presumably at the mention of their insect saviors. Hamming it up for Luisa's and Logan's benefits for sure.

"Were you able to extract any information from it during its possession of the fortune-teller?"

"Yes," Velvet said. "But you're not going to like it."

"Don't worry about what I'll like or not like, Velvet. This is business. We deal with what comes our way, now, don't we?" The station agent's voice was as sweet and childlike as ever, but underneath it was the strength of generations of body thievery as the head of her own Salvage teams.

Velvet considered it and then opened the floodgates. "It said something about the departure. That it was coming. That we couldn't stop it." She edged forward in the chair.

Nick spoke up, "What are you guys talking about?"

Velvet's and Manny's heads jerked in his direction.

"If you don't mind me asking," he added.

Velvet pulled the wadded flyer from her pocket as she watched Manny's reaction. The woman stroked her neck and stared at the ceiling. "No, Nick. We don't mind."

I do, Velvet thought. *Who does this guy think he is? Being hot and all doesn't give him carte blanche to horn in on my investigation.*

She handed the crinkled flyer to the station agent.

Manny sighed as she perused it, set it down on the couch between them, and continued, an empathic expression on her face. "Purgatory isn't the happiest place you could have ended up, kid, and I'm sorry for that. We've got our share of problems. Chief among them is a small group of revolutionaries who don't care for how the system works." She stood and paced the room, stocking feet padding against the stone.

Nick followed her movement intently.

"The City of the Dead is no different from anywhere else; we have rules. People don't always like them. Are you aware of the principal rule, Nick?"

"No haunting?" Nick offered, looking to Velvet for approval.

Velvet tilted her head in agreement.

"That's right. No hauntings, Nick." She used his name like a punctuation mark, a warning. "Hauntings are wrong, terribly wrong. They can be addictive and disfiguring, as you've no doubt seen tonight. Trapping daylight-bound souls." She shook her head, eyes dark with worry. "What a horrible thing. A soul who has taken to haunting is not likely to deal with their remainder, their unresolved life issue, the reason for their presence here rather than . . ." She paused. "Elsewhere."

"Um . . ." Nick bit his lip before continuing. "But isn't that what Velvet, Quentin, Logan, and Luisa were doing when they saved me? Haunting?"

Manny prickled. "No. I realize it seems like there's no distinction, that it seems contradictory to the message, but Salvage missions are controlled, targeted. The time spent among the corporeal is intentionally brief. The problem with hauntings is they tend to linger, and with uncontrolled roaming comes repercussions here in purgatory. Sometimes quite awful consequences."

Velvet had heard this speech before, and her mind wandered.

She was unable to divorce her thoughts from Bonesaw as Manny's measured voice filled the space. She imagined him sharpening the knives, lining them up on his shiny metal workbench, polishing the fingerprints off their blades. Getting ready for the worst kind of things imaginable. The more she thought of it, the angrier she became.

Oh, haunting serves a purpose, all right.

As a matter of fact, Velvet planned on *serving a purpose* as soon as she could slip away, and she didn't care what could happen. After a reasonable amount of sleep, of course.

She wasn't crazy, after all, just antisocial.

"The punishment for haunting is a revocation of your ability to dim and move on to somewhere else." Manny crouched next to Nick, made eye contact. "Dimming is going to sound scary to your human brain, but it's not at all. Not in the slightest. Dimming is a wonderful thing. It's the best thing that can happen to you. The best thing of all." She glanced up at his hair and brushed it away from his forehead. "And you don't want to mess that up, do you?"

Nick's Adam's apple bobbed as he swallowed. His eyes focused on Manny's, and he licked his lips. He did everything but pant.

Velvet shook her head. *The guy is captive to his groin. Just like any other boy. Nothing special. Pathetic.*

"But what does it mean?" Nick asked, cocking his head.

"It's when you move on. Do you remember the lights passing above you through the glass dome of the station? I'm sure you saw them, looked like shooting stars?"

Nick nodded and glanced at Logan, who cocked an eyebrow knowingly.

"We believe those are souls from Earth passing on to another place."

"Heaven?" Nick suggested, shrugging as though it were an obvious assumption.

"We don't know, really. But we . . . The Council of Station Agents is able to prevent it from happening, if we need to. It's really the only punishment we can effect here. Of course, it's a deterrent only if the soul believes they'll be moving on to a better place when they dim."

The boy stiffened. "So, wait a minute. What do you mean you don't know where we go when we . . . dim? You have proof there's a heaven, right?"

"He's gonna blow!" Logan shouted, holding his hands over his head to avoid the imaginary shrapnel.

"Shut up, Logan!" Luisa shook her fist at her brother, now up on his knees and examining Nick's every movement for signs that he'd break down or run screaming for the hall, or any of the other reactions that people have when they find out that their questions about death, when it's finally upon them, are still answered with more questions. Nick's eyes were already wild with terror.

"The universe is a strange place, Nick." Manny whispered in her most soothing tone. She pressed him against the seat back by his shoulder. "Now settle down and listen closely; we're not going over this again."

He nodded and chewed at his lips.

"Like I was saying, the universe is much stranger than we knew when we were alive. We don't even really know if this is *the* purgatory that religious scholars spoke of in the Bible and other texts. We just know this: We continue to exist. We know other things, of course, like that we retain our shapes, our memories, our desires."

"Obviously." Velvet stood up and flopped onto the davenport, wrestled with the pillow, fluffed the crap out of it, and finally shoved it behind her head.

Manny gave her the evil eye, only hers was a pretty one, of course. That Velvet was strapped with an afterlife full of comparisons to such a beauty came as absolutely no surprise to her.

"Are you serious with this, Manny?" Velvet fluttered her hand toward Nick, flustered and feeling the exhaustion weighing on her. It was funny how comfortable furniture triggered the body's sleep response. "We have more important things to discuss than how the world works. I can give him the rundown later. What about the banshee?"

"The banshee is in a cell downstairs, if I'm not mistaken. You did say the flies took him, didn't you?"

Velvet crossed her arms against her chest and breathed a haughty, "Yes!"

"Then, we have a moment to be polite and offer a fellow soul the common decency of an explanation for all of this." She waved her arms about, really amping up in her condescension. "Don't you think?"

Velvet sighed and turned her face toward the back of the couch.

What is it about this guy that's got me so messed up? she wondered. And then it came to her. It was that he was still around. He was, like Mrs. Allerdice had said, her problem. She shot the back of his head a look. *It's not like he's all that cute.*

Only he was, and she knew it, and just as she was thinking that, she heard him whisper to the others, "Is Velvet always such a bitch?"

On any other day, she would have gone off like fireworks on the Fourth of July, but today, with Manny breathing down her neck and so much crap going on with the shadowquakes, the revolutionaries, and Bonesaw's latest victim, she figured it would be best to take the high road and ignore his petty comment.

Luisa didn't share her resolve. "It comes and goes."

Logan exploded into laughter.

Velvet seethed. Now they were all ganging up on her. She

shot up from the couch. "I'm only trying to keep us focused on the job at hand. If you all want to make jokes and chit-chat, well, then I guess we'll just wait around for the next shadowquake to hit. Doesn't matter to me."

She stomped off toward the French doors that led to the station agent's balcony. Someone was following. Velvet didn't need to turn around to recognize that the soft, whispery footsteps were Manny's.

"It's not like you to be so selfish," the woman whispered. "I realize the stress you're under."

If only, Velvet thought. Manny didn't know the half of it. Try adding a clandestine haunting to the mix.

"I'm sorry, but—" Velvet started.

Manny cut her off. "My primary concern and that of the council is the increasing severity of the shadowquakes. We lost twelve buildings in the Latin Quarter alone, and seven in the Slavic Sector, and you know as well as I that it will be years before we're able to Salvage enough material from the other side to rebuild, let alone the soul power required."

"Yeah, that's gonna be—"

"The cracks are spreading beyond the station," she cut in, casting a dark gaze on Velvet. "Far beyond."

Velvet was planning on asking more, but quickly shut her mouth. She hoped that the look on the station agent's face wasn't suspicion.

Had someone seen her slip into the hidden passage next to the Paper Aviary? Was she to be accused of haunting? Were they right now building a case against her?

Manny sighed. "We're certain this is how the souls are escaping. Take the example of this banshee. Banshees aren't bred in purgatory. It takes multiple hauntings to produce such a powerful force. And a dark intent." She turned up her nose.

Velvet nodded absently. She wondered if her own intentions were honorable enough to keep her from going banshee. Maybe she was deluded. She'd certainly been accused of worse psychological issues.

But was it possible that she was villainous simply because she was working toward building up the nerve to climb into her killer's body and help him commit a little suicide? It seemed like a win-win to Velvet.

A goddamn public service.

She decided to put it out of her mind and follow Manny back into her parlor.

"Of course." Manny raised her finger. "We have word that others, nonrevolutionaries, are escaping clandestinely. We suspect a rise in generic hauntings."

Velvet tried to stifle a gasp.

The station agent furrowed a perfectly arched brow. "Oh. Have you heard word of these? Has it become public knowledge?"

Velvet stumbled for the words, wishing she'd never pushed the issue of the shadowquakes and the banshee at all. Rather, she should have let Manny ramble on about the goings-on of purgatory, and Velvet could simply have taken a nap on the comfortable davenport. She could have pressed her cheek into the soft nubby fabric and pretended that her obligations in the daylight weren't jeopardizing her life there in the City of the Dead.

Their discussion seemed more and more like a trap with

every word the station agent uttered. Velvet opted for brevity.

And lies, of course.

"It's just that I'm horrified that more people would be doing that kind of thing, particularly with all the shadow-quakes. Surely they must know"—as she did—"that even minor hauntings can cause tremblers and shadow clouds."

"There is no such thing as a minor haunting!" Manny's teeth were clenched.

"No. No. Of course not. I only meant that the threat of either of those things should be enough to prevent souls from—"

The woman silenced Velvet with a terse wave of her hand. "I know what you meant. But what you need to know, and it would be helpful if you'd spread around this knowledge among your peers, is that the hauntings are creating their own cracks."

Velvet noticed her knees beginning to shake, and stilled them. Expressions of fear, even one so slight, disgusted her. Surely what Manny was suggesting was just a theory. A ridiculous one at that. Velvet had searched for weeks before discovering the alley crack, and even that had been an accident. She'd merely been looking for a shortcut and had hit a dead end, so to speak.

The idea that she could be causing damage, too, incensed her. She felt the anger coiling around her insides, constricting. Damage came from intent, from dark magic. Velvet's motives were pure; her actions were just.

Luisa stood up. "You mean here . . . in the station?"

"No." Manny cast her gaze toward the darkened window. "They've been found outside in the district."

"Jesus!" Velvet shouted, throwing up her hands. "Don't we have any spackle?"

The station agent ignored her. "We think this activity may be related to the departure."

"The revolutionaries?" Velvet was shocked and relieved at the same time. If the revolutionaries were behind the increase in hauntings and thus the shadowquakes, then her work with Bonesaw might not be under scrutiny.

She could only hope.

She'd also prayed that her hauntings had been controlled and quick enough to avoid any repercussions. Velvet was a professional, after all. She could handle it.

Even as she thought the words, she knew she sounded like an addict. Images of drunks sitting around gyms in circles came to mind. Smoke curling up from their cigarettes. Stale doughnuts littering coffee-ring-stained card tables. Addicts.

God, what am I doing?

"Yes. Now, keep that part to yourself, Velvet. We can't have a panic on our hands, can we?"

"No. Absolutely not." She glanced over to the sitting area. Luisa and Logan were punching each other over the expanse of Nick's knees, and he watched their volleys with a pleasant smile, enjoying himself. She looked away. "We'll finish briefing Nick on purgatory on the way back to the Salvage dorm."

"Very good," Manny said, cutting off any further word on the matter. "Good talk as well. Do check on our prisoner in the Cellar before you leave, won't you?" Her face changed from pleasant to vicious in a second. "And I do mean for you to interrogate it . . . ruthlessly."

A shudder rolled through Velvet.

Not of fear. Of something else entirely.

The Cellar was no fun at all for normal people. In fact, it was pretty horrific, what with all the trapped souls moping about screaming, covered in flies and hatching maggots. But despite her desperate need to get away and relax, the Cellar's dank horrors called to her.

Being murdered changes a girl. It can turn the peppiest cheerleader into a bitter hissing crone and an already morose lover of art films and blue-black hair dye and combat boots into a violence junkie.

Interrogations always took her mind off the maelstrom of crap she dealt with. It was the action, the hands-on quality of the work. It was a distraction, and Velvet needed those even more than usual, now with the added problem of Bonesaw's new victim weighing heavily on her shoulders. Madame Despot had been an awesome diversion, as had Nick to no small extent, if she were to be honest. But neither could occupy her mind like a nice brutal questioning.

"Oh, look at that face," Manny said, misreading her—a rare mistake on the station agent's part. "It's not that bad. Used to do that job all the time back when I was body thievin'. It felt like sort of an honor. There's the key."

There was that, too.

Velvet glanced at the kidney-shaped writing desk in the corner, with its mirrored drawers and elegant cushioned chair. She thought it must be French. There are plenty of antiques in purgatory. Anything that people lose interest in becomes marked for Salvage. If the council could only work out electricity, the place would be loaded with VCRs, she was certain.

"Now run on and get it, and I'll say goodbye to your team."

"You know I have this, right?" Velvet promised.

"I hope so. For all our sakes."

Velvet jogged for the desk and pulled the glass knob of the top drawer gently. Inside, skeleton keys cut in various profiles and hues were strung on ribbon, grosgrain in Easter colors and velvets in jewel tones, but what dazzled her most were the baubles that hung from the key loops—charms and glass beads, tiny skulls carved from human bone, sometimes pearls. She dug through them until she found the right combination of charms and ribbon.

The key was gray and mottled, oxidized from both age and the trip to the City of the Dead; its looped end circled a strip of black velvet, a dangle of obsidian beads as dark as night, and a shiny silver skull, eyes sunken and seeking, yet more alive than anything else around her. Velvet slipped the ribbon over her head and straightened the key against the front of her shirt. Just as she was about to slide the drawer shut, a glint of light caught on something shiny in the very back. She reached in and pulled out the tack that secured a key she'd never seen before to the back wall of the drawer. It was as light as air and lacquered a deep crimson. The scroll-work at its pinch point reminded her of Victorian lace.

"Is this one new?" she asked, lifting it up for Manny.

The station agent stormed across the room, her gown cutting grooves into the thin layer of dust on the floor. Snatching the key from Velvet's hand, Manny glared at the tiny artifact for a second and then turned her fury on Velvet.

"Don't be nosy, Velvet. It doesn't suit you."

"But I . . . ," she began.

Manny leaned in close, her jaw as tense as knuckles in a fist, her eyes blazing. "You have a job to do, girl. I suggest you do it."

With that, the woman turned and slipped away, never once looking up from the little red key.

Damn, Velvet thought. She'd never seen Manny lose her temper like that before. Even through some of their toughest cases, the station agent always managed to present herself as calm and direct. That key must open more than a few tumblers and gears.

A whole lot more.

Chapter 12

As Velvet closed the door to Manny's office, she noticed Nick staring at the atrium's glass ceiling. She joined him where he stood at the high railing. Below them, the crowd had thinned a bit and the bustle mimicked the purposeful machinations of an ant colony, lines ticking along.

She glanced skyward. Nick was watching the traveling souls, their trailing arcs of light like comets, portents, reminders that Velvet, Nick, and the rest were trapped in a world of remainders. They were ghosts that didn't really fit into either heaven or hell, if those were even actual places.

"Don't look at them. It'll only depress you, and you're really doing very well," Velvet said.

He smiled thinly, and Velvet imagined what it would be like to pat his hand, to grip it. Would he look at her then, as she had seen him do on the stairs?

So intently.

Did she want him to? She was beginning to think she didn't know what she wanted, but one thing was for sure, purgatory was sorely lacking in the mood-stabilizing medication department.

Instead of patting Nick's hand, or reacting with any of the many possibilities of comforting gestures, she crossed to a smaller door at the end of the landing, opened it, and beckoned the boy to follow her.

They passed onto a covered balcony overlooking the Latin Quarter and the other districts beyond, a dark rooftop world. Street after street of slate-topped buildings stretched from the hill and into the horizon, and from as far to their right and left as could be fathomed. Chimneys puffed writhing arms of smoke into a night sky twinkling, like with diamonds in a coal vein.

A ratcheting clamor rose from beneath them. Nick leaned over the iron railing to find hundreds of boxy railcars, wooden and caged in filigreed iron, shuttling souls down parallel rails into the depths of the vast city.

"It goes on forever, you know?" It was Luisa, nestling up beside them. "It's the biggest city ever. Bigger than New York, even."

"Nah. It don't go on forever. Nothin' goes on forever." Logan blinked. "Goes a long way, though." He leaned in as if to impart a secret, and whispered, "I hear it wraps around the whole planet, if that's even what this is." He spoke as though this were some great mystery of purgatory.

"What do you mean?" Nick asked. "What is it if it isn't a planet? If not Earth?"

"Don't listen to him." Velvet hoisted herself up onto the rail, giving Nick a little startle. He reached out to steady her, but she slapped his hands away. "Of course it's a planet. It's Earth. Just a different side of it, is all."

She sat there a moment, head cocked at an angle, examining Nick's face.

"Somethin' wrong?" he asked.

"Nothing. Nothing is wrong. Everything's just different."

The boy nodded slowly, and Velvet hopped down from the rail. "We better get goin'."

She strode back through the door of the landing.

"Yeah, 'cause Velvet will be tired and grumpy after what she's got to do." Logan whistled behind her.

"You mean grumpier than normal," Luisa offered.

Her brother giggled. "Yeah. Right? Hard to believe it gets worse." He grew silent, serious, as though about to impart some terrible secret. "But it does."

Then he burst into laughter, Luisa chiming in with her own chorus of giggles.

"You guys are nuts." Nick shook his head.

Velvet smiled, too, but a commotion mushrooming below stripped the smile from her lips. The crowd surged toward the giant iron doors, souls jumping up to see over the heads of the people ahead of them. A booming squelch blasted through the room as the filigree uncoiled and the doors opened, revealing a wide stone ramp. The whooshing sound of a thousand whispers filled the mammoth room and bounced from the walls, getting louder and louder as Velvet descended the wide stone steps.

"Oh, Lord," she muttered, shaking off the sight with a cringing shudder. "We better get through there before—"

"Too late," Logan groaned as the bottom of the stairs was blocked by a wall of spectators.

Nick stopped and leaned over the rail to get a better view. "What?" he asked. "What's going on?"

Long wheeled racks sped from the opening, black garment bags flapping from their rails like oily tentacles, reducing the souls propelling them to shuffling, disembodied feet. Behind them gray footmen balanced teetering stacks of hatboxes on their heads like those African women on the National Geographic Channel. Another wave of workers, these dressed like Sherpas, in thick furry coats and hats pulled over their ears, heaved massive crates.

"Careful with those, Yang!" a woman's voice boomed. "Those are the finest peep-toe boots from the 2009 Paris fall season! Do you know how many people I had to glamour to secure that shipment? Imbecile!"

A tall caricature of a woman swept from the opening. Everything about her face was pronounced. Her nose was as sharp as a shark fin, her eyes were narrow slits, and her mouth was huge and belting out orders as loud as a police bullhorn.

"Wang Xu-Wei! I'll have you permanently lit up if I see even the tiniest frazzle on those hand-knit Givenchy capes. We didn't raid that sample sale for nothing. Lit up, I tell you!"

The woman sliced through the crowd, almost literally. She wore a gown of concentric blue rings that sparkled on the edges like the sharpened blades of butcher knives. Her hat stood nearly three feet above her head, wound with tulle and skulls, feathers, and possibly even live rats or something. It was hideous and probably expensive.

Velvet couldn't stomach another moment of the spectacle. The Cellar called to her like the biggest plate of fettuccine Alfredo ever. She might actually have been salivating. She turned to her team and shouted over the ruckus, "I'll meet you in the square! Fill Nick in on the rest!"

The twins tossed off some obligatory waves, but Nick just gaped after her, his expression quickly turning into the kind of frown you reserve for the departure of a loved one. It was at once confusing and sort of hot, and forced Velvet to stop dead. When he noticed her reaction, though, he shook his head, squinted, and went back to witnessing the madness of the parade.

What the hell?

Either the boy was on the top of his game at manipulating girls, or Velvet was losing her mind. She tried to shake off the weirdness and made a beeline for a gap between the Collectors' parade and the bystanders shouting for cast-off garments. But just as she rounded a column, Isadora and Shandie planted themselves directly in her path like they *wanted* to be beaten.

"Oh, hi, Velv," Isadora drawled. Shandie crinkled her fingers in a cutesy wave that made Velvet want to break off the hand and feed it to her. "And kudos . . . I guess." Isadora rolled her eyes at her lackey.

Velvet sighed and peered around the stockade of bitchy, to

see a tall gangly figure poke his head from behind the next column down, and then disappear just as quickly. Quentin. So creepy. She tossed a sneer Isadora's way. "So you enjoy shadowquakes, then. I didn't need to protect you two clothes whores? You were good with the whole tentacle thing."

"There's no need to get vulgar," Isadora chided, then added to her friend, "She's so common."

Before Velvet could utter another word, the two were off, meandering through the racks of clothing, snatching prized items and holding them up for the other to judge. Stunned and irritated, all Velvet could do was glare after them and try not to vomit at their wretchedness.

Finally Velvet huffed and darted toward the hidden door to the Cellar.

The Cellar guard was a burly gray soul with a lisp, named Rancho Cucamonga. The first time Velvet spoke to the man, he told her the story of his name. Apparently, when Rancho was alive, he was accident-prone and particularly predisposed to head injuries. Motorcycle accidents, falling chandeliers, fly baseballs, whatever, Rancho was sure to connect with a nasty case of amnesia at the drop of a hat, or an anvil. He ended up in the emergency room with great frequency. On one of these visits, he was laid up next to a tattoo artist named Mook. (Velvet didn't have a clue as to the derivation of said inker's name.) Mook nonchalantly asked for his clinic-mate's name, and when Rancho couldn't recall, he simply told Mook the first thing that came to mind. Mook laughed and laughed and told Rancho how much he loved the name, and since he, being a tattoo artist, carried his needles with him, and since the emergency room was busy on that particular day and they had plenty of time to commit the moment to indelible art, Mook freehanded Rancho's name on his forearm so he'd never forget it.

The fact that Rancho's real name was Franklin Norbert didn't make one bit of difference, because from that day forward he was never known as anything else but Rancho Cucamonga. And the tattoo was awfully pretty, if Velvet did say so, drawn in a scrolling cursive with gardenia blossoms instead of Os.

The weird thing was, ever since that day—ever since the tattoo—Rancho never again had an accident with his head and never again had amnesia. He had some close calls, like the time he fell off a ladder while putting up Christmas lights and ended up in the soft cushion of the hedge, just inches from the sidewalk. The tattoo became his good luck charm, until he was hit by a bus in 1992, which wasn't very lucky at all.

"Velvet!" Rancho threw open his arms and rushed toward her, enveloping her in a soft squish of a hug that, had her friends seen, would have registered with a haughty scowl—on principle.

"Hi, Rancho," she said, muffled into the thick ruffles of the powder-blue tuxedo shirt he wore, so it sounded more like "My, Mantho."

He pushed her away and beamed with pride, the reason for her visit becoming clear. "You got your fifty-seventh soul! Congratulations on the record!"

She grinned, nodded proudly. "Absolutely. I always get my ghost."

"That you do, sweets." His smile faded, and he glanced

nervously toward the weighty iron gate behind him. "I'm afraid whatever it is you've sent me isn't nearly as happy for you as I am."

As if to prove Rancho Cucamonga's point, a shuddering bellow escaped the Cellar and echoed about them. "Release!" it exclaimed, and then unleashed another scream so earsplitting, the travelers in the station must have been able to hear it, and stopped dead in their bustling. Velvet slapped her palms over her ears, whereas the guard merely grimaced.

"Been yelling like that for an hour solid. I've a mind to go down there and give it the what for." He held up a fist the size of a pie plate and flexed it so his knuckles popped up like gnarled teeth fighting their way through some frighteningly hairy gums.

"Manny wants me to interrogate it," Velvet said.

Rancho shook his head sympathetically. "Well, good luck with that. I don't see as how you're going to get much information out of that one. All he seems capable of is disrupting my morning reading." The guard picked up a book from his stool and handed it to Velvet.

"*Relaxation Techniques for the Stressed and Distressed* by Dr. Callus McKellar," she read aloud. She looked up at Rancho, and saw the worry around his eyes, the clear skin there creasing like an old jellyfish left to dry on the beach. "Are you stressed?"

He snatched the book back from her. "Well, of course I am. Who in their right mind wouldn't be? Why, if you heard half of what I do echoing up from the Cellar, then you'd be climbing the walls with hypertension. Why . . ." Rancho paused, tensing up

"Why what?" Velvet asked.

He looked around her, past her to the hall where she'd entered, and, satisfied that there were no souls lurking in the shadows, leaned forward conspiratorially. "They say the departure is coming soon," he whispered. "They say purgatory will empty out and the living will be their shelter."

"Could they be vaguer?"

"Apparently not."

Rancho straightened, and fear creased the skin around his eyes deeper than before. The spirits in the Cellar had convinced him that the revolutionists were capable of getting their way, whatever that meant.

She reached out and placed her hand over his. "It's not going to happen. Manny is aware, and so is the council. And so am I, Rancho. The station agent has a theory, and I think it's a good one, and soon she'll have a plan. We'll put the screws to the revolutionaries soon enough."

"I'm glad to hear it. Until then, I'm going to be following my deep breathing regime set forth by Dr. McKellar." He sat down on his stool again and opened the book. "In through the nose, out through the mouth. In through the nose, out through the mouth."

Velvet chuckled as Rancho wheezed in a breath as hollow as a dog whistle, slumped loosely in his exhale, and then repeated, again and again. He was a good guy and the only soul in the City of the Dead she'd ever considered telling her secret to. She really needed someone to talk about it with, especially now that Bonesaw had taken another girl to the shed. She imagined the girl's eyes upon waking in that charnel house, the sounds of metal scraping against metal rousing her from her chemical slumber.

Velvet shook off the memory of her own abduction.

Of course she could never tell him. She'd never do that to him, make him an accomplice to her treachery.

"You're doing a good job there, Rancho. Lookin' real relaxed."

He nodded, breathing all the more deeply for her benefit.

Velvet turned toward the gate. Without realizing it, she'd clutched the key in her fist while they'd been talking, the velvet ribbon digging a groove into the back of her neck. She opened her hand and saw the marks from its teeth denting her palm.

She hunched over and slipped it into the lock. The mechanism clanged and clattered, the gears grinding inside, scraping. The gate swung open with a groan, and Velvet descended the wide stone steps into darkness, pausing a moment to light a wooden torch off a nearby gaslight. Her shoes scraped against the loose stones, which skittered downward in near constant tiny avalanches. About halfway down, she stopped dead in her tracks.

The banshee screamed.

It was louder in the bowels of the Cellar, and once again she shielded her ears from the horror. "Shut up, banshee!" she yelled. "I'm coming for you!"

She hoped she sounded menacing.

"Looking forward to it!" he shouted back.

Not so menacing, then.

She sucked at her teeth. If the banshee's shouting wasn't enough to grind on her nerves, his insolence certainly was. Damn him. Didn't matter one bit what the revolutionary and body thief thought. He was going to talk. She'd make sure of that.

She was not above torture.

"Good," she mumbled.

Velvet descended in the slim circle of light from the torch, squinting to see beneath her. She could never shake the fear that a prisoner might be out of its cage and waiting in the shadows, reaching toward her with its glistening fingers dewy with condensation from the Cellar's gas deposits.

She'd been down there enough that you'd think the prisoners' taunts wouldn't bother her, but they did every time— not that she'd ever mention that to anyone. No matter what happened, Velvet had to be strong for her team, stoic.

"You comin', body thief?" the voice asked.

Velvet steeled herself at the base of the stairs. The torches were lit among the cells, and so she tamped out her torch and trudged onward. "That I am, banshee."

"Sure are taking your time, little girl. I don't have all day to wait for you."

"That's where you're wrong, banshee. You've got eternity." Velvet glanced toward the first cell. A naked man glowed through dirty smudges, his eyes grim with hate as he followed her progress. He began the cacophony of hissing she was accustomed to on each of her visits.

"Hisssss!"

"Hiss, yourself!"

The prisoner rushed to the cast-iron bars of the cell and hissed even more vehemently. He was joined by the woman in the neighboring cell, her face so black with mud from the cell floor that her eyes floated between the bars as though the darkness of the Cellar were some cartoon blackout.

Velvet quickened her pace, heading for the far end of the hall.

The Cellar ran on for several miles in different directions, mazelike. But at the first intersection, there was a central holding cell used for interrogations of new prisoners.

The banshee waited for her there.

Before the cage a single ladder-backed chair sat lonely in the hall. A ball of gaseous flame hung above the circular cell like a substitute sun, illuminating the cavernous Cellar to some degree, but not enough. Velvet sometimes wished she could witness the full scale of the place, imagining that it stretched on forever. That would, of course, freak her out, and so she didn't think about it much.

She eased herself into the seat and stared at the solid representation of the ghost before her.

As dark as night and not from ashing but mud, the banshee paced the edges of the cage, the grit of a thousand years whirring beneath his feet like sandpaper. He passed her several times before he spoke, each time sneering or glaring or presenting some other expression that let her know she'd made him very angry.

"Time to use your big boy words," she said.

"You'll get nothing from me, body thief."

"Why so nervous, then? There's nothing I can do to you. You're already dead." Velvet tried to sound sweet. "And I certainly mean you no harm."

He stopped and gripped the bars, the sound of his dirty fingers curling around the metal akin to the dry-paper rustling of a reptile slithering. "You and I both know that's not the case."

Velvet's eyes narrowed shrewdly. "Do we?"

"We do. So what's it to be, a nerve reading?"

It took all of Velvet's willpower to still her expression and appear unscathed by the banshee's remark. How did he know about Salvage techniques? Sure he was a body thief, and a strong one, but as far as she knew, none of the teams had been led by the kind of vile villain that would end up going banshee. The council would never allow it. Nerve readings were a highly secretive talent, one that took months to acquire. Velvet herself wasn't all that good at picking around inside a purgatory-bound soul, but this fiend didn't need to know that.

"Perhaps." She crossed her legs elegantly and relaxed into the chair a bit. In through the nose, out through the mouth. Thank you, Dr. McKellar. "Well, then, if you're aware of what I can do, why don't we spare some time and just get to the question and answer portion of this game show."

"Ooh, yes. Let's do." He grinned, a glow breaking through a crack in the dried mud beneath his chin like light catching on a choker.

"Let's start at the beginning. Did you acquire the captured soul yourself, or did you find him on some antiques store shelf or something?" Velvet knew the answer to this one without the banshee uttering a word, but it never hurt to start small.

"Don't be ridiculous. Of course I imprisoned the soul. Masterfully, too. Just slipped it right inside that crystal ball like an eight ball in the pocket. But that's not the information you're after. You want to know when the departure is coming."

She did indeed want to know that, but it hadn't occurred to her that he'd offer up such important intelligence. She nodded.

"Well, I won't tell you," he said smugly.

"Of course not. That'd be too simple."

"Exactly."

"Well, then, let's stay with the incident at Madame Despot's Fortunes and Favors."

He nodded in an overly congenial sort of way.

"What was the purpose of possessing that particular woman?"

"The choice of Madame Despot was entirely incidental. A mere hack as a medium, the woman was less talented than a late-night infomercial psychic. She simply had a space for me to ply my trade. A comfortable one, too, don't you think? Roomy."

Velvet considered the Goth trappings of the fortune-teller's rooms, creepy but warm. She had to admit she kind of loved it, but that was beside the point.

"Well, if you know so much about my ability to nerve read, then you must've been aware that we'd isolate your activity from the shadowquake. Did you think we wouldn't come for you?"

"Of course I knew. We expected it, with a disturbance of this magnitude."

Ah. He'd slipped. "We?" she said, smiling slyly.

"I meant that in the royal sense." He bowed deeply, flourishing the movement with a flutter of his wrist like she'd seen many times in movies about kings and queens and such.

"I don't think you did."

"Well, regardless of what you think, little girl, I meant what I meant. Or we meant what we meant, as the case may be."

More rigmarole, she thought. A word her mother used to use when Velvet was being "gamey," as she'd put it. Most of the time, Velvet was just trying to talk her way out of some mess or another, missing curfew, getting an F on a science test, roughing up her brothers.

Same thing with this guy.

"It doesn't make sense. You say you expected us to come. Well, then, why do it? An act of civil unrest? Terrorism? Have the revolutionaries turned to shadowquakes to make their point?"

"All of the above." The banshee cackled and slapped his knee, clearly impressed with his response.

Velvet was not.

"What's your name, banshee?" she asked.

"I'm certainly not going to tell you that."

"Yes, you will."

"No, I . . ." His voice trailed off. His eyes widened.

Velvet fondled the key and the charms dangling from its thick pinch point. She pieced out the sterling image of the skull and held it between her index finger and thumb. It was so delicate.

And the key was so sharp.

She lunged forward, throwing her shoulder against the bars of the cell, with such speed and ferocity that the banshee didn't have a chance to back away. The key punctured his glowing forehead. He bucked a moment, spasming, fists pumping around the bars, and then he dropped to the dirt floor like a sack of flour. Velvet dropped to her knees along with him, the ribbon attached to the key still around her neck, linking her to the fallen soul. He was on his face, one arm extended past the bars nearly to his armpit. She maneuvered around and rested her weight on his bicep.

"Try getting up," she whispered. "Just try it."

All around her the hissing of the inmates echoed, becoming louder and louder as it washed through the prison like a tsunami. She wished that hushing them were as simple as screaming "Shut up," but that had never worked before, and it certainly wouldn't have worked then. She lifted his head and felt for the edge of the charm. What she found there made her stomach jerk inside her. The fall had forced the charm deep inside. She shuddered, braced herself, and gave the ribbon a tug.

Once. Twice.

A thin drizzle of clear ooze dropped from the hole and puddled in the dirt. It glowed there for a moment, and Velvet resisted the urge to vomit upon seeing the squirming phosphorous worms that she knew were only displaced nerves. Pressing her fingers around the edge of the charm, she asked again, "What's your name?"

She closed her eyes and let the banshee's thoughts flood into her. There was blackness mostly, a dark as evil and unwelcome as the curling inky shadows that filled the streets during a shadowquake. But occasionally, and only briefly, those black clouds broke and Velvet could see his memories, sparking from his phantom nerves.

A street in Chinatown, but not from the Asian section of a city in America. It was from Vermillion there in purgatory. Velvet had never been to the district, but she'd definitely heard stories of it. Exotic and grand, Vermillion's walls were laced with Salvaged pagoda tiles and hung with paper lanterns folded around the gaslight globes. A gigantic tower of stacked roofs was the district's station. The Grand Pagoda sat atop a cliff, an atoll amid the murky glow of the city, the ascent to it cruel and forbidding. In storefronts, crimson robes and scrolls and ancient musical instruments hung from hooks, instead of the more traditional roast duck. She saw a narrow stairwell and a door with a sign that read Dr. Chan's Homeopathy. Underneath that, intricate Chinese characters were carved directly into the door. As the door opened, she saw not a waiting room full of ailing patients but a printing press and stacks of paper as high as the ceiling, each piece imprinted with a similar logo.

A red panda.

The darkness clouded her vision again. She dug the charm deeper into the banshee, nearly all the way up to the knotted velvet ribbon. But Velvet was already listing into a deeper trance, and the sound of the banshee's cries muffled to whispers.

Then she was walking down a thin alley. Cracks split the stone walls at regular intervals, and above her the sky was black, not with the ink of shadow but with an all too regular view of nighttime. No souls passed over. None.

She shivered. Something horrible was going to happen.

Horrible.

Her head was filled next with a confusing collage of crystal balls all lined up in rows on metal shelves, stacks of the paper figures—a few so closely resembling Manny it seemed she'd have had to sit for the artist while he or she worked—leaned limply against the wall like the fallen victims of a firing squad, and the sound of a man laughing, his cruel snicker a warning of horrors to come. The laughter brought her mind instantly back to Bonesaw.

He'd chuckle under his breath as he did his worst—as though the curls of skin he removed were wooden shavings from a perfect, adorable decoration he was carving, and not disfiguring torture.

The dread fueled her anger. The images flickered and decayed, and Velvet slowly returned to the Cellar, to the droning hiss of the prisoners.

It was enough.

She had her lead.

In front of her, the banshee was seizing like bacon in a frying pan. She scowled at the evil soul and let him squirm a few moments more before jerking the charm from the wound in his forehead.

He let out a long scream and scuttled into the center of the cell, beyond her reach. "You only think you know," he whimpered.

"I know enough," Velvet said bluntly, rising to her feet and brushing her knees of dust. She turned to leave him alone in the dark.

"Wait!" he called after her. "You'll need to know a lot more if you expect to stop what's already in motion."

"Oh? And you'll tell me?" She didn't bother to turn back and look at the soul.

There was a slight pause, and then he offered a weak, "I might."

His was a feeble ploy and a complete waste of Velvet's time. The banshee would no more tell her his secrets than she would ever visit him again. Little did he know, this would be their last contact. It was enough to learn that Nick's soul imprisonment was connected to the departure, as were the crystal balls. But for as many leads the interrogation derived, there were twice as many questions.

Were the paper figures the key? The effigy had certainly played no small part in the revolutionary's plans this evening.

She'd have to talk to the only person she knew skilled in making such intricate things from paper. Mr. Fassbinder. He was sure to point her in the right direction.

She smiled wanly at the prisoner.

"I might be back. You never know," she lied, and marched straight to the stairs, past the cursing souls in their cells.

The last one hissed, "He knows your sin."

This time Velvet hissed back.

Chapter 13

Slow shimmying descents were perfect for napping. Something about the rhythmic clanking of the railcar's wheels and the droning whoosh of air against the windowless frames lulled Velvet like nobody's business. And God did she ever need the rest.

She leaned her head against the wall and leveled her eyes on the horizon, where the inky sky met the gray rooftops and ash fell like dreary rain on the black umbrellas of a funeral. The night was circular, she decided, a tedious loop of tasks and responsibilities. Moments recalling moments, followed by the same and more of the same.

The exhaustion was taking hold.

After the events in the Cellar, Velvet had met with Manny in her private curtained sitting room, candles beating their shadows against the fabric walls like a stiff, quiet breeze.

They'd both agreed that the visions required the utmost discretion.

"The revolution is amping up," Manny said, her eyes downcast, the glimmer fading with her mood. "It has to be stamped out before something terrible happens. Something horrible."

Velvet leaned forward in the wingback chair, her fingers tracing the ridges of its dense brocade. "Do you think this goes beyond the Latin Quarter? I mean, if Vermillion is involved."

"No. I don't think so. The disturbances have been fairly isolated to our district. And, let's face it, the Latin Quarter has always had its share of rabble-rousers. We're a militant bunch. We're fighters. You know that better than anyone, I suspect."

Velvet nodded. Their team was consistently called to consult with other districts when the other districts experienced problems. Primarily because the Latin Quarter's Salvagers never hesitated to settle issues with violence. Their reputation as the muscle was both well-earned and widespread. And the citizenry of the Latin Quarter weren't a whole lot different—back alley brawling was a favorite pastime. Maybe they'd learned to raise their fists instead of their voices in the same way a child learns to be abusive by watching her parents. Imitation is the highest form of flattery. Was that the saying?

That didn't explain Velvet, though.

Not at all.

Manny delivered her directive with a sigh. "Follow up on your leads, and I'll set someone to the task of investigating this Vermillion connection. You've done righteous work this evening. It's appreciated."

Velvet stood up. The religious connotations of the station agent's words weren't lost on her, but it seemed that, like everything else in purgatory, good and evil, the righteous and the sacrilegious, all the big issues were less black-and-white and more gray.

Mind-numbingly gray.

She'd never been a religious girl, and she still wasn't. Until there was proof that anything existed beyond purgatory, Velvet would simply do her job—Salvage souls that didn't have any business in the daylight, and that would be that.

It didn't make her a good person.

Just a good worker.

The railcar jerked forward, jarring Velvet from sleep. The platform on the square appeared on her right, along with Quentin, Logan, Luisa, and Nick, crammed together on the single bench, their heads tossed back in sleep, mouths open and spewing light in columns like modern art sculptures. The twins' feet dangled above the cobblestones, and Nick's arm lay across their laps like the lap bar of a carnival ride, the posture protective rather than creepy.

She slipped from the car quietly and watched them a moment. Truth be told, she wanted them to rest, even if she never seemed able to get the chance. They deserved it. Deserved whatever they wanted. They were the best Salvage crew in the world, and she didn't tell them that enough.

Of course, if she did, there'd be plenty of eye rolling and "whatevers." But that was beside the point.

She was about to bite the bullet and express her admiration, when Quentin twitched, his knee jumping slightly. Then, as though some unconscious language existed between them, Logan and Luisa responded; the boy by brushing away an invisible fly, the girl by emitting a gentle moan, nearly a whisper.

And then, from the other side of the bench, Nick's long leg flopped absurdly. Talk about some fast bonding.

She glared at it. At Nick. And then all of *them*. Leave them alone for an hour and look what happens, cozied up like BFFs. Stabby thoughts were swimming all around her. What did they see in the guy? And Luisa! What could she possibly think might happen between Nick and Velvet? *Like* him? She didn't even know him.

Velvet cleared her throat, but the sound came out a pathetic choking gag.

Quentin yawned loudly, stretched, and peered up at her through squinted eyes. "It's like the next day, right?"

"Try the next night," Logan muttered, reaching his arms over his head and belching.

"Ugh." Luisa groaned and stood, tossing Nick's hand to the side brusquely. "That must have been some interrogation."

"It was. I'll tell you about it . . . later." Velvet planted her hands on her hips. It was going to take more than shoptalk to distract her. "You're all looking pretty cozy."

Quentin nodded. "Yeah, Nick's almost got me talked into approaching Shandie."

Her mouth dropped open, and she turned her gaze on

Nick, gawping in disbelief. "Seriously? What are you, a wizard?"

Nick shrugged like it was no big deal.

The most girl-phobic boy ever had been completely cured by a few minutes with this guy? Really? Velvet wasn't buying it. She stomped down the ramp, waving them off. "You guys are fucking with me."

"Oh, no. It's true. Yeah," Quentin said, heading her off. He straightened and puffed out his sunken chest as far as it would go. "I'm gonna get my girl." He let the word "girl" stretch on with swagger, and Velvet felt her stomach turn.

"You certainly seem to think so."

"Well, to be fair, in a roundabout way, it was sort of Shandie's idea," Nick said from behind her. "The guys were showing me around the square, and all the weird paper stuff for sale here, like I'd died and gone to Office Depot. And I noticed this girl hanging around in the background. Giant Mickey Mouse hair, expensive clothes, smirk."

"That's Shandie," Velvet agreed.

"Yeah. The same one Quentin was drooling all over back at the station."

"You mean the one he was *stalking*?" Velvet asked, glaring at Quentin.

"Yeah!" Nick materialized at her side. His elbow brushed her upper arm as he bounced on the balls of his feet with pride. "Only this time, she was the one doing all the stalking." He swatted Quentin on the shoulder and winked smugly. " 'Cause our man here is smokin'. Right? Right?"

Quentin beamed. There was no denying it: he was pumped

up on whatever crack-fueled advice Nick was pushing, and was itching to throw himself at the enemy. Bile rose in Velvet's throat.

"No way." Velvet stepped aside, putting a little air between her and the boy throwing a monkey wrench at her team. "That's sort of awesome, Quentin."

"That's what I said," Luisa quipped, strutting past and down the center of the main street. The rest of them followed her.

"So, you're ready, then, Quentin?" Velvet asked, gearing up. "Sigmund Freud here has cured your panic attacks in one session?"

"Aw. Come on," Nick wrapped his arm around Quentin's shoulder as they walked. "Fear of rejection is the killer of many romantic teen scenarios. It's the scourge of adolescence. All I told him is to embrace the possibility that Shandie won't like him and go for it anyway. She is, after all, pretty hot."

"Yeah." Quentin beamed. "What's the worst that could happen?"

She could tell you to eat shit and die, Velvet thought, but kept her mouth shut.

But it was Nick who said, right after, "She could tell him to eat shit and die, right? Words. Just words. That kind of stuff never lasts. People are fickle; they may laugh at you and stuff, but they always move on to the next tragedy as soon as it happens. In the end, it's more about Quentin than it is the girl. It's about courage. The act of talking to her. Exposing himself."

Logan busted up laughing.

Nick rolled his eyes and crammed his hands into his back pockets. "Not that way. I mean, being vulnerable with her. That's what's gonna make you a man. It's going to kill that fear and bury it as deep as the bodies he thieves are kept."

"What are you, some sort of guidance counselor?" Velvet asked.

Nick nodded. "I'm the fucking Geek Whisperer, dude."

Quentin slipped past them and joined the twins already nearing the main entrance to the Retrieval dorm. Velvet snatched Nick's arm and stopped him dead in his tracks.

"You think you know him? You've been here for thirty seconds." She tried to hold back her anger as much as she could, stay cool, but a threat was looming, and she wasn't going to be able to hold her temper back. Nick's brow furrowed with worry. "That's my friend, Nick. Quentin's not just my undertaker. He's my friend. You don't know how he struggles, what he goes through about this stuff. He hurts, dude. And if you just sent him off on a crash and burn, you'll be lucky if I don't kill you. Got it, sport?"

Nick stood there nodding his head, mouthing silent apologies.

"I hope you're right," she said, her eyes drifting to the lanky kid jogging toward the dorms. There was something charged about him, and Velvet realized there was a possibility this could actually work. "I hope so."

She turned back to the boy and found that he'd followed her gaze to Quentin. There was a wan smile on his face and a wistful look in his glowing eyes.

"Me too," he said.

And despite her initial impression of the boy—"dumb jock" came to mind—and the weird, almost tumbling effect he had on her moods and thoughts, she believed he really did have Quentin's best interests at heart.

Could he actually be a decent guy?

Hard to imagine.

He was pretty to look at, though, she thought. Boys weren't objectified nearly enough, and turnabout was *always* fair play. Velvet trudged off through the dwindling crowd to the Retrieval dorm door.

Nick stumbled forward. "Is this the dorms?"

"Yep." Luisa grinned devilishly. "You get to meet Miss Antonia. You're going to love her."

"Who's she?"

Velvet reached for the doorknob and swiveled back to face him. "She's the Salvage mother, and Luisa is messing with you. No one loves Miss Antonia. Respects, maybe, but never loves."

"Why?" He scanned the tall doors, nearly the height of the first floor.

Velvet's chest heaved with laughter. "You'll see."

Velvet swung the doors open and bounded through the short breezeway and into the bustling courtyard full of gabbing cliques of gray souls, and a few powdered white instead of ashed, as Isadora occasionally was. The souls played games set up on bistro tables. Tiles and cards. Music billowed about them like a cloud, eerie and tinny sounding from the gramophone. The place had completely recovered from the shadowquake.

Even Bethany, recovered fully from her run-in with the

shadow tentacle, gabbed noisily about her horrifying experience. Something about a carnival ride and clowns.

Whatever.

Velvet glanced skyward to where even the burn marks on the upper walls had been scrubbed and the gaslight globes replaced. Miss Antonia ran a tight ship; there was no doubt about that.

At one end of the courtyard, a pair of children sat amid the risers of the wide stone stair, one reading to the other from a book the size of a Christmas ham. Nearby a couple of girls in flowing, vibrantly colored saris twirled and gyrated to the music.

Velvet's approach signaled a change in the crowd. Some souls gasped audibly, games were tossed aside, and the music ground to a mopey halt. They left their conversations and gathered around, applauding wildly, pumping Velvet's hand and shouting congratulations. Other souls merely hated and crossed their arms belligerently, chatting among themselves the way the entitled do.

Kipper rounded the stair and trotted across the courtyard to hoist Luisa and Logan each onto one of his broad shoulders and parade them through the cheering crowd. Quentin, his previous enthusiasm turned to a driven focus, scanned the room for Shandie, but he couldn't maintain his focus in the presence of such a homecoming. The clamor of the crowd swept him in, and soon enough his intensity turned into uproarious laughter.

"Velvet!" a woman's voice bellowed above the din.

Velvet watched Nick get his first glimpse of Miss Antonia.

He peered over the heads of the crowd as the tall rail of a woman descended the stairs. Her robe was thick and matronly, as gray as her ashen face. She wore her hair up tight in a bun held together by two dangerously long divining needles.

Nick shuddered beside Velvet, slowly massaging the palm Mrs. Allerdice had pierced. Velvet resisted the urge to lean over and say, "Yes, *those* needles."

The crowd parted, and she shuffled toward them. Her face was as severe as her apparel and hairstyle, narrow eyes sunken in above a thin spindle of a nose. Her lips were a mere shadow around the gash of her mouth. She greeted Velvet with a brief but brutal hug, hoisting the girl off her feet. Since it was useless to struggle, Velvet merely went limp, combat boots dangling in the air an inch above the courtyard pavers. She heard her own pained groan squeak from between her lips.

And then she was set back down, surprised and relieved at the same time. She hadn't expected any appreciation from the woman, and buoyant declarations weren't in the woman's toolbox, by a mile. The two were alike in that sense.

Velvet nodded a quick "You're welcome" before either of them felt the urge to vocalize any niceties. "This is Nick," she said instead.

Nick stepped forward. "Hello, ma'am."

"Number fifty-seven, eh?" She reached for and held Nick's arms out to his sides, assessing his frame. The boy's face registered the appropriate degree of shocked embarrassment. Miss Antonia could have said, "Look at this pretty dress. Isn't it adorable." But what actually came out was less complimentary in tone. "And he's meant for Salvage . . . I assume?"

"So I'm told," Velvet said, her eyes drawn to a thin break between Nick's shirt and the waist of his trousers; the tight flesh of his belly glowed there like a smut beacon. Velvet found herself wanting to touch it, before shaking off the idea as being completely inappropriate and, frankly, bizarre.

What the hell was wrong with her?

When she glanced back up at his face, he was grinning at her, and she spun away, flustered.

"How did you do that?" she wanted to scream. He had some kind of magical magnet or something to know when girls were looking at him.

Every single time.

"Well," Miss Antonia muttered noncommittally. "We'll figure out a place for him. If anything, he can sweep."

Nick scowled.

Miss Antonia snapped her fingers. The sound cracked through the courtyard like gunfire. "Attention! These are your heroes." She swept her bony arms toward the quartet of Salvagers and Nick. "Do something special for them, as they've saved your lazy butts from the shadowquake." She paused, sighing thoughtfully. "I know what you are asking. You are asking, Whatever could we do to show our vast and immense appreciation?"

The faces of the gathered souls sunk into grimaces, but their groans were met by a harsh sneer from the Salvage mother.

"You may take on their chores! For starts, clean up this

courtyard and restring the lanterns! It's far too dark to have a proper salon, so we'll postpone it until tomorrow. But until then, your heroes can't be expected to live like filthy animals, can they?"

There were some shrugs, primarily from the groups on the opposite side of the room. But mostly the tenants of the dorm nodded in agreement.

"Then," Miss Antonia continued, "you may go back to enjoying yourselves!" She snatched one of the needles from the bun in her hair and held it out. It glinted in the dim light, menacingly. "But not before. Or else." She drew the weapon across her throat.

Miss Antonia smirked, her lips disappearing into her mouth, eyes glowing rabidly.

The tenants of the Salvage house stared at her, eyes skittering around at each other, and then as the Salvage mother lurched forward at them, they scrambled wildly away, scuttling like cockroaches caught in a surprise flick of a light switch.

"Wow," Nick muttered.

"She ain't always that nice," a deep voice spoke, thick without any accent at all, like a newscaster or something.

Kipper settled Luisa and Logan onto the ground and held out his hand to shake Nick's. "I'm Kipper. Gary Kipness is my real name. You Velvet's latest conquest?"

Oh, my God, she thought. *Really?*

The boy made it sound like Velvet had picked Nick up at some sleazy bar. Which probably would have suited Nick fine, but it totally wasn't her style. She'd never even been in a bar.

"Yeah, I guess," Nick agreed nervously, losing his hand in the guy's massive grip. It fit around Nick's like a baseball glove, thick and padded and enormous. The shaking was long, forceful, and rolled up Nick's arm like Kipper had snapped a whip.

"Number fifty-seven." Kipper shook his head as though he couldn't quite believe he was meeting Nick. "Congratulations, Velv."

"Uh . . . thanks?" she said.

"People keep saying that," Nick said. "Though why it's important, I don't know."

Kipper waved the comment off. "Just a number. Ain't nothin' else. But . . ." He leaned in close. "Happens to be the highest number of souls retrieved by a single Salvage team leader, so it's kind of a big deal. Velvet's sort of a hero, and she's still young, so she's all set for an amazing record. Major-league shit. She'll be completely excruciating to be around now."

Nick rubbed his hand. "Well, that's a relief. People been saying 'fifty-seven' so much, I figured it was a nickname I'd have to get used to."

Kipper laughed, a great booming laugh. "You got an actual name, Fifty-Seven?"

"Nick Russell."

"Well, tell you what, Nick. As new as you are, and looking like you do, you're gonna be girl food."

"Jesus," Velvet sighed, but as she scanned the room, she noticed a pack of girls prowling near the stage, alternating between chatting and looking over their shoulders at the two boys. Or rather at Nick, as if *he* needed a bigger head on his shoulders.

"I guess that's a good thing." Nick smiled and waved in their direction.

Kipper shrugged. "Could be. Those ones bite, but they're nothing compared to Isadora and her group." He pointed out the girl, standing, of course, with Shandie.

Isadora's eyes locked onto Nick's and didn't blink, and a sinister smirk curled on her perfectly painted lips, as if she were picking him out of the pastry case, a piece of cheesecake or something. That the devil of the Collector set would have eyes for Nick was a given.

"You gotta be careful with that one," Kipper said.

"She's pretty hot," Nick agreed.

Velvet rolled her eyes. "Jesus," she said again.

Kipper nailed it. "Not what I meant. She's psycho. This guy I know, Graham Polosian, went out with her one time and came back completely messed up."

Nick nodded his head. "She looks like the type to mess with a guy's head."

"That ain't it. He came back all made up like a living guy. White skin, lipstick. Hell, even eyeliner. He was like Thirty Seconds to Mantyhose."

Nick chuckled but didn't quite seem to catch Kipper's emo slur.

"Mantyhose?" Velvet added, butting into the conversation. "Those skinny jeans they make the boys wear are like shackles." She glowered in Isadora's direction. "Oh, yeah. I agree one hundred percent. Isadora is a piece of work. Master

Emasculator if there ever was one. Probably carries around a collection of balls in her purse."

Nick ventured another look at the girl, and shivered.

Velvet's eyes were set on Isadora's friend.

Quentin had emerged from the darkness and was striding, quite deliberately, toward the girl. The distraction of Nick's appearance having been quickly discarded, Shandie had gone back to chatting with Isadora, her face scrunched up a bit in judgment as Quentin stepped up to them and began to speak. Velvet wished she could hear what Quentin was saying. She suspected some of the words came out stuttered, fast, probably rambled. But she was so proud of him.

And to Velvet's surprise, Shandie was smiling. She touched her neck, the international symbol for being interested.

Nick nudged her slightly, and Velvet gave in and gave him an appreciative nod. It certainly appeared that Quentin was a go. They weren't the only ones spying. Kipper pumped his fist in the air while Logan's mouth lolled open with surprise. Luisa wore a wan, hopeful expression and clasped her hands over her heart in a wholly girlish attitude, belying her viciousness.

The sound of people gasping brought Velvet's attention back to Quentin and the girl. In fact, the crowd of souls were backing away. She rushed forward. Had the girl slapped him or something? Quentin wasn't the kind of guy to ever be a complete douche. He didn't even have those words in him, unless he was repeating something Kipper had told him.

Velvet darted the short distance to see what was going on.

When she broke through the throng, she stopped dead.

Her heart sank. Nick stumbled up behind her and touched his hand to her arm, likely to hold himself up. If his knees were as shaky as hers, they'd both need the support soon enough.

Quentin lay on the crooked cobblestones, his legs splayed out like a discarded rag doll, his head in Kipper's lap. Shandie had retreated a few feet away and sobbed quietly into Isadora's shoulder.

"Go on, Quentin. It's your time. You're the man." Kipper's voice was choked with tears. "You're the man."

Quentin's skin flickered. He glanced at Velvet and Nick and smiled the briefest of smiles before the glow beneath the thin layer of ash flashed brightly and then dimmed. The light behind his eyes died out. Kipper lifted the boy's head and slid from underneath him, setting him gently back onto the cold stone ground.

He backed away, as did everyone else nearby. Velvet felt a hand slipping into hers and looked down to see Luisa, her expression a confused mix of pride and grief. Velvet reached out for Nick and pulled him backward.

As though a dark fire had been set within Quentin's prone form, his skin began to crackle and expand, puffing out where it wasn't constricted by clothing. It dimpled and shed like dandruff, falling off in chunks and exploding into ash against the cobblestone, spilling into the indentations between. And then, as if a jetty of wind swirled about the corpse, ash curled from Quentin's exposed flesh in big flakes and floated around him. The depressions caved, creating sinkholes on his cheeks, in the hollow of his throat. His clothes caught fire and were consumed in an instant. When all was said and done, all that was left of the boy was a pile of ash, as gray as a storm front.

Velvet shivered, her body suddenly a hollow shell.

Remainders were silent mysterious, things. No one knew what exactly anchored them to purgatory's ashen shore. She had suspicions—everyone did—and often figured hers had to do with feelings, or the lack of them. The confusion of emotion. And really, if she thought about it at all, that quiet moment in the Shattered Hall, huddled over Nick, wrapping him in the warm solidity of the woolen peacoat, could very well have been her cue to flash burn and turn to ash.

You just never knew. Quentin had learned everything he'd needed to, and there was no reason to be sad about that, she supposed. At least, that was what the Council of Station Agents told them to believe.

Velvet turned to Nick.

Hurt clouded his face. A feeling weighed at the corners of his mouth, heavy and funereal. His eyelids sagged and the light in his eyes turned to shadowy eclipses.

It was guilt. Nick was mourning.

She felt an unfamiliar twinge and for a moment thought she was experiencing guilt over her friend's passing, too. But that wasn't it. It wasn't guilt at all. It was jealousy. The realization bit into her like the jaws of some black creature, grim and nightmarish. And she shook it away.

And thankfully, it fell.

If she could count on her particular affliction for anything, it was the rapid sloughing of unwanted and unexpected feelings. Accessing the ones she needed was the issue.

Which brought her back to the boy in front of her.

She wanted to be able to reach back into their history and recapture the moment in the Shattered Hall, but she couldn't. It floated between them like a dust mote caught in a slant of light.

She should hold him, she decided. But she didn't.

"It's fine. It's a natural thing," Velvet found herself saying. "Just follow my lead."

She touched Nick's arm to slip past, her hip brushing his. Nick tensed, and for a second, Velvet thought he would wrap her up in his arms and never let go; to cover her face with kisses.

But he didn't.

Velvet squatted beside the pile of Quentin's ashes and dug her hand deep into it, rubbing the gray powder on her face and neck before moving on. The residents of the dorms had formed a loose line, and each in turn did as Velvet had, spreading a small handful of Quentin's remains on their skin.

"It's an act of respect," she muttered to Nick, who held back and watched.

Miss Antonia was the next to last to pay her respects. She sidestepped the line and guided Nick to the dwindling pile of ash. "The rest is for the pots; just take a small handful."

He did as he was told, hands shaking as his fingers sank into the pile. He rubbed the ash into his cheeks in stiff strokes, where it crumbled and rained down the yoke of his dress shirt.

Chapter 14

Velvet crouched in the corner of her room, her fingers wound in the cording of the drapes. Everything around her was deflated, as though made of sagging, half-empty balloons. Her bed, dresser, even the wardrobes, sagged into slick plastic piles, punctured by Mr. Fassbinder's spiky nest of monk parakeets, which hung from the ceiling like the world's scariest nursery mobile. The prickly globe kept getting bigger and bigger, like a set of lungs filling up with air, heaving in and expanding until there was more room inside than out. The needles scraped the walls with a horrible grating sound, nearly shutting out the chirping of the hundred birds in their cells. Velvet threw her arms up and clinched her eyes shut as the spikes pressed closer.

Moments later, Velvet was staring into a soul-streaked sky. She noticed one thing immediately: she wasn't alone. Bonesaw crouched beside her, his face placid, slack. His black eyes bored into her mind.

Don't ever leave me.

The words hissed through her head, splitting her brain open until there was nothing but pain and the killer's sad longing inside her. She tried to push away, but they were both trapped in a parakeet's cell, nestled among strips of finely shredded paper. She pulled them around her and stuffed them into her ears, even as she heard his next plea . . .

Love me.

His face so close.

His waxy lips puckered.

His eyes full of need.

Velvet sat bolt upright in her bed. A shimmer of gaslight filtered through her window, over a collection of origami birds from the Paper Aviary, and settled on the peaks of the tussled blanket like a dry layer of snow.

She stared into the shadows and tried to calm herself. The silence helped. The dorms were asleep at that hour, and normally she'd take the opportunity to slip out and check on Bonesaw, watch him as he stared at his new acquisition and whispered horrible things to her until she screamed back. Velvet didn't have the stomach for it just then. She needed to recharge. The previous hours had worn her down more than she'd realized. Bonesaw, Nick, Quentin—the dream had been proof of that.

No.

Velvet rested her head back into the soft, pulpy pillow and closed her eyes. She began to pray that she wouldn't dream of her killer, but it was too late. The memories were flooding back.

The shed was cold in those first two days.

Dead insects drifted into the corners and accumulated like snowbanks, and the dust hung in the air like a million constellations of rancid, stinky stars. She'd tried to escape, but the ropes and rubber tubing had dug into her flesh like fingers tightening.

She'd screamed and screamed, but nothing had ever answered except the incessant rain pounding schizophrenic melodies on the tin roof.

Then there was Bonesaw.

His waxy face close to hers, his clammy fingers on her skin, his whispers.

Tell me you love me.

Velvet shook her head, rubbed her eyes. She wished the memories were bound up in fishing line and rubber tubing as well.

She sat back up in bed and listened to the sleeping dorm.

Soft sobs echoed through her open bedroom door from the darkened courtyard below. Or at least she thought that was what they were.

"What now?" she moaned, and tore the comforter aside and crammed her feet into her boots. She hung over the balustrade outside her room and glared into the darkness, watching for movement, listening for the mysterious weeper.

There was nothing for precious seconds, but then she heard it again.

A sharp intake of breath.

A quiet moan.

Velvet trod quietly down the uneven stairs—no easy task in the heavy boots—and, upon reaching the courtyard floor, squinted. A pair of glowing eyes blinked at her from the front door alcove.

"All right. Who's down there?" she whispered.

A rare girly moment passed with Velvet fantasizing that it was Shandie, mourning the loss of a really great guy who was never going to be pining away for her again. But when the figure shifted, wavy gray hair, not the girl's teased-out puffs, poked into a dim column of gaslight.

"Nick?" Velvet crossed the courtyard and crouched beside him, her fingertips digging into the grooves between the stones to hold her upright. The boy's legs were splayed out before him, as loose and limber as a rag doll's. Pale white tears fell from under his lids, stripping ash off his cheeks in thin rivulets. The glare from his skin spilled out and cast an odd glow between them.

"Oh, crap," Velvet said uneasily.

Nick winced. "Figures it's you. Couldn't have been someone nice."

"I'll let you have that one, because you're . . . incapacitated and probably missing your family. But watch it from now on, okay?"

He nodded, and Velvet reached out to catch a gray teardrop from his chin. It clung to her fingertip like a dirty pearl, and she stared at it a bit before rubbing it off on the boy's sleeve.

Nick sneered and pulled away into the shadows, shaking

his head. "It's just that I thought I could handle it. But after Miss Antonia took me to my room and the door closed behind me . . ." He paused. "After I was alone, it just kind of hit, you know? Like an earthquake."

"Yeah."

"Why are you up?"

"Stupid dream. It's nothing."

She rested on her heels and sighed. Nurturing wasn't the kind of magic she carried around in her bag of tricks along with the penchant for violence and the really cool fashion sense, but there was something about this boy that made her want to protect him. Though Velvet wasn't sure she had it in her.

She glanced toward the opposing sets of stairs—no one stirred in either wing of the dormitory. Probably exhausted from Quentin's dimming and the gloomy ceremony of cleaning up that followed. Velvet rubbed the ash further into her cheek at the thought.

What am I even doing down here?

She had her own shit to deal with. She didn't have time to help this boy through his. Like she needed one more thing on her plate. Thwarting serial killers and banshees, investigating revolutionaries, keeping secrets? Yeah. All she needed was to take on a depressed, albeit hot, boy. But there he was, his shoulders softly heaving and his big bare boy foot poking out into the light.

"I'll never see them again?" Nick's voice was heavy with sorrow, but the sobs had stopped. Thankfully.

Velvet wasn't a fan of crying, as if you couldn't tell.

"Not for a while," Velvet said, conjuring up her most empathetic tone. "But maybe. Someday."

"Maybe?" His sleepy glowing eyes sought out hers and held them in his gaze.

"Maybe."

She slipped in next to him, sliding down the wall until her butt hit the cold stone and her hip nestled next to his.

"It's a matter of perspective. So it's like this. Time is on our side, right? It's not like we're going to die again. So lots of stuff falls into the realm of possibility. Way more than when we were alive."

He scrunched up his face, the skin around his eyes crinkling.

"Give me your hand," she directed.

Nick slipped his hand tentatively into hers. She thought his hands would be rough. But they weren't. They were way bigger than hers, mannish, but soft skin lay beneath the fine layer of ash. And a warmth. A tragically welcoming warmth. She began to massage his palm with her thumbs.

Nick's head rolled on his neck, and she thought she heard a quick gasp.

"Hand massages have a miraculous effect on mood. And since I like you better not so weepy, let's give this a shot," Velvet said.

A small smile made its way onto his mouth. "Is that right?"

She looked up from his hand. "Huh?"

"You like me?" His face was creepily hopeful. Well, as creepy as he could look with perfect bone structure and those fat boy lips stuck to his face like candy.

"Uh . . . not so fast with the semantics, dickweed. I said I like you better not bawling your eyes out like a little girl. There's a difference."

"Gotcha," he said with a grin that quickly faded.

Why couldn't people just let her be nice? She'd been doing so well.

She went back to work on his hand. "It's all about pressure points. You gotta get in there real good. Sometimes it hurts, but in the end, you'll feel great. Take this spot here in the web between your thumb and index finger."

He glanced down at their hands.

"Rubbing it just right relaxes the brain. Chills you out."

"Feels nice." His voice was deep, dreamy. It vibrated as thought they were both asleep. Floating. Safe.

He turned her hand in his and caressed *her* palm this time, the grit grinding between them magnificently, sending tiny earthquakes through Velvet's skin, up her arms and all over, until her whole body ached for his touch.

"Do you like me, Velvet? I mean, do you like me at all?"

She shrugged, bit her cheek. "I don't know you."

And that was when she did it.

Broke yet another rule.

Partly because she was, like Kipper had said, lonely. Or maybe it was because things had just gotten out of hand and she was nervous all of a sudden.

Everything was so nuts. So out of control.

Bonesaw's latest. The departure. Quentin.

Velvet leaned forward, probably a little too abruptly, and found his lips, brushed the soft flesh there with her thumb before tentatively pressing her mouth to his. Nick's hands slipped around either side of her neck, lingering on the curves, caressing the soft hollows of her throat, her shoulders. He pulled her toward him, kissing her deeply and then in soft pecks that trailed down one cheek and then the other, as though it had been Velvet crying before.

"I could take care of you," he said, his breath hot against her neck. "We could care about each other."

Just like that. Like it was a choice.

The words surprised her. Not that he'd spoken them, but that he seemed to know she needed some relief. As though he'd read her mind. She thought a moment, or rather tried to think, to gather her thoughts into a tidy little pile. It was tricky to do with Nick's hands fumbling with her T-shirt, his fingertips drawing across her belly. In the end she gave up.

She knew it wasn't right. Hell, she didn't even know the boy, let alone love him, or like him, for that matter.

"We could." She spoke the words softly against the flesh of Nick's throat.

He quivered beneath her, and Velvet pushed him farther into the shadows, pressing her body to his.

Chapter 15

A railcar lumbered past, rattling the thin greasy window-panes and dusting her cheeks with a fine rain of ash from the rafters.

Velvet's eyes fluttered open.

Gaslight streamed in from outside, not the full glow alerting them to working hours but a dingy yellow slanting across her bed. Time worked differently in purgatory. The imposition of night could stretch on and on as the stations that studded the planet cleared out their backlogs of incoming souls.

When death lulled to a manageable trickle, the gaslights blazed up.

She pushed up onto her elbows, yawned one of those big quivering yawns that make you see squiggly lines, and stretched. Velvet twisted her neck to the right, trying to crack it, work out the kink, and noticed something strange about the blankets.

Something horrifying.

She wasn't alone. Nick lay sprawled out beside her.

"Uhhhh." The sound spilled out of her like a leaky tire. She'd woken thinking their liaison had been a semi-pleasant dream, but clearly—unless Nick was extremely agile at slipping into girls' beds unnoticed—it was less dream and more like a hazy reality with consequences she didn't really have time for.

Ash had been rubbed from Nick's bare shoulder, revealing the dull glow of sleep threading through his nerves. *Not dreaming,* she thought. He would be brighter. His hair was tousled, his face slack with slumber and something else . . . satisfaction?

She hoped not.

He lay on his back with the white sheet bunched up under his right arm and his palm up and clawed, clinching something imaginary. A soft whisper spilled from his parted lips. Lips she'd been more than happy to taste not so long ago.

What else had they done?

She pinched the edge of the sheet and lifted it up. Skin, and lots of it. Nick had on the brown wool trousers from earlier, only now they were beltless and open where the trail of gray hairs disappeared down his glowing stomach into the exposed band of his boxers.

Pants were a good sign, she decided. Not case-closing, but something.

Velvet poked him in the shoulder, and his face instantly scrunched up uncomfortably.

Nick groaned, rubbed his eyes, and winced in her direction. "Jeez. What?"

"What are you doing here?" she asked, biting out each word.

He grinned, like she was playing with him or something. "Um . . . we kind of made out and stuff, remember?"

"Yeah. I got that. I'm just a little hazy on the part where I invited you to sleep in my bed. I'm gonna need to see your permission slip."

Nick smiled broadly and started to lift the sheet, his eyes motioning downward.

"Not what I meant." Velvet slapped his hand, and the sheet fell from his fingers.

"Hey, it's no big deal, right? We were both tired. I kissed you good night, because I seriously can't get enough of your mouth." He sighed. "I think I was just dreaming about those lips."

"Don't." Velvet's eyes narrowed viciously, and she balled her hand into a fist.

"I couldn't find my room, but I remembered where yours was."

"If you tell me we did stuff and I just don't remember . . ."

"No way. I mean, God. No. You don't know me. I get that. But you gotta know that I wouldn't take advantage." His jaw clenched with conviction. He sat bolt upright and covered her fist with his palm. "Your honor is unblemished, if that's what you're worried about. You were pretty tired."

Is this guy for real? she wondered, glancing down at his hand, so much larger than her own, strong. Protective.

The imagery didn't sit right.

"All right, Nick. I believe you." She twisted her wrist until his hand fell away, and then she slipped out from beneath the covers, thankful she hadn't stripped off all her clothes in her exhausted state. It would have been really difficult to make her point if she'd had to deliver the next bit totally naked.

She tugged a sweater on over the T-shirt she wore and settled back at the foot of the bed. Nick followed her each and every movement, poring over her like he would an exam or maybe his playbook, if they even had those in basketball.

"This . . . ," she said, poking the space between them and leaving a dimple in the blankets. "Is *not* a love story."

He squinted, shook his head. "No?"

Definitely not, she thought. Velvet needed to get that through to the boy. His cocky smile, the way he deflected stuff with humor, everything about him was wrong for her. If anything, he'd have to settle for her eyes wandering over his body. And that face and those eyes. And the way he was tracing the indents between his stomach muscles.

Velvet gripped the thin slip of fabric covering the mattress. "No."

"Then what is it?"

"Depends on the day. Mostly horror."

She stopped short of telling him the real story. Girls punched through like college rule paper. Tortured. Packaged. Instead, Velvet shrugged and bent to fish a pair of jeans off the floor. "Everything that happened was a mistake. I was bestowing a kindness on your pathetic grief act."

"Harsh," he said matter-of-factly.

Velvet thought about it, glanced back over her shoulder. "Coulda been way harsher."

Nick rested his back against the headboard, as if he were posing. He was ridiculously gorgeous, even with bed-head—maybe because of it. It made her sick—like violently ill. He could at least be polite and have some scars, a third nipple, or a low-hanging ear on the side of his head. But no. He was perfect and adorable and in her bed. And, oh yeah, she felt like punching the shit out of him.

"You must be going soft," he mumbled.

"Unlikely." Velvet pulled on the jeans and crammed her feet into her black boots.

"Going somewhere?"

She nodded, rolling her eyes. "You're very observant, aren't you?"

"I'm like a detective that way."

Velvet resisted an almost impossible urge to smile. The guy was charming for sure, and a smart-ass, which, of course, she couldn't get enough of, but seriously. Enough was enough.

She spun around. "Listen, Nick."

His face took on a stern mocking. "Yes, Velvet."

"You need to be gone when I get back. This whole thing was a giant mistake. Huge."

Concern wiped the humor from his face. "So, wait. That's it? We make out and it was awesome and you make me feel things I never have with any other girl, and then you run? I gotta say, I'm feeling a little slutty here."

Velvet nodded, cranked the doorknob, and pointed into the hall. "Yeah, well. I can't do anything about that."

He groaned, looked wounded, and pulled the sheet up around him.

Meanwhile, Velvet was close to breaking. It was hard to be mean to the guy. He'd been so vulnerable just a short while ago. "What do you want, a ring?"

"Well, no," he said. "But I was hoping we could skip the teenage heartbreak part."

She nodded sympathetically. "Well . . . just this once."

"You mean it?" He brightened.

She glared back. "No."

Nick shoved the sheet off and bounded from the bed, head swinging from side to side, squinting into the dark corners of the room. "You can really be a bitch, you know?"

"I have training."

He snatched his shirt from the floor and tugged it on over his head. "Yeah. I'm being a little bit serious."

"I know, and that scares me in a restraining order kind of way. So let's plan on forgetting that all this happened and agree to simply be polite when we run into each other again, and leave it at that."

She left him scratching his head as she pulled the door closed behind her and made off for the stairs.

What the hell had she been thinking? As if she didn't have enough going on in her afterlife, she had to go and throw Nick into the mix? Insane.

It really was too bad souls couldn't take medication.

Velvet needed a lot.

Lots and lots of psychiatric medication.

What with Bonesaw's mountain of crazy spilling into her dreams, an inability to follow even the most basic of rules, and now a seeming lack of decision-making skill other than the kind that would have her end up standing in front of the Council of Station Agents.

Problems. Lots of problems.

And Nick. And his eyes. And his body. And those hands.

If only he weren't such a good kisser. She was going to have to put his mouth up on the same pedestal with egg rolls and linguini with clams, all things she'd miss so freakin' bad.

Game face.

The tables in the courtyard were polished to a high sheen, obsessively so. There wasn't a streak in sight. In the tables' reflection, Velvet could see the grid of ropes and hoses strung from the balconies, stripped free of clothes and rags. The bubbles of gaslight were dimmed to a mute flutter, and beyond that was the streaked glare of passing souls. The chairs were pushed up under the tables with precision, like someone had had all the time in the world—which they just might—a nasty case of obsessive-compulsive disorder, and a ruler.

Miss Antonia did insist on cleanliness.

The stage was set and draped with rich woven tapestries, candelabras, and stacks of sheet music teetering precariously atop a big mahogany lectern, though most people just sang stuff they remembered—or mostly remembered, or just thought they remembered when really those weren't the words at all. It was shaping up to be a pretty momentous salon, Velvet guessed. Particularly after the crappy night they'd all experienced. First the shadowquake, then Quentin. Then Nick.

Of course, she'd been the only one to experience that last one.

Still. Too much.

She clung to the shadows as far from the soft glimmer of lamplight as she could, crouching behind tables as she slunk toward the breezeway door. She lingered briefly, listening for the sounds of night owls, gas addicts creeping back from their drug dens, but there was nothing. It might just be too early for that, she hoped. As it was, she had no freaking clue what time it was. The gaslight told them when it was time to be active. She glanced at the dim glow as she crept through the courtyard and out into the square, stepping softly toward her secret.

Ahead of her, she could just make out a form winding its way from the shadows. Someone familiar. The soul's heels clacked purposeful steps against the cobblestone. Even Miss Antonia's outline was stern and stiffly postured. Velvet resisted the urge to bolt in the opposite direction before the Salvage mother could catch a glimpse of her.

But then something odd happened.

The shadows snagging on the sharp angles of her face, Miss Antonia crept from the darkness. As the woman neared, she began to stumble and stutter uncharacteristically, "Uh. Oh. Vuh-Velvet. I didn't see you there. You must be off for another of your walks."

If Velvet hadn't been so on edge, she might have launched

into questioning. The woman seemed so guilty about something, but as it was, Velvet thought she'd be better off distracting her and moving on.

Miss Antonia seemed to readjust herself, ridding her voice of the weird vulnerability. Suspicion took the place of the Salvage mother's alarm, crackled there like a fire.

Velvet tried not to bristle. "Just can't sleep. All the excitement of yesterday, you know."

"I do know." The Salvage mother nodded, studying Velvet for any tiny hint of a lie.

And she did know, of course.

Miss Antonia had been a well-known undertaker in her day. Her team had even set a record at thirty-seven. Those were quieter times, Velvet thought. Nothing like the outbreaks of psychic phenomena they had to deal with and fend off now. But kids always think they have it worse than older people, or at least that's what parents and teachers love to remind them. *Sometimes it's true, though,* she thought.

"I rarely slept when I was on Salvage," Miss Antonia said in a rare moment of wistful nostalgia.

Velvet snatched at the opportunity to redirect the woman, veer her off course from scrutinizing Velvet's intentions for the evening walk. "I love hearing about your cases."

Miss Antonia brightened immediately. "Perhaps I'll share one at the coming salon."

The Salvage mother loved telling her stories—they may have been the only thing she loved—though they always seemed to lead back to the one about the body thief on her team, back in the day. Aloysius Clay was his name. He went missing after a botched mission where one of their poltergeists disappeared. Just went up in smoke during a raid on a séance.

Nasty business.

But Velvet thought there might be more to Miss Antonia's obsession with Clay's disappearance than simple camaraderie or the mystery of it all. There was a glimmer in her eye when she talked—and since she was a spirit, there was no way Velvet could mistake the bigger than normal glow for anything other than extreme nerves. Velvet thought Miss Antonia had been in love with Aloysius Clay.

Possibly had even been his lover.

The woman could never say so. Fraternizing with your teammates, while convenient, could really end up in some messy situations.

"I wish you would. I'd love to hear another." She held the woman's gaze, smiling, nodding, trying to be as pleasant as she could, until she realized that was completely out of character. So she shifted her weight, planted a hand on her hip, and sighed, breathing some annoyed life into the situation. *Normal,* she commanded herself. *Act normal or she'll catch on to the ruse.*

Miss Antonia relaxed.

"Well, then. Be careful on your walk, Velvet. It's early. There's probably a few more hours in this long night, but not enough to rid the streets of hooligans. And . . ." She narrowed her eyes as she said, "You'll want to get a little rest. We're going to start testing Nick tomorrow."

Velvet thought she might have actually gulped. "Wh-what?" she sputtered.

Miss Antonia pressed her palm to the gray lapel of her matronly suit. "Oh. I thought you were aware. Now, with Quentin's dimming and all, your team does have an opening."

Velvet stood there with her mouth agape. She couldn't find the words to describe her horror. Her big-ass mistake had just turned into something a hundred times worse. Training Nick? Working alongside him? Hell, she could barely keep her hands off him last night. But now, if they expected him to be a part of her team, she could never have him. It was against the rules.

No fraternization.

Never again.

And seriously? Why the hell did they think he was so special?

Nick had the strength for the job, certainly. Her memory wandered to his glowing flesh, the curve of his muscles, the smooth strength of his jaw. His bright smile. Normally she wouldn't have thought twice about a guy like Nick. The type made her nauseous. Or used to, rather.

Perhaps, but that was a long time ago. The old Velvet had been replaced by a warrior. Mostly. Still, the attraction was undeniable. And attractions were distractions, no matter how cute, and totally dangerous in her line of work. Dangerous and deadly.

"I see" was all Velvet could bring herself to say.

Miss Antonia's gaze sharpened. "You disapprove."

"Of course," Velvet said flippantly.

"Well, that's par for the course." The Salvage mother sneered. "Disapproval is your middle name."

Velvet huffed and stomped off into the shadows.

"Don't be long!" Miss Antonia called behind her.

Velvet waved without stopping, passing through the town square quickly. Souls milled about, even at that early hour, chatting under the soft glow of the gaslight flames flickering behind charred glass, or rushing home to catch a few moments of rest before the day started all over again. The streets narrowed, and in the distance, the funicular rails hummed with the distant shuttling of souls. The farther she traveled, the sparser her company, and soon her footsteps were the only ones echoing against the stone walls. Velvet could hardly see her feet beneath her.

At the Paper Aviary, she slowed. It was dark, and Mr. Fassbinder was sure to be asleep inside. She'd make certain to pop in on the way back, not only to add whatever special bird he'd made for her to her collection, but to ask him questions about the effigy. About the paper from Vermillion. She knew she could count on him to help, unlike others, who were merely obstacles.

Velvet made a sharp left into a narrow alley. The light did not follow.

But something had.

"Where are *you* going, then?" The voice was crisp, bitchy, and distinctly British.

Isadora.

Velvet, astonished at her terrible luck, stiffened and felt her fists balling up for a fight. "A better question is, what is a mere Collector doing out in the early morning hours, Isadora?" The girl's name caught in her throat like phlegm. "It's still night, you know."

Turning, she saw Isadora leaning against the thick glass of the Paper Aviary, the last of the gaslight glinting off her wolflike teeth in the moonlight. Isadora wasn't nearly as tall as Velvet, but she fought like an animal. They'd never had a skirmish, but Velvet had seen the girl take on a boy twice her size and swat him down, all without disturbing a stitch in her Jean Paul Gaultier gown.

"I won't lie." Isadora's eyes narrowed to slits. "I *was* following you. I know you're up to no good."

Velvet held her breath. What could the girl possibly know? If she even had an inkling that Velvet was on the haunt, the brat wouldn't think twice about reporting her. As a matter of fact, Velvet knew Isadora would be more than happy to see her stripped of her duties as a body thief. She'd totally get off on it. No question.

"Sneaking off from the dorms in the middle of the night? I've seen you."

"I'm simply taking a walk, Isadora. There's no rule against that."

"Hmm. I suppose."

"I could say the same thing about you!" Velvet barked, her grasp on her temper slipping. She heard a clang of something dropping inside the shop, as though they'd roused the origamist.

"No, you couldn't." Isadora's grin was even bigger than before. "And look at you getting defensive. Now I really do know I've caught you doing something bad. What is it? You've got a secret boyfriend or something?"

"No!" Velvet started to shout, and then hushed to a whisper. "Of course not."

Hell, she couldn't even make the words sound convincing.

"Well, what is it, then?"

"Just walking."

"Down a dark alley?" Isadora crossed her legs and made a show of examining her fingernails. "Gotta tell ya, Vel. I'm skeptical."

"What you are, Isadora, is a bitch, and I'm done talking to you." Velvet spun and stomped into the darkness.

The other girl chuckled.

"Well," she said huffily. "I guess I won't tell you about meeting your fancy new boy."

Velvet stopped dead in her tracks.

Isadora continued. "You got a thing going with him yet? 'Cause the lad's got yummy all over him and Isadora's in the mood for a snack."

"Did you just refer to yourself in the third person?" Velvet snipped.

"I did."

Velvet fumed. She'd be damned if the snotty Collector got her mitts on Nick. She'd sooner be banned from dimming than let that happen. *Wait a minute,* she thought. *Why should I be jealous? I'm not. Nick was a mistake.*

Wasn't he?

"Well, since you've no response . . . ," the other girl said.

"Oh, I've got a response." Velvet spun back toward

Isadora intending on punching the girl in the face, but there was no one there.

Nothing but a thin wisp of mist. Isadora loved to get the last word almost as much as Velvet hated not getting it herself.

"Gah!" Velvet spat, looked around nervously for onlookers, and rushed back into the dark gap between the buildings. She stripped off her clothes, wanting nothing more than to put a great deal of distance between herself and the vermin that was Isadora. Instinctively she found the crack and slipped into the fracture and away from purgatory.

Her body shuddered, and the blackness gave way to a rush of vibrant light as she sped along a brilliant surging vein of phosphorous. The experience stripped her of all the hate she felt toward Isadora, the confusion over Nick, and the sorrow about Quentin, leaving her calm and ready for Bonesaw.

Velvet fell from the crack in the tree and onto the forest floor. Exhausted, she felt a strong urge to curl up in the ferns and the coils of ivy vines forever. There was definitely something comforting about the dewy undergrowth. Of course, with things as stressful as they were, a bed of nails seemed snooze-worthy.

She glanced back at the tree and sighed.

"Rachel + Jimbo = TLA" was carved inside a heart with horns and a little tail like a devil. Velvet remembered chuckling the first time she'd seen it. Jimbo must have thought himself quite clever. And really, if Velvet were to be honest, if Jimbo had carved it for her, she might have given a tiny pause before rolling her eyes. It was a winning move—a little cliché, sure, but nonetheless romantic—for some.

She wondered if Nick was the kind of guy to carve meaningless symbols into perfectly healthy unscarred trees.

Nick.

"Bah!" she shouted, banishing the boy from her mind, and stormed from the copse of trees.

And stopped.

The sun was halfway up the sky, but warm, melting ice from the stiff, sugared blades of pasture grass. All around her the world was crisp from an overnight freeze. The oak branches behind her crackled from the weight, and birds caught by frost's surprise attack cawed with a newfound urgency; their sound echoed like a warning over the hills and gullies.

The ghost of Velvet's heart skittered with excitement. Bonesaw might have already left for the day. It wasn't her first choice, but his absence would free her up to work on releasing the madman's victim.

She darted for the meandering gravel road that ran from farm to farm to slaughterhouse horror show and finally to nowhere. Her stomping and kicking stirred up dust storms and devils that twisted away from the phantom pressure of her feet and the memory of the Fluevog boots surrounding them.

As the Simanski farm came into view, pegging the horizon like a gray knife handle stabbed into the ground, Velvet was oddly reminded of her mother.

And a movie, naturally.

A Clockwork Orange had played a brief run at the Hallmark theater two towns over from New Brompfel Heights, where people drank coffee in small cups, read things that didn't have celebrity gossip in them, and mused about the state of the capital *A* Arts in America. Velvet loved the place, with its gold burnished alcoves and private curved balconies with thick curtained entrances. The seats were a plush velveteen, and sitting on them made a twelve-year-old-Velvet feel like she was in the exact right spot; her mother's homage to her love of cinema was Velvet's proper name. Most people suspected "Velveteen" referenced the sappy children's story about the bunny that wanted to be real, not a luxurious mass-produced fabric.

"It's subversive," her mother had said of *A Clockwork Orange,* not her choice of name for her daughter. Though there was definitely a foreshadowing in the selection, any idiot could see that.

Velvet had watched the horror of Stanley Kubrick's film unfold in stunned silence. Alex and his "droogs" tore up a totally dystopian future Britain with bats and their fists and used weird slang that began to make some sort of sense the longer she listened. There were rapes and murders and all number of horrible things in the film. But when the main character was finally convicted of his crimes and prescribed an aversion therapy, it was just as horrendous as his crimes. And it didn't work.

It was terrible.

And brilliant.

Afterward, her mother treated her to an espresso at the Café des Artistes and they discussed satire and violence like grown-ups, eating tortes with long names and watching sweat drip from the windows.

Later, as Velvet had sat outside the principal's office, dressed as Kubrick's Alex DeLarge in a white shirt and pants, bowler hat, codpiece, and one eye done up with impossibly long fake eyelashes, she'd listened to the man berate her mother for "parentifying" Velvet.

Whatever that meant.

The principal couldn't have been more wrong.

If anything, just knowing other children made Velvet not want to be a parent. Kids could be horrible, too. Her costume had been a satire. No one had seemed to get that. Except maybe Stanley Kubrick.

But he was dead.

And Velvet wished she had a bat.

"Time for a little ultraviolence," she muttered through a grim smile, and trekked the remaining half mile up the road, hoping Bonesaw hadn't left for work. She was certain she could find a two-by-four or a piece of old pipe to break his kneecap or something . . . or maybe, if she could conjure the courage, she'd possess the freak and drive the stupid minivan off a cliff.

The thought made her wistful and moony.

But then it occurred to her that the girl might have already been cut, that the killer had changed his pattern in some small way, turning up the volume, skipping crucial steps. The bloody raised welts might already be there, like mementos on her forearms and thighs.

The thought of it made her run faster and faster.

The house stood at the top of a small hill, the roof of Bonesaw's nearest neighbor just barely visible behind the overgrown grass swaying in the adjacent field. Velvet noted the absence of Bonesaw's van.

"Well," she sighed. "That changes things. Ron Simanski lives to see another day."

Pushing her disappointment aside, Velvet padded across the lawn and peeked her head inside the door to the outbuilding. The girl sat bolt upright, tied to the chair where she'd left her. Her eyes were weak but open, and her lips were slack like she'd just had a big shot of Novocain and was feeling a little droopy in the jaw. Velvet scanned the girl's arms and sighed in relief. Her pants were still on her legs, too. Once those were off, there'd be no question she'd be marked. The more he cut, the more he wanted to, and then there was no stopping him.

But there was nothing yet.

Nothing but the soft dew of pale blond hairs and tiny port-wine stain on her right hand, a beauty mark, Velvet's mother would have said.

"That's a relief, isn't it?" she whispered. "I'd untie you, sweetheart. But I can't manage the knots in the fishing line. Ghosts just don't have that kind of dexterity."

She glanced around the workbench, scanning for something suitable.

"I'll need a knife. Something big enough, where I can really whack at those ropes and stuff. Sawing is not really in my repertoire."

It was hard enough to manage throwing stuff with precision, let alone gripping a handle and cutting through something using all those intricate little movements. Ghosts

just weren't built for that, and the one time she'd commandeered a body for the purpose, things had not gone well for
the body.

Not. At. All.

Velvet didn't want to think about that. Though, to be clear,
he'd been completely closed off from his pain receptors—she
always made sure of that, whenever she possessed—and
she had helped secure a very cushy job and residence for the
man's dearly departed soul. So. There was that.

The times she had tried to untie the girls with her fingers, they'd always struggled and made the knots tighter as
soon as they'd realized that something invisible was touching them and creating little indents in their loosening skin.
Screaming, fainting, that kind of thing was usually what
came next.

Hacking was the only viable solution.

"Oh, Ron. Where do you keep your cleavers?"

Drawn onto the black Peg-Board that formed the wall behind the workbench were chalk outlines of various cutlery—
butcher knives, paring knives, deboning knives, et cetera.
And usually, inside of each one was its shiny metallic match.
But today, the outlines were as vacant and empty as an old
crime scene. There were none on the table or floor.

Nowhere.

"Seriously, Ron?" she shouted. "What kind of serial killer
doesn't have any knives?"

Her eyes wandered over the outlines, and she remembered
that he took all the sharps, as he called them, inside at night
so they wouldn't get damp. His victims could grow mossy

and mildewed, but not his precious knives. It did bring a smile to her face that he must've been so busy with the kitchen flooding that he'd forgotten to bring them back out and arrange them with crazed meticulousness.

Velvet remembered something else, too. She couldn't help it. Staring at the workbench for too long always triggered the memories.

She hadn't been nearly as late for the bus as she could have been, but when she'd arrived at the stop, Velvet could just see the tail of the big silver metro bus taking the corner.

"Dammit!" she'd yelled, and tossed her book bag onto the bench in the little bus carrel. If she hadn't been on texting restriction, she never would have gone into the Round Up Grocery asking to use the phone.

That was where she met Bonesaw, and she'd suspected nothing. How could she have? He was a pleasant guy with a big broad smile and a goofy expression on his face that had actually been kind of endearing to a girl like Velvet, who'd been used to people judging her about the way she kept her hair or the fact that she wore all black and listened to mopey music and stuff.

"You wanna use the employee phone?" he'd asked.

"Sure, sir. Thanks."

He'd taken her behind the meat counter and shown her the black phone hanging on the wall—one of those older ones with a coil of cord connecting the receiver to a big plastic box. If her mother had answered the phone, it probably would have ended there.

If. If. If. Woulda. Shoulda. Didn't.

"You need a ride home or something?" Bonesaw had asked.

And despite everything she'd ever learned about strangers, despite her natural instinct to be suspicious of just about everyone around her—due to the fact that she'd found most people were assholes—and particularly people who were nice to her, Velvet had nodded.

"Well, lucky for you, I'm just about ready to clock out." He'd taken off his blood-smudged white coat and hung it on a hook next to a puffy winter jacket, which he'd thrown over his shoulder. "You ready, then?"

Velvet had nodded again.

Moments later they'd been in his van.

Moments after that, she'd been unconscious.

Velvet didn't want to think about it anymore; she had serious haunting business to take care of. She marched out of the shed and across the lawn to the back door of the farmhouse. She would have gone inside eventually anyway. The pull of the kitchen's devastation was just too strong.

A Shop-Vac sat in the middle of the dry linoleum like a sentinel. The kitchen door was propped open with a box fan that whirred and clanked intermittently, pointed at a wet patch of carpet that she was certain was almost dry. Even the molding around the floor seemed fine.

"Bastard!" she screamed, kicking over the fan. It fell with a loud clunk and sputtered to a stop. She slouched over and picked up the empty vacuum and tossed it at the bistro set.

The cheap plastic tub bounced ineffectually off the wrought-iron table, crashed back down onto its wheels, and rolled quietly to a stop by the fridge.

Velvet stared at the lack of damage with a combination of shock and mild appreciation. Ron Simanski clearly had an angel looking after him. A dark demented angel with a boner for cutlery and pasty white jackasses who loved condiments. And likewise, someone or something—God, whoever—wanted her to fail.

"Dammit!" she yelled, stomping to the sink.

She suddenly wanted to be anywhere but there.

Bonesaw's knives lay lined up in the bottom, steel against porcelain, both gleaming like a showroom. She picked up the cleaver and managed to tote it almost to the door before it slipped through her hands and impaled the plastic flooring, quivering. She snatched it up and threw it at the window in the back door. Unbelievably, the cleaver clinked against the window sharply and cracked it rather than breaking through, and then it dropped to the floor with a *bonk*.

"Come on!"

She knelt to try again, the fury of the situation blistering through her. Velvet snatched at the cleaver's handle, and her fingers barely moved it an inch across the slick sheen of the linoleum. Her next try was even more infuriating. She was on her knees at that point, but at least she was able to send the damn thing skittering.

"What the crap?"

She had to calm down; in her anger, she'd forgotten to focus. And that did the trick. But when she stood, the cleaver held tightly in her phantom fist, the first thing she saw was Ron Simanski's face framed in the cracked pane of glass in the door.

He wore a fresh scowl, and his eyes were intent and focused on the cleaver. To him, it must have appeared to be floating.

To Velvet, the cleaver needed to find a new spot to dwell.

She aimed for Bonesaw's forehead and flung it with every ounce of energy she had.

It banked off the opening door and clattered loudly as it sailed across the counter and fell back into the sink. By the time Simanski had crossed the threshold, nearly everything was back in its place, except the fan. The killer's mouth crept open, a question dangling there, before he shook his head, crossed to the refrigerator, and withdrew a paper lunch sack. He peered down into the sink, his lips moving soundlessly as though counting. Satisfied, he shrugged, gave the room a final odd look, and walked back out. He hadn't even noticed the fan lying on its side.

Velvet shook her head. The whole trip had been a complete waste of time. She hadn't freed the girl, and she'd missed her chance to bludgeon a psycho. What good was she?

Then she heard the minivan engine spark to life.

Velvet didn't stop to think about it; she sprinted through the door and across the grass toward the moving vehicle, and then leapt at the driver's side door, already focusing on a takeover.

Darkness surrounded her, and a low hum—the muffled sound of the van engine—vibrated the space inside him.

Velvet set off to corral Ron Simanski's mind, but his thoughts were so vulgar, so hateful, she couldn't help but look, to witness his madness. He imagined himself as red as a cartoon devil, fresh blood painting his skin a dark crimson. His tongue darted for the corners of his lips, blotting them back to pink. Fire danced about him like an aura. He was the god of his world.

And batshit crazy.

Velvet reined in her terror and refocused on forcing the blazing image of Bonesaw into the little box she conjured for it. The act took a little more meditation than another body. Images, like postcards of the man's insanity, fluttered around her: Meat extruding from grinders. Girls walking on sidewalks. Bonesaw's desire. She heard a low, steady moan. Letting her anger build the box's wall helped to distract her from the horrors. But once it was formed and Velvet looked inside, she gasped.

The box, her carefully designed jail for Bonesaw's mind, was already full.

A body lay curled up inside, tight and fetal and so red.

A girl. Her hands covered her face protectively. Wounds stabbed clean through her palms into her cheeks.

Velvet didn't want to know who the girl was. It wasn't her intention to explore the freak's psyche, just kill him quickly. But the girl's hands were already falling. It was too late to look away.

Velvet saw the girl's face and it was her own. A glassy-eyed version of Velvet stared back at her, dead lips parted, tongue as gray and dry as cigarette ash. Then the rest of Bonesaw's victims spilled into the box, dropping in dull thuds. His dark proclivities were so strong that she couldn't keep his twisted obsessions out of her construction. The box bowed and bulged, then collapsed.

She lost her grip and fell from Bonesaw's body, through the undercarriage of the moving minivan, and landed painlessly on the dirt farm road. The van disappeared in a cloud of dust that trailed it until the cloud disappeared around the forest bend.

"Oh, my God," Velvet said, shaking and hugging her knees to her chest.

She rocked like that, trying to forget what she'd seen. She blamed her curiosity. If only she hadn't wondered about his thoughts. If she could only take the last few minutes back, she'd still be able to hang on to the idea that Bonesaw could be forced to kill himself. That she could kill him.

If only the girl's face hadn't been her own.

Pull yourself together. You're projecting. There was nothing in that box but your fear.

After uncoiling herself slowly, Velvet made her shambling way back to the copse with the oak tree. It wouldn't do any good to let the moment destroy her plans. They just needed revising, she told herself. Tightening up. Streamlining.

"Focus on that," she muttered. "You just need to focus."

Getting back to work would help.

Chapter 16

A vine of little paper bells, shellacked and clacking, shook from the doorknob as Velvet pushed into the Paper Aviary. It was quiet inside, the monk parakeets perfectly still and no sound of Mr. Fassbinder's busy, sometimes frantic, humming. Tempted to change that, Velvet approached the globe of spikes, eager to hear the funny chirping sound from the tiny bellows.

She reached out to touch one of the sharp spines, but stopped.

Pitch-black eyes glowered back from inside the hollows, each parakeet cold and utterly, completely alone.

Velvet's dream pushed its way back into her mind. In a moment, she was like the parakeet again, trapped. The feeling of imprisonment knotted in her stomach, chilled her to the very core of her being.

"Velvet!" Mr. Fassbinder's voice tore her attention from the cage of papery needles as he rushed from behind the storeroom curtain, thankfully interrupting her creepy state. *Pull yourself together, girl,* she thought.

Velvet returned the origamist's greeting. "Hey, Mr. Fassbinder."

"Velvet!" he scolded. "Look at your eyes. They're so dim. It's like you're carrying the weight of the world in that pretty head."

He rushed over and put his arm around her shoulders, herding her toward a pair of chairs standing guard over his desk and a dusty abacus in a mahogany frame. "Why don't you sit down and we'll talk. I'll just run in the back and get the special bird I promised."

Velvet sank into the chair, managing as polite a smile as she could, and Mr. Fassbinder disappeared behind the dark plum curtain. She could hear him rummaging in the storeroom and wondered what kind of epic projects he carried out in private, if the monk parakeet would was suitable for display in the store.

What is he working on next? she wondered.

She shook off her exhaustion and tried to focus on why she'd stopped by at all. The nerve reading; the banshee's memories of effigies and Chinese printing presses and all that paper. Velvet didn't think Mr. Fassbinder would know anything about the rows of crystal balls, but he was sure to know all about the paper.

"Here it is!" he called out.

When he returned, he held a small black cube in his hand,

a sleek matte origami box with a hinge of tightly woven paper. Velvet forced a smile as she took it and opened it slowly, wary of tearing the precise folds.

Inside sat a miniature black dove.

It was never enough for Mr. Fassbinder to merely create lifelike copies; he was all about capturing a moment. The dove was cleaning itself, and one shiny black eye was all that peered from underneath its ruffled outstretched wing.

"I love it." Velvet smiled up at the man and she said, "It's genius. Just like you."

And it was true, though her mind was far too focused on the task at hand to really enjoy the present fully.

Mr. Fassbinder clapped his bandaged hands together and slipped into the other chair. "I'm so glad, dear. It's not much. Just a little dove to carry away the gloom of this dark existence."

Velvet looked up from the bird. "It's not always this bad. Just sometimes, well, my work . . ."

"That last shadowquake was a terror. I can't imagine what you must go through. Don't suppose you care to talk about the horrors that caused such a menace?" Mr. Fassbinder's eyes were hopeful, and he leaned forward as though he expected Velvet to spill, as if Velvet were allowed to share specifics about any of her missions.

"Nice try. But you know—"

He broke into a fit of deep booming laughter. "Of course, but I have to try. You know how I miss being an insider. Getting all the information before it spreads among the souls. Now I never hear anything first, only through my customers, and by then I'm certain I'm the last."

That had to be true.

As far as Velvet knew, Mr. Fassbinder rarely left the Paper Aviary. All his supplies were delivered. She'd invited him to attend the Retrieval dorm salons on a number of occasions, but he'd always declined. When he'd been alive, he'd been quite the society gentleman, to hear him tell it. Parties nearly every night of the week, expensive restaurant openings, art gallery galas.

But something had happened to change all that—something Mr. Fassbinder had never shared with Velvet. Something more than just his death.

"Well," Velvet stretched the word out conspiratorially, a sinister smirk spreading across her lips.

The man leaned forward and clasped his hands together eagerly. "Yes?"

"I do have some questions for you. I can't tell you why I need to know or answer anything about the shadowquakes other than to say that the answers to the questions I have could have a major impact on the case."

"Ooh," he moaned saucily. "Now you definitely have my attention."

"You know about the departure, right?"

His eyes narrowed, but he nodded slowly, intently.

"Well, when we returned to the station, there was a demonstration of sorts."

He shook his head, his mouth crinkled up in disgust. "Nasty business. Yes. I've heard about it. Something was set ablaze. Neanderthals!"

"Well, it's exactly what was on fire that brings me to you."

"Oh?" Mr. Fassbinder reclined in the chair and crossed his legs, rubbing at the knot of his chin.

"The effigy, if that's the right word, was made of paper. Possibly origami." Velvet studied the man's face for his reaction. "It looked exactly like the station agent. A picture-perfect replica."

"Oh, my. That is disturbing." He shook his head but didn't seem surprised. "Now, why would the revolutionaries do something like that?"

"We don't know."

"Have you heard rumblings? Has Manny been accused of something?"

The words startled her.

Accused of something? Velvet thought. *Where did that come from?* Manny had never done anything that wasn't for the betterment of the Latin Quarter and purgatory.

"Of course not," she barked, irked.

Mr. Fassbinder shrugged. "I wouldn't have thought so. What do the revolutionaries have against her, then?"

Velvet shook her head and glanced at the monk parakeets in their cells. She wondered if perhaps that was how the revolutionaries felt. Trapped. Isolated. But even if that were the case, why take it out on Manny? And what kind of departure were they planning, anyway?

As if he'd heard her thoughts, Mr. Fassbinder added, "Perhaps the revolutionaries believe that dimming is being kept from them by the Council of Station Agents. That it's being lorded over them. That they're being kept in this place against their will."

The idea startled her. "What? That's ridiculous." She paused, considering the notion in light of her dreams, of the demonstration at the station. "You're suggesting that we could all dim at any second but somehow aren't allowed to based on the whims of Manny and the others? Have you heard something to that effect?"

"No. No. Not at all." He shook his hands out in front of him. "Don't get me wrong here. I'm just trying to help."

Velvet sighed. "And you have, Mr. Fassbinder. Those are definitely interesting ideas. But we kind of got sidetracked, because I meant to ask about who, besides yourself, is skilled enough at origami to create such lifelike paper effigies?"

He stood up and skirted the desk. "Well. It's a pretty rare profession, but there are quite a few, mostly in Vermillion."

"Oh?" she said, eyes widening at the possibility of a significant break in the case.

The Chinese newspapers had certainly been in Vermillion. If there were an origamist who could be linked to the newspapers, then Velvet was on to something.

"Do you know any of them?" she said quickly.

"I know *of* them." He paused, brow furrowing.

"Is there someone? Someone you suspect?"

He shook his head. "It's probably nothing—though, perhaps. . . ."

"Well, just spill it, then. If it's nothing, it won't make any difference."

"Aloysius Clay."

Velvet gasped. "The missing body thief?"

Could Miss Antonia's lost love possibly be involved?

Velvet had no proof, of course, but at the mere mention of his name, she was reminded of her certainty that Clay and Miss Antonia had been lovers. It just seemed right. And despite being completely paranoid lately, Velvet usually trusted her instincts.

Mr. Fassbinder leaned forward, glancing cautiously at the front door of the shop to make sure they were still alone. "I have heard that Aloysius Clay didn't disappear randomly. He didn't dim. He wasn't kidnapped, as so many have hypothesized, but rather, like so many Hitchcockian characters, took on a secret identity far away from his home here in the Latin Quarter. And . . ." His voice trailed off.

"And?" Now it was Velvet leaning in, hanging on her friend's every word.

"And he has become a great—no—a *master* origamist. Some say he produces the finest paper mimicry in all of Vermillion. Though that's just talk. I have no proof to speak of."

Velvet rubbed her lips and thought about this news.

It made some sense. If Clay was the creator of the effigies, he might have had contact with the banshee she'd interrogated in the Cellar.

She nodded finally. "Thank you, Mr. Fassbinder. You've been very helpful."

"I do hope so. This departure business is all very disturbing, and the shadowquakes have slowed business, I'm afraid."

Velvet employed as sympathetic a smile as possible and stood, ready to leave. "Tremendously helpful. I'll be back in a few days so we can have that film talk. I'd really love to chat with you about *The Birds,* and your parakeets, too."

"You'll be amazed at what I have planned next," Mr. Fassbinder said, doing his best villain impression.

"Something positively evil, no doubt," she joked back.

"No doubt," he said, the sternness fallen away in favor of a chuckle.

"Oh, but wait," Velvet said, remembering that in proper questioning, it's important to cover all of one's bases. "One more thing. Where do you get your paper?"

Mr. Fassbinder shrugged. "Local suppliers." His eyes darted toward the little black box, now closed in the cage of Velvet's fingers.

She looked at it again and then back to Mr. Fassbinder. His smile was as gracious and pleasant as ever, but Velvet couldn't help wondering if the man was telling the truth. Immediately following the thought, though, she felt suddenly, immeasurably ashamed. She had friends in purgatory but so few confidants. It just wasn't possible that this man who treated her so well could be involved in something so heinous. And why would he lie? There was really no reason. Who would he be protecting? He didn't seem to know anyone but his customers and some delivery boys. He hardly ever even left the Paper Aviary.

Still, his ideas were very interesting, and in light of those ideas, the appearance of Aloysius Clay as a suspect, and the visions pulled from the banshee's skull, she needed to meet with Manny.

Velvet thanked Mr. Fassbinder, squeezed the box into her

pocket, and let herself out into the murky shadows of the midday. She trod quickly but focused on her footing all the way to the square. Even with the gaslight cranked to high, it was difficult to see the funicular platform in the distance, and Velvet had to rely on instinct to guide her to the ramp and to the basket of paper and pencils. She jotted down a quick message to Manny, folded the note into fourths, and added delivery instructions to the station post. As the railcar ground up to the platform, Velvet tossed the note into a box on its side marked "To: Station," and tromped back down to the cobblestone street below.

The walk back to the dorm was the same as ever, with one notable difference. The flyers and handbills announcing the coming departure were more frequent than she'd seen before. The red paper spattered the walls around her like at the scene of a crime. She stopped to tear one off the wall, crumpled it up, and tossed it into the gutter.

Back at the dormitory, Velvet had no more than crossed the threshold when Miss Antonia slipped her hand into the crook of her elbow and whisked her off through the bustling residents to a table in a well-shadowed corner of the court-yard. The stage was being readied, salon imminent.

Her phantom heart skipped inside her chest.

Did Miss Antonia know about Nick? Or was it Velvet's frequent trips to the charming farmlands of New Brompfel Heights to haunt a certain serial killer that was prompting this discussion?

Miss Antonia sat across from Velvet, her chin in her palm, scrutinizing her carefully.

"Yes?" Velvet noticed that her voice was shaking.

"Well?" Miss Antonia returned, eyes narrowing. "Isn't there something you'd like to tell me?"

Velvet's stomach turned, twisting into a pretzel shape in her gut. Her eyes darted around the courtyard. The first person she lit on was Nick, of course. Nothing like a reminder of how she'd screwed things up. The real question was: Had she been running away from him because he was making her crazy, or was she just plain crazy to begin with?

She was beginning to think the latter was the blue ribbon winner.

The boy leaned against the wall, hair tousled in the same sexy way she'd seen it the night before. He was watching her, his mouth crooked with a stupid, ridiculous grin. Distracting her.

Why does he have to be so frickin' gorgeous? If he just had prematurely thinning hair and a pie face, it wouldn't be an issue. Though she supposed she'd still have her haunting situation on the table.

Who am I kidding? she thought. *I'm stockpiling secrets like Isadora hoards ugly clothes and girls to worship her. I'm screwed.*

She turned back to Miss Antonia. The woman's pursed lips and the way she drummed her fingers on the tabletop told the whole story.

Someone had spilled.

"You're awfully squirrelly." Miss Antonia studied Velvet and then sighed morosely. "Must not be good news."

Velvet was thoroughly confused but momentarily hopeful. Maybe she'd misjudged the situation. "What must not be good news?"

259

"Your investigation," another voice chimed in.

Velvet spun to see Manny sauntering toward them. "Don't look so surprised. I was eager to hear your report and came to get it firsthand. Plus"—she slipped into the chair next to Velvet, her hand resting on Velvet's shoulder—"this way I get to take in a little entertainment while we chat. Won't that be nice?"

"Ya-yeah," Velvet stuttered, noticing the commotion on the stage: kids straightening the backdrop, stacking sheet music next to the lectern, dusting the creepy box of doom with her name stuffed inside it like a threat. "Salon is gonna be awesome," she lied, and quickly changed the subject. "You got my message, then?"

"I was expecting one," Manny said reproachfully. "But since it never came, I decided to swing by to find out what was keeping my best body thief as quiet as a church mouse."

"I did send one, just recently, though. I'm sorry." Velvet squirmed in her chair. Despite the fact that Mr. Fassbinder may have burst the case wide open with his theories, there was nothing like an inquisition after a hard day of illegal haunting to make a girl uncomfortable. "I did find out tons of stuff."

Manny grinned and slapped her hands on the table. "Well, thank goodness. The Council of Station Agents was beginning to doubt your abilities. But I insisted you were the best team leader we had. 'If Velvet doesn't get to the bottom of this,' I said, 'no one will and we'll all be doomed.'"

No pressure there, Velvet thought. *And what is with the speedy time line?* She'd barely had time to blink, let alone solve the case and get a message back to the station, in time for them to be worried.

Something must have them seriously spooked.

Manny's expression darkened, her eyes narrowed to dim slits, and she leaned in to whisper, "We have reason to believe the departure, whatever shape that may take, is to occur sooner rather than later."

Velvet cringed and glanced at Miss Antonia, who nodded.

"Much sooner," the Salvage mother whispered.

At that moment, Kipper bounded up like a shaved yeti, all massive boy muscles and jocularity. "So what's new?" He plopped down in the chair opposite Velvet.

"We're kind of having a meeting, doofus," she said, rolling her eyes.

Manny set her hand atop Velvet's. "It's all right. We've asked Gary to attend this impromptu meeting. We're going to need his help . . . and Nick's." She suddenly beamed as though just remembering. "Happy dimming, by the way."

"Happy dimming," Miss Antonia aped.

Neither Velvet nor Kipper returned the morosely cheerful sentiment. People said it when close friends passed. Or in this case, a close friend and coworker.

But Manny had mentioned Nick.

Nick's help?

It must have been decided. Nick was in line to be her new undertaker and was therefore officially, indubitably off-limits to her and her lusts and ogling. It was like she'd taken a punch to the gut. All the air went out of her. She felt faint, which totally sucked, because more than anything, Velvet preferred to put out a tough bitch persona when it came to work.

"What's wrong, girl?" Miss Antonia asked.

She shook her head, peeking across at Kipper. The boy's mouth was tight, and he was definitely avoiding her gaze. He'd probably talked to Nick. He knew. He had to.

"I'm fine." Velvet inhaled and sat up as straight and stoic as was manageable under the circumstances. "We'll do whatever it is you think is necessary for our mission to be successful."

Manny winked at her. "Good girl. Now tell us what you've discovered."

Velvet went over the nerve reading with their prisoner again, for the benefit of Miss Antonia and Kipper—the visions, Vermillion, the printing press behind the doctor's office door, and the rows of effigies and crystal balls.

She told them about her meeting with Mr. Fassbinder and his idea that the revolutionaries might believe that the station agents were keeping the souls trapped in purgatory, and finally, after only the briefest hesitation, Velvet held out her hand for Miss Antonia to hold. Dramatic, yes, but the action served another purpose: to hold the woman close so Velvet could watch her reaction.

The Salvage mother didn't move at first, her mouth twisted up in a quizzical expression. "What's this now?" she asked.

"It's about Aloysius Clay."

Miss Antonia's eyes widened to saucers, and Velvet could have sworn the Salvage mother shot a reproachful glance in the station agent's direction. Manny was stoic—she showed no reaction at all to the name. Miss Antonia gripped Velvet's hand so tightly, the nerves under her fingers glowed through the creases of her knuckles.

"Mr. Fassbinder said that he's heard a rumor that Aloysius Clay . . ." Velvet paused as Miss Antonia's hand fell away and her eyes trained skyward, lost in some distant memory. ". . . became a master origamist, and he lives in Vermillion under a secret identity. He says it's just talk, but it does explain a lot."

Manny rubbed her temples. "Which explains the banshee's knowledge of our ability to nerve read. Clay would have known that; he could have briefed the revolutionaries on our ways."

Kipper whistled. "These guys aren't foolin' around."

Everyone at the table nodded in agreement. Velvet was just relieved the topic had shifted. She'd already made all these jumps in logic. She was sold on the theory.

"And neither shall we," Manny said finally. "Kipper, I want you to follow up on this lead in Vermillion. See if you can find Clay there and take him into custody."

"But what about Nick's testing and training?"

Velvet cringed. Kipper was the primary Salvage trainer, but with him gone on a mission, that would mean . . .

"Why, Velvet will take over the proctoring and tutelage, of course."

She sighed and slunk in her chair. *Of course,* she thought. *Of course. Of course. Of course. Why couldn't she catch a break?*

"Do you have a problem with that, Velvet?"

She didn't have an answer, not one that didn't include a metric ton of F-bombs.

Chapter 17

After the discussion, Velvet was left to wrestle with the whole Nick thing by herself.

Kipper darted for his assignment. Manny was likewise swept away from the conversation by the grotesquely over-dressed Connie Lawrence. She was wearing something on her head that Velvet guessed was supposed to be a hat but looked more like a bloated old boot, the leather soggy and listing to the side. A moment after that, Miss Antonia breezed off toward the stage, chatting with the various groups gathered around the tables as though she were host-essing a cocktail party.

Velvet wondered whether she could sneak all the way across the courtyard without drawing any attention. It wouldn't be the first salon she'd skipped out on. She glanced at the stairwell as a pair of wingtips appeared there, followed shortly thereafter by a certain tall blond boy.

Now was as good a time as any, she thought. They would have to talk about everything sooner or later, and the way she'd left it felt so cold and final. Now, of course, she realized that there wouldn't be any closure on their interlude at all. Just a constant reminder in the form of proximity.

Velvet pushed herself up out of the chair, just as Tony Falk took the stage to sing along to Stephen "Tin Tin" Duffy's "Kiss Me."

"Kiss me with your mouth," he sang, and several girls were sucked toward the stage like lint to a sock fresh from the dryer. He preened, running his fingers through his longish black hair, and swiveled his hips suggestively.

Velvet stabbed a finger in her mouth as if she were gagging, for the benefit of a table of Salvage guys, spies or other support staff, who seemed to readily agree. Though after she moved on, Velvet wasn't certain they were talking about the same thing.

Up ahead, blocking the stairs and Nick like some underworld hit squad, was Isadora Lawrence and two henchgirls—Shandie, and another one with a nose like a rat and close-set beady eyes to match. Isadora wore a miniskirt nearly as short as her temper and a vicious smile that seemed to broadcast her intentions—those being to devour Nick like a praying mantis.

Velvet opted for a shadowy spot to see how Nick would handle the temptation. Purely for supervisory purposes, of course.

"Look at this, girls," Isadora said, inspecting him up and down. The other girls did, too, running their eyes over him like he was a bar code. "Little boy lost. You lost, Nick?"

"Um . . . no."

Velvet raised her brows, tying her lush mane of hair up with a strip of leather as she watched.

Nick tried to squeeze past, but Isadora threaded her arm under his and pressed in tight. "Well, never mind. I just wanted to say, we Collectors have been a little lax with our welcoming party and thought you might like us to show you the ropes."

"Ropes," Rat Girl repeated, and giggled sinisterly.

Velvet didn't doubt they had a stockpile of ropes in their warehouses, probably handcuffs, too.

"No, thanks. I've got to—" Nick began.

Isadora reached up and took hold of his chin, directing his eyes toward hers. "Maybe you're not understanding what I'm saying here, Nick. I'm asking if you party."

"Yeah," he said. "I got that."

Velvet tensed.

But then Nick did something remarkable. He shot the girl a clearly identifiable look of disinterest.

Isadora's mouth dropped open, even as her fists balled up tight and her cheeks glowed with embarrassment. Shandie and the other girl covered their mouths, chuckling as they backed away from the beautiful girl, as though she might explode.

"I see how it is." Isadora glowered and shot a look across the courtyard, possibly looking for her, Velvet thought. "You're after *Velvet*." She shook her head, and a look of nausea grew on Isadora's perfectly made-up face, even as actual nausea blossomed in Velvet's stomach. "Well, I'll tell you this, because I like you and I know we'll be great friends some-day. Velvet's crazy. Certifiable. Clearly insane, huh, girls?"

The other two nodded adamantly. Rat Girl added, "So crazy."

"Why, she even sneaks out at night, you know? I found her in an alley early this morning."

"Ew," Shandie said. "Wallowing in the gutter, no doubt."

Velvet had to hold herself back. She was furious. And she hadn't had the satisfaction of beating anything to a pulp lately. The interrogation, while fun, hadn't been nearly as aggressive as she'd have liked. If only she'd launched that cleaver at Bonesaw a second earlier.

The idea of the weapon quivering from a deep hold in Bonesaw's skull made her smile grimly.

Maybe Isadora *was* right. She felt herself relax.

But when Velvet looked back at Nick, she saw a shadow of doubt spread over his face. He was squinting, his gaze askance. He was remembering something.

"You're too good for her, Nick." Isadora pulled back and assessed him again. "And far too pretty. Besides . . . she's a whore."

Velvet flinched as Isadora's backup dancers nodded, and Velvet began to stride toward them, ready to fight.

She was stopped by a flush that sparked on Nick's cheeks brightly.

"We're not going to be friends, Isadora. We're not going to be anything. You think you can talk like that about the girl that saves your butts every other week?" He leaned in close—close enough that Velvet couldn't hear.

But as she approached the stairs, she heard this . . .

"I know you. You're a predator. There's nothing good in you. And I bet . . . I just bet that if you ever found something good in yourself, you'd move on to wherever it is souls go after here. Or are you afraid it's the frying pan for you?"

Velvet nearly choked on her laughter. Isadora had spotted her and was seething. Velvet just shook her head and grinned.

"And you," Nick said, turning on Shandie. "After seeing what Quentin was willing to do for you, and you're in on this little lynch mob. It makes me sick."

They weren't impressed—or pretended not to be. Nor did they back down.

Isadora just shook her head and laughed. "Wow, you really don't get it, do you? Things aren't like before. You better figure that out quick. Maybe your whore can fill you in."

She stabbed a finger in Velvet's direction.

Velvet returned the favor and a different finger.

Nick turned to Velvet and shrugged playfully.

"Shit!" Isadora cried. Then she pivoted and snapped for the other girls to fall in line—which they rushed to do like the lemmings they were. The three stomped off, a snotty drill team wobbling away on the unlevel cobble.

Nick joined Velvet in her laughter.

"That was impressive," she said.

He shook his head. "Nope. Just necessary."

She nodded. "You're not nearly as soft as I pegged you as, Nick Russell."

"Wow!" Nick staggered back clutching at his heart. "A compliment? Was that— I didn't   Really?"

She slugged him in the arm and was about to launch into her spiel about training him for the team, when a familiar voice bellowed through the courtyard.

"Good evening!" Miss Antonia shouted from the stage. "Welcome to another exciting salon."

The chattering dorm tenants sank into their chairs, and the din quieted to an eerie silence. Miss Antonia licked her lips, nodding pleasantly to various people. Taking note.

"I thought we'd change things up a bit this evening. Considering the hardships we've had to endure over the past days, let's start with a story. I'm going to forgo the box entirely and choose someone special this evening."

The audience clapped and wooted uproariously.

"Nick Russell, come up here!" Miss Antonia pointed at the boy, and he turned and searched Velvet's face for a clue.

She shrugged. "Good luck."

A moment later there were hands on his back, leading him forward through the crowd.

Velvet climbed the stairs and found a spot on the balcony.

Nick was already standing on the stage. The courtyard was silent, waiting. His knees shook, his voice wobbled; he looked adorable. "Wha-what am I supposed to be doing up here?" he asked.

"Tell us!" the crowd members hissed, like mythical beasts, threatening, beseeching.

"About my death?" Nick asked as he crammed his hands into his back pockets.

"Yes, dummy!" Luisa barked from a table she'd commandeered in the front. Velvet hadn't even seen her come into the courtyard. She wished she had, though. After the night and day she'd had, Velvet was in dire need of a little girl time.

Logan sat next to his sister rubbing his hands together greedily.

Nick's head craned around, scanning the crowd, the foot of the stair, and finally his gaze landed on Velvet where she stood on the balcony. His smile was unforgettable and unfortunate. It was the kind of smile that made knees shake, wicked and divine. Velvet clutched the railing and waited for the weird feeling shuddering through her to abate.

"You guys are really morbid," Nick said, and finally broke the intense stare.

There were nods of general agreement all around.

The boy shrugged and went right into the story. "All right, then. You're lucky I remember it at all. When I first came through the crack there was nothin'." Nick rapped his fist against his skull, adorably.

Velvet was certain actual swooning was occurring among the girls and a few of the boys.

"I was in this coffee shop with my friend Joe the day I died," he began.

Velvet rested her chin in her palm as she watched Nick speak. He was a natural storyteller, and the residents seemed to be rapt. Velvet supposed that was a good thing. The Salvage team could use a spokesman who didn't rouse people to reach for their pitchforks.

He told of a killer in a brown hoodie, a man Nick called the Mad Monk. The man stalked him from a coffee shop near his high school through the New York City subway system before chasing him ultimately and finally into the path of an oncoming train.

"I didn't die right away, though," Nick said, holding up his hand. "I lay there in agony. Screaming in pain. Slipping away even as the Mad Monk bore down on me. In his hand, the crystal ball, glowing as brightly as the Mad Monk's eyes."

And with that, the crowd exploded with applause. Logan and Luisa whistled bombastically, and even Isadora's crew graced the boy with a standing ovation. Velvet found herself shaking her head incredulously. Nick wasn't just pretty; he was actually kind of fascinating.

How had that little tidbit slipped past her?

Stilling her attraction just kept getting harder.

Damn him.

After salon began to clear for the night and she was sure no one of any importance would notice, Velvet padded down the stairs, crossed the courtyard, slapped her palm into Nick's, and dragged him out into the square.

"We have to talk," she said, avoiding the sappy look on his face in favor of not tripping on the cobblestone and losing her power position publicly. There was no way to regain the upper hand while wallowing on the ground. The heels on her boots wouldn't help her out any with that, either.

Nick tagged along behind her, caught up in her wake like a leaf in the breeze.

"We do," he agreed, shouting over the bustle of night shoppers and bellowing vendors. "I mean, I know we do. I've definitely got some things I need to say, but I just didn't know you had things to say, too. . . ."

"You're rambling," Velvet snapped, and tugged at his hand.

Ahead, black wrought-iron gates cut a gap between two other dormitories, both housing paper workers, if she remembered correctly. Velvet slammed her palm against them, and she and Nick spilled inside. In a space no larger than a small house, trees made of bent wire and wrapped in crepe paper and hung with newspaper leaves provided a dense canopy around the garden. Newspaper-print bushes were set off with bright pink origami flowers, and beneath them, from a low creeping vine of bound paper, sprang lavender buds that smelled of memory.

Velvet sat down on a little bench at the far end of the garden. Nick slipped in beside her. She glanced at him and shook her head. The boy confused her; there was no other word for it. She waited for some calm to find her, for some epiphany to wrap her up in its understanding arms. It was times like these that she longed for her mother. Regina Monroe always had an answer. It wasn't necessarily the right answer, but it was something. A direction.

And she always paired it with a visual aid.

Velvet could use a movie with a moral right now. Something that suited the situation. Something dark. *Harold and Maude, Heathers*—a movie that would validate that she wasn't wrong to think that being in a relationship was bad

272

for you, made you crazy. Well, crazier than she already was. Velvet stared at the wall on the right side of the garden, waiting for an imaginary projector to start whirring in a booth that wasn't there.

And then she felt Nick's fingers lacing between hers, and cocked her head to find him smiling that crooked beautiful smile of his. Velvet almost melted and gave in. He could have done anything, but he just sat there.

Like he was happy just to be with her. What was worse was that she was starting to think she was happy, too.

Velvet jerked her hand away and stood up. "Jesus! You're making me nuts."

He smiled again. "And that's bad?"

"Yeah, it's bad. I've got too much going on for this." She waved her hands around wildly. "Whatever this is."

"What is this? I'd kind of like to know, too."

Velvet started pacing. "It's nothing. It's . . . well, I don't know. But things have changed since last night. You're on track to take Quentin's place, and that makes this a nonthing."

"I know."

That stopped her in her tracks. Velvet craned her neck toward the boy, who didn't seem to get that he'd said something upsetting.

"And how, exactly, do you know?"

"Kipper told me."

"Oh, my God. You didn't tell him anything, did you?"

Nick scoffed. "Of course not. Not after everything he said."

"What did he say?"

"He said that if we were caught, I'd have to move away from you. I don't think I could stand that, you know?"

"Jesus! How did he know something had happened?" Velvet snatched his collar threateningly.

"He just . . . we were talking . . . and he just knew. Said he saw me looking at you or something."

"Great. That's great."

Nick stood up and touched her arm. She didn't pull away this time but instead let him speak his piece. It couldn't hurt, and who knew, maybe he could say something to relieve her oncoming breakdown.

"Kipper won't say anything. He just thinks I'm into you— which I am," he added, eyes going suddenly sad. "Hopelessly."

Velvet let out a long sigh and tried to think, tried to get a handle on the situation before it spiraled out of control. But try as she might, she couldn't pull together a coherent or helpful thought. Kipper. Bonesaw. The departure.

Nick. Nick. Nick.

Her brain was scrambled. Fried. Over easy. No. Not easy. Over hard. She tried taking some deep breaths. When her head started to clear, it was too late to avoid Nick's incoming lip bomb.

He swept in close, pressing his body to hers. His fingers curled behind her neck as he drew her toward him. A shudder rolled through her, and even as she was certain that letting him kiss her was a mistake, she couldn't resist letting it happen.

Nick's lips were feather light. Nothing more than a whisper at first, but so electrifying that she felt the weight of his intentions course through her. And then the kiss became more forceful, his mouth parting and releasing the softest of moans, before lunging more passionately, touching his tongue to hers, sucking at it gently.

Velvet couldn't stop herself. She'd flung her arms around him like any number of idiot girls who knew better, and kissed him back. She ran her fingers through his wavy hair, which was softer than she'd imagined. It sparkled like the night sky. His skin was on fire beneath the ash.

Before she knew it, she was off the ground, her head thrown back and Nick's mouth whispering promises against her throat, professing his . . .

"Love . . ." The word was no more than a sigh.

She pushed him away, and he dropped her to the gravel floor of the garden. She had to stop him. She couldn't hear it again.

Velvet stared at the boy, her jaw hung open like a Venus flytrap. "Snap out of it, Nick! We're not having a secret affair. That's. Not. Happening."

"That's the part that makes it okay. The fact that it's secret. It's a stupid rule anyway. Any rule that says two people who are clearly meant to be together can't be is stupid." He reached for her, but she slapped his hand away.

"It's not love, anyway," she said. "It's just your out-of-control hormones. It's lust or something."

"What's the difference? Lust is like a gateway drug for boys."

"You're ridiculous." She stared at him, furious and excited at the same time. And certain they were *not* experiencing the same emotion. "You will never be my everything. My job is too important to risk."

He smiled, reached for her again.

Velvet glanced toward the gates and thought she saw a shadow. Someone was close. Someone who'd question what they were doing.

"Hide!" Velvet spat.

Nick dove behind a tree. At the very least, the boy could follow directions.

She planted her butt on the bench and tried to look calm, look normal, look like anything other than the girl who'd been thinking vile sex thoughts just moments before.

"Velvet?" a familiar voice called from the gate.

Luisa's face was pressed between the bars, stretching her expression of concern into a weird grimace. Velvet relaxed a little. Concern was better than shock.

"Are you all right, Velvet?" the girl asked.

"Of course," she said, and jumped up from the stone bench. She wound her way through the rows of paper box hedges until she stood before the little girl, feigning nonchalance as best she could. "Why wouldn't I be?"

"You seemed like you were deep in it, you know. Really depressed or something."

Velvet shrugged. Changing the subject seemed to be her best option. "Did you come looking for me special? You know how I love to feel needed," she said.

Luisa laughed. She knew Velvet too well to buy it. "Yeah, right. You could give a crap."

Velvet shifted her weight to her hip, blocking Luisa's view into the garden, and tried to cock her head in the most light, casual way possible. "Anything for you. Though the rest of them . . ." She waved her hand at the passing shapes in the square and scrunched up her face like she smelled something nasty.

"You don't mean that," Luisa said, deadpan.

Velvet relaxed as the girl's attention drifted off to somewhere past the cathedral that studded the opposite end of the square. "What's up, Luisa?"

The girl squinted, bit her cheek, and wrung her hands. "It's really not a big deal, but . . ."

Velvet mimicked Luisa's behavior, exaggerating the girl's nervous fidgeting. "It's nothing, I'm sure. That's why you're super calm."

"Could you come with me?"

She glanced back into the garden and saw Nick peering around the bottom of the paper tree. "Where to?"

Luisa shook her head, the disappointment etched into her frown. She hesitated and then spilled it. "Logan's down at the gas chamber, again."

Velvet sighed and shot a glance in the direction of the square's most infamous alley. Men stood at its entrance, slapping handbills onto the chests and palms of passersby and promising unspeakable pleasures. She rankled. "Really?"

"I know. I know." Luisa turned and stomped off, weaving through the street vendors, stragglers, and wanderers. "Let's just deal with it."

Velvet trotted along behind the girl. "He can't keep doing this, Luisa. You hear me?"

"I said 'I know.' Are you deaf?"

"I'm just saying, if we had a shadowquake right now, we'd be so screwed."

Luisa spun on her and snapped, "You think I don't know that? Why don't you save your guilt-trip for him?"

Velvet winced. "Sorry, Luisa. I'm having a bitch attack."

The gas chamber was at the bottom of a steep hill, and getting back up the hill was a chore without a railcar. But Velvet figured, if nothing else, it might take her mind off all her recent dramas.

Gas Chamber Alley wasn't nearly as awesome as you'd expect. Once you braved the gauntlet of perverts hawking prostitutes and peep shows, there weren't any actual gas chambers, or electric chairs or hangman's nooses. The street vendors didn't even sell those little guillotines that chop off the ends of cigars. There were, in fact, so many missed opportunities for parody that it made Velvet a little sad. Velvet had, of course, been on this exact same journey alongside Luisa a few times before.

Logan had the same problem as lots of souls; he was chronically bored. Most of the time, that was cured by relieving unsuspecting poker players of their pressed paper coins, books, or whatever else he felt had some value. But sometimes, like tonight, he needed something else. Something stronger.

Trippier.

"Look at that," Luisa said, pointing at a block of grimy citizens surrounding a man on a raised dais.

The alley had opened into a wide square big enough

for an open-air theater to spring up. The speaker, a grim-looking man, was framed by a clash of red, a banner of some sort that draped over the flat roof of the building. An image of a black crack was painted down the banner's center and disappeared into a big iconic letter *D*. It didn't take an art teacher to figure out that the crack was both a metaphor for the fracturing of purgatory's populace and a literal depiction of the results of the shadowquakes. And the *D* went without saying.

It was a different type of depravity going on down here. Departurists.

The guy towered over a wooden lectern, a tattered black top hat stretching him taller and not quite shading a face as pointy and pinched as a rodent's. His hand gripped the sides like claws. Velvet had never seen the man before.

"Your time is coming!" he shouted cheerfully. "The tyranny of the Council of Station Agents *will* come to an end, good souls! Never fear. Our departure is eminent."

The thirty or so men and women gathered raised their fists, wooted, and shouted their approval. One voice, blisteringly tenebrous, cut through the rest, "When? When do we depart?"

"Soon, brother!" The man's voice bellowed across the space. "The Departurists are hard at work for your benefit. Your days of waiting, of toiling in this grimy cesspool, are coming to an end."

Velvet couldn't take her eyes off the crack in the banner. She thought of dams and how they fail and flood out from the smallest crack, and she couldn't hold back the feeling that something horrible was going to happen. Something worse than Bonesaw, worse than a few shadowquakes, a few banshees.

The scariest part was the religious-like fervor with which the crowd cheered and stared and clasped their hands together reverently. Some fell to their knees and held their hands aloft, not skyward but directed toward the banner.

Velvet couldn't stand to listen to the instigator ramble a second longer. She stepped forward, elbowing her way to the front of the dais. The man's eyes needled in on her approach. He stabbed a crooked, bony finger directly at her and cackled wildly.

"Look here. A representative of the council! What is it, dear? Have you come to abdicate to the revolution's good cause?"

"Hardly," Velvet snipped. "I'm just disgusted that so many"—she glanced with contempt at the faces around her—"that so many sheep are buying your bullshit."

"Boo!" the crowd responded, and the man grinned, raising an eyebrow.

Velvet turned to plead with them. "You have to see that whatever this man tells you is the worst kind of solution. You can never circumvent what nature or God or whatever has in store for you. You can't escape your demons!"

She knew that better than anyone.

The man roared over her final statement. "We can and we will. Nature has been manipulated by the station agents for long enough. You'll see, little girl. Just wait until it's your turn to dim, see what happens."

"Nothing! Nothing!" The shouts were unanimous and horrifying.

Velvet shook her head; she didn't want to hear it. But it was impossible to block out. *Of course* something happened when a soul dimmed. How did they explain the passing souls above purgatory? Dimming wasn't arbitrary like human death. It was absolutely related to a soul's remainder; everyone knew that.

The Departurists were insane.

It was only after Luisa had dragged her away by the arm that Velvet stopped shaking enough to notice the glut of departure flyers plastered on the alley walls. The pressed paper bricks were practically crimson with the things. They'd certainly been busy over in Vermillion, giving that printing press a workout.

"Did you hear that?" Velvet said, still riled up.

Luisa shrugged. "They're crazy."

Velvet steadied herself against the nearest wall. "At least we know what their motive is. That's something, regardless of whether they're wrong. If they believe that dimming is final and they can avoid death through this departure . . ."

"But where do they think they're going when they *depart*?"

"Who knows? I'll talk to Manny about this as soon as I can."

They pressed on toward the end of the road and Logan.

The alley quieted beyond the buckle and thinned to no more than a hallway before the hill leveled off. At the bottom stood the entrance to the gas chamber. There wasn't a sign to point it out, but everyone knew it was there. Word spread about available vices in purgatory, quicker than a teenage boy could sneak in for a kiss.

The alley ended abruptly at the rounded walls of a structure covered in rags, banded and knotted here and there. The roof was a tarpaulin dome, with gas leaking from the seams in thin snaky spirals that greased the air colorlessly. The building was a bellows of sorts. Inside were the gasworks and escape valves to deal with variance in pressure and other stuff. Velvet had only a breezy understanding of the system. She had seen a documentary, with her mother, of course, about Indian sweat lodges, places where ceremonial purifications took place—though the gas chamber was all about the opposite.

Luisa grabbed one of the rags from a basket near the small door of the place and clamped it over her nose, tossing another rag to Velvet. They held their breaths, crouched, and crossed into the chamber.

"Shut the door!" came a shout from the shadows. Not Logan, one of the many other people flailing on the floor or propped up around the edges of the round room.

There must have been a hundred souls in various states of inebriation. Some laughing, some making out, but most just zonked and plastered flat on their backs.

Velvet clamped the rag to her face tighter as they carefully found footholds within the tangle of bodies.

Luisa pointed toward a lump near the center of the room. A child clung to an obese woman in a red dress, like a monkey clutching a wire mother in some pathetic psychology experiment. Logan was slack-jawed, his tongue lolling from his open mouth and his eyes mere slits. Completely stoned.

Velvet didn't need directions. She stumbled over to the boy, unwound his fingers from the fabric of the woman's dress, and grabbed one of his feet. Luisa picked up the other. Logan twisted and groaned. Velvet scanned his eyes for some small hint of recognition flickering behind his blown-out pupils. The light in him diffused like a rolling blackout. Waves of dull gray alternated with whitecaps so bright she had to look away.

Totally gone. Huffed out of his mind.

Velvet wondered if things would have been different for him had he and Luisa not been on the road with the drunk driver who killed them, if Logan had been able to grow up, grow taller, get out of that ridiculous costume, become a man. What would he have been like?

Those thoughts led down the same road.

Every time.

Velvet knew enough to realize Logan was doing the same thing his father had, though the man was a drunk, not a druggie. A functional alcoholic was how Luisa had put it once. Logan would probably have been smoked out by his senior year anyway. It happens like that.

As they dragged him through the labyrinth of drug addicts, his head bumped over shoes, discarded or still attached to feet, newspaper bolsters, and wadded-up rags.

"Ow. What are you two . . . ," he slurred, drifting into and out of consciousness.

They hauled him into the alley, careful not to breathe in too much of the gas when they tossed the rags aside.

"Shut the door!" the crowd called in unison this time.

Velvet slammed it. "Damn, I'd hate to release their valuable drugs."

"Right?" Luisa agreed, shaking her head.

"Wha?" Logan mumbled, a doped-up look on his little face.

"Oh, I'll tell you what," Luisa replied, grabbing his cheeks in her fists.

The boy tensed with a pain that cleared his eyes somewhat.

"You gotta cut this shit out before you end up down here for good. You hear me?"

He shrugged.

"That means no more poltergeisting. You won't get to cross the veil. It'll just be you and your stupid gas chamber."

Logan winced when he saw Velvet. He pulled away from Luisa, lay down in the street, and curled up on his side into a ball.

Velvet held back, watching so intently that she didn't notice Nick approaching from the direction of the square until he was almost on them.

"Hey, you guys," he said softly. "Do you need some help?"

Velvet sighed. The boy had followed them. Perfect.

"How did you know we were down here?" she asked, feigning ignorance.

Luisa rolled her eyes. "Cut the crap, Velvet."

"What?"

"Look at Nick's mouth and ask me that question again."

Velvet assessed the boy's face and this time noticed the rouging from their make-out session. She looked back at

Luisa and shrugged. "So what? It's probably a nervous condition. He rubs his mouth or something."

"I am kinda weird," Nick offered.

Luisa nodded noncommittally. "It's just that, well . . ." She pointed at Velvet's face as she strode past them. "Your mouth looks exactly the same."

"Dammit," Velvet said, and trudged behind the girl, grimacing at Nick as she passed him. "Would you mind carrying Logan?"

She caught up with the girl where the alley bowed out. The revolutionaries had dispersed, and Luisa had taken a seat on the little stage. Velvet found her grinning wildly.

"I knew it," Luisa said.

"It's not going to happen again." Velvet flopped down next to her.

Nick stomped by with Logan draped over his shoulder like some laundry. He tipped an imaginary hat in their direction and smiled sheepishly.

"He's very cute," Luisa said.

"I know."

"I'll keep your secret. You don't even have to ask me, or talk about it again. You know that, right?"

"I know."

The girl patted her on the knee and sprang up. "Just don't get caught." With that, Luisa strode off after Nick and her brother and out of sight.

So Luisa knew. It was sort of a relief, Velvet realized. But it wasn't permission. Luisa had meant what she said.

Which didn't matter, because it wasn't going to happen again.

Chapter 18

Before she even opened her eyes, Velvet reached out under the sheet to make sure Nick wasn't haunting her bed again. Her fingers slipped over the fabric, but when they didn't find skin, instead of feeling relief, Velvet left her fingers there as though the boy might magically appear.

Her disappointment stung.

She wasn't supposed to be like this. Wasn't supposed to want, or desire, or need anything but her work, both sanctioned and the volunteer work she did over at Bonesaw's shed.

"This is ridiculous." Velvet sighed, tore off the sheet, and launched herself out of the bed. She pulled on a black tee, some pants, and a plum-colored jacket, stuffed her feet into her boots, and tied her hair up in a knot. If anything, Velvet would *look* ready for an intensive day of Salvage training, even if she wasn't looking forward to it. She was about to leave when she noticed the box Mr. Fassbinder had given her and pocketed the sturdy little thing.

Outside, the tenants of the dorm were waking, shuffling onto the three levels of balconies framing the courtyard in their pajamas like loose newspaper blown across vacant streets. Velvet followed suit, closing the door behind her. She stood at the rail, yawning, and looked down at the third floor.

"Good morning," Luisa said cheerfully, buttoning her jacket as she bounded toward her.

Velvet leered at her. "I guess. It's morning, anyway."

Luisa rolled her eyes and leaned over the banister to watch Nick, a floor down, shambling from his room and rubbing his eyes. His hair was tousled, and his pajama bottoms narrowly clinging to his hips. He was, of course, shirtless and wickedly aware that Velvet had noticed, if his grin was any indication.

"Morning!" Luisa called, waving. "Thanks for helping with my dumb-ass brother."

Nick nodded politely, bit his lip, and stretched his arms up over his head. His muscles rippled and tensed like some guy from an Abercrombie & Fitch catalog. Velvet couldn't stand it anymore. She had to look away from his erotic pose. Seriously, he had to know what he was doing; even Luisa had raised an eyebrow.

Logan, heavy-lidded and cringing, stumbled from his room with a pair of earmuffs on. He wasn't the most hungover person Velvet had ever seen, but he was definitely the youngest-looking hungover person she'd ever seen.

Luisa groaned in his direction and trotted off toward the stairs.

"I guess she's not speaking to me," Logan said, and yawned.

"Probably," Velvet agreed. She was going to say something else, but Logan was already retreating into his room, a train of blanket sliding across the hall floor.

"Good morning, Velvet," Nick called from below, in a tone that suggested he thought she was ignoring him. She glanced in his direction, only to be greeted by that painfully beautiful smile, those perfect teeth. "Did you sleep well?" he asked.

"Always."

Nick continued to stretch. "Well, I had a rough night. Mattresses are a little lumpy down here in the ghetto. You were probably curled up on your pile of down feathers like a kitten?"

"Like a web of gossamer." She sucked at her teeth, trying to look as disinterested as possible.

He nodded, catching on. "Right."

Velvet strode toward the stairs, and Nick started to follow suit. She stopped and shot a look in his direction.

"Are you going to dress, or were you hoping for a camera crew?" she asked, lips pursed.

"What?" He glanced down at himself and smiled. "Oh, yeah. We've got that test thing, huh?"

She cocked her head in his direction, as though he were the biggest doofus ever, which was a distinct possibility. "Yeah. That test thing."

He shrugged like it was no big deal. "Really, your team's

got a lot going for it, Velvet, but what it doesn't have is a Nick Russell."

Cocky bastard.

A smile curled skeptically on her lips. "Oh, yeah?"

"Yeah. He's pretty awesome."

Velvet cocked an eyebrow. "I hear he's kind of annoying. Needy."

"Oh, no." He laughed, leaning casually against the stair rail and scratching his bare belly. "No way. Not at all. He's super smooth."

"Really? Not completely arrogant and douche-baggy? Are you sure?"

Nick shook his head aggressively. "Well. If he is, it's because he's awesome, like I said earlier. And quite a storyteller, come to think of it."

"Well, then. I'll make of note of all that. Thanks for the reference."

Nick shoved his hands into the pockets of his pajama bottoms and shrugged his shoulders. "No problemo."

"Except for one." She raised an eyebrow at his state of undress.

"Oh, yeah!" He nodded excitedly and ducked back into his room. Clangs and thuds echoed out into the gap between the balconies, but thirty seconds later, the boy had managed to put together an outfit and tousle his hair in that effortlessly sexy way that is impossible for girls to do.

"Let's get you tested," she said, annoyance threading through her words. "The first one's the math portion. That won't be a problem, will it?" Part of Nick's salon story had detailed a terrible math phobia for which a tutor had needed to be called in. It was important to remember these things about potential employees—keeps the hierarchy straight.

Nick's gulp was audible a floor up.

Velvet smiled and trod the uneven stairs down to the second floor. Miss Antonia's office was off to the right. The door was open a crack, and Velvet couldn't resist stealing a secret peek before announcing herself.

The woman stood bone straight with her back to Velvet, looking down at something in her hands. There was a sharp clicking sound, and then Miss Antonia placed one item into her pocket gingerly and, after stepping precariously onto a stool, placed the other on the highest of her bookshelves, dusting the space around it.

It was a tiny black box, similar to the one Velvet carried in her pocket, the one Mr. Fassbinder had given her.

Velvet rapped on the door. "Are you busy?"

The woman glanced behind her, her expression mournful, as though she'd been crying.

"Are you all right?" Velvet strode across the room to get a closer look. "You look like you've been crying. Was it something Isadora said? Because I'd be happy to beat the—"

"Of course I'm fine. Foolish girl," she spat, stepping down. "Why are you here? Don't you have business to take care of? The last time I checked, that boy hadn't been tested and you're short one undertaker."

Grumpy, Velvet thought. "Yes. We're almost ready to head out for the Salvage trials."

"Well." Miss Antonia sank into her desk chair and spun toward Velvet. "I suggest you get on with it. And do the third test today, too. Time is not on your side with the revolution."

"No," Velvet agreed, but between her kiss with Nick and—well, just the kiss, if she were being honest—she'd nearly forgotten the nastier bits of last night. "I was just going to say—"

"I fear it's only a matter of time before the shadows fall on us again and this whole world starts to crumble." Miss Antonia's jaw clenched, her face a jumble of emotions—fear, sadness.

Wow. Velvet hardly ever saw the Salvage mother look frantic or confused. Her expression brought to mind the look that had shot across the table between Miss Antonia and Manny when Velvet had brought up Aloysius Clay. There was something going on there, but the timing was definitely not right to discuss that.

God, no.

Velvet would be lucky to survive that discussion with her last few nerve endings still in her head. "I'm on it, Miss Antonia." And as much as it pained her to add it, she said, "I'll get Nick processed and ready for extractions and all other Salvage duties. If he doesn't cut it as an undertaker, I can move Luisa into the position. She's adept."

"Fine. We'll need to talk further after tonight's salon. When Kipper returns with news from Vermillion."

Miss Antonia sniffed, and Velvet backed out of the room. "Do you want me to shut the door?"

"Gah!" Miss Antonia shouted, waving her off.

Velvet backed away quickly.

In the courtyard, Nick was surrounded by a handful of Collector girls and one boy, all seemingly hanging on every one of his no-doubt brilliant words like he was the second coming of Jared Padalecki. If only she had a box cutter, Velvet could remedy this situation real quick.

"Fall in line, Mr. Russell," she said as she swept past him, not stopping to endure a moment of his fans' googly-eyed fascination. She darted out into the square with him trotting at her heels like a puppy.

"When we're on team business, there'll be no smart-ass comments, no cute quips or come-ons. You got me?"

"Yup!" he shouted.

"Do you?" She stopped and spun toward him, stepped in close, and pressed the palm of her hand against the flat of his belly. He tensed up immediately.

He shrugged. "No problem. I can be professional."

Velvet wasn't convinced. "Can you?"

"Absolutely. But then later . . ." His hand reached for hers, and she pulled away abruptly.

"No. I'm not joking around here." She leaned in close. "You keep up with that crap, and I'll have you transferred somewhere really gross, where all the girls look like Kipper. You got it?"

Frowning, he nodded, backed away a bit. "Yeah, I get it. Business. I'm fine with that. I'm all about the business."

If the rejection hurt him at all, to his credit, Nick didn't show it. Velvet couldn't back down, though. Things were too hot in purgatory—she couldn't risk the kind of distraction Nick posed. Purgatory could fall into civil war, for all she knew.

"That's right. It was just something that happened. It's over. We need to be mature about it and move on. We've got to work together. Dark times ahead, Nick. Pitch-black."

His face screwed up quizzically. He was silent.

"Okay." Velvet had suspected a snappy comeback. When it didn't happen, she turned and stomped away. Nick chased after her, stumbling on the pavers with loud clops. About halfway to the dry fountain in the center of the square, she swiveled to look back at him.

He showed her open palms and said, "Sorry. I don't mean to be a dick."

"You've just got to let me lead," she said. "You've got to."

He nodded and followed her the rest of the way to the funicular platform in silence. Velvet forced her hands into her pockets and felt the little box from Mr. Fassbinder, just as sturdy and pristine as when he'd given it to her. Just having the paper bird, a gift from a man who'd never been anything but kind to her, somehow gave her comfort from the sadness.

Velvet and Nick sat with their hands inches apart, resting against the wooden bench seats of the railcar as it rattled and lurched up the mountain to the station. The minute Velvet was certain she'd have to break the silence, Nick cleared his throat.

"I scared you when I said 'love,' didn't I?" he asked. He chewed at his nails but didn't wait for her to answer. "I don't love you in a romantic way. I mean, I think you're hot and all, and I love making out with you, but that's different. I love you because you saved me, because you make me feel less alone."

Velvet mulled over the words. She guessed they made a sort of bizarre boy-sense, but it didn't change the fact that he was still talking to her like they could continue any sort of physical stuff.

She bit the inside of her cheek. Maybe Nick would never get it. How horrible would it be to have to fend off his attentions and work side by side with him for weeks, or months? Years?

Finally she decided to take a cue from his tack. Hers, she thought, clearly wasn't working.

"Yeah. I totally get what you mean. The kissing and stuff is sexy, and it takes our minds off of all the bad shit. But in the end"—she shrugged pleasantly—"I don't really know you and you don't really know me. So we should probably work on being friends and coworkers."

"Oh, I know you," he said, smiling broadly.

She gave him a sideways glance. So much for reverse psychology.

He caught on to her edginess and huffed. "Jesus. I'm flirting again, aren't I?"

"That's kind of your fallback position. Why don't we just change the subject? Okay?"

The railcar jogged forward as they crossed into the station proper, and they both bounced in their seats. Their fingers touched, and neither of them moved. They just sat there like that, pinkies creating arcs of heat.

Velvet held her breath and closed her eyes. They were much better like this, she thought. Still. Not talking. It was perfect.

Finally Nick pulled away.

She decided to pretend it hadn't happened and continued. "So, the tests!"

Nick nodded and crossed his arms, tucking his hands into his armpits. "Maybe we could call them something else," he said. "'Tests' sounds like something involving needles."

Velvet thought about the second part of the test and the nursing home where Nick would have to try to possess a body. "Well, there might actually be needles," she said, trying to remember.

"Oh, good."

The platform came up on the left, and they scooted out onto the smooth cobblestone along with the few other passengers. There weren't nearly as many travelers in the station as the last time she'd been there, and so they breezed quickly up to the Shattered Hall.

"The tests are actually kind of fun," she told him as the coiled lock on the gate spiraled open. "Plus, we'll get a chance to know each other."

He straightened, developing a swarthy look befitting a lusty pirate in those old Sunday afternoon movies.

Velvet almost giggled. "Not like that."

He slumped over dramatically.

Velvet laughed. She couldn't keep up the tough love. It was just getting exhausting, and she did, despite her better judgment, like the guy. It wasn't in her nature to develop an easy rapport with anyone, let alone a boy. And this guy actually liked her back . . . or at least wanted to make out, which was something.

"Or maybe . . ."

"What?" Nick lit up.

Velvet started to remove her pants, unbuckling her leather belt with delicate movements. She knew Nick was watching and, God help her, she wanted him to. She glanced at him and found him quietly chewing at his lips.

Velvet looked up at him and shook her head. "This isn't a seduction, you loser. Get your clothes off. We're going through that crack there and doing a job."

Nick scowled and tugged his shirt from his pants.

Velvet briefed the boy to the best of her ability, gave him the same three details for the pull-focus that they always used. Yellow plastic mop buckets full of moldy rags, a Girls of Glassware calendar perpetually on the June photo depicting a busty redhead leaning over two vases, and a barely used doorknob, covered in dust.

"You need to get a move on the second we arrive at the factory," she directed.

And he nodded.

Velvet thought she'd been very specific. Succinct, even.

So why was it that when she followed Nick through the crack, Velvet wound up collapsed directly on top of the boy, right between his legs?

"Jesus, Nick. You've got to keep moving." She disentangled herself and passed through the door of the small closet where the crack had led them, and into a vast warehouse. After a moment, she huffed in the direction of the door. No Nick. She crammed her hand back through it and pulled Nick out.

"Thanks." Nick found his footing and inspected their surroundings.

A grooved metal ceiling towered above them. The glass transoms were cranked fully open, and birds fluttered between the steel rods, chirping like a bunch of girls gossiping at a coffee shop. Row upon row of racks stretched the length of the building, and perched on each rack were crystal vases, wineglasses, and ashtrays.

"What is it?" he asked.

"It's the Caruthers Family Crystal warehouse." Velvet began to walk between the rows. "Well, one of them. This one is full of factory seconds, and they rarely move any of these pieces anywhere but into the garbage."

"What do you mean 'seconds'?"

Velvet crossed in front of him and drew his attention to a candlestick that looked like a column on a really old building—only glass and small, obviously. Nick leaned over and examined it closely. The carved edges sparkled in the sunlight beaming in from above. Pretty, if you liked that kind of thing, but Velvet thought it would look much better smashed into little glittery bits on the floor.

"Do you see all those little bubbles?" She pointed at the candlestick's base, where, like a pile of frog eggs in a pond, there were dozens of little bubbles settled inside the thick glass. "That means they're no good. They can't sell 'em for top dollar."

Nick nodded, his normally expressive face gone dull with boredom.

"So where's the test?" he whined.

Velvet grinned and swept her arms toward the city-bus-sized towers of factory second crystal as though she and

Nick had just arrived in some defective fantasy wonderland. "This is it."

"What do you mean, 'This is it'? You want me to blow glass or something?"

"When you're done blowing yourself," Velvet joked.

The boy chuckled. "Funny."

She reached out with her amorphous hand and picked up a candlestick from the metal shelf. She handed it to Nick. "Take it."

Nick lifted his hand to circle the piece of glass. His brow scrunched with concentration. When Velvet released it, the crystal toppled from the boy's nonexistent grasp and shattered on the concrete floor between their feet, glass shards dancing like a hard rain.

"Oh, crap!" he shouted, and instinctively crouched, as though the workers or guards would come running. "We better get out of here."

"Not until you've completed the test. All you've proven is your lack of natural ability in poltergeisting, but you still have to learn it to get by in the daylight. It's unacceptable to simply be able to do one job and not others. Where would you be if you got separated out there on the streets? You'd be nothing. A lost soul. Useless."

"What do you mean 'daylight'?"

" 'The daylight' just means 'the world of the living.' "

"Then, why don't we call purgatory 'the nighttime' or something?"

Velvet scowled and stabbed a thumb toward the shelf. "Just shut up and try again. This time focus your energy on the candlestick or whatever. Don't think of anything else but moving it. Really want it."

Velvet would have been amazed if Nick had taken to moving objects right out of the gate. It took a natural poltergeist to achieve that kind of dexterity. The thought reminded her of her problem with the knotted ropes and fishing lines circling Bonesaw's girls. If she'd only been a natural, things would be so much easier.

If only. If only.

She brushed the thoughts aside before they infected her mind with the darkness of the situation, before the image of herself in Bonesaw's mind became her only focus.

Nick chose a crystal ashtray from a stack of the things and stretched his hand toward it. He touched the edge of the glass and pressed straight through.

"You don't feel anything, right?" She stepped up close to him. "It's a matter of perspective. To you, it's like the glass doesn't exist, rather than the other way around. You have to focus."

And so did she.

"Focus!" Velvet demanded.

Nick glanced in her direction, his face filled with a steely determination in the gauzy light. On his second attempt, his finger caught hold for a moment before giving way to nothingness.

"Dammit!" he shouted.

"Just concentrate," Velvet said. "It'll come. Imagine your hand is solid."

This time, when the boy reached out, the ashtray's edge

nestled into his palm. He slipped his thumb underneath and lifted it off the shelf, drawing it toward them. It scraped and hopped against the open grid in the metal. He held it out for Velvet.

"Holy crap." She grinned proudly and gave him a great big theater clap.

Then.

The ashtray fell, slapping against the floor, bouncing once and then breaking into a million pieces, scattering across the floor like a crowd dispersing.

"Shit!" Nick yelled.

"That was really good. Until you lost your focus and screwed the pooch."

He straightened, and puffed his chest out proudly. "Heck, yeah. It was awesome, is what it was. Damn fine ashtray lifting."

"Uh." Velvet shook her head. "I wouldn't go that far. But it was a start!"

Nick agreed, nodding. "A start. So what now?"

She shrugged. "The next test."

Velvet waited for Nick to bounce from the crack. She sat on a cushy couch, her legs were crossed elegantly, her ankle popping in her boots.

Nick slipped from the crack in the ballroom wall and tumbled across the freshly oiled floor.

"Took you long enough," Velvet chided, giving him a sheepish smile.

She hopped up and sauntered across the room, feeling his

gaze lower to her hips. Velvet couldn't deny that she took some degree of pleasure in him watching her, and if she were being honest, she'd have to cop to swiveling her butt around a little more for the boy's benefit.

She couldn't help but think of their night together. She could pretend she didn't remember, but she'd been all over him. And their kiss.

Holy crap.

When she turned back to look at him, his eyes were dark with something completely unwholesome and his tongue played in the corner of his lips. Her heart pounded a haunting rhythm in her chest, and for a second, she was sure that he'd seen something in her expression. Something she had not meant to show him.

Desire.

Velvet turned away quickly. What was wrong with her? What was it with the boy? He was like a hormone magnet. And she was stuck in a perpetual loop of teenage lust and poor impulse control. But this wasn't the place.

But what if it was? she mused. What if it could be?

"Welcome to the Friendly Acres Retirement Community and Skilled Nursing Facility," she said, sweeping her arms out toward the space around them.

"Lovely." He scanned the lavishly decorated walls dutifully, but mostly he just watched Velvet. "I guess."

"Oh, it is. It's also sad, and you'll see that." She glanced off to her right. "Or feel it, in a minute."

They passed through a narrow wood-paneled hall that opened into a grand lobby, richly appointed with plush chairs, Oriental carpets, and a massive fireplace that was blazing and crackling. A group of elderly residents sat in front of it warming themselves and gossiping. The sound of the fire joined the squeaking of aluminum walkers and wheelchairs and the soft *shurr*ing of crepe-soled nurse's shoes. At the opposite end of the hall was a front desk of dark mahogany the size of a Mini Cooper. From behind it a man in a maroon cardigan and glasses with beads hanging from the arms glanced in their direction.

"Did that guy just wink at me?" Nick asked Velvet, pointing in the deskman's direction.

"Barney is legally blind, so I seriously doubt it." She pursed her lips and shook her head in judgment. "You're really full of yourself, aren't you?"

Nick took a defensive posture. "Absolutely not. I just thought he could see us, is all. He definitely seemed to notice us passing through."

"Well, some people can, but they don't really know what they're seeing. I've heard that we kind of look like when you catch something in your eyelashes and the light hits it just right so you can see it in your periphery. Glowing orb things."

"Yeah. Or maybe people are just crazy and want to see things."

"Well, there is that." She smiled.

She led him through a closed door into a hall lined with wheelchairs, gurneys, and chests of drawers. Nurses in paper hats crisscrossed the hall in front of them, darting from room to room, like some live-action video game.

Velvet paid them no attention, and when they passed through her, she didn't even flinch. The same couldn't be said for Nick, who spasmed nearly every time one of the busy nurses clipped him.

"In here!" Velvet yelled as she watched Nick recover from a particularly heinous body violation by a nurse nearly twice as big around as he was. She pointed toward an open door into a shadow-filled room.

Nick stepped past her onto a floor as glossy as spun sugar. The sound of machines beeping echoed off the walls, and a gray curtain hung from the ceiling in a half-moon around a hospital bed. They peered around the corner to find an elderly woman harpooned by breathing tubes, the blankets on top of her stretched so tight that she seemed to be sunken into the bed, paper thin.

"She's a vegetable," Velvet said without a hint of empathy in her voice.

"You mean 'comatose,'" Nick snipped.

She shrugged. "Sure. Yeah, that works, too."

"What's her name?"

Velvet crouched to read the chart hanging from the foot of the woman's bed. "Rita Renjette. It says here she has lung cancer."

Nick circled the bed, breezing across the woman's exposed hand with the tips of his fingers. "Her face is so slack."

Her skin hung from her cheekbones like the clothes from the lines in the courtyard, limp and saggy.

"It's like there's nothing underneath," he whispered.

Velvet studied the creases around the boy's light eyes. His sympathy was so apparent, it made her sad. It came so easy for Nick.

He cared.

"But we know that's not true." Velvet sat down in an emerald-green wingback chair, the fleur-de-lis pattern of the fabric obscuring her figure as she did. "You need to get on in there."

"What?" He looked down at the old woman again, at her breathing tubes and wires and permanently sealed paper-thin eyelids. "She looks like a coffin," he said finally. "Not *ready* for one, but like an actual coffin herself." He glanced back at Velvet, beseeching her to excuse him from the task.

"I don't think I want anything to do with body thieving, Velvet. It scares me." Nick's voice quivered.

Velvet nodded; it wasn't for everyone. It took a certain degree of coarseness to pull it off, to commandeer someone else and strip away his or her humanity. It might *not* be for Nick. Poltergeisting certainly hadn't been. But the test had to be done.

"We're not here sightseeing, Nick." She tried to speak softly. "This is part of your test."

He shook his head and glanced at the prone figure. "Not this one. She reminds me of my own grandmother."

Velvet stood up and joined him next to the bed. "Really?"

"Yeah." He pointed at the thin skin on the woman's wrists, bunched up like saggy panty hose. "I think it's that."

"I know what you mean." She turned and caught his gaze. "We used to visit my great-aunt in the nursing home up until she passed away. She was always so . . . like, alive. And then the old age just took her and she got like this. This woman is just waiting to move on. She might not know it, but we do, right?"

He nodded his head, but his expression was grim.

"You're not going to hurt her. She's beyond that now. Just lie down in her place and see what happens, okay?"

He gulped. She'd never seen him look so horrified, and that was saying something, considering the panic she'd witnessed as he'd broken free from the bonds of the crystal ball. "You won't hurt her. I promise."

Nick flinched, but climbed atop the bed, seemingly worried about putting any weight on the woman's frail frame. He flipped and crab-walked over the woman, his hands and feet barely making dents in the hospital blankets, and then with a deep breath of nothing, he sank down into her.

Velvet sat back down and waited. The clock above the door ticked away in time with the hushing *shh* of the breathing machine. She'd trained a boy named Gregory a few months ago—she wasn't sure what district he'd ended up Salvaging for—much younger than Nick, but fearless. That boy had plopped down into one of these coma patients, and not a second later their eyes snapped open and he sat them right up and winked at her.

If Nick couldn't do that, she decided, she'd still have faith that he could be an undertaker. Operating a living body was totally different from getting a dead one up and moving. Plus, the fly production was the real skill there.

Velvet was beginning to hope.

If he did end up being her undertaker, they'd get to spend time together.

It might not be so bad to work with Nick. And the eye-candy fringe benefits were clearly epic.

305

A groan brought her attention back to Mrs. Renjette, and Velvet stood and raced to the woman's side. Her eyes had crept open just a bit, and Velvet could see Nick moving inside, turning the glassy cataracts in her direction. The woman's hand moved shakily to the bed rail, and Velvet patted it.

"Took you long enough," she said.

Another groan, and the woman's shoulders shrugged.

"All right," Velvet said, and nodded. "I'll give you this."

Nick jutted up out of the woman, beaming. He twisted around to see that the woman's face was just as placid as before, and that seemed to be okay with him. He leapt from the bed and stood next to Velvet, bouncing on the balls of his feet.

"A 'Congratulations' is in order, for I believe *that*"—he pointed toward Mrs. Renjette—"was some masterful body thieving," Nick said.

Velvet rolled her eyes. "If by 'masterful' you mean 'sluggish' or 'inadequate,' then, yeah. Masterful. You are the grand master of incompetent body thieves."

"What? I was just getting comfy with my new friend Rita."

Velvet glowered and sauntered out of the room. *Must not laugh,* she told herself. Though Nick's cocky self was a far better companion than the mopey version.

"Velvet!" he called into the hall. "Wait up!"

"Yeah, yeah," she said.

Nick came up beside her, and they walked back toward the lobby.

"That was amazing. Rita was so nice, too. Really helpful."

Velvet stopped dead and spun toward him. "Hold everything. You talked to her?"

"Yeah, totally. She even helped me out."

"You're like the coma whisperer, then, because I've never heard of that happening."

"She was really very helpful, told me what to do. She even apologized for being so atrophied. Crazy, right?"

Velvet wondered if, in some horrible way, that was what had happened when she'd entered Ron Simanski's head. Maybe he'd communicated.

"Maybe no one's ever told you," he said.

"Maybe." She wasn't convinced.

"So what's next?" he asked breathlessly.

Nick actually sounded excited again. The tests had distracted him from hounding her. Definitely a good thing.

Velvet led him through the nursing home halls and back to the ballroom crack.

Chapter 19

She was dumped out into a hilly field. A barn was the home of her traveling crack, which was still shimmering as the passage sealed itself. A path stretched out to the left and right, and before her was a long berm fitted with rows of mounds, some heavy with dirt, others thin and lumpy with their rotty inhabitants.

When Nick hadn't appeared by her side moments later, she remembered she hadn't given him details for the passage. She slapped her leg and shook her head. "Stupid!" she chastised.

But then something astonishing happened. The crack in the old boards shimmered and Nick spilled out. He bounded up beside her with a broad smile and a wicked look in his eye. "Found ya," he said, and reached out to push up Velvet's jaw, which had dropped open in amazement.

"But how?" she asked. "I didn't—"

"I thought of you," he said, his tone misty and serious. "I could describe you in a hundred different ways. And I figured, as long as you were already here, that was all it would take." He shrugged. "Guess I'm lucky it worked."

It took a moment for Velvet to recover from this. She was left without words. If she'd been alive, her breath would have been sucked from her lungs. As it was, she felt a gentle vibration pass over her ethereal form.

"Where are we, anyway?"

"The body fields," Velvet whispered, staring at him, uncertain whether he was something special or just so obsessed that he'd follow her anywhere. At that moment, she decided she'd be happy with either answer.

Nick's eyes traveled over the tiny hills and valleys. "What are they?"

"You know how people give their bodies away for science or donate their organs and stuff?"

"Yeah?" Nick answered, his mouth left hanging open.

"Well, sometimes the whole body comes here. But it's not so they can give a kidney to some poor kid that needs one. It's so scientists can watch how the person rots, so they can tell things about how long they've been dead, or what it looks like if someone sprinkles Liquid-Plumr all over them, or how the flesh around a stab wound caves in over time."

Nick clutched the spot over his phantom stomach. "That's some *CSI* crap right there."

"Totally."

Velvet crossed the path and climbed the small hill, gesturing toward the nearest mound and a little sign stuck at the foot of it like a garden marker.

"See, this one's already covered in maggots." She squatted next to it. "Male. Thirty-four. Hear them?"

Nick squatted next to the grave, but he didn't need to. You couldn't help but hear the sound of something snapping, crackling, and popping, so clear and unmuffled. A bowl of Rice Krispies could have been sitting nearby. But there was none.

"What's that sound?" he asked.

"You don't want to know."

She pressed on down the first row, reading each of the little signs, looking for the perfect one. A challenge. Something disgusting but mobile. There'd be no point in testing the boy in a body that was just going to fall apart.

Velvet stopped before a shallow hillock and brushed some spatter from the white metal marker. Nick peered over her shoulder. The gray nose and cheeks of a cadaver poked from freshly crumbled loam, as though the body were wrapped in a blanket instead of lying in a grave. Velvet turned in time to see the shiver tear through him. If he'd had flesh, the goose bumps would have covered it.

"Oh, man," he said. "That's creepy."

"Subject number twenty-seven," Velvet read. "A John Doe found prone on the banks of the Elk River. Multiple stab wounds, postmortem bloating."

She looked up at Nick, raised an eyebrow.

"I'm fine," he shot back. "I'm not going to vomit."

Velvet grinned. "I've actually never seen a ghost puke. Souls, sure. You're a perfect example of that. I don't think ghosts can, but if anyone could prove me wrong, it's you."

She stood next to him and looked around the farm. It was early still, and a light mist clung to the undergrowth in the forest surrounding the hilly field. Velvet couldn't tell it from the air, but she thought it might be cold, as though her breath would have turned to fog if she'd been a living, breathing girl.

"We're alone," she said without glancing in his direction. "You ready?"

He exhaled heavily, staring at the placid corpse at his feet, and sat down next to the mound. Then, taking a deep but useless breath, he dropped into the space occupied by John Doe.

Velvet stood back and watched. She was filled with both hope and dread. The zombies were a necessary evil, but they were gross and creepy and she never got used to working around her undertaker's rotting flesh suits. But Nick needed to be able to do this. Sure, she could train him to be a body thief, but with the revolution looming, she didn't have the time for that.

Time was something everybody was running a little short of lately.

She glanced around at the walls of trees surrounding the body farm and thought of the girl in Bonesaw's shed. Velvet needed to get back there. After her last run-in with the man, he'd be on edge, and that was never good. It made him more aggressive. More invested in his gouging and grating.

She shivered, and a second later, the corpse's eyelids snapped open and Velvet screamed uncontrollably. Nick chuckled. The corpse's vocal cords were gravelly, like it had strep throat or laryngitis or worms coiled in the back of its esophagus. Velvet composed herself and nodded in his direction.

"That was quick."

Nick sat up and shook away the dirt from the zombie's shoulders and bare chest. The body was wearing a pair of decomposing jeans, and he brushed the rest of the mounded dirt from its legs before hoisting himself up.

"Good thing he's got jeans on. Would hate for you to feel awkward," he said.

She rolled her eyes. "Gross."

Velvet started walking back toward the barn.

Behind her, she could hear the cracking heavy-footed machinations of the corpse. Nick maneuvered the thing like a pro. Velvet felt something well inside her that she thought might be pride, but then he tried to run and tripped over a garden marker. He dropped like a sack of potatoes and jarred an eyeball from its socket. It rolled across the dirt, getting coated with the dark soil like a meatball in bread crumbs.

"Ah, crap. Hang on a minute, will ya?"

Velvet bent over with laughter. "You lost something!"

He searched through the dirt for the dark little orb, but in that single moment of looking up at Velvet, he'd lost sight of it, so to speak.

"Yep," he said. "Eyeball."

She laughed again, intentionally morbidly, like a mad scientist. "Muhahaha!"

Nick stood up, giving up the search, and jogged forward

again. On his second step, he landed square on the missing organ, and it splattered beneath his bare foot. Velvet felt a gag rising in her throat.

"Sorry, dude," Nick said. He stumbled down the far side of the hill to where Velvet stood at the corner of the old red barn. The doors were chained shut, and a combination padlock was looped through the chain.

"Let's test your manual dexterity." She flipped the lock up, and it clanged against the door, making the chain jingle.

"Um, brilliant idea, boss. Except I don't know the combination."

She glared. "Yeah, I know. I'm giving it to you."

"Are you?" he asked. The tone was salacious, she guessed, but Velvet couldn't tell whether he was trying to start something, not with the remaining eye twitching like it was inside the socket.

"Not that you're not completely gorgeous like this, but if you're looking for some romance, might I suggest one of these lovely Jane Does?" She stabbed her thumb in the direction of the fields.

Nick gagged a bit.

"Defeat!" she cried, savoring the victory.

He opened his mouth to retort, but a thin strand of mist flew out—ectoplasm—forcing wild guffaws of laughter from Velvet. Back in purgatory it would have been a spark, and she would have really keeled over busting up.

"Seriously," she said. "Let's get this open and move on. There's another salon tonight, and I'm hoping Kipper is back from his mission with news on Aloysius Clay."

"Who's that?" Nick asked.

"Clay's a lead we're following up on. He's probably involved in the revolution and is likely involved in your death and soul imprisonment."

"That guy sounds really awesome," Nick said sarcastically.

Velvet suppressed a laugh and continued. "If it is him, then Kipper can find out what exactly the Departurists are planning before their magic causes another shadowquake. That's why it's so urgent that we complete your tests. We're not sure what's going to happen or when. The departure could be happening right now."

Nick whistled through the corpse's loose lips.

Velvet recited the combination, and Nick spun the lock open with ease, jiggled the shackle from the chamber, and left the chain to dangle, all in record time. She ran him through some more tests, lifting tools, jumping through hoops, mostly physical stuff that Nick seemed to have no problem with.

"You know," he said, "I realize salon has its purposes and all, but I could really go for some nachos."

"Ooh, yeah. Or some fried cheese." Velvet bit her lip and glanced off into the distance, lost in a great big food memory.

"I love mozzarella sticks!" Nick added. "Dipped in ranch."

Velvet brightened. "Shut up! Everyone thinks I'm crazy 'cause I don't like the marinara dip."

Nick shrugged the corpse's shoulders and winked his eye at the girl.

Her expression crinkled. "You do know that's not cute, right?"

"Hey!" he garbled. "*You* try to be charming when your skin is sagging around you like a shar-pei's!"

"The real test will be whether you can generate the flies." Nick shivered. "Now?"

Velvet looked him up and down, wondering if she'd misjudged his stamina. But rather than sagging away from the task, Nick puffed out the corpse's chest and shrugged nonchalantly. "One fly machine, coming up."

"Yeah," she said. "Right now. And don't bother asking me how it works. I could never get them to do it when I did the test."

The boy bounded up the hill and planted himself in the groove of earth where they'd found the John Doe. He pulled the dirt up around himself like a kid on a day at the beach.

Velvet followed and stood over him, brow furrowed with confusion. "Getting comfy?"

"Yes, gots to concentrate. Shh "

Velvet stepped back and crossed her arms. She studied the corpse for signs of an eruption, but the only thing Nick seemed to be able to do was cause a maggot to dance on the puckered flesh of the empty eye socket.

"Come on!" she chided.

"Just a second!" the zombie graveled.

The corpse tensed, and a scream bellowed from the body's slimy lungs like a ship's whistle. There was a low buzzing sound and then a whoosh of air, and then, suddenly, the flies buzzed around Velvet everywhere. She grinned down at Nick, who beamed with pride and nodded.

"Who's a stud?" he said.

Velvet crinkled her nose, but she was definitely impressed. "That was good work, dude. Seriously."

Without a clear target to devour, the flies dispersed quickly, and soon the body farm fell back into silence.

Nick bounced to his feet and planted his translucent fists on his hips heroically. Thankfully, he resisted the urge to do a douchey fist pump; that would have stripped away any admiration Velvet had developed.

"So does that mean I get to be the undertaker?"

Velvet ignored him and stomped away over the edge of the berm.

"Hey!" he shouted. "Seriously?"

She tossed a quick grin over her shoulder and slipped into the undergrowth of the surrounding forest.

The woods were dense but stretched only about twenty yards before they opened onto the grounds of what looked like a college campus. Young people bustled about carrying backpacks over their shoulders, or sat around under trees reading books and crap. Velvet felt a pang of loss at the sight. She'd dreamed of going to school for filmmaking, directing.

Her mother had definitely helped to push her in that direction. She wondered what it would be like to actually do it. To be like these young adults, bustling back and forth to classes, piecing together student films about ice cream melting or kisses that make your lips turn black.

She glanced over at Nick and thought she recognized the look in his eyes, the regret, the grief.

They were all grieving, she suspected. Logan and Luisa, too—despite their love for the Salvaging life and missions and junk. But especially Nick. There was a sadness in him, playing out just behind the cockiness like some off camera backstory. When she thought about it, that's what connected them.

"What did you want to be?" he asked her, sinking onto the grass.

Velvet sat next to him, leaning back on her elbows and crossing her legs out in front of her. "Flight attendant."

Nick spat laughter. "What? You?"

Velvet shrugged. "Just kidding. I wanted to make movies."

He raised an eyebrow. "You wanted to act?"

She shook her head. "Oh, God no. I'm definitely more the directing type."

"Well, you *are* bossy."

Velvet ignored him. "My mother took me to the movies. Lots of movies."

She trailed away into memory. It seemed that the cinema was all they'd had. It had been her mother's response to every problem. Kids bullying? Let's go see *West Side Story*. Down in the dumps? Willy Wonka will clear that up!

"Yeah?" Nick was watching her out of the corner of his eye.

"Yeah! What of it?" She punched his thigh playfully.

"Nothing," he laughed. "You just make it sound like you've thought about it a lot."

"All the time." Her voice was small, nearly a whisper. "What about you?"

Nick turned toward her, resting his head in his palm. "I wanted to write."

"Yeah? You don't strike me as much of a reader."

He chuffed. "What gave you that impression?"

"I guess I've judged a book by its cover." She shrugged and shifted toward him a bit. "Jock boys aren't typically the well-read types, you know. They're more the groping-girls-in-the-back-of-their-trucks types."

"I don't have a truck."

"That's a relief," she said. "So what was your favorite book?"

"The Velveteen Rabbit."

Velvet sputtered. If she'd been drinking something, which she would have loved to have been doing, she'd have spit it across the lawn. "It is not!"

He shook his head. "Just fucking with you. No. It's *Slaughterhouse-Five.*"

"Mmm." Velvet bit her lip. "A boy who digs Vonnegut."

She stopped short of letting him know that made him at least 50 percent more attractive. "Vonnegut's not an easy guy to love," she said instead. "He was weird, rambly, jumped from point to point, and didn't give a crap about linear storytelling. Probably why the film version of *Slaughterhouse* wasn't so well liked."

Nick's excitement was evident. "You dig Vonnegut?"

Velvet shrugged. "I prefer *Cat's Cradle.*"

A couple passed them, their hands in the back pockets of each other's jeans. They were the chatty, chuckling sort. The kind that Velvet would normally sneer at, but she didn't. The moment looked kind of sweet, and she found herself smiling.

"You have a really pretty smile."

Nick had that look in his eye again and that smile on his lips. The knee-melter.

Her eyes narrowed to slits. "You're full of shit."

"What? Okay." He held out his hands, pretending she was about to assault him.

"You've got to stop with this. It's not going to happen, again."

He scooted in closer, until their faces were well within kissing range. She didn't pull away. "Just one kiss. Then I won't bother you. Swear to God," he said, eyes serious.

She sighed. And then heard herself say, "Just one."

Nick leaned toward her slowly. Her stomach twisted. Her vision blurred. He held up his hand and brushed her cheek; his knuckles slipped across her phantom skin like an electrical current. She closed her eyes as he pressed his lips against hers. Velvet loosened up, turning her hips to him and slipping her hand around his waist to pull him closer.

Soft murmurs played in her throat.

Inside her head, fireworks exploded. *Probably literally,* she thought. She wanted more. Nick was like no one she'd ever been with, and certainly different from any boy she'd ever kissed before. He was light and glowed so brightly, he seemed to have no trouble climbing out of his own darkness and letting that optimism shine on her.

In that moment he was everything.

Chapter 20

*Y*ou *better get it together, girl. Before you screw up every-thing!*

She glanced back down the path to see Nick staring at her again, following her back through the forest toward the body farm. *But how can it be a mistake when it felt so . . . awesome?*

Hormones, that's how. Damn things must still be swimming around in these dead bodies, she thought.

But especially now, with so much going on, so much drama, how could she let him kiss her, again?

So stupid. Stupid and sloppy.

No more. And not again, she promised.

"What now?" Nick asked, jogging up beside her and beaming ridiculously.

She shot him a suspicious glare. He probably was after a little more tongue action. Actually, from the look of him, there was no "probably" about it. He was swollen with pride over his fly hatching, over their kiss. "Salon," she reminded him, rolling her eyes.

The boy darted ahead of her, leaping and twisting as though shooting a basket. "I'm just completely amped up from all this, you know?"

"Yeah, you're totally tweaking. Are you sure you didn't snack on some leftover meth in one of those bodies?"

Nick chuckled and rushed back to her side, head lolling on his shoulders. "You're hilarious."

His smile was infectious, and she found herself studying his face, the way the skin around his eyes crinkled, the depths of his dimples, the pale blue of his eyes. Even in the transparent, Nick was insanely gorgeous. And despite it being completely irritating, Velvet found herself returning his grin.

So she punched him.

"Ow," he said, rubbing his arm. "What'd you do that for?"

"Seriously, let's get moving." As they descended toward the barn, she quickened her pace, grazing the damp grass of the hill like a bullet. Nick had fallen behind, and when he spoke, she stopped dead in her tracks.

"I'm infatuated with you. Is that the word? I think that's what I mean, like you're all I think about." He was rambling, and the deep baritone of his voice played across her ethereal form like the ripples of a stone skipping across a crystal lake.

She would have blushed, had she been a real girl, but instead she spun on him. "Who says things like that?" she demanded.

He spread his arms out and shrugged. "I guess I do."

"Yeah?" Her thoughts were racing.

Unreal. He'll never let up.

Still . . .

There was something about Nick that she had been drawn to immediately. Why else would she have gone to him like that on his first night? Even in that first moment back at Madame Despot's Fortunes and Favors, she'd noticed something in him, all the while calling him "ass" and "douche bag" in her mind and, sure, sometimes to his face. But there was something there. She wasn't sure what it was, because she'd never been that close to a guy before. She'd had boyfriends. Jakub and Greeley, specifically, but she hadn't really been "into" either of them. Not emotionally.

Jakub Chesel was hot in a pierced punk kind of way. He always wore band T-shirts—the Ramones and the Buzzcocks were his favorites—and sneered at people when they got too close. And sure, she'd made out with him, because that's kind of what you do, but Velvet had never really felt anything more than a physical attraction, and he could kiss really well.

Greeley Franks was a different sort.

She'd adopted him and let him hang out with her, much to the chagrin of her few friends. He was gangly and had the most enormous nose, but his hair was long and really amazingly soft when she'd run her fingers through it. He never talked all that much, but she could tell he was into her. And she'd even let him feel her up a few times. Under the shirt, too, for what that was worth. But one day he just didn't come to school anymore. Left home and disappeared.

Not quite in the way Velvet had, but, you know, gone, like a runaway or something. He'd probably end up in the porn industry, if he wasn't rotting in one of the forensic graves.

She scanned Nick's face and found sincerity lurking in his eyes. And something else. It wasn't lust exactly, though that was lurking just under the surface of every boy. This was different.

"So you think you care about me or something?" she asked, wincing at her own words.

"I know it." Nick ran his fingers across the sheen of her arm. Where hairs might have prickled, she felt something else rustle beneath the surface.

A longing.

It came over her all of a sudden. As they stood there in that field surrounded by the dead. She wanted him. More than anything she'd ever wanted in her life—or death, even. And it surprised her that she hadn't been thinking it all along. A fire burned through her, ignited by her desire and coursing inside her, consuming her.

Nick reached out for her then and pulled her close, already masterful at the delicate art of touching another spirit, his focus so intent. He pressed his lips to hers, and she nearly collapsed.

His kiss weakened her, made her legs feel like rubber bands, like overdone spaghetti, like Aunt Sylvia's flavorless gelatin jiggling on a plate.

Her last resolve melted away and she threw her arms around his neck and let him press his body close to hers.

She collapsed against him, relishing his soft kisses, the way he parted her lips gently with his tongue, his hands stroking the hollow of her spine.

In the end, it was Nick who pushed away first.

"I'm so happy," he said. "I know it sounds ridiculous, but all this"—he swept his hand out toward the grave mounds—"is worth it just to spend time with you. Death is worth it."

She stepped back, shaking her head. "Don't say that."

"It's true. I—" he started.

"Don't say it," Velvet interrupted before he could finish.

Their position flooded back into her mind. She was his team leader. She couldn't be emotionally involved with him. It would never work.

"I love you. And I won't take that back, because it's true," Nick said.

"It's Stockholm syndrome," she snapped, pulling the term from a paper she'd done for her Intro to Psychology class back at New Brompfel Heights High.

Nick cocked an eyebrow, unimpressed. "What's that supposed to mean? Did you give me a Russian virus or something?"

"Stockholm's in Sweden, dork. Besides, it's not about the city. It's a phenomenon where prisoners fall in love with their captors. It's really weird." She glanced up at him. "Like you."

"I'm weird? Me? Okay. Yeah. But not you. You're not weird at all."

She flipped her hair. "Of course not."

"Well, you're not my *captor.*" He wrapped the words in

air quotes. "So it doesn't really make sense to me. I'm not a prisoner, Velvet. I'm just a ghost. Just as dead as can be. And so are you. And we've got all the time in the world to spend together. So don't try to make it weird."

She turned toward the crack and sighed.

He didn't get it. How could he?

"It's because I saved you, Nick! You feel like you owe me this. Would you really be attracted to a girl like me if we were in the halls at your high school? Would the basketball star really be caught dead with the dark mopey Goth girl?"

"It could happen."

She shook her head. "Not likely."

Velvet felt his hand on her shoulder. His lips close to her ear. "We'll keep it a secret. No one needs to know. That's what you're worried about, isn't it? Manny? Miss Antonia? The rules?"

It was against the rules, for sure. The way Velvet figured it, she was breaking enough rules as it was, almost daily. Though if she thought about it, that was almost an excuse to go through with Nick's suggestion.

Rules seemed to be a waste of time in purgatory anyway.

Most rules were created to keep people from hurting themselves in some stupid way or other. "Don't touch the stove." "Don't stand too close to the edge." "Don't ride on the roof of a moving car with reins around the hood ornament like it's a rodeo bull." Blah, blah, blah. None of those were even valid anymore.

Take "Don't steal."

The Collectors did that daily. It was a part of the afterlife.

The Golden Rule? If Velvet didn't do the kinds of stuff "unto" others that she did, whether they did it back or not, where the hell would she be? Apparently gold fades away when it's covered in ash.

As far as rules go, "Don't fall in love with the hot boy who needs to follow your orders" seemed to be on par with "Don't wear white after Labor Day."

What was the purpose?

Who were they hurting?

Velvet was starting to think that that rule had been established specifically for leaders who were girls. Whoever thought that crap up must have believed that the girl couldn't wear the pants in the relationship. Ridiculous.

Everyone wears pants!

She knew she was rationalizing and that there might not be enough fate left to tempt, but she needed it. She needed this distraction.

Upon their return, the courtyard was packed with souls, and Velvet left Nick to the endless interrogation of Luisa and Logan and sought out Miss Antonia. The woman was in her quarters, penning a letter to someone with a big feather pen when Velvet knocked on her open door.

"Miss Antonia?"

The woman looked up, a hopeful expression on her otherwise somber face.

"He's going to work out perfectly," Velvet said.

The woman nodded and returned to her work. "I knew

that somehow. In fact, I'll just confirm that in this memo for the Council of Station Agents. Manny will be so glad to hear it." She jotted a few extra lines, folded the paper into thirds, and slipped it into an envelope before returning her gaze to Velvet.

"He was way better than I'd hoped. Quentin could barely get the zombie moving his first time, but Nick just jumped in and drove the body like a motorbike or something. And he was really strong." Her voice rose with excitement recounting the story.

Miss Antonia's eyes widened. "Really? All that? You sound quite enamored of the boy."

"Oh, no!" Velvet was mortified. "I'd never. I mean—"

"Calm yourself, child. I know you're a consummate professional and would never overstep your bounds or compromise your authority in such a way."

"No." Velvet had never been gladder that souls didn't sweat. "Has Kipper returned from Vermillion?"

"Not yet."

"I wish I could have gone."

Miss Antonia didn't make a sound. She was lost somewhere in her thoughts about Aloysius Clay and his disappearance, most likely, thoughts that her long lost love—allegedly—could have been involved in the departure. It must have hurt desperately.

"Are you all right, Velvet?" Miss Antonia stood and reached her hand out to Velvet.

She nodded quickly, suddenly embarrassed to be the one in need of a supportive touch.

"I'm fine."

"Good." Miss Antonia pulled a familiar box from a drawer in her desk, and Velvet cringed.

The story lottery.

"Run on and get ready for salon," Miss Antonia said. "You know I'll be telling my story shortly, and you don't want to miss that, do you?"

Velvet smiled. "No. Absolutely not. I can't wait to hear about your adventures."

"Then run."

Velvet hugged the woman and turned to leave, but stopped. The appearance of the box had forced a memory into the front of her mind. "Miss Antonia?"

"Yes?"

"Were you going to call my name the night of the shadow-quake? Was I next?"

Miss Antonia's expression didn't change. She simply shook her head briefly. Velvet stared at her a moment, and when it became clear that the woman had no intention of responding further, Velvet turned and trod out of the Salvage mother's office and down the stairs into the courtyard.

Nick's grinning face was the first she saw amid the crowd, handsome as always. That he liked her seemed like some kind of miracle.

"You guys are meant to be together." The voice came from her left, Luisa tugging at her sleeve.

"Shh!" Velvet chastised, and immediately felt awash in pesky guilt. "You know that can't happen."

Luisa shrugged. "Who says? No one needs to know. It's a stupid rule anyways."

Velvet glanced across the space and found Nick searching her out in the crowd. When their eyes met, his face lit up and he gave a little wave.

"See?" Luisa said.

"He's just horny."

"Well, yeah," Luisa said, and shrugged. "But that's just basic boy science. Two boobs plus one snootch equals boner. But there's something else, too. It's the way he looks at you when you don't even notice. Even Logan's said something about it, and he never picks up on anything that's not about bashing skulls."

This was what it was always like with Luisa.

"Did you see him in the antechamber of the Shattered Hall?" Luisa asked.

Of course she had.

"He glows like no one else I've ever seen," Luisa added.

Velvet nodded.

"And in all the right places," Luisa said saucily.

She was right on the money. Nick seemed to be perfect. And now there he was, smiling and chatting with Logan and . . . Isadora.

Isadora!

Velvet rushed forward into the crowd, rudely pushing people to the side to get at the girl who was clearly flirting with Nick, batting her eyes and clutching her fist to her chest in a totally unsubtle attempt to draw attention to her abnormally large cleavage. She and that evil mother of hers had undoubtedly uncovered a cache of push-up bras in some warehouse somewhere, because those breasts were altogether wrong.

Weapons-grade boobage.

As Luisa sat down at their table, she sneered at Isadora.

"Isadora?" Velvet said, stumbling the last few feet to plant herself directly between Nick and the other girl.

"Hello, Velvet. So good of you to join us," Isadora said with a brilliant grin. Her teeth even sparkled.

Velvet wanted to knock them out and watch them tinkle to the ground like a broken strand of pearls. If only she could scream and pounce on the monster without anyone noticing, or thinking her completely insane. Instead, she just balled up her fists and nodded as pleasantly as she could, though it probably appeared she was barely choking down some horrible food at a family dinner just to be polite, something nasty like gefilte fish.

"It was nice of you to invite Isadora to sit with us," Nick said, eyeing Velvet skeptically.

She shrugged, not really caring to make a scene just then. "Heh. What can I say, I'm a people pleaser."

Luisa spat with laughter and even slapped the table.

Logan followed suit, and before long they were all laughing. Even Velvet, though her chuckles were forced and completely fake. She wasn't certain she could keep it up long. The more she looked at Isadora, with her high-fashion dress tight against her body like a sausage casing, the more she wanted to punch her. Luckily, the gaslight dimmed and the stage curtain opened to reveal Miss Antonia beaming uncharacteristically.

"Welcome to salon, ladies and gentleman!" she shouted, and the crowd hushed to a barely audible whisper in response. "We've quite the spectacle for your consumption this evening, including the marvelous and harrowing adventures of . . . well . . . me!"

The crowd broke into wild applause and whistles of approval.

"Do any of you remember the story of the psychic in the early 1900s whose séances were known far and wide for their horrifyingly realistic finales?"

Velvet had no clue what she was talking about, but Isadora nodded, of course. She was one of the few in the crowd who did. Though Velvet suspected the girl knew nothing.

"Well, it was said," Miss Antonia continued, "that he channeled the spirits of the dearly departed. And when they were through using him as a vessel, they became solid and spewed from his every orifice in a milky translucent cloud of gas that all present could see."

There was a waller in the audience. No one had seen such a thing, and few had even heard of it. Velvet certainly hadn't. In all her days of body thieving and breaking up sham séances, there'd never been any indication that the laymen had ever witnessed her presence, and she didn't recall ever seeing a soul conjured in such a way.

Nick leaned over and whispered, "Have you ever had gas at a séance?"

He was such a dork. But despite Velvet's decidedly highbrow sense of humor, she couldn't contain a giggle, and elbowed him in the ribs. "Stop it. You're going to get us in trouble."

He shook in silent laughter next to her, his leg quivering

against hers. The sensation rippled through her, and she couldn't help but leave her leg right where it was.

"Well, it was long believed that this medium was, in fact, legitimately gifted and that no one before him, nor since, had such an ability," Miss Antonia continued. "That was not the case, however. In the summer of 1952, I was called to a Salvage operation in the small coastal town of Newport, Oregon. Shadowquakes weren't nearly as violent in those days, and this one barely registered as an inky smudge obscuring the passing sparkle of souls above us. The station agent warned us, however, that there was something different about this disturbance, some undercurrent of evil that seemed to link directly between the lands of the living and the dead. Our team's body thief's name was Aloysius Clay."

There was a familiar darkness in Miss Antonia's eyes as she spoke the name, a tension to her jaw that Velvet suspected only she'd picked up on.

"He was a bright young man in the prime of his experience. He led us through the cracks to a string of beachside cabins called the Oasis Motel. It was rainy and clearly the off-season, as the streets were predominantly empty, except for several cars scattered around this one particular cabin, a gray clapboard box with a single window obscured by thick curtains. I remained ethereal on this particular mission, as the nearest dead were several miles inland and Clay reassured us he'd be able to handle the situation with little trouble. The motel clerk was his target, and he made short work of securing the use of the elderly man's body. If only he'd found someone with more strength."

Her words were ominous; her tone suggested that this story was not going to end well. Velvet scooted in closer to Nick, drawing Isadora's foul gaze. She reveled in it, making a point to rest her head on the boy's shoulder in a pointedly affable, totally non-girlfriendy kind of way. The other girl scowled and whipped her head back toward the stage.

"Clay rapped on the door to the cabin, but there was no response. Using the clerk's keys, we entered and found the twin beds disassembled and propped against the wall. The lone table from the room had been moved to its center and was surrounded by several stunned men and women. Farthest from our vantage, a young woman, twenty-five years old perhaps, tossed her head back and belched a clammy fog from her mouth. It curled and glugged into the air, syrupy and sickening. One of the women in attendance fainted, falling forward onto the table with a bang."

Velvet noticed that Logan was on the edge of his seat, mouth wide open, probably still hungover. Luisa grimaced as the Salvage mother continued her tale.

"Jerry, one of our poltergeists, sprang across the space and attempted to tackle the girl. She did appear to be possessed, after all, and the cloud of pearlescent gas was still issuing from inside her. What happened next marked the end of my tenure as an official undertaker, stripped down to the bone my will to protect purgatory. Jerry did not tumble out of the back of this girl but rather howled in pain from inside her and churned out of her mouth, transformed into what we now understand to be authentic ectoplasm. His cries of pain were excruciating."

Logan clamped his hands to his mouth.

"Clay rushed forward, gathering all the strength he could muster from the withered man's frame, and struck the girl. She rose from her seat, hands still clasped to the men at her right and left.

"She bellowed, 'Die in this mortal coil, unclean spirit.'

"And the cloud dissipated, her eyes cleared up, and she sat there looking around, bewildered and confused. Later, Clay questioned the girl, and she told him that she didn't remember a thing, that she didn't even live in Newport but in Salem. How she got to be in the Oasis Motel surrounded by these people, with the death of our poltergeist Jerry on her hands, remains a mystery."

Miss Antonia leaned forward and held up one excruciatingly long finger as a warning. "But there are theories that this girl was an instrument of some unidentified spirit acting from purgatory through her slight frame to disrupt our Salvage team. And disrupt our team, it did. Jerry was gone, Clay disappeared shortly thereafter and was never seen again near the dormitories, and our second poltergeist transferred to another quarter. As you can see, I stayed, but in a different capacity entirely."

Why is she telling this particular story now? Velvet wondered. Did she suspect that the revolution and Aloysius Clay had access to the kind of horrific power that had killed Jerry?

Velvet raised her hand.

Miss Antonia scanned the crowd with tortured eyes. Storytelling might be sustenance for some, but it certainly didn't work that way for this storyteller. Her eyes brightened slightly when she lit on Velvet waving madly. "Yes, child?"

"Is there any indication that the events of that night might be happening again?"

Miss Antonia shook her head. "No one knows for certain. There've been instances of Salvage teams arriving late at the locus of a disturbance and finding nothing but bewildered humans with no memory of anything happening at all."

"Yes," Velvet said, "but couldn't those have been . . ." She hesitated to say it aloud.

The crowd around her gawked, wide-eyed and clearly disturbed by the Salvage mother's story.

"Go on," she said. "In light of the revolutionaries popping up everywhere, it's important that we discuss these things openly."

"Couldn't those people have simply been the targets of rogue body thieves, who dispossessed them prior to the team's arrival?"

The audience turned in unison toward Miss Antonia. The woman had no response. But Velvet could think only of that horrible creature lounging in the bowels of the Cellar, of its struggle to keep Madame Despot in its grasp and Nick in his crystal cell. And for what purpose? For nothing more than to create shadowquakes? To disrupt the fabric of purgatory? None of it made sense. And what about this ectoplasm stuff? Surely that wasn't real. Some parlor trick to hide Jerry's escape into the world, perhaps. The alternative—that Jerry had been processed as though the medium's body were no more than a ghost blender—was too horrible. Velvet shuddered at the thought. But if it was real, then what had torn apart Miss Antonia's team?

What had happened to Jerry?

What had made Clay run away and get involved with the revolution?

Velvet looked around the room and noticed Isadora glaring at her intently, not with her regular pious judgment but with something else. Fear lurked in the soft glow of her eyes.

They sat and listened to one of the singers accompanying a new record that had been swiped on a recent Collection run. It reminded Velvet of the disco her mother used to sing and dance to while doing the dishes. Velvet even used to join in—when she was younger, of course—her mother twirling her around and bumping her with her hip. Those were good times, but she rarely called upon the memories for comfort. It was better not to. Sadness could take hold of you in purgatory like nowhere else. She saw it all the time, people sobbing on the railcar, on benches, even within the dorms. She'd been awakened by the tortured cries of someone who couldn't leave the memories well enough alone. It's as though souls forget that there is an afterlife and they're living it, which means that those who have been left behind will eventually be in purgatory themselves, or, hopefully, somewhere less gritty and crowded.

Nick stood up beside her and wandered into the crowd. Her eyes followed him as he slipped up the stairs and out of sight.

With Nick gone, her focus returned to Isadora.

Isadora reached across and patted Velvet's hand. Her touch sent shivers up Velvet's spine, shivers that threatened to spike through her head. She slapped the girl's hand away.

"Oh, so infantile," Isadora hissed. "Clearly you're intimidated by my looks and ability to snatch your man right out from under you. Because, really, what do you have to offer? That sour expression? Terrible hair? You could benefit from an actual personality, Velv. It'd counteract all *this*." She swept her hand around Velvet's general vicinity.

Velvet tried to calm herself, but the girl leaned in farther and really put her foot in it.

"I wouldn't be surprised if you were a revolutionary, like everyone's been saying," she hissed into Velvet's ear. "Creeping around like you do."

Without thinking how it'd look to the gathered crowd, Velvet clenched her fist and drove it straight into Isadora's jaw.

There wasn't a crack, as there would have been had living flesh and bone connected, but all the same, Isadora dropped off her stool and thudded against the stone pavers like a burlap bag full of flour. The powder coating her skin puffed away from her in tiny mushroom clouds, and she even coughed up a wad of sparks that bounced around on the bodice of her far-too-dressy dress.

Velvet expected the girl to get up, return the punch, and turn the altercation into one huge brawl, but instead, Isadora just lay there, her expression wounded and pitiful. The girl sought out the help of the strangers around her, reaching for them to help her to her feet, playing the victim for all it was worth. Velvet turned to Luisa for support.

"Jeez, Velvet. Harsh" was all the little girl had to offer.

Velvet turned toward the staircase, but Nick hadn't returned. Nor was Miss Antonia anywhere to be seen. The rest of the dorm tenants were glowering at her now, shaking their heads in disapproval. Velvet felt the nerves exploding in her cheeks, across her chest, the humiliation of being seen as the brute in the situation setting in and finding a home.

When she peered over the table to see Isadora explaining the horror of the attack to a miraculously reappeared Miss Antonia, Velvet nearly exploded. She ran through the crowd to the breezeway and out into the streets.

Chapter 21

Velvet needed to hit something.

To break. To destroy.

To kill.

When she broke out of the Retrieval dorm it was at a full run, boots pounding the cobblestone in blunt echoing clops. Scissoring through groups of people chattering and vendor carts rolling away for the night, Velvet rushed toward the only purpose that could effectively employ her anger.

Moments later, she burst out into the forest glen. A crunch of leaves nearby heralded a deer stunned by her presence. She kept going, her pace quickening toward the desolate farmhouse, itself a dark smear against the pastoral scenery. She blew through fencing and livestock before stepping foot on the gravel approach to the Simanski farm. And pressing forward, Velvet sprinted past the house quickly, then the van, rushing headlong into the small shed stinking with hate.

Bonesaw loomed over his victim from behind the chair. He'd set her chin and head in a horseshoe-shaped binding. A prong jutted downward from the device, ending in a loop attached to a belt strapped tightly about her chest. It looked like a tuning fork, and the girl's cheeks were indented so painfully that Velvet could swear she felt the memory of the thing biting into her own flesh. The tool's purpose was clear and sickening. The girl struggled to turn her head but couldn't. The binding prevented all but the most minor movement. The girl's eyes flinched and blinked painfully as she tried to see what her captor was doing.

You don't want to see, Velvet thought.

It was bad enough that Velvet could see the man arching in, the grater nearly scraping against the girl's ear, ready to abrade the cartilage down to hot bloody gristle. His doughy face was flushed. His eyes were mad with lust.

Velvet rushed to the workbench and began slapping her palms against the table. Knives and cleavers jumped and clattered together, and when she peered over her shoulder, Bonesaw had dropped his grater. It lay tilted and askew atop his big bare foot.

But it wasn't the lack of a weapon in his hand that made Velvet smile. It was the fear written across his face in a trio of Os—his gaping mouth, his wide eyes. She grabbed a paring knife and tossed it toward the door with enough force that it grabbed a hold in the wood about a foot above the floor, right between a pair of bare legs.

Velvet gasped as her eyes traveled quickly upward past the long satiny basketball shorts, the tank, to Nick's beautiful face, turned ugly in a shocked grimace.

"What the hell?" His eyes darted between Velvet, Bonesaw, and the man's terrified victim. "What the hell is going on here?"

She staggered backward, completely at a loss as to what to do . . . or to say. But when she shot a glance back at Simanski, just in time to see him recovering the grater from the floor and beginning to cross through the shed to check out the paring knife, she acted.

"Nick! You've got to follow my directions really closely. This man is a maniac. If you can possess him, even for a second, try it. I haven't been able to, and we've got to save this girl!"

Nick nodded and watched the man as he approached, lumbering over in his black rubber apron, which was slick with God knew what. Velvet watched as the boy bit his lip, steeled himself by puffing a short burst of air from his mouth and hopping a bit, and then lunged into Bonesaw.

The big man staggered, reached out, and braced his palm against the door. Nick was doing it, she thought. Velvet turned to the girl, and her heart sank as she saw the craziness invading Simanski's victim's face. There was no getting around that, though. Insanity had been Velvet's only escape from the shed.

She didn't waste another second. Velvet dove into the girl and quickly went to work shutting down her thoughts and ruminations—if nothing else, she could provide a little

341

vacation from the horror. As traumatized as the girl was, Velvet was easily able to tuck her into the little mind-box.

Velvet opened her eyes and looked out through a veil of tears.

A big blurry version of Bonesaw shambled about recklessly, bumping into things. His knives fell to the floor around his ankles, clanging noisily. He stumbled toward her, tripping and very nearly falling. She braced the girl's body as best she could as the man's bulky frame barreled into the chair. It tipped and, try as she might, Velvet couldn't shift the girl's center of gravity enough to right it.

She hovered there for the briefest of seconds. Dread filled her, and then a violent crash against the floor jarred her ghost loose from the body. Velvet hung half out of the girl. She twisted back to look at her and noticed the girl's face turning blue. The brace about her neck had caught on a gap between the floorboards and forced her windpipe closed.

The girl gagged. Spittle flew from her lips and drizzled down her cheek.

Velvet wriggled away, flipped onto her butt, and focused on the legs of the chair. She kicked upward and out, over and over, until her foot caught against the wood and the whole thing jumped, chair, girl, ropes, and most important, the choking brace. The bar dislodged from the crack in the floor, and the girl fell over onto her side, gasping for air.

"Have you got him?" Velvet screamed as she saw Bonesaw settle and still himself next to the worktable.

But when Simanski turned around, he held a knife in his fist and his face was red with determination; his eyes were black and soulless. Where was Nick?

Velvet scrambled to climb back into the girl before the knife started plunging into her. She'd take the girl's pain. She owed her that much. But he was coming fast. So fast.

By the time Velvet sank into the girl, working the possession as rapidly as she knew how, Velvet could feel the stainless steel blade pressing against her skin. Moving slowly, purposefully.

Sawing.

"You bastard!" she screamed.

Bonesaw's hands were on the girl then, hefting her upward until the chair was upright.

Velvet closed her eyes. The man's breath was hot on her face.

"Don't," she whispered, and felt the slow hot trickle of blood drawing a line around the girl's wrist. He was cutting her now.

But she didn't feel it. The only pressure she could feel from the depths of the body were the slowly loosening bonds around her chest. The brace falling away.

"Nick!" Her eyes snapped open, and the killer's eyes crinkled pleasantly, a faint glow blistering around his pupils like a solar eclipse. "You did it!"

He nodded and slipped the knife as carefully as he could between the fishing line and the girl's right forearm. The thin plastic thread broke free, and she found that she was grinning, giddy for Nick's success, for the girl's impending freedom.

For the first time, Velvet smiled broadly at her killer out of happiness rather than spite. But what she saw there made her heart skip a beat. Nick was slipping away. The man's eyes were going from a safe glow to dead black and as dark as murder. He slashed the knife at her brutally, and Velvet held out the girl's hand to defend her face.

She didn't realize Bonesaw had succeeded until a spurt of blood showered the dry floorboards. Velvet fell from the chair onto the girl's knees, clutching the wounded hand to her chest, grasping the rapidly soaking shirt like a makeshift bandage. Her ankles were still connected to the chair by taut rubber tubing.

The man growled and squatted down next to her, teeth bared and eyes narrowed in suspicion. "What's going on, girl? You got somethin' special in you?"

Velvet's eyes flew open wide. *How can he know I'm inside the girl?* she wondered. He couldn't.

Behind him, Nick was rushing forward, falling into a crouch and then straight into the killer's back. For a second, Velvet thought she saw the struggle at play. Bonesaw's eyes flashing with light, and then he was biting his lip in the same way Nick did when he was thinking. The knife in his hand turned back toward himself.

Velvet panted, licked at the girl's lips in violent anticipation. *Make it brutal,* she pleaded without speaking.

Make it worth it!

Nick plunged the knife into the man's leg hilt-deep and cried out from the pain. His ghost stumbled forward, breaking free from his Bonesaw suit and landing next to her on the floor.

"Ugh!" The man lurched a bit, snatching the knife from the wound in his leg and falling to the floor, moaning. As he did, Nick shot upright.

Velvet wasted no time stripping the rest of the restraints from her ankles and was nearly halfway to the door when the man reached out and snatched her ankle, drawing her body to him. She swung around him, climbing atop him rather than pulling away, figuring he wouldn't expect it.

Another thing he wasn't expecting was her index finger widening the hole in his leg, scratching at the bone, twisting the sinew. Bonesaw screamed, a loud mewling sound that rolled over Velvet's borrowed flesh.

She heard another sound and realized it was laughter.

Her own, projected through the girl.

"Damn," she heard Nick say, and she pulled herself off Simanski.

He lay beneath her, eyes closed, his breathing shallow.

Velvet looked up at Nick. His mouth hung open, and he wiped it with the back of his hand. "Is he dead?"

Velvet shook her head. "Still breathing."

Standing up, she surveyed the scene. The man's body was twisted in the center of a puddle of blood that pooled around the guy like ink draining from a broken pen. His rubber apron was bunched up around his waist like a tire, and the wound gurgled from a spot high up on the inside of his thigh.

Velvet felt like she should know why there was so much blood from such a little cut, but it was Nick who answered the question.

"Femoral artery," he said somberly. "I wasn't aiming for it. I promise I wasn't."

Bonesaw spat, and his eyes crept open, training on Velvet, and he started screaming.

She couldn't take another moment in the same room with him, and the farther Velvet could take the girl's body, the better. She turned, threw open the door, and bolted, Nick breezing along behind her.

They ran not back toward the road but around to the back of the shed. Velvet expected Simanski to come tearing around the opposite side and head them off at the pass, but he was still screaming from inside. Cursing her. No. Not her.

Cursing the girl.

Velvet hefted her body onto the back fence and tossed herself over, never breaking speed. A path zigzagged through the forest and on the other side let out into a children's playground, thick with mulch to pad the inevitable fall from jungle gyms or to cushion heroic leaps from the swing set, her personal favorite activity when she was a kid.

"Help!" Velvet screamed.

A pair of mothers in designer tracksuits sprang to attention from a nearby bench, and upon seeing the girl covered with blood—so much blood—began shouting insanely. One grabbed her cell phone and called 911, and the other drew Velvet up into a hug.

"Oh, my God. What happened? What happened?" The woman's eyes pored over the cuts on the girl's arms, and she brushed the girl's greasy hair away from her face.

Velvet spoke a single word and pointed toward the path to the shed. "Bonesaw!"

And then she fell out of the girl and onto her back, exhausted.

Nick ran up amid the clamor of the two women caring

346

for the teenager and gathering their own children. He kept swiveling back toward the forest, an expression of dire emergency on his face, as though he were sure that Bonesaw was bound to come barreling toward them, fully prepared to kill both the girl and her rescuers, but he didn't come. Nick crouched down onto his knees, and Velvet curled close to him, resting her head in his lap. She was crying, but the tears weren't wet; they were clear and dropped to the ground like pearls.

"Are you all right, Velvet? What can I do?" He wiped the tears from her eyes as she shook her head.

There was nothing he could do. Nothing anyone could do.

Nick lowered his head to hers and planted soft kisses on each eye.

"It'll be all right. Everything will be fine."

It was later, as Nick supported a sobbing Velvet in his arms and led her back down the path, giving the psycho's property a wide berth, that she realized that she was crying out of relief, but now there was a new issue.

Nick knew.

And not only did he know that Velvet was totally guilty of haunting; now, in effect, so was he. And it was all her fault.

"You don't think I'm horrible, do you?" Velvet asked, the words muffled in his sleeve.

Nick reached down and pressed his palm against her cheek, turning her toward him. "Never. You're wonderful. The most amazing thing that's ever happened to me."

"You can't tell, Nick. You shouldn't have followed me."

He shook off her words. "I'm glad I did, and I won't tell a soul unless you want me to. Not a soul. Ever."

They held each other for a while, Nick's back pressed against the dead tree with the lightning-blackened crack, and Velvet against him. His breathing was soft and shallow against her face. He stroked her hair and cradled the back of her neck as he gazed into her eyes.

"We have a secret. It bonds us." He nodded, suggesting she should agree.

And she did. They settled onto the squishy loam of the glen floor.

"You want to tell me what was going on back there?"

Velvet's brow furrowed, and she looked away. "It's what you think it is."

"Haunting?"

"Yes, but . . ." She jerked away from him. "I didn't mean for it to go on like this. It's just that he's such a monster and he kept picking up new girls. I couldn't let him. It wasn't right."

Nick finished her thought, "No matter what the consequences."

She slunk back into his arms. "No matter what."

They lay like that for a few moments, a pair of gelatinous ethereal creatures, barely visible except for the shimmer of dew that caught on their flesh for brief moments, before drifting through them and settling on the clumps of dry pine needles carpeting the glen.

Velvet felt herself drifting away, losing herself, slipping through time. Bonesaw's blood had been so black. It pooled and pooled, and he screamed and screamed.

Still alive.

She shot up then from the waking dream, startled, and crawled toward the gap in the trees. Nick chased after her, catching her around the waist.

"I have to go back. I've got to finish this. I can't go on. Not now that you're involved. Now that I've sentenced you to the same fate as me. The lies. There are so many to keep track of. I'll be caught eventually. And now . . . you." Velvet rolled onto her back, and Nick crawled across her until their eyes met.

"What you've done is right. No matter what the rules of purgatory are. And if saving that girl's life means that neither of us ever get to dim and move on to heaven or hell or wherever, then I'm fine with that. There's something here." Nick reached up and placed his hand over his heart, and then gestured toward Velvet's chest. She reached up and gently took his wrist, drawing his palm close to her breast.

"And here," she agreed. "It's true. I know it."

"So you understand that it doesn't matter to me if they find out. As long as I'm here. With you."

Velvet sighed and started to turn her head, to resist.

"Shh," Nick whispered, and pressed his lips to hers, softly.

Velvet moaned quietly.

Nick studied her face. She smiled for him.

"Well. That's a welcome change."

"The kiss?" she asked.

"The intent and the smile. You should do it more often."

She poked him in the ribs, and despite the fact that they were both technically ghosts and shouldn't have had any access to physical sensation at all, somehow the two of them were connected. Attached by something bigger than them, bigger than purgatory, and much bigger than the dark secret they shared.

"What are you going to do if I fall in love with you, Nick?" she asked.

Nick nodded slowly, eyes intent on the question. "I don't know. That sounds kind of dangerous."

"Good answer."

Chapter 22

Velvet pushed herself up from the rubble beneath her. Her ankle was twisted between the tangle of Nick's legs. All around them purgatory was crumbling, stones dropping free from mortar shaken back into powder. She heard screams in the distance, the warbling moans of the injured, and couldn't help but think that what they'd just done was completely to blame.

Her second thought was that her first impression was ridiculous.

"Shadowquake!" she shouted, pounding against Nick to get moving.

She reached for a mound of stones that rose a bit taller than the others and dug out the crate where she'd left her clothes. She pulled them on recklessly, inside out, torn, the boots finding the correct foot by sheer chance.

"Hurry up, Nick!"

He scrambled up next to her and slipped his hand into hers.

"Follow the walls when we get out to the street. There'll be stuff falling everywhere," she said, and pulled him after her.

They were nearly past the Paper Aviary when a building up ahead exploded into a cloud of dust. The gaslights shot flames into the air like Roman candles.

"I guess we're not going that way," Nick quipped, and pulled her in the opposite direction, across the street and around the block.

Souls trying to get to the safety of the station crowded the nearby funicular platform, and Velvet searched the faces for Logan and Luisa, but they weren't there, or if they were, they were obscured in the stampede of frightened denizens, most of whom had abandoned hope for a railcar and were shakily traversing the tracks in droves.

"Look at that!" Nick yelled.

In the distance, one of the spires of the cathedral cracked apart and plummeted to the square below, crushing the gaslights and bringing down their hoses. The souls rushing into the church for some chance at safety screamed and scattered.

Velvet sped off toward the next street and at the intersection was relieved to see the dorm at the far end still standing, its columns unmarred by cracks. The front door was open, but plastered there like a threat were hundreds of flyers for the revolution. But these were different from before. These read:

The Departure Is Now.

Velvet tore one from the door and stumbled across the shaking breezeway and into the courtyard, Nick hot on her heels. What she found inside chilled her to the bone.

One of the gaslights had broken open, and a fire blazed up the interior wall. Beyond that, a group of souls gathered around the foot of the staircase. A shower of pebbles created a haze in the air, and as Velvet and Nick broke through the crowd, Velvet saw why.

The frieze from above them had fallen and crushed someone, the impact diminishing the victim to ash. Velvet screamed. She dropped to the floor next to the shadowy remnants. Luisa crawled in beside her.

"It's Miss Antonia," the little girl said softly.

A low moan loosed from Velvet's throat. Miss Antonia was gone. Velvet couldn't imagine it.

"She asked for you in the end," the little girl said, her face a study in sorrow.

Velvet shook her head, not understanding. "For me? Why? What did she say?"

"That you'll fix all this."

Velvet gasped and stared at what was left of the Salvage mother's face, a crumbling mask of curled ash, like the flaking of aged paint peeling away from garden statuary. The pieces dropped away and caught on the wind that lapped the inside of the courtyard like waves.

"What did you mean, Miss Antonia?" Velvet murmured. She felt strong hands on her shoulders and knew they belonged to Nick. She sensed his warm feelings and somehow knew that everything would be all right. A shadow crossed over the crowd, and she looked up to find Logan standing there, a shallow smile playing across his lips.

"The shadowquake didn't get her, Velvet. She dimmed. It was her time, and she was fine with it." For some reason, Velvet had found, little kids were much more accepting of the whole dimming thing than she was. And despite the bravery on Logan's face, Velvet wanted to scream.

Nearby, another chunk of the frieze fell and shattered into a pile of rock and pebbles that scattered across the court-yard, popping against the uneven pavers like popcorn.

It was almost too much to take.

What had just happened with Bonesaw, the secret she'd been keeping about haunting, the revolutionaries, the shadowquake, the revelation of Nick's feelings—hell, her own feelings about him. The thoughts wound around her brain like searing-hot barbed wire. And now this—Miss Antonia's death. She sighed, closed her eyes, and tried to make sense of it all.

She refused to believe that her brief trips to hinder Bonesaw had caused the current catastrophe. The level of the disturbance and her intent didn't even compare to killing a teenage boy and trapping his soul in a crystal ball. So she planned on shelving that theory in the *not* category.

Velvet knelt beside Miss Antonia's ashes, thrust her hand inside, and drew a fistful back. She smeared it across her face like a warrior's stripe. When she glanced back at the pile, she caught sight of something bright glinting in the mound. She reached in and pulled out a tiny, familiar red key. Velvet recognized it immediately.

It was the same as the one Manny had had hidden in her drawer.

Velvet casually palmed it, not wanting to start a conversation or draw any attention to the item. She wasn't sure what it meant, whether the women were in some sort of secret club. She just didn't know.

Nick smiled empathetically. He squeezed her shoulder and pressed in close to her ear. "Time for you to do what you do best."

Velvet glanced to her right and left. Logan stood stoically amid the dark clouds of gas swirling about them from the whipping broken hoses that fed the lights. Luisa gave her a quick grin and a thumbs-up. And from the breezeway another figure stumbled into the courtyard.

Kipper.

He held his head up high and strode toward them.

"You're gonna need all the help you can get," he offered, his face resolved.

"Thanks, Kipper," she said. "I'm definitely taking you up on that."

She stood and trod to the center of the courtyard. A fire lapped up the wall that used to be covered in posters of exotic travel destinations and musical acts. Now curled and charred to ash, the posters fell in piles like snowdrifts against the walls. But the flames were subsiding. The building, constructed primarily of stone, didn't lend itself to feeding the fire much, and soon the blaze would be out. Above her, from the balconies, she heard the whimpering and cries of the tenants. "Mrs. Lawrence!"

The Collector mother popped up from a crouch by the stage.

"You'll have to take charge of both dorms," Velvet said. "Make sure our people are safe, and if it looks like the building can't take much more, evacuate them to the funicular track."

Mrs. Lawrence nodded and ran toward the stairs. "Clear the floors!" she called out.

Velvet summoned her team around her.

"We're going up to the station. Manny will know what to do. Though I suspect this operation is going to be our hardest yet." She glanced at Nick.

His expression was grim. "Am I really prepared for this?" he asked. "Haven't really had a ton of training, have I?"

Kipper stepped in next to him and addressed Velvet. "I'll watch out for him."

Velvet knew that if anyone could protect her team, Kipper could. But there was something there, a struggle in the tension of his jaw, in the tight balls of his fists. He had been very close to Miss Antonia. She knew he'd be taking it hard, but with Kipper, for all his macho posturing, you never could tell when he'd break down and let his emotions flood out. The last thing she needed was another pile of ash right then. She cocked her head in his direction and asked, "Was the mission to Vermillion successful?"

He shook his head and looked away. "Nothing."

"Damn." Velvet had been certain he would find a lead to Clay. She straightened. "Well, then, if we could just catch some luck and find the railcars in working order," she said, leading the team toward the breezeway. "That's probably asking too much."

Logan sped past and into the street. The black clouds were finally descending into the streets, signaling the coming of the fiercest quakes. Visibility was about to become impossible.

Velvet turned to Luisa and grabbed her hand. She slipped it into the back of her waistband and balled it up. "Tight," she ordered, and then raised her fist to the others. "Tight, like this. Link up. We've got a long hike, I'm afraid."

They were just barely connected, a string of fragile pearls amid the sharp edges and falling buildings. All around them walls crumbled and metal screamed as it bent and gave way to the weight. The ground shook and the quintet stumbled and sidestepped on their trek to the ramp at the far end of the block.

Velvet led them up and over the curb and onto the tracks. She stooped, gripping the tracks as she had done only a day ago, and felt nothing. Nothing besides the tremors they'd felt everywhere else. No movement.

The funicular wasn't engaged. It was broken. Velvet's eyes turned skyward, toward the monolithic mountain and the station and the miles of track between them.

She screamed in frustration and stood up.

"Let's go!" she called back to her team, eyes lingering on Nick's solid frame bringing up the rear. Velvet thought she saw Kipper notice the exchange. He stood just beyond Nick, and she could see a question forming in his eyes, burning there like coals. Velvet wondered if he'd be the one to tell, out of jealousy or whatever. She definitely didn't have time for the argument, though.

They traveled close to the rails, trying to keep a steady pace as the tracks began to slope upward toward the great mountain of the station. It wasn't long before they found themselves crammed into a crowd of refugees, all with the same idea, heading for safety. The tracks were probably tight with the thousands of residents of the Latin Quarter all the way to the tunnels, a veritable logjam. The darkness had descended, and as they squeezed along to the track wall, pushing past the throngs of moaning, frantic souls, Velvet felt Luisa's small hand slip from the waistband of her pants.

She spun toward the girl. A woman, head wrapped in a scarf and as dull as the last moment of dusk, slipped into the girl's place. Velvet pushed her aside, perhaps too brutally, and to no avail—behind her was a little boy, face pressed against the hip of a middle-aged man in a long wool overcoat. He glowered at Velvet and clutched the boy even closer to his side.

"Luisa!" Velvet screamed, and vaulted out of the canal of tracks, out of the shuffling herds of souls and up onto the street level.

To her right, Nick and Kipper were dragging an exhausted and limp Logan from the clamor. They fell back onto the cobblestone. Nick was checking the boy for wounds with such intensity, you'd think he were the boy's father.

"Where's Luisa?" she shouted in Nick's direction.

Nick shook his head, and Logan, who'd been holding on

to his sister, was wild-eyed with horror. "I lost her. Couldn't hang on."

As they talked, the crowd continued sluicing on toward the station. The street sat on a shelf above a deep groove where the railcars traveled, and Velvet crawled on her hands and knees up to the edge. She reached into the crowd, pushing shoulders away, trying to get a peak between the refugees.

"Luisa! Have you seen a little girl?" Velvet yelled into their faces, terrified that the Salvage team would have to go on without her favorite poltergeist. Her heart pounded. Her skin glowed as hot as the brightest gaslight.

Then Nick was by her side, then Kipper. Their horror, their fear, cut through the ash in shimmering spikes from their panicked faces. The sheer passion of their conviction shone through the black ooze of the shadowquake, piercing it like columns of sunlight shining into a dark basement, or the first rays of morning shining into the tiny windowpane of a farmhouse shed—Velvet shook off the memory.

The sight of the Salvage team aura stopped the herd of souls in their tracks, and a hush fell over them, screams dying, replaced by a sudden calm.

Velvet took advantage of the break. "Luisa!" she screamed at the top of her lungs.

"Here!" a thin voice called out.

Ahead, near the edge of their glow, Luisa's face poked up from the heads around her. She was climbing atop a man in a baseball cap.

Velvet rushed forward, relief swelling inside her, and

motioned for the man, whose pleasant face nodded in her direction. He knew what she wanted without being asked. It was like they were all connected in a common goal. He hoisted Luisa up, and using a couple of strangers' shoulders as stepping stones, she hopped across the crowd—shouting "Sorry"—onto the curb, and into Velvet's arms. She glanced back in the man's direction to thank him, but the souls had already rushed forward.

"This isn't working," Velvet said, and sighed.

"We're going to have to go up another way," Kipper said, suddenly at her side.

"I agree." Nick's hand slipped around Velvet's waist protectively.

"No," she whispered, and shook it off. "Not now." She glanced toward Kipper, who thankfully was scanning the crowd instead of playing hall monitor.

The street went only so far before it gave way to a nearly impassible rocky cliff face. Velvet knew that, on even the most placid of days, the climb would be treacherous, but in the midst of a massive shadowquake the climb would be impossible. Her head swam with the sounds of the buildings collapsing, the screams. The dorms were in danger. There had to be a way.

"What about the alley?" Nick suggested.

"The alley?" She shook her head, not really comprehending.

"Where we just came from."

She pulled him close and whispered, "Are you suggesting that we reveal the secret?"

He shook his head and gave her a grin that clearly implied

she was being an idiot. "Of course not, just the crack. We found it. No big deal."

The idea was brilliant, but it would involve a lie and it would invite tons of questions. Velvet rankled, but as she watched the mass of refugees tumble over each other to climb to the station's safety, she couldn't think of any other way. And the pull-focus would be the same they used each time they returned from purgatory. Easy.

"Follow me!" she shouted.

Velvet gestured for the team to link up again, and she led them back toward the heart of the Latin Quarter, first balancing on the thin curb above the funicular tracks and then dropping down into the gap, once the crowds thinned to only a few stragglers. The inky clouds that accompanied the shadowquakes became denser, pooling around the roofs of buildings and drizzling over the sides in wiggling streaks. As they reached the mouth of the alley, Velvet knew they'd made a mistake.

A solid shadowy mass blocked the street on the opposite side of the Paper Aviary, so large that even as she noticed the threat, it filled in behind them, trapping them. She peered into the slender alley and the total blackness, but that didn't bother her as much as the noise issuing from its depths, rhythmic and wet.

*Thwap*ping thuds.

Dripping, dreadful splats.

Velvet felt a grim shiver travel the length of her spine and settle in her head like a cramp. Beside her, Luisa gasped and Logan took a step backward. Kipper bit his lip, and Nick simply looked around for the source.

He'd see them soon enough, Velvet thought, and pressed into the alley a bit—far enough to see the blurry outlines of tentacles stretched down the sides of the walls, lapping at the Salvage team like tongues reaching for that last little taste of a delicacy. The tentacles licked at the stone, curling back and slapping, searching for unwilling souls to broadcast their horror shows into.

Velvet scrambled to come up with some other solution, an alternative that would take them far away from this place. But there wasn't one. She glanced at her team, clearly in the midst of similar thoughts.

"There's no choice," Nick said.

Velvet shuddered. She said grimly, "This isn't going to be easy, but at the end of this alley, there's a crack in the wall."

Nick jumped in. "We found it earlier . . . by accident."

Kipper narrowed his eyes, scowling into the abyss. "You seriously want us to go in there? Do you hear those things?"

Velvet straightened. "No. You're right. Let's just wait here and watch the walls crumble. It's a nice night for it."

He shrugged, "All right, then."

Luisa and Logan wore steely determined expressions, as usual, which gave Velvet the boost she needed to get the ball rolling. "Link up, now!"

She slipped her hand into Nick's and nodded for him to grab Luisa, and so on back to Kipper. They crept forward like that, boots treading crookedly over the shaking rubble scattered across the ground. The unlevel surface made each step into danger even more unsettling.

The darkness didn't help, either.

About halfway to the secret crack, Velvet jerked to a halt. Her team crashed into each other, crumpling up at her back like a squashed tin can. The alley had gone as silent as a grave.

"What's going—" Nick started.

"Shh!" Velvet held up her hand in the universal shut-the-hell-up sign just as a whisper sliced through the air past her cheek. In that next second, the screams began, and, still linked, the entire chain of them were jerked backward and up. Her hand tore from Nick's amid the jostling, and she turned, snatching and pulling him down into a low crouch.

The screams belonged to Logan. Joined a moment later by Luisa's horrified cries.

Velvet had to squint to see what was going on. The inky shadows turned everything into dull outlines. Gray against gray. Barely there.

But what she could make out horrified her.

A figure floated above them, arms and legs dangling limply from its torso like the leads on a hot-air balloon. Kipper. The tentacle had him around the waist and was cinching his stomach until it was impossibly thin around the column of his spine. Logan leapt and snatched at Kipper's hands, futilely swiping the air beneath them, while Luisa merely shook her head, her hand clasped over her mouth and her eyes wide enough to glare spikes of light up at the scene.

All my fault, Velvet thought, and bolted upright. She should never have brought them down the alley. Especially not after seeing the shadow creatures.

The tentacle shifted and Kipper's body contorted, dipping

closer to them and then farther away and then back like a crank. As Kipper drew close, Velvet caught a glimpse of his face, waxy and slack around the cheeks and mouth. Images drifted across the glassy curves of his sightless eyes like the reflections of blackened clouds.

Velvet tried not to look at that, but rather back to the way his body dipped as the tentacle repositioned itself. There seemed to be a pattern emerging.

Lift. Lift.

Dip.

Although Velvet had never seen anyone try it, it occurred to her that she might be able to jar the boy loose if she timed it just right.

"Nick!" she yelled. "Basket your hands for me and give me a boost."

"What?" Nick climbed to his feet, shaking his head incredulously.

"Just do it and then lift when I say!"

The boy wove his fingers together and crouched. Velvet planted one boot solidly in his palms, and as the curling appendage brought Kipper up for the second time and began to sink, she shouted to Nick, "Heave!"

Velvet launched upward, caught Kipper's arm halfway between his wrist and his elbow, and climbed until she had a solid grip on the back of his neck.

Her fingers instantly felt a little numb. A chill seeped into her from Kipper's skin, and flickers of something big and lumbering blinked into the corner of her eye. Something coming to get her.

To tear her from Kipper's limp body and show her . . .

Things.

Velvet had seen enough horror to know she had to act quickly. She clutched Kipper tightly, and as the tentacle unfurled to its most tenuous grip, she bounced violently. She thrashed and grunted, and just as she thought it wouldn't work, the two of them fell through the air. Nick threw his arm around her waist, cushioning her fall, while Logan and Luisa did the best they could to buffer Kipper's significant weight.

He landed with a groan and his eyes fluttered open.

"Wha . . . ?" he moaned.

Totally out of it.

Velvet's gaze shot skyward. The tentacles stabbed deeper toward the floor of the alley, lapping at the walls angrily. She leaned over and slapped Kipper's cheek. Hard.

His eyelids snapped open and he glowered. "Why are you being such a devil bitch?"

Back to normal, she thought, and screamed, "We have to go! Now!"

Velvet scrambled over the debris, ankles buckling and hands outstretched in the darkness. Behind her, Nick pounded the gravel and loose paper bricks littering the alley, kicking rocks into the backs of her legs and shouting to the others behind him. It had to be just ahead. She braced herself for impact with the dead end. The last thing they needed was an unconscious leader.

But Velvet knew they were short on time. The shadowy tongues were dense toward the middle of the alley behind them, crowded tight and writhing, a black wall of horror. The tentacles would search each of them out if she didn't find the crack quickly. They weren't going to have time to discuss the details of a pull-focus, either.

"Meet up in the Shattered Hall, people!" she shouted.

Her hands slid over the vibrating stone before her, until her nails found the broken seam and began to glow, to draw her in. She couldn't risk slowing down to remove her clothes; modesty be damned—along with her awesome combat boots—they would just have to end up shredded. Luisa pressed in underneath her, her own fingers turning gaseous and long. She slipped away, followed by the rest until Velvet was left standing amid a pile of shredded fabric and leather.

She focused on the imagery and felt the familiar pull.

A moment later, Velvet landed in the Shattered Hall atop a tumble of limbs and bodies, her face smashed into the gritty floor.

"Ow!" she cried.

"Sorry," Nick said from somewhere beneath her.

"Sorry," someone else said, Luisa or Logan. It was hard to hear over the clambering of her team, poking about for clothes from the crates around the hall. Candlelight filled the room with such a warm glow, Velvet let it wash over her like a shower, let it wash away the inky darkness. Footfalls alerted Velvet to Manny's rapid approach, her shiny silver gown flapping about her legs.

"I knew you'd find a way to get here!" Manny said, leaning down to help Velvet to her feet. "You are brilliant."

Velvet ignored the compliment. The hows and whys of their arrival were best left in secret.

Manny glanced up and must have seen Kipper standing among the group.

"Perfect. I'm glad to see you, boy. We need to talk."

Velvet turned to see the big guy pulling on a pair of pants and handing some clothing to Nick.

"Don't bother," Velvet said, her hands draped across her privates casually. "We're not going to be here long enough for modesty."

Manny nodded a quick agreement. "But there's something I need to show you first."

The woman clipped off down the hall, followed closely by Kipper and the twins.

"Hurry up, Nick!" Velvet chided in her most official tone.

There was no sense in giving him any slack, especially in front of Manny. She'd be able to sniff out an office romance like a hound. It was sort of second nature to her, having been a pinup girl and sex symbol in her time.

"I'm comin'. I'm comin'," Nick said.

Manny led them to the gate and pointed out into the station. Souls drifted aimlessly, some brand-new and un-ashed wandering from the primary crack. The guides had left their stations. But that wasn't what Manny wanted them to see. It was the curved walls that ringed the atrium. A multitude of cracks rose from the station's cobblestone floor.

Velvet scanned them with a mixture of confusion and horror.

The cracks were everywhere. Even running across the floor like veins.

"Look at all of 'em," Logan said, a note of awe stretching the words into something ominous.

"I don't need to tell you what this means, do I?" There was uncharacteristic fear in Manny's voice.

Velvet met the woman's stern gaze and tried to remain as stoic and resolved as possible. Of course she knew what the cracks meant. If *she* had been able to find one and use it for her purposes, the Departurists wouldn't have any difficulty figuring out what to do.

"It's the revolution," Velvet said. "It's begun." Her memory flashed on the flyer she'd torn from the door of the Retrieval dorm.

The Departure Is Now. "It has begun." Manny reached out for Velvet's hand. "The expanding cracks are giving them more and more points to enter the daylight and to complete their heinous plans."

"And what are those plans?" Nick asked from behind her.

"Look around you, Nick. It's an invasion. The departure of which they speak is a full-scale invasion into the daylight. An exodus from purgatory."

It wasn't until then that Velvet noticed souls slipping away. Tendrils of their evaporating selves, dozens of smoky ribbons receded into the chasms, into the daylight.

It didn't take a criminologist to put together the pieces.

The revolutionaries wouldn't have any intention of floating freely as ghosts in the daylight. Why would they? They'd be merely whispers of themselves. That wasn't really living. Not when they could find a perfectly good person to inhabit and experience all the things life has to offer all over again, or things they missed out on.

"Body thieves," Velvet breathed angrily. "They'll possess the living!"

And saying it out loud felt like the answer to what she

hadn't been able to figure out until now. The revolutionaries' ultimate goal.

The banshee had been certain that it was going to happen. Rancho and Mr. Fassbinder, too. Velvet hadn't wanted to believe that souls would be so selfish as to think they deserved another shot at living, especially at the expense of someone who wasn't finished living their own life.

"It's got to be Clay," Kipper said. "He wasn't anywhere in Vermillion because he's here. Or he's already crossed over."

"So he wasn't there at all?" Velvet asked.

"No." Kipper shook his head. "My sources told me that he hadn't been there in some time. But the rumor was that he had never left the Latin Quarter."

Manny gasped. "You have to stop him," she said, leading them frantically back toward their departure crack. "If it is Aloysius Clay perpetrating this particular shadowquake and he's still powerful enough to rattle the station this way, then you've got your work cut out for you."

She pointed toward the long crack in the wall again and began to deliver the details for their crossing. "Neon chopsticks lifting hot pink noodles from a bright blue bowl. A sweaty single-paned window with the name Sal drawn onto it in a big greasy cursive. And a red flyer for the South Hadley Chamber of Commerce Haunted House Spectacular."

"Then we go. Now!" Velvet cried.

Always ready for a battle, Logan dove for the crack with a snarl. His body thinned and stretched out, slipping through with ease. Luisa was right behind him, followed in short order by Nick.

Manny gripped Velvet's arm and hissed, "Be careful. The darkest of evils is being committed to create what we're seeing here."

"Are you afraid?" Velvet asked.

The woman shook her head, the soft curls of her hair drifting from side to side about her powdered face. But Velvet could sense that something horrible waited for them on the other side. And for the first time, she sensed that they might not all make it back.

She might not make it back.

She thought of Nick and his soft lips, and the horror of the situation rocked through her. What if she made it back and Nick didn't?

Velvet dove for the crack without saying her final goodbyes to Kipper or the station agent.

Chapter 23

They stood in a parking lot. In front of them, a completely unremarkable strip mall, the sort you'd find in Anytown, America, stretched hundreds of feet in each direction. There was a nail salon and a sub shop, a check-cashing place, and what Velvet was looking for: a dive called the Quickie Teriyaki.

The neon sign fluttered in the same greasy window that framed the scribble of letters spelling out "Sal." The Halloween flyer was taped at an odd angle on the glass.

Velvet moved, instantly on task. A Closed sign hung on the door, and beyond the sweaty windows the restaurant was dark.

"There. It's coming from there," she said.

They each pivoted toward the place in turn. "Why there?" Nick asked. "It doesn't look any different from the Super Nail or Lucky Dry Cleaner. It's not even open."

"That's precisely why. It's closed," Velvet said. "Doesn't it seem like an awfully busy day for them to be closed?" She pointed at the people coming and going from the other shops.

Nick shrugged. "Point taken."

Logan passed them, his blue furry Grover feet shuffling along the pavement, and peered in the front window. "I don't see nothin' in there but dirty tables and people's half-eaten food. What a mess!"

Velvet perked up.

"See? What kind of a restaurant doesn't clean up before they close and closes on a busy day?" she asked. "Doesn't make a bit of sense."

"She's right," Luisa said.

Velvet passed through the front window, the others following close on her heels.

The inside of the Quickie Teriyaki was as Logan had described, as though the customers had simply disappeared. Forks stuck out from plates of kung pao chicken and spicy yakisoba, and flies congregated on a lonely California roll, nibbling away at the fake crab salad stuffed in its center. Velvet glanced to the table next to where Logan stood and noticed a steaming hot bowl of egg drop soup.

"Look at that." She pointed to the plastic spoon floating in the bowl's center. "It's still hot. Whatever happened was recent."

Velvet shot a glance over at the twins. "You two, do the rounds. Check the kitchen, the storeroom, see if there's a parking lot out back. Check inside the cabinets, even!"

Logan and Luisa padded across the room, their ghostly forms passing through tables, chairs, the counter, the back wall, and into, presumably, the kitchen.

"What about me?" Nick asked. "I don't smell a morgue around here. No graveyard. Do you? Don't I need a corpse or something?"

"I don't know," Velvet said, shaking her head. "It could be that you'll have to snatch up someone living. We don't have the time to search out dead bodies."

Nick flinched.

Velvet wanted to sock herself for being insensitive. The last time Nick had possessed a living person hadn't ended so well, depending on how you looked at the situation.

"You guys!" Logan popped into the pass-through from the kitchen. His blue mask seemed pale, as though the costume itself sensed his disquiet. "You're probably not going to need to go outside to find a body."

They scrambled toward the boy and into the kitchen space.

On the floor, amid fallen pots of broth, piles of sticky noodles, and unknown brown sauces, lay the corpses of the diners, their arms and legs akimbo, their bodies twisted and contorted, their eyes staring into some unknown vista.

"What happened to them?" Luisa knelt beside a blond woman, her pregnant belly protruding into the air. The girl straightened the woman's shirt around the mound. A trail of foam trickled down the woman's cheek from her open mouth.

"Poisoned?" Nick asked.

Luisa shook her head. "I don't know."

Velvet crouched down over an obese man with salt-and-pepper hair and a nose like a pale dill pickle. She pressed her ear close to his chest and listened.

"This one's heart is still beating."

"Maybe I should jump in?" Nick surmised. "See what's happening behind those eyelids."

Velvet sat up into a squat. It was just three bodies, but that would mean purgatory was still in for a whole lot of shadowquaking. Nick's had been a single death—one imprisoned soul was bad enough—and that quake had been nearly disastrous. Velvet glanced around her and didn't sense the presence of new souls, so none of the victims' ghosts were hanging around waiting for the light.

They must have been taken, she thought.

And there were no possessed dead or living bodies lurching toward them to pin this disruption on, either. Velvet had certainly expected to run into another possession, possibly even another banshee.

Or worse. A group of them, given the severity of the shadowquake.

Were they too late?

"What about behind the store?" Velvet asked the twins. "Did you look back there? I'm not sensing any spirits here. And I'm certain that's what we're dealing with. This is no wayward medium or some retarded psychic overstepping his bounds. This is something far more nefarious."

"For sure," Luisa agreed, and darted off in the direction of the back door.

Logan hesitated. "Are you sure?"

Nick peered up at Velvet strangely.

She chewed at her lips, stressed and not at all certain, if truth be told. Her hands shook as she ran them through her hair, trying desperately to come up with some solution that made sense.

Then, from the corner of her eye she saw Nick dive into the man's body and settle into his much larger frame. "What the hell?" Velvet heard herself mutter.

Nick popped back out. "This guy says he was poisoned. Something in his egg drop soup."

"Did you just talk to that guy?" Logan asked, his hands on his hips and his mouth stretched into a surprised oval. "That's so cool. Isn't that cool, Velvet? How'd he do that, Velvet?"

She shrugged and waved Logan off, turning her attention back to Nick. "Ask him what he remembers."

Nick dropped back into the body. It twitched a bit on the linoleum. The man's legs kicked about, and then Nick sat up at an odd angle, his hips and legs still inside the body.

"He was eating soup, waiting for his spicy chicken teriyaki," Nick said.

"Spicy chicken teriyaki is awesome," Logan agreed.

"He said there wasn't anything really weird going on, but get this . . ." He paused. "The waiter was wearing sunglasses. Possessed."

"Look at this!" Logan yelled from where he'd wandered to the large walk-in pantry in the rear of the kitchen.

Velvet followed him through the stainless steel kitchen morgue, Nick padding up behind her. Logan pointed at a shattered glass object. She squatted beside it. The edges were jagged, but large rounded chunks of the thing remained intact.

"Do you think this could be a crystal ball?" Nick asked.

Grover tilted his head sideways.

"Just because that's what you were trapped in, doesn't mean . . . ," Velvet began.

"But what about the ones at the crystal warehouse?"

Velvet shifted impatiently. "What are you talking about?"

"Well." Nick's brow furrowed. "After you went through the crack at the warehouse, I thought I heard something. So I investigated. I didn't find anything except row upon row of crystal balls. Lots of them. Hundreds!"

"When did Caruthers start making crystal balls, Velvet?" Logan asked.

She stared at the boy, a thought dancing just beyond her comprehension. The clue was far too convenient to be a coincidence. The crystal company where Salvage tested their staff just so happened to begin crystal ball manufacturing?

It was beyond fishy; it was a freaking Swedish smorgasbord of fishiness.

Velvet stared at Nick incredulously. "You're just remembering this?"

Nick shrugged. "Yeah. I didn't think much of it. Crystal balls at a crystal factory. No big deal, right?"

There was a commotion at the back door as Luisa tore open the screen, entered, and dropped an empty cardboard box onto the mottled linoleum next to the still foot of the pregnant woman.

"There are more bodies in the back," Luisa said. "Six in the bed of a moving truck and one in the walk-in refrigerator by the Dumpster."

"That's nine total," Nick said, stepping up behind the twins and clamping his hands onto their shoulders. "Plus the survivor." He glanced at the obese guy. Even from their position, they could all hear the man's lungs rattling.

"What's the box for, then?" Velvet nodded toward the thing.

Luisa kicked it and it spun around, revealing a familiar company name.

Caruthers Family Crystal.

"Holy crap," Velvet spat.

"See!" Nick shouted, and then slapped his forehead.

"Yeah, yeah. This is starting to make sense." Velvet paced between the bodies, not really paying them any attention, shuffling through them as though they were snowdrifts.

She explained the visions she'd torn from the banshee's brain, the printing press, Aloysius Clay, and the rows of effigies and crystal balls. "Only someone familiar with our testing would have access to the crystal warehouse crack."

"Someone who'd already been to the seconds warehouse?" Nick added.

"Since when did they start making crystal balls?" Luisa chimed in late, her hand on her jutting hip and her face screwed up in disgust.

"The whole thing stinks," Logan added.

"Yeah, it does," Velvet said, her eyes narrowing. "It stinks of Clay. Aloysius Clay. He would have been trained there himself. Might have trained others there, too! We've got to find that guy!"

She moved toward the door to the dining room, but before she could take a step, a bright light exploded from underneath the chrome stove vent, brighter than any lightbulb. Luisa and Logan backed away and turned to face the wall. Velvet fell into a crouch and shaded her eyes but soon became aware of Nick staring at the portal.

She should have prepared him better. Especially knowing that the obese man would likely die. Nick's face took on a placid calm, and he slumped over against the wall, smiling wanly.

The room grew so bright that she almost didn't see the spirit standing next to the poisoned man, identical to the now still corpse in every way, except translucent. Not merely see-through as ghosts were, but glowing as brightly as an un-ashed purgatory-bound soul. The light coiled around him in gossamer threads, guiding him.

Extracting him.

"Nick!" Velvet waved to the boy, her eyes shielded by the visor of her palm. "Look away. That's not meant for you!"

In the last glimpse before Velvet turned and buried her eyes into the sleeve of her shirt, the man's form was hovering in midair, the light bisecting him at his waist. Tentacles of light danced over his limbs in such a beautiful diaphanous manner. Velvet felt a dangerous calm wash over her. A calm not meant for her, either.

But in a second, it was over and the room was still and lit only by the fluorescent bulbs above them.

"What was that?" Nick screamed, thrilled by the experience.

Velvet grinned. "That was someone dying and *not* going to purgatory."

"Wow. I just wanted to dive in there."

"Exactly," Luisa said. "That's why you don't look. It's not right. The light was meant for him, not you. We look away so we don't get tempted to move on before our time. It's another rule."

Nick whistled. "There seems to be more of those every day."

Logan grinned mischievously and rubbed his palms together.

Velvet nodded and turned, barking orders as she wound her way through the tables and out the main door. "Run a quick search of this strip mall before you return through the crack. I need to speak with Manny about this."

Luisa and Logan were on task in an instant, darting into the dry cleaner next door.

Nick followed behind and grabbed her by the arm. "We can all go with you. Clay is not likely to be around, you know?"

"I have another motive." She glanced around to make sure Luisa and Logan couldn't overhear. "I need to talk to the banshee one more time. Something doesn't add up. Remember what I told you? He doesn't just know about Clay and the departure. He said he knew about *my* secret."

Nick shuddered. "Well, you be careful. I've lost a lot this week, you know? I don't want to lose you, too."

She clutched the collar of his jacket and pulled him toward her forcefully. "I don't want to go," she whispered into his ear. "I don't want to ever be anywhere but right here."

Nick grinned. "In a strip mall parking lot?"

"No, doofus," she said, smiling. "But thanks for lightening things up. It was getting pretty intense."

Then she pushed him away completely and ran toward the crack, waved, and dove into the fissure in the concrete, leaving Nick standing alone.

The first thing Velvet saw as she burst into the Shattered Hall was an antique settee positioned at an odd angle atop some rubble and Manny pacing wildly in front of it. Velvet coughed and drew the station agent's stern attention.

"What's going on?" Manny asked, leaning over and tossing clothes at Velvet from a nearby crate.

"I don't know," Velvet said, jerking a shirt down over her head. "But I'm going to figure it out."

She started to move toward the gate, but felt a hand curled over her shoulder, stopping her still.

"Hold on just one minute, Little Miss Savior of Purgatory. You're not going to go stomping off into danger without running your theory by me. Not a chance."

Velvet flinched apologetically. "Could you walk with me, then? I need to interrogate the banshee one more time."

"You better know what you're doing, Velvet. This is no time for hunches."

"No one knows what they're doing in this, Manny. But if I can't trust my instincts, then I can't trust anything."

The station agent fell in alongside her, nodding as Velvet described the scene at the teriyaki place and the bodies, and Nick's revelation about the crystal balls. Before she could even mention it, Manny jumped to the appropriate conclusion.

"So the Departurists have the souls they need to shake the Latin Quarter apart, create all the cracks, and free the rest of the local revolutionaries." She staggered a bit, reaching for the wall of the cavern to right herself. "You have to find Clay. Now."

Velvet gaped at the woman. Didn't Manny think she knew that?

"I know. And the only person who seems to know anything about all this is the banshee." They passed the gate and rushed through the emptying atrium toward the secret entry to the Cellar.

"And the crystal balls at our testing facility." Manny shook her head and whispered, "Clay."

"Clay," Velvet said, and nodded. "It has to be. What other body thief has such connections? Plus, we've already linked him to the effigies. I have to ask, because I think it could help, did you know him, Manny?"

"I knew *of* him, like you. The council was aware of the trauma he'd suffered as a result of losing Jerry like that. But we've been unable to locate him to offer support. All these years his bitterness must have grown." Her expression fell.

"He must blame purgatory," Velvet mumbled, watching the woman closely. Velvet didn't have the nerve to bring up the uncomfortable glances between Manny and Miss Antonia. But her instincts told her there was something connecting them all and that Manny wasn't telling her everything.

Manny nodded slowly. "Perhaps. But whether he blames purgatory, God, Santa, or his very own mother makes little difference. We have to find him. He has the trapped souls, wherever he is." She held up her finger between them like a warning. "And until we find them, this shadowquake is going to continue to damage purgatory."

Velvet nodded. The timing wasn't right to confront the woman about her relationship with Clay and Miss Antonia. They had to move.

Halfway across the nearly empty station, they came upon a small crowd gathered around the smoldering embers of another effigy, this one only partially burned. Manny stomped toward it and shooed away the gawkers.

"Go about your business!" she cried.

Velvet crouched down beside the pile of ash and folded paper and pulled apart a piece of the figure's foot, unfolding the intricate creases until she could see the paper clearly. Bold strokes of Chinese characters littered the page—pictures, too, city scenes and businessmen holding plaques. A newspaper. A red panda with another character set in its center seemed to be the logo.

She held the red panda logo up to Manny, who merely grunted an acknowledgment.

"It's from my vision," Velvet said. "It's from Vermillion."

The massive station hub had fallen silent, and the crowd had dissipated to a few hundred wandering souls. Velvet peered up at Manny. "Is it nearly done? Have most of the revolutionaries already passed through the cracks?"

Manny nodded, a veil of sadness across her porcelain face. But there was something else there, too. Hope. At least Velvet *thought* that's what she saw. "Thankfully, it's still isolated to the Latin Quarter. We can still stop this."

Velvet nodded stoically and followed Manny as they continued across the station floor, hopping cracks and sidestepping boulders until they reached the entrance to the Cellar.

The wide stone stairs were torn up in places, and descending them would be an obstacle in itself without the near constant shaking of the quake. Still, Manny slipped off her shoes, turned, and trotted down the stairs.

Velvet steeled herself and followed.

Ten dead, and nine souls trapped in crystal balls—God knew where.

Purgatory under attack.

The cracks were impossible to defend against escaping revolutionaries.

Velvet shuddered to think of what the departure could really mean for them. What would happen as other districts got word of what was going on in the Latin Quarter? Would the revolution spread across purgatory, filling the daylight with escaped souls? Velvet tried to imagine a world populated by possessed human beings living as hosts to parasitic souls. It was too much.

Too horrible a sentence.

But the other question was more niggling: Who *wouldn't* leave? That seemed to be the bigger question. Given the choice of waiting in the gray doldrums of the City of the Dead for some ultimate thumbs-up or thumbs-down on their fates, would anyone choose to stay? Would the souls take the righteous path and leave the living to their limited existences? Velvet suspected the worst.

The departure could become a global invasion of the daylight.

Rancho Cucamonga met them at the bottom of the stairs. The hissing nearly drowned their speech in its earsplitting constant wail. The sound coursed around them in waves, striating the inky clouds of shadow gas and tingeing them a pus-colored yellow.

"It's been going on for well over an hour now!" Rancho shouted.

"Since the shadowquake began?" Velvet asked, leaning in close.

The burly guy nodded, head twisting toward the black cast-iron gates. Velvet's eyes homed in on the lock. She reached for the key around her neck and realized that it didn't hang there. And of course it didn't. It'd been days since she'd worn the Cellar key.

"Dammit!" she yelled.

Manny twisted toward her, a question on her face.

"The key!"

"You'll have to go, Velvet. Run. Run to my office." The woman pointed back up the stairs, now bucking wildly from the machinations of moving rock underneath them.

Whatever the revolution had planned utilized the most horrible of magic, an evil so fierce and destructive that Velvet, for the first time staring at the task at hand, doubted her ability to stop it.

"Go, girl," Rancho begged. "Quick!"

Velvet launched herself up the stairs, clambering over them on all fours, falling back and then thrusting forward. She reached for the rail, only to have it give way in her hand. The entire chunk of black metal tortured itself from the bolts in the wall and clattered against the undulations of the stone risers. It swung toward her, and she dove over it, coming down hard on her knee. The phantom of her bone felt as though it splintered; strands of nerves sparked and slithered from a gash in the side of her leg. The final few steps were torturous, and her knee cried out in wave after wave of radiating pain.

At the top, she rolled across the cobbles and gained her footing, limping through the thinning crowds.

People gathered together and held each other to stay on their feet as the ground beneath them rocked and forced pavers to pop up and down. Velvet was nearly to the circular stair leading to Manny's office when she heard the glass dome begin to crack. The sound echoed across the space before the first shards fell free of their leaden bonds. Fresh screams filled the station below as hoards of people panicked and bolted en masse for the arches to the tunnels.

Would this night ever end?

Velvet made for the stairs while they still managed to cleave to the wall. The thought of the floor falling from underneath her feet fueled her, forced her to pound the steps through the pain, to run the last yards and barrel through the doors. The doors banged against the office walls, but the sound was muffled by the clatter of stone cracking.

Manny's writing desk lay on its side, its contents spilled

into a pile beside it like the insides of a stabbing victim. Velvet dropped down next to it, wincing in agony as her knee hit stone, and started to dig through the different keys. She knew exactly the one, but there were so many. So many.

The little spirit charm dangling from the loops of the skeleton key glinted in the flames of a nearby gaslight, and Velvet snatched it, and then she saw the other one. The small crimson key—the same as Miss Antonia's—and pocketed it as well, reminding herself that she'd need to retrieve the one she'd pulled from the Salvage mother's ashes from her shredded clothes in the alley. She retraced her steps and dodged even more destruction on her return to the Cellar.

The moments after the key turned in the lock and the gates flung open and off their hinges were a blur in Velvet's mind. Rancho Cucamonga rushed forward into the dark cave of the stairwell. The steps had devolved into a gravelly hill because of the rolling in the earth. Manny followed Rancho, and the two were swallowed in the inky black depths of the Cellar.

The hissing turned into a roar and then into screams.

Velvet tumbled forward, skidding down the slope on her hands and aching knee, pebbles popping up at her face and into her mouth. She jerked her head to the side and pivoted, trying desperately to gain her footing, or at the very least to dig her heels into the softening stone to slow her descent. What finally did it was a jarring bash into the rock wall, its surface still very much solid and hard enough to dizzy Velvet's senses.

It took a few seconds for her to realize she was in the Cellar. A lit torch lay in the center of the dirty floor, and she stumbled over and snatched it.

"Rancho! Manny!" she screamed.

"Rancho!" one of the prisoner's mocked in response.

"Manny!" another chimed in, their tone much whinier than hers, she noted.

"I see you cons have taken time out from your busy hissing schedule," Velvet said, zipping past their cages, and speeding up as she noticed the bars were decomposing into chilling bends and curves. She thought back to the gate above. Nothing was going to hold these monsters in place if they couldn't find Clay and the stolen souls in time. Banshees and other criminals would flood out into purgatory.

Velvet quickened her pace, limping toward the interrogation cell. The hissing rose up anew from the cages on either side of her, and she swung her torch left and right, not caring whether she set the prisoners' reaching hands afire.

One hand caught and blazed briefly before the prisoner jerked it back into his cage, pouting and rocking it in the crook of his other arm like a baby.

"Serves you right," Velvet said.

Another light glowed in the near distance, and Velvet broke toward it, hoping desperately to find Rancho or Manny nearby. Surely they'd had time to reach the interrogation cell. But as she neared the cell, she ran straight into the bars. At her feet, Manny lay unconscious. Inside, the banshee sat calmly on the dirt floor, the torch lapping in front of him like a campfire. The monster's face was so serene, Velvet thought, that he could have been toasting marshmallows over the thing.

She knelt and gently took Manny's face between her palms. "Are you all right?" And then she screamed into the darkness, "Rancho! Where are you? Come to the center cell! Rancho!"

The only response was more hissing.

"You!" she screamed at the banshee. "What are you doing? Answer me!"

His face remained placid; his arms hung limply at his sides. It was like he was in a coma. Velvet narrowed her eyes, crouched, scraped a handful of dirt and gravel from the ground, and threw it between the bars. The debris hit its mark, but the banshee still didn't move. She turned the key in the lock and swung open the door, rushing toward the prone figure. A second later she realized her mistake.

An effigy.

She ran her fingers over the tightly folded paper that made up the thing's form, the perfection of the work, and rolled it over. Behind her, Manny gasped.

"He's gone. Disappeared. Just like Clay." Velvet's voice quivered on the brink of insanity. "One day he's locked up, and the next he's gone."

"Uh." Manny clutched the crown of her head and glowered in stupefied horror at the masterwork of origami before them. "Well, at the very least, Kipper's idea to investigate the Latin Quarter's origamists wasn't a dead end."

Velvet's eyes shot toward the station agent. "What did you say?"

"Yes. Kipper is searching for Clay among the few master origamists in our district. Including, I believe, your friend. What was his name?"

"Mr. Fassbinder?"

"Yes, that's it. He's been helpful so far, right?"

"Certainly," Velvet said. But as she said it, she wondered what exactly Mr. Fassbinder had helped with. The rumors he'd spoken of, about Clay residing in Vermillion, had been a wild-goose chase for Kipper. And he really ought to have known something, oughtn't he? The level of skill involved in the origami effigies was unparalleled. Velvet hadn't seen such artistry outside of the Paper Aviary.

If Mr. Fassbinder is involved . . .

Velvet pushed the thought aside. It wasn't a possibility. He was her friend, and if she was nothing else, she was loyal.

Without waiting for a response, Velvet ran, the key bouncing against her hip, the torch crackling and leaving a blazing red wake in the murky dark. She heard the pounding of feet in the dirt as Manny gave chase, Rancho shouting his presence in the distance.

Velvet wished she could send a message to Nick, to tell him to come back from the strip mall. They had to fight something worse than the murder and capture of souls.

The departure.

It could still be stopped, couldn't it? Or reversed?

Aloysius Clay couldn't be allowed to get his way and release all of his followers into the daylight.

Hell, it might happen anyway, she thought.

All. These. Cracks.

She scrambled over the fallen gates and out into the main hall. Souls were busy mending those injured by the falling dome, pressing stolen cloth into the gashes. Velvet passed one woman with a cut on her head so deep, white tentacles writhed from inside. A little boy in a football jersey and a newsboy cap used his tiny fingers to quickly shove the tentacles back in. He jerked away from each spark that jumped from the end of the dendrites and crackled down the front of the woman's robes.

An unusual wind whipped through the hall, twisting the inky blue shadows into cyclones of dark trouble. The ground beneath them churned, and the crumbled stone caught in the swirling air and showered the cowering masses of souls.

Velvet flanked the curved wall of the atrium and raced toward the Shattered Hall near the entrance to the funicular and ducked inside. She traced her delicate finger against their crack, itself shattered into a web and barely recognizable as the port to the strip mall. Then she disrobed quietly and slipped through into the light.

It was good to have her feet on solid ground once more. She'd almost gotten used to the constant shaking, but the absence of it made a profound impact and she took a moment to let the stillness calm her fragile nerves before heading toward the Quickie Teriyaki. Inside, Nick stood in the doorway between the kitchen and the loading dock behind the strip mall, watching Logan and Luisa and the bodies in turn. When he turned toward her and smiled, it was as though a light went on inside her. Velvet was filled with a warmth and happiness that she'd not felt since she was alive, and much, much younger.

"Nick!" she cried, and raced across the room to fall into his arms for a quick hug. He held her tight, and Velvet felt a stitch of regret as his face wilted when she pulled away.

Velvet leaned out the back door. Luisa poked her head out of the side of the truck, and Velvet waved for the girl to join them.

"Did you find anything?" Velvet asked, knowing perfectly well they hadn't—they wouldn't. Those souls were long gone.

Luisa shook her head. "You look funny. What's going on?"

She searched for the words to tell her team what was happening back at their home. Finding no easy way to put it, she said it the only way she knew how. "Purgatory is falling apart. Whatever happened here"—she pointed to the prone figures on the floor— "is destroying the City of the Dead."

Logan's mouth dropped open, and Luisa slouched into a discouraged curl. Nick reached out and drew them both close to his sides.

"It'll be okay. Won't it?" The look in Nick's eyes is what directed her to answer the question the way she did.

"Of course," she said. "We just have work to do to make sure of it. And we have to leave now. Manny is waiting for us."

Chapter 24

Manny was waiting for them to return when they spilled back into the Shattered Hall, her arms crossed and her hair uncharacteristically frizzy. The station agent had been busy. Clothes had been laid out for them on the out-of-place settee from her office. One of the sofa's legs had fallen into another crack, adding to the general imbalance of the hall.

"Hurry up, then," Manny urged, tapping her foot.

Velvet rushed forward and snatched up some of the mismatched garments, dressing amid a flurry of flapping fabric and elbows. They followed the woman out into the station, and Velvet fell into a jogging gait beside her as they drove straight through the throngs of refugees huddled inside. Though "inside" was more of a relative term, considering that the shattered dome of the station above them had turned the room into something resembling a courtyard.

Manny headed toward the staircase rather than the arched

entrances to the platforms. Velvet glanced at Nick and shrugged.

"Where are we going?" she yelled ahead.

Manny looked back over her shoulder and held her finger to her lips. "Secret," she said.

"Because this is a good time for secrets," Velvet snipped. "You know, this is something my team and I can handle."

Manny ignored the comment and kept on. The last thing Velvet needed was the station agent's tagging along to the Paper Aviary. It was too close to the alley. Too close to her lie.

Velvet winced at the smattering of people they passed, each face a study in exhaustion. Heads hung between knees and swayed with the sporadic shimmy of the floor. The rows of refugees could have been on a train, bound for anywhere, covered in the dust and ash from the building's slow and shuddering collapse.

Eventually it would fall. That was very possible. *But please not now*, she thought. *Let the station stay up a few more hours. An hour. Something.*

They followed Manny up the stairs to her office on hands and knees, scrabbling over mounds that looked more like rock piles than risers. Once inside the office, they watched as Manny pulled back the pale blue curtains draped behind the empty space where the settee normally stood and led them into a dark cavernous space that Velvet hadn't been aware existed.

She gawped in amazement. Manny, it turned out, was keeping a lot of secrets.

The walls here were made of brick, and small orbs of

gaslight cast a dusty glow onto a raised wooden beam, rounded at the top like a spectacularly elongated horse's back. Between the lamps, thick swatches of leather hung from hooks, belts and carabiners attached to them. Velvet peered into the distance, where the hall-like room seemed to descend rapidly into darkness. A cliff of some kind.

"What is this?" she asked. "Some kind of slide?"

"Exactly." Manny snatched one of the leather pieces from the wall and laid it across the wooden rail.

She strode across the room into the shadows and returned pushing a rolling cart. Atop it were metal teardrops, each affixed with a loop at the pointy end. With some effort she attached one to each of the four corners of the leather.

"So that's like a sled?" Nick asked, and grimaced.

He shuffled out to the edge of the precipice, where the slide began its downturn. When he turned back toward them, he wore a look of terror. "It sure is steep."

Manny straightened and looked them in the eye, one after the other. "The slides are built into the walls of every station in purgatory, as a means of escape should something happen. I'm sure you'll agree it's important to keep the Council of Station Agents safe, particularly in times of disaster and political unrest."

They nodded.

She ran a hand across the smooth, oiled leather. "This slide will take us to the foot of the mountain, depositing us less than a mile from the Latin Quarter's main square. We'll be within a stone's throw of the dorms and, if I've done my homework correctly, very close to the Paper Aviary, the shop of Velvet's friend, Mr. Fassbinder." She winked at Velvet, but the sentiment seemed oddly forced.

Velvet wasn't sure what to make of it all. Surely Manny wanted to stop the destruction. What would she gain from any of this? If anything, Velvet was the one being fake— going along with the station agent's presence, when she didn't want the woman anywhere near the epicenter of her lies. The closer they got to the alley, the closer Velvet would come to having her coil of secrets unravel. It was only a matter of someone mentioning that they'd used the secret crack to get to the station, before the station agent's questions would start.

"How did you know it was there, Velvet?" Manny would ask.

"How did you know it was viable, Velvet?"

"How many times did you cross into the daylight without permission?"

And worse . . .

"What were you doing?"

Ugh. The answers would spell disaster for her future, she was sure of it.

Manny continued, "I have a good feeling about this. We'll learn more from this origamist. We'll learn enough to point us in the direction of an end."

Velvet wasn't so certain. She felt a familiar hopelessness begin to settle in. But she had to be hopeful for her team, or at least appear that way, so she nodded firmly for all of them to see.

It was Luisa who lifted her brow suspiciously, and Velvet

wondered if her carefully constructed lie was beginning to crumble.

Manny continued, "Each of you grab a swath of leather and fit it as I have. The weights will keep the leather snug against the wood slide." She loosened the belts atop it. "These strap around the rider. Make them tight; it's going to be a very quick ride."

Velvet pulled another of the leather sleds from the wall and draped it over the slide.

Manny straddled the piece of leather, belting herself to it, and bucked herself backward toward the edge of the drop-off. She paused just before the slope. "Before you get on, slide the leather close to the drop-off. You don't want to have to shift it as much as I did. Good luck!"

And with that, Manny thrust her hips and slipped backward into the blackness.

"Ohhhhhh, aaaaaand haaaang oooooooon!" Her voice echoed from the chasm, the last note stretching into a terrified scream.

"Sweet Jesus," Nick said.

"Oh, what are you, scared?" Velvet teased, rubbing her arms. "Should I go first so you'll want to get to me? Or do you need me to push you?"

Logan went next, shouting a high-pitched "Yahoo!" as he dropped out of sight.

"It's gonna be fun, Nick. Don't be a pussy," Luisa said, and scooted down the incline without another peep.

Nick straddled the cowhide and looked up at Velvet, his worried expression shifting into something else. "How about I'll go first, if you flash me a boob."

Velvet rolled her eyes. "You think this is a good time for a negotiation?"

He shrugged.

She sighed and reached up toward her shirt seductively. Nick's mouth dropped open, and just as he leaned forward with anticipation, Velvet rushed up to him and gave him a big shove, shifting the leather sled over the tiniest hump.

"Velvet?" he asked, hanging there for a moment, quivering. Then he was splitting the air as he slipped through space.

Velvet fastened the weights as they'd been instructed, jumped onto the flat of leather, and kicked off. The slide was much steeper than she'd expected and she fell forward clawing at the edges of the leather, squeezing her thighs around the wooden rail in a ridiculous attempt to slow her descent.

She clenched her teeth and closed her eyes. Her hair flapped around her face as she plummeted, and her stomach seemed to have detached and was making its way up through her other organs in some mad, self-serving attempt to be free of her body.

She fell through a cascade of pebbles, which caught in her mouth and hair, and a couple of times, the whole leather sled seemed to take flight for a moment.

She arrived with such speed that the echo of her voice, a scream she didn't recall making, showed up a second after she reached the bottom. That sound gave way to another— welcome voices hooting and hollering and cheering the ride.

"What a rush!" Logan shouted.

She hopped off and threw her arms around Nick. "Wasn't that fantastic?"

Nick's jaw tensed. "Um."

Velvet didn't let him finish. Instead she quickly withdrew and socked him in the shoulder like a buddy before the others had a chance to question her affectionate embrace. "You can thank me later."

She sped off after Manny and the twins, leaving Nick to catch his breath and his footing.

Manny had been right about one thing. The slide had ended in very close proximity to Mr. Fassbinder's shop. As soon as they turned the first corner, Velvet recognized the cobblestone street. The street had been left mostly dark, from the ongoing quake and push of shadows, but a single globe of gaslight three blocks ahead lit up the advisor's office, the Paper Aviary, and the alley that sat in between them.

The group trudged forward, and a familiar shape stepped from out of the darkness and into the cone of flickering light.

He stood close to the alley's mouth, which told Velvet that the tentacles had moved on. The boy might have been as tough as stone, but no one who'd been coiled in the shadow's grasp ever wanted to put themselves in danger of it again.

"Over here," he called, waving them closer.

"Ah, Kipper, darling," Manny said, clutching his shoulder dramatically. "Have you found our origamist?"

He shook his head slowly. "Shop's closed. I've hammered on the door for ten minutes, and nothing. I figure he's probably found shelter somewhere else. Or, you know . . ."

Velvet did know. Kipper had stopped short of implying that Fassbinder had escaped with the rest of the Departurists.

"Oh, dear." Manny scowled. "That is disappointing."

"He wouldn't do that," Velvet said.

Manny studied Velvet intently. "How do you know?"

She shook her head. She guessed she didn't want it to be true. "I don't. He was just so adamant about helping us find Clay. Why would he do that if he wanted to depart himself?"

"Perhaps it was a ruse," Manny suggested.

"A what?" Logan asked.

"A ruse," Velvet repeated. "A trick to mislead us from the truth."

"Oh."

Velvet didn't want to even think about what that meant. Mr. Fassbinder was her friend, he'd been like a father figure to her. She'd even fantasized that in a perfect world, they'd all still be alive and Mr. Fassbinder would sweep her mother off her feet, making her fall madly in love with both his quirky style and his knowledge of film.

She refused to believe that he was a traitor.

But just as she was about to rebut Manny's statement, Nick appeared from the darkness of the alley. She flinched. What was he up to? Nick pulled her aside while Kipper and Manny continued their heated discussion, seemingly oblivious.

"What were you doing in there?" she asked.

"I went to search for this." He held out the black box.

"Mr. Fassbinder's gift?"

Nick shrugged. "It fell out of your pocket when you ran from salon tonight. I'd almost forgotten that I brought it with me when I followed you to the crack, but all this talk of origami reminded me."

Velvet snatched it from his hand and tore it open. In her haste, the paper bird waiting inside fell to the ground and opened slightly. A strip of crimson poked out from a ruptured fold. Velvet squinted and crouched next to it.

She began to slowly unfold it, careful to avoid tearing the heavily creased paper. What she saw there chilled her to the bone.

The paper drifted to the floor, and Manny snatched it up.

Velvet knew exactly what the station agent was seeing.

She didn't even have to look at her face to know that the woman was putting two and two together. And it wasn't nearly the mathematics running through Velvet's head. Mr. Fassbinder had lied about where he obtained his paper. He used the same paper as the one from the effigy, the ones in the memories she'd snatched from the banshee's head.

With the same red panda logo.

He'd lied about everything, and Velvet's heart was plummeting.

"What's this, Velvet?" Manny asked.

Velvet's voice was beyond shaky. She couldn't control it. "It's an origami bird that a friend gave me."

"The origamist." The station agent nodded, urging Velvet to continue.

Velvet's mind was in a blender. Ideas, plots, predicaments, and motives whirred inside. Kipper had said that Clay had never left the Latin Quarter. The banshee had shown her that the Departurists were led by a master origamist. There was no one more masterful. She'd suspected.

She didn't want to believe.

"Mr. Fassbinder is Aloysius Clay." The words fell out of her mouth like bricks.

"Why would Clay do that?" Kipper scowled at her, judgment in his gaze. "Why would he send us on a path of discovery that would lead us right back to him? Why would he want to be found out?"

Mr. Fassbinder had seemed to connect with her on so many levels—their mutual love of film, of animals, birds in particular. There had been an easiness to their talks that had made her feel comfortable. Loved. Like when she'd spend time with her mother apart from her rambunctious brothers.

Why would he give himself away? Did he want her to know the truth on some level? He'd talked about the departure with such understanding, too. She couldn't wrap her head around it.

"Maybe he didn't care—he was confident we wouldn't be able to stop him," Velvet announced finally.

She picked up the unfolded bird, the paper crinkled so completely that the opened folds looked like goose bumps on the sheet.

The realization struck her suddenly. "He loves the intricacy of his ruse. Just like the intricacy of his origami creations. There's no one better than him at the art of mimicry. He doesn't even look as Miss Antonia described. He's completely different. Arty, even. He's disguised himself in every way."

"An egotist," Manny agreed, nodding.

An ego is right, Velvet thought. The man had tricked her

completely, getting her to believe he was her friend when really he had been using her as part of his plan somehow. She felt violated.

Livid.

And in moments like these, only one thing could help.

Revenge.

The display of *The Birds* scene in the front window of the Paper Aviary was destroyed. The big picture window lay in shards on the cobblestone, along with the black crows and even the miniature Tippi Hedren, crumpled and torn.

Velvet glanced in Nick's direction, stone-faced and purposeful. She was back in the game, focused. Nick nodded and followed her as she crawled up over the ledge of the broken window and down into the shop. The great spiny globe lay against one wall, rattling and wheezing and chirping along with the slow rumble of the earth beneath them.

She glared at the thing, and the dream came back, only this time with clarity.

The monk parakeets had been Clay's biggest clue, his great big cinematic metaphor. The one any self-described film aficionado would have figured out to begin with. Mr. Fassbinder was the one who was trapped. Purgatory was the prison.

It was like the whole philosophy of the revolution in one great big art project. But how did he become so embittered? Was it simply Jerry's death, or was it something else? It still didn't make any sense, and Velvet refused to buy the insanity plea that everyone else would certainly jump on.

Tables lay on their sides, and with every step farther inside, origami birds were crushed into the ashy ground. Velvet stomped through a swinging door into the back. Clay's workroom. Stacks of newspaper and reams of stolen printer paper lined the edges of the room, with a single desk and chair in the center. Laid across it, and totally still, was the figure of a man. As Velvet approached, her eyes grew wide with horror and she froze. What she saw struck her like a bat straight to the gut.

"Is he dead?" Nick asked, and crossed the gap to the desk.

"Is who dead?" Kipper leaned in with wide-eyed curiosity. Bonesaw.

Velvet's killer lay as silent as the grave on Clay's desk—brought to purgatory completely whole, pasty pink, through some sick means only the origamist was privy to. Regardless of the means, her secret—their secret—wasn't going to be a secret anymore.

"What's this, then?" Manny strode into the room. She crossed to the body quickly and scanned Nick's and Velvet's stunned faces for an answer. Then she reached out to touch the body.

"No, don't!" Velvet shrieked.

Manny pulled her hand away as though she'd very nearly patted a blazing fire. "What, then? What's happening here, Velvet? This"—she pointed at the body—"is certainly not Aloysius Clay."

In the corner of the room, Velvet noticed a thin mattress piled with more paper. The bed was empty. Clay was gone.

Velvet stood up and approached the prone figure and the station agent. "Bonesaw. He's my kuh-killer," she stuttered.

"Your killer? I don't understand. How could that be? Killers don't come to purgatory. Their path is a certainty."

"I don't know," Velvet said, pale arcs of tears clearing the ash from her face.

Velvet closed in on the body. She noticed a clean line across Bonesaw's left thigh. No blood on his clothing. No knife wounds. On instinct, Velvet balled her fist and brought it down on the figure's abdomen.

It caved in with a plume of dust, crinkling around her wrist.

Manny leaned over it, too, squeezing the "flesh" of its face and watching as the tightly folded paper ruffled and creased.

"It's another one of those damn effigy things!" Kipper yelled.

"It's a message," Velvet muttered. It had all come together in those short, tense moments. Mr. Fassbinder—Clay—had followed her through the crack to the farmhouse, to the shed. He knew her secret, and that's how the banshee knew. Clay had made it his secret, too. But what was this creature for? She turned away from the hulking paper mannequin. A joke?

"You have something to tell me?" Manny asked. "You thought you knew this thing. You called it Bonesaw?"

"I'd hoped you hadn't heard that," Velvet said, knowing the question could lead only one place: to a connection between Fassbinder and her killer, and to the crack outside in the alley.

Nick slipped his hand into hers and whispered, "It doesn't matter. I'm not going anywhere."

Manny's eyes narrowed. "Velvet?"

"He killed me." She slapped her hand against the paper carcass. "Not him, obviously. This is some kind of trick, Mr. Fassbinder's paper fraud," she spat.

"What do you mean, he killed you?"

"He looks just like the guy who murdered me, Manny. His name is Ron Simanski, and he was a serial killer in my hometown. Aloysius Clay found out." She hesitated. "Somehow."

"How exactly? And don't hold back. As you can see"— she threw her arms up to note that the building was still shaking, the floor sending ripples up their legs as they stood there—"things aren't getting any better."

Manny was right. Secrets weren't going to help anything.

Velvet took a deep breath, squeezed Nick's hand, and vomited her entire secret into the room—the extent of her haunting of Bonesaw, how she'd saved girls in that tiny shed, but not all of them. Those visions she kept to herself, kept them locked away in the deepest recesses of her mind like nightmares.

"I see." Manny stared off, deep in thought, ruminating on the information, or at least Velvet hoped that was what she was doing. For all she knew, the station agent could have been planning her eternal damnation. But then Manny spun around and stared at each of them intently, including the twins, who stood at the swinging door, mouths open with shock at the revelation of Velvet's crime. "Well. There's not much we can do about that right now. I'm going to keep it in my head until we've resolved all this madness. If we . . ." Her voice trailed off.

"It's not so bad!" Nick added. "Velvet's saved a lot of girls from this guy!"

Velvet's heart sunk. It was one thing that she'd done it, but revealing that he knew, too? Not good. She let her hand slip from the boy's grip.

"She's actually a hero, don't you think?" he implored.

Manny glowered. "So you knew?"

Velvet reached out and stroked Nick's arm. He was shivering with fear, and even her touch didn't seem to help. He'd meant well, but now he'd implicated himself.

"It was an accident that Nick followed me," Velvet said, and sighed. "He wasn't even aware—"

The woman held her hand up, ceasing the conversation. "I don't need to hear any more about this. For now we must figure out what the purpose of this effigy is. You've said it's a message. Do you believe it is simply to show you that he's on to your scheming?"

Scheming.

Velvet winced at the word, at the idea that the station agent thought less of her, thought she was a criminal.

"I think . . ." She didn't want to finish. She wasn't even sure what it meant, but she knew where the answer would lead. "Mr. Fassbinder—Clay—passed through into the daylight. The crack we used to get up to the station tonight is in the alley on the other side of this wall. I think he wants me to follow."

"Ah." Manny nodded. "But what if it's a trap of some sort?"

"It probably is," Velvet agreed. "This whole thing has been leading up to this point. The banshee, the crystal balls, the shadowquakes, the trapped souls. The revolution. But it feels right that I should follow him."

Manny nodded.

Nick gulped.

"He's at the farmhouse, and there's no question whose body he's walking around in."

"Then, you'll go," Manny said, but her eyes were narrowing cruelly. "But don't you forget your goal. Stop this shadowquake. Bring back Clay. Any score you feel needs to be settled between you and Aloysius is secondary to that. Understand?"

Not to mention Bonesaw, Velvet thought. She was hoping that that part had been taken care of naturally. That he'd bled out on the shed floor.

Dead.

Velvet nodded and stormed from the room. "Come on!" she called back to Nick.

He followed behind her down the crumbled alley, over piles of rubble and to the crack, which was barely discernible on the now quake-fractured wall. The others were still at the mouth of the alley, but nearing.

"Holy crap." Nick stared at the passageway, discouragement clouding his expression.

"Where are you guys going?" Logan shouted, clambering over the mounds of crushed brick.

Velvet shuddered. For the first time, she didn't want her team with her on a mission. She couldn't risk their safety. Not this time. "Stay here, Logan. And make sure your sister doesn't follow."

The boy scowled but stilled himself. "Fine."

Then she turned to Nick and held out her hand. He slipped his into her palm and squeezed. "You stay, too. Stop the others from following," she said. "This is my battle."

He shook his head. "No," he said. "Don't ask me to do that. I can't."

The sound of rocks scattering turned his attention toward Luisa, who'd joined her brother, the same look of confusion on her face. In that moment, Velvet slipped through the crack.

Chapter 25

The moon hung high over the glen, shining through the web of leaves and branches in thin white bars. Dim light played across the carpet of glistening pine needles. The moment would have been serene and welcoming, if Velvet hadn't just shared a secret that doomed her soul to an eternity in purgatory, and maybe Nick's, too. Despite the station agent's affection for her—and she didn't doubt that for a second—Manny wouldn't be able to keep this secret from her superiors.

Velvet was screwed.

"Dammit!" she cursed.

She rolled onto her knees and pushed herself up from the dirt, tossing her hair over her shoulder to get a better look at the burnt-out crack that ran up the tree like a wound, secretly hoping the rest of the team would be spit out.

"That shouldn't happen," she muttered to herself. She deserved to face Aloysius Clay alone.

Deserved whatever happened to her.

It wasn't right to bring Nick along or get him into any more trouble, especially if that meant his damnation. She couldn't have that on her head. Not with him. It wasn't his fault.

But just as she rose to leave, she heard the crack open to another ghost, a quiet spurting sound. She turned to see the boy's body roll across the ground, his tank tight across his chest. Nick got up and rolled his head on his broad shoulders. He fixed on her gaze immediately and smiled at her with such warmth that she questioned how she could have ever done anything without him.

Dammit! she thought. *I sound like a movie of the week.*

Those sorts of eye-batting lovey-ass thoughts were meant for much weaker girls. How had it even happened? She'd been just going along, minding her own business. She'd had a stellar career in her afterlife, good friends, and, sure, a little secret that could blow everything apart.

But who didn't have a few skeletons in her closet?

"Are you okay?" Nick's deep voice vibrated across her skin like a personal massager. Tingles coursed through her.

She smiled and held her hand out to him, and Nick closed the gap, pulling her into a tight embrace.

"That was rough, right?" he said, brushing back some hair from her face. "It wasn't just me?"

"No, Nick." She chuckled at his understatement. "It was definitely prickly."

He hugged her tighter, lifting her until their noses nearly touched. "Maybe we just run away together and never have to worry about all the crap that happens in purgatory."

She pushed him away, clenching her jaw with anger, grinding her teeth. "Don't even joke about that!"

"Who's joking?" He shrugged. "We could find a couple of high-school-aged bodies and hang out for a while . . . or sixty years." He paused, grimacing at the disgusted look Velvet was cultivating. "Or not. It's just a suggestion."

A horrible one.

The idea was just gross. Brief possession was one thing. But what Nick was implying just wasn't right.

"Well, Nick. That's not going to happen, you understand? What we *are* going to do is march up to that farmhouse and take care of what I should have taken care of a long time ago."

"I hope you mean kill the bastard."

"Well, something like that. Besides . . ." She planted her hand on his chest. "It is my job." Velvet stomped away toward the road. When she shot an angry look back at Nick, he was grinning proudly.

Shit, she thought. He'd tricked her.

"You were just getting me riled up for what's ahead, weren't you?" How had she fallen for such a sneaky bastard, she wondered.

Nick cocked his head as if he didn't understand, but then bowed dramatically, like a court jester or something.

"Dude," she chastised. "Come on."

* * *

As the road crested the hill, the pulsing red and blue lights of a police cruiser became more and more distinct. It was parked sideways, blocking the road ahead. Velvet glanced at Nick, who shrugged like he wasn't surprised to see the police. It had been only a few hours, regardless of how much had happened in the space of time since they'd been there. Bonesaw's victim must have managed to identify the farmhouse.

Velvet expected to see a uniformed officer nearby, hand on his holster, ready to hold back traffic from entering the crime scene, but there was no one. Just a little past the cruiser, the yellow tape began, furled around the chunky wooden pasture fence and stretching across the driveway. Three other police cars, a couple of black sedans reeking of FBI, an ambulance with its back doors wide open, and a white crime scene van littered the dirt road. But beyond all those hints that some major shit had gone down on this lonely stretch of countryside, the property was eerily quiet.

There was no bustle of officers. No paramedics rushing a gurney across the potholed drive up to the house. No shouting about keeping away the media, or messing up someone's crime scene.

Nothing.

Not a peep.

She glanced at Nick. His mouth was wide open.

"Doesn't make sense," he said. "Where is everyone?"

Velvet tried to shake off the feeling that something was

horribly wrong, and offered up an excuse. "Maybe they're all inside, or around back?" It sounded more stupid spoken aloud than inside her head, where it should have stayed.

"And mute?" Nick offered, shaking his head to indicate that it didn't seem very likely.

And of course, it wasn't.

They passed through the tape, across the lawn pocked with dandelions, and into the house.

What they saw there filled them with the cold chill of realization.

Several men and women—way more than ten—filled the living and dining rooms of Bonesaw's farmhouse, and they were as still as the people in the Quickie Teriyaki. These people had been shot, though. Blood gurgled from their mouths in pink bubbles, and the carpet was soaked with the stuff. Some were dead, Velvet was sure, but others still clung to life. A policewoman clutched the cabinet the TV sat atop, still struggling to reach her gun, smoke rising from its barrel a few feet away. Another officer, no more than a few years out of high school, held a sopping red couch pillow to his gut and shivered as though feverish.

"Holy crap," Nick said. "I thought for sure we'd at least disabled Bonesaw. The way he dropped like that, like a sack of potatoes. I thought he was down for the count."

"Apparently not." Velvet pressed forward, searching through the two small bedrooms, both as pristine as hotel rooms, sheets tight on the beds like shrink-wrap. He wasn't in the bathroom, with its encyclopedia-of-sushi-motif shower curtain and jars full of motel soaps still in their paper wrappers. She did notice that the edge of his toilet paper was folded into a polite triangle, though she doubted it was for his guest's convenience. Bonesaw had only one kind of guest out to the house.

And they generally ended up dead.

But not always.

Velvet and Nick stepped though the wall from the hallway into the kitchen, where a moaning sheriff sat in a chair, holding a rag to a deep gushing wound in his thigh. Another cop, who appeared to be uninjured, knelt before him, shaking his head and whispering, "I think it's the femoral artery. You gotta hold that tight, man. Hold it real tight."

Just like Bonesaw, Velvet thought. *Did he hold it real tight?*

But the man's words went unheeded, and the sheriff, a mustached man with crinkled eyelids and sandy blond hair, went slack in the chair. His arm dropped away from the rag, and a ton of blood leaked onto the floor.

Velvet couldn't take any more of it.

The pain of all these injured and dead people hit her suddenly. She dove into the body of the young officer and quickly wrestled his mind into submission. For him this day would be over in a minute, and at the very least he wouldn't have to deal with the fear and anxiety that these people were in further danger.

Velvet would see to that. *Into your box.*

Then "Follow me," she said to Nick, the man's voice foreign in her throat.

The minivan sat in its regular spot, so unless Bonesaw had swiped a cop car to get out of there, she was pretty sure he was still around. And not just him, either. He'd be filled to the brim with that douche bag, Clay, and neither would be at all pleased to see her and Nick.

They were halfway to the shed when Velvet heard a voice.

"Officer?" High and a bit whiny.

Velvet directed the cop's body toward the sound, her hand settling on the handle of his gun cradled in its holster. A young woman in navy slacks, an official-looking badge on her hip, and an awkward smile on her pointy face approached wearing a pair of aviator sunglasses, despite a complete lack of sun or any glare, for that matter.

Why was Velvet not surprised? The revolutionaries must all have taken their fashion cues from the Big Book of Possession Clichés.

"Get into the shed," she whispered to Nick out of the corner of the man's mouth.

Nick stumbled toward the scene of the earlier bloodshed.

Velvet needed to lure the spirit out of the woman's body, but she needed confirmation of possession. She needed to get it to reveal itself with some incorrect response. "We're conducting an investigation here, miss," she said.

The badge on the woman's belt loop glinted against the lunar rays. *She should lambast me with official fervor for such a demeaning comment,* Velvet thought, *if she is in fact a detective,* and Velvet was pretty sure the body was.

"Oh, I'm sorry," the woman said, and grinned, still approaching.

Velvet stepped back. There was something familiar about the smile. Something that reminded her of long afternoons talking about film and watching a certain soul folding and folding and folding.

"I just saw all the cars and thought . . ."

"Thought you'd just see what you could do to help out, huh?" Velvet glanced at the woman's pants legs, wet with something that turned the navy into a slick jet-black. She didn't even have to think about it. Not for a second.

Blood. The woman had been wading in the stuff.

Mr. Fassbinder—Clay—had possession of her, *and* he was clearly a sexist. He hadn't even bothered to notice that the woman was an official. Her outfit was exactly the kind of thing those women wore on those serial killer shows. Not to mention the damn badge.

Velvet shuddered, stumbled backward.

She glanced back over her shoulder at the tiny shed. Visions of her killer's spirit, fighting the dark light of hell and grappling with Nick inside, flooded her mind. She had to get a grip.

"What's wrong?" The woman's head tilted slowly to the side, examining her. "I only want to help. There's no need to be afraid, Velvet."

There were no words to describe how hearing her own name gripped her heart at that moment.

"Why, Mr. Fassbinder?" she mumbled. "Why did you do it? Why here?"

"Why? Oh, Velvet, do we need to have that conversation? You interest me. We're friends, and I like to know all about my friends."

The words spun about in Velvet's head. Fassbinder's tone

was seriously grossing her out. It was too familiar, too pleasant. She guessed having a conversation wasn't really a good idea after all.

But even as the voice came from the woman's mouth, she was reaching behind her, into the waistband of her pants.

A gun!

Velvet had to protect the body she was in. She scrambled toward the shed, nearly tripping out of the officer entirely, before snagging his mind again and maneuvering the door between him and the approaching figure. There was a loud crack, and a bullet tore through the wood as Velvet slammed the door closed behind her and latched it shut.

She scrambled over to the workbench and crouched down, the officer's body panting from the workout. Velvet turned to see a nightmare come to life.

Bonesaw.

Gray and slack-jawed, her murderer limped across the floor toward her, his hair matted with cobwebs and gore. She screamed, a deep terror escaping her throat.

He lunged, arms fumbling and reaching for her, his face shaking left to right. A word played on his lips, stuttering there like a digital satellite TV feed in a rainstorm.

Bullets pounded the shed from outside, and one tore through Bonesaw's abdomen, sending a spasm through him that should have knocked him to the ground. But instead he heaved forward, pressing his face tight against a knot in the shed door, peering outside as bullets pinged and thunked all around them. He squatted and slipped in beside her, cowering under the workbench.

"So you noticed the detective was wearing sunglasses at night?" he asked, shrugging when she didn't respond. "What's the matter with you, Velvet?"

Nick. Velvet sagged with relief.

But she still couldn't look at him, couldn't rationalize the fact that it was her love's voice coming from the man who'd killed her. She didn't want to put that together. Better to pretend it wasn't happening at all. She shook off the disturbing image and looked away.

"Yeah, I saw the sunglasses," she said. "Not sure how many bullets Clay has, but I'm not going to have the death of another person on my head. Not when I don't have to."

"What are we going to do?"

Shivers ran up her chosen body's back with every word Nick drew from Bonesaw's vocal cords. She could barely process the words, let alone come up with a plan.

She pounded her fist against her legs and winced, focused on the pain and not the horror whispering inside the shed.

Get it together, girl, she thought. Velvet knew what they were up against and almost regretted shelving Luisa and Logan from the mission. Their role was instrumental in relieving a spirit from the body the spirit had possessed. There had to be something else that would work. Some way to capture Clay or Fassbinder or whoever the hell was inside Agent Scully and keep that spirit until Nick could do the old fly trick.

And then it came to her. Suddenly. The irony of it made her smile.

They were going to need a crystal ball of their very own.

"We're going to need a vessel to trap him in. We've already got a body," she said, and jabbed a thumb in his direction.

He shook his head. "You mean the fly thing?" He paused. "I don't really know how I did that. What if it was a fluke?"

She ducked a fresh round of bullets, this time from the tiny window.

"Oh? Now you don't know how you did it? What was with the big victory dance, then?"

Bonesaw shrugged.

Velvet desperately wished the twins would magically appear to tackle the spirit out of the detective like they always did. It'd take all her strength to wrestle the bastard, and she didn't relish getting that close to him again. And she didn't see much point in the flies taking him, actually. Especially when there wasn't a plan for him to return to the Cellars. Not again and not with the prison in the shambles it was in.

She'd just have to trust that Rancho could handle it. That he had things under control. What choice did she have?

If her suspicions were right, the crystal balls would be nearby. Nine of them. Nick and Velvet could capture Clay and then shatter the magic that was imprisoning the souls, which would stop the shadowquakes. If only they could get a message back to Luisa and Logan, explain where they were.

She shook away the possibility. It wasn't going to happen.

"I'm afraid we're on our own." She glanced in Nick's direction and flinched, seeing Bonesaw's corpse look at her with that kind of affection. She'd only ever seen his vicious dark intentions, the bizarre desire that had sparked within him when he'd cut her.

Wait.

Velvet remembered a time, near the end of her life, when her killer had brought the shiny metal urn into the shed, the one she'd always avoided on his mantel, his mother's ashes. He'd smiled like that when he'd set them down on the workbench, like he'd needed his mother there to witness the killing blow, to approve of him, maybe. Sick.

But the urn.

"You've got to get into the house, Nick." She said his name intentionally, tricking her mind into seeing the boy and not the dead monster before her. "There's an urn, like the kind you keep ashes in."

He nodded.

"It's on the mantel in the living room. Grab it and bring it out here, and I'll do the rest."

Bonesaw rose and shambled toward the door, and Velvet rolled the officer's body farther under the workbench, as tight into the corner as possible, readying herself to dispossess it. With as many bullets flying at the shed, she figured that once the officer was conscious again, he'd catch on and not try to get up anytime soon. As if to accentuate her point, Nick opened the shed door, turning into a silhouette of Bonesaw against the moonlight, and took several shots in the chest. Thick globs of black blood were flung across the interior of the shed as he spasmed, splattering the butcher's diagram on the wall. He steadied the corpse and darted into the yard.

Outside, the woman belted laughter, though it sounded more like shrieking to Velvet's ear.

Velvet watched the officer position herself between the shed and Bonesaw's lumbering form, firing round after round into his back. The zombie shuddered and stumbled but kept moving. Velvet could only pray a bullet wouldn't hit the zombie's spine. Then they really would be up shit creek. But as Velvet slipped out of the officer's body and onto the dusty floor, she could see Nick make his way to the house and into the kitchen.

Fassbinder chased after him, but as his stolen body approached the steps, Velvet shouted, "Aloysius Clay!"

The detective spun around and glowered, the sunglasses finally falling away. The stolen body's eyes, Clay's eyes, stared into the shadows of the shed, waiting for Velvet to make her official appearance, for the two of them to meet again without the pretense of Fassbinder between them.

"We know everything." Velvet stepped out into the moonlight.

"Well," the detective said, and grinned. "I doubt that. But it doesn't much matter now. The departure is done. The crystal balls are of no use. The magic that holds them is fading. . . ."

"Where are the crystal balls, Clay? The stolen souls?"

"Doesn't matter. As we speak, the disenfranchised of the Latin Quarter are flooding into the world and making my dream a reality. Imagine it, Velvet, a world free of fear. This time, we'll simply occupy these mortal bodies without concern for sickness or cancer or violence. If something happens, we'll just move on to the next like a new pair of shoes. A utopia!"

"It doesn't make any sense, Clay. The living will fight you. *They* can do that. We can't possess everybody—some resist."

"That may be. But even now, it's happening. And there won't be enough resistance to warrant concern. If the revolution spreads, like I know it will, we'll have the majority." The detective's eyebrows cocked menacingly. "And you know it."

Velvet did know. Even if a minority of the dead took on Aloysius Clay's cause, if news of this spread to other districts, that number would fill the world in a heartbeat. She glanced into the trees and thought she saw movement in the undergrowth. Dim glowing orbs floated in the darkness.

"Look." Clay laughed. "Even now they're surrounding us. Watching the end of all this. It's my day, girl. It's my achievement. And they want to applaud me. Come out!"

He shouted for the ghosts to come forward to show themselves. Velvet stewed; she felt as though she'd explode. Her world was falling apart in a way she'd never imagined. She focused on nine figures moving toward them. In their phantom hands the waning light glinted from the damned crystal balls.

The sight infuriated Velvet.

She was murderous.

She screamed and charged the woman's frame, focusing on the spirit inside, the shimmer of smoke and haze that was Clay's perverted, deformed ghost. She passed into the body and felt a chill course through her, as though she'd jumped into some icy river like those crazy people in polar bear clubs. She hung there for a moment before falling back out and onto the ground, where she rolled onto her back.

The woman's feet protruded from Velvet's abdomen, her cackling still exploding from her mouth like machine-gun fire.

It hadn't worked.

She couldn't force his soul from the woman's frame.

The agony of failure rushed over her, and she thought she might be reduced to wimpy girlish sobs, until she heard the screen door slam open and saw Bonesaw's bloody corpse emerge. He juggled the urn in his hands, the lid popping like there was boiling water bubbling just underneath.

"This one?" he yelled sweetly.

And though she knew she was cringing, Velvet nodded. She watched with amazement as Bonesaw opened the lid and dumped his own precious mother's ashes in a wide arc. They caught on the breeze and turned into a cloud that coated the detective's body in a thick layer of death. She sputtered and coughed.

"That was all sorts of wrong, you know," Velvet called in Nick's direction, but she couldn't help laughing. He nodded and raised an eyebrow saucily.

She backed away and gave it another run. Clay was distracted this time, covered in the grime and rubbing his borrowed eyes. But as Velvet lunged, she felt the presence of two other ghosts flanking her, matching her pace, one a streak of cartoonish blue. They hit Clay's ghost in unison and rolled across the lawn.

Or rather, two of them did.

She lay on the ground panting, Logan beside her.

"Where's Luisa?" she cried.

Anxiety coursed through her. She imagined Miss Antonia's

story of the soul churning and couldn't let that happen to Luisa. It might have been an irrational fear, but still, Luisa was trapped somewhere inside the detective's body, Clay coiling around her, squeezing the life or ectoplasm or whatever from her soul, only to vomit her out like a bad meal.

That was not happening.

Velvet plunged her outstretched fingers into the body, clawing and connecting enough with the battling spirits inside that the woman began to jerk and spasm in wild fits as though she were being electrocuted. Velvet submerged her face inside the woman's skull, half expecting to come nose to nose with Clay, gone full banshee, but all she saw was gray matter and blood pulsing through thick rubbery veins, the firing of neurons.

"Come on out, Detective," Velvet commanded of the woman. "Take your body back."

She didn't feel the woman at first, with the raucous fight swirling all around her like wild hamsters circling a metal wheel, but then there was a shallow muted grunt.

"Now! Run for your life!" Velvet screamed, trying desperately to supplant Clay's hazy spell over the woman with enough urgency to startle her awake.

Velvet pulled away, settling back against her ghost heels and staring down at the woman's seizing form. Bonesaw panted over them. When she noticed, she flinched for a moment, the look in his eye reminding her of her last moments on earth.

"I'm sorry. So sorry. I didn't hurt you, did I?" he had asked, false concern clouding his vision like cataracts. Then his lips, as thin as worms, had pressed against the bloody tracks, smearing them rosy.

Velvet shuddered at the memory, banishing it from her mind.

Now the killer's body sagged, and the urn shook in its sausagelike fingers. Despite knowing Nick was inside, that this monster before her was nothing more than a shell, Velvet was filled with hatred. She wanted to see Ron Simanski burned, like the effigies of the revolution, wanted to watch him turn to ash and blow away.

A moment later, the detective rose from her gauzy slumber and clawed through the grass, detangling from the ghostly forms of Luisa and Clay, as though sloughing off a memory.

It was as though Velvet were finally seeing the truth behind Fassbinder's lies in all its deformed, stretched-out obscenity. Clay was a fully formed banshee, wriggling and writhing like a giant snake.

Velvet toppled over, mixing into the fray. Luisa threw punches, and Velvet wrapped her legs around Clay's slithering form as though she were climbing a rope in PE, and probably not as gracefully. A second later, a wailing Grover leapt on top of them, landing blows with his big furry fists like a champ.

Velvet reached out to Nick. "The urn!" she screamed, bouncing against the grass as Clay bucked and growled.

Nick steadied himself above them, holding the metal jar in one hand and the lid in the other like he was ready to clang them together as cymbals. Luisa held Clay down by the shoulders, while Velvet tried to wrangle the thing's snakelike tail. Whatever evil had turned Clay into this monster, she couldn't imagine.

"Dude!" she shouted at Nick. "Before we all catch the banshee virus or something!"

Nick scooped the end of Clay's tail up, Bonesaw's arm falling away and Nick's own ethereal hand gripping the squiggly thing tightly. Velvet threw herself back onto her haunches and helped Luisa and Logan cram the banshee into the urn, scooping and shaking off the slithering tentacles, even as they slapped around their faces, their torsos. Clay's head was the last to go, and he let out a long growling roar as Nick clamped the lid down tight and gave it a quick screw to lock him in good. After setting the urn down on the back steps, Nick took off Bonesaw's body like a jumpsuit. It crumpled around his ankles in a wet heap.

"Ew." Nick shuddered and rubbed at his arms. "Was that as creepy as I thought it was?"

"Yeah. Worse." Velvet glanced toward Luisa, who lay on her back, stomach rising and falling rapidly. Exhaustion.

Logan stood in the distance, stunned. "Man," he said. "I'm glad that's over."

Behind him the lady detective stood up and brushed the grass from her pants, shaking her head like she'd just seen a ghost—and, of course, she probably had (or at least, felt it). A ruckus like every tool in the shed had fallen to the ground at once preceded the young officer's appearance in the doorframe. Velvet heard the screen door of the kitchen bang open.

They turned just in time to see the very dead sheriff, eyes glowing like candles, unscrewing the cap from the urn.

"No!" Nick screamed, arms stretching toward it.

"Grab him!"

But it was too late. The banshee flooded from the container like a genie, stretching out to its full length. Aloysius Clay towered above them. Hell, towered over the roof of the farmhouse, pole-thin and laughing riotously.

"How long have we known each other, Velvet? You ought to know that I'm a little smarter than to be trapped by a move like that. I knew you didn't have the wits to take me on. I'm just happy to have such a fine, familiar place to start my rule." The head of the thing surveyed the view. "New Brompfel Heights. Lovely. Where did you say your family lives, Velvet?"

The words came at her like a slap to the face, and before she even realized what she was doing, she was on Clay. She slashed at him with her fingernails, kicked at the base of his stocky trunk, but he didn't waver. He didn't move in the slightest.

"Poor Velvet," he said. "Whatever will you do now? Join us, I suspect."

"Never!" she screamed.

"I was afraid of that." The banshee almost sounded disappointed, until the mad giggling began. "She won't join us, friends."

Velvet dropped to the ground and saw four of the dead and injured cops shuffling across the grass toward them, each carrying a different vessel, a coffee can, a flour canister, a tin first aid kit, and a rusty toolbox.

"No," she gasped.

Luisa and Logan gathered in close beside her. She jerked

her head toward Nick, in time to see him pulling Bonesaw's body back on like a jumpsuit and rushing to the silver mini-van. He climbed onto the back bumper and heaved himself on top.

"Now what's he up to?" Clay muttered.

Velvet didn't have a clue, but he'd slowed the cops from bearing down on them with their little makeshift ghost pris-ons, so she didn't care. All she could think was *GO NICK!*

He struggled to right himself on the roof, a little wobbly in Bonesaw's bloodless corpse, but defiant nonetheless. Nick spread out his arms and closed his eyes tightly as though in deep concentration. Velvet swiveled to see Clay intently glowering at the event transpiring before him, assessing. He didn't utter a word, until . . .

Bonesaw's body began to bloat; his skin bubbled into wet blisters and a weird buzzing cut through the night. A mo-ment later, Velvet watched as her killer's body split nearly in two and exploded outward, filling the sky with the largest swarm of flies Velvet had ever seen.

"Holy shit!" Logan yelled.

Luisa heaved with laughter.

Velvet smiled, sat back, and watched her killer disappear into a spray of blood and bone that basted the minivan red.

It looked like freedom.

It felt like it, too.

Clay screamed as the flies came at him. Millions of them gnashed and ground the top part of the towering evil spirit into tiny travel-sized pieces. It was loud. Electric. A cacoph-ony of crackling, buzzing, humming. Velvet was reminded of the power company substation near her elementary school, that low monotonous hum.

But then the banshee's tail whipped toward her, mingling with her form in the ether, and the flies descended, eating their way toward her. She could hear Luisa and Logan screaming, and in the distance, a heartbreaking sob from Nick before the flies covered her.

Chapter 26

Velvet thrashed amid the swarm, slapping and swatting, each assault as futile and ineffective as throwing punches in a pool of molasses. The insects clung to her like spandex, everywhere, so tight that she couldn't tell where their tiny bodies began and she ended. She tried to tell herself they weren't hurting her, they were just doing their job, serving their purpose, but if nothing else, they were buzzing her to death.

The sound was deafening.

As if that weren't bad enough, the grinding whir of wings beat vile rhythms against her flesh. Tickling. Tormenting. Her internal organs rattled inside her, and she flew into another panic as she remembered how they'd flooded into her.

Chewing. Twisting. Tapping their pointy legs against her insides.

It occurred to her that they *were* inside her still, bloating her abdomen, pushing, looking for exits.

Looking for her mouth.

She screamed, and her eyes snapped open as a thousand little nightmares erupted from her throat, blasting past her lips into the darkness around her. A few lingered on her lips pecking horrific kisses, driving her to the brink of madness.

Velvet choked and clawed at her throat. Sputtering to expel the remaining bugs from her mouth, she plucked a stubborn one from the tip of her tongue like a hair and shuddered.

For a moment she thought she'd lose consciousness, but something in her distant vision caught her attention.

Velvet thought she was seeing fireflies flitting about, tiny orbs of light dancing on the horizon, but then she realized she was witnessing the violent whipping of gaslight globes on their quaking, writhing hoses.

They were in purgatory.

She felt the gravity next, the pull of the floor. She was on the ceiling. Twisting, Velvet saw Clay bucking out of a mountain of flies as though being born. His internal glow flickered throughout his naked chest with each convulsion.

It all came back to her in a rush of images.

The bastard had wrapped himself around her when Nick's flies had descended. Quick thinking on his part. Her heart sank, imagining the boy watching her being eaten along with the monster Clay had become.

Clay.

"Clay!" she yelled, and lunged toward him, her hands curling into claws. But as much as she stretched, she couldn't pull free from the anchor of flies festering about her waist.

Aloysius didn't respond, but a smile spread across his face as he contorted and slithered and, finally, broke free from the dark brood, dropping like a lead weight past the dim lights and out of sight somewhere in the dark depths beneath her.

"Dammit!" she cried out, and struggled all the more ferociously. Swatting at the flies, she was able to expose her hips and the top of her legs, but the more she looked at the point where her knees disappeared in the glossy insectile mass, the more frightened she became. The bugs weren't holding her back, imprisoning her on the ceiling like one of those dangling glue strips.

They were stitching her back together!

With each rub of their tiny legs, more of her body appeared. It looked like they were secreting her flesh in little globs from their mouths and then spreading it around, solidifying it. Puked out of an insect's guts! She felt her stomach heaving, bile rising in the back of her throat.

"Don't look. Don't look. Don't look," Velvet repeated to herself, swallowing back her disgust.

She flopped away from the horror and hung limply, focusing back at the floor, trying to key in on Clay. The more she squinted, the more she became aware of the room. Light glinted off metal, and a few phosphorous streaks scurried about. If she listened really hard, she could just make out a familiar sinister hiss.

Of course, she thought. The maze of prison cells that made up the Cellar. And if the flies hadn't abandoned their jobs like the rest of purgatory, then Clay had fallen straight into a holding cell.

"I'm coming for you, Clay!" she screamed. "You won't get far!"

The second after the feeling came back to her feet and she was able to wiggle her toes, Velvet was falling.

Plummeting.

The air whistled past as she sliced through the inky darkness. She felt a few flies still working at her feet. It tickled, but she didn't dare look for fear that they'd fly away and leave her with a pair of stubs where toes should be. She figured it was best to just trust them. Don't think too much. And don't scream.

Well, not again.

The swaying lights below grew brighter. Her insides tumbled. She wondered how long she would fall, if it would hurt horribly when she hit, and if she would be so lucky as to land on Clay, like Dorothy's house on the wicked witch, and smash his ass flat.

She wondered how she had so much time to wonder.

Her speculation was cut short by an excruciating impact with something super hard and metallic. Pain ripped through her and she bounced a bit, airborne, before slamming back against it, sliding down sideways, and skidding on her butt across the gravelly floor of the Cellar. Velvet came to an abrupt stop against a wall of cell bars, the wind bellowing from her lungs along with some white squiggly memories.

They flopped on the still-shaking floor like worms, before dimming out and turning to ash.

Across from her, the holding cell was in shambles. The iron bars had toppled over into an impossibly twisted rib cage. That she'd landed at an angle and not impaled herself on one of the jutting rods like a piece of meat on a fork was a miracle. The cell itself was empty, except for the hissing column of light emanating from the gaslight swaying above.

Empty.

Like, with no Clay in it.

"Dammit!"

Velvet tried to scramble to her feet, but ended up kicking at the gravel ineffectually and plopping back down on her ass. She'd just found her footing and was pushing upward on the bars behind her when a whisper blew past her left ear.

Hissssss.

She gasped as a pair of claws clamped around her arms and pulled her roughly back against the cell behind her.

"Who's got who?" The raspy voice curled its way into her ear like a tongue. "I've got her, Aloysius!"

The soft *shurr*ing of shuffling feet announced Clay's approach. Grit and gravel popped, and the dim glow of soul flesh hung in the air, fox fire. Clay was coming for her, and this time he had no need of a body to hide inside.

"Come to turn yourself in, Clay?" Velvet struggled against her captor, clawing at his talonlike fingers as she watched the aura in the darkness become more solid.

Clay's bare feet smoldered in the cracks of a dusty coat-

434

ing. The monster had found some clothing. A torn shirt and pants, but no glasses, no charade that he was her old friend, Mr. Fassbinder.

That was over.

His smile was brilliant and easy. It turned her stomach and made her fight all the more against the damnable prisoner behind her, pinning her to his own cell.

"Now, Velvet, that's no way to act. Pierre there has had a very rough day. All his compatriots have abandoned him and taken their rightful places in the daylight. How would you feel? Trapped in this pit? Oh, wait. But you *are* trapped and you just don't know it yet."

"What is that supposed to mean?" she spat.

"Feisty," Pierre quipped.

"Isn't she?" Clay held out his hand and stopped when she flinched, only to go ahead and brush her cheek. "I have a special place in my heart for our Velvet. We're quite good friends. Did you know that, Pierre?"

The other soul grunted.

Velvet jerked away from Clay's touch, repulsed. "How dare you touch me, after what you've done?"

"And what exactly do you think I've done?"

"I think you've been possessing a lonely butcher and making him kill girls!"

Clay sputtered with laughter. "No. No. Velvet, you're too smart for that. Don't get stuck in some easy theory that can be explained away by simple psychosis."

She shot a glower of hatred in his direction. "Then why don't you explain it? I think you owe me that much."

"Owe you?" His voice turned shrill. "Well, maybe just a taste."

He paced as he delivered his speech—one, Velvet suspected, he'd been practicing for a long time.

"I learned about Bonesaw from you, not the other way around. I never possessed him, nor watched any of the filthy things he did to his victims. To lump my work in with his, well, that just makes me sad. I'd hoped you'd think more highly of me."

Velvet sneered. "That's a laugh. And even if it is true, you've still destroyed the Latin Quarter, ensnared hundreds of people through possession. That's unconscionable!"

"And one hundred percent justified."

Rocks scattered in the distance, drawing all of their attention to a shaft of light slanting into the Cellar from above.

"Velvet!" Manny's voice echoed across the cavern a moment before an explosion tore through the grid of rubber hoses above them, striping the darkness with flame and blasting the gloom away. The sound stole Pierre's attention just enough for Velvet to wriggle free of his grimy clutches. His clawed fingers whistled through the air behind her.

The station agent scrambled down the broken shambles of the Cellar stairs, Rancho in tow, their feet clouded in dust and an avalanche of shattered stone.

Velvet allowed herself the briefest smile and was about to respond to Manny, when Clay leapt the gap between them, a blur in the air that slammed into her like a bag of bricks. She dropped flat onto her back. Before she had time to react, he wrapped his thick hand across her mouth.

He slid in close to her face, his body heavy against her naked vulnerability. Clay's lips threatened to press hers, and whispered, "You want so desperately to know what happened to me, don't you? What could turn a perfectly reasonable Salvage man into someone like me? Well." He glowered in Manny's direction. "Your answer is rummaging her way toward us. Ask *her* why some people seem to never dim. Even though they progress and change and could not possibly have anything remaining to learn."

Velvet was stunned by the implication.

Manny wouldn't hold someone back from moving on. Would she? It was a trick. Another ruse. How could Velvet believe a murderer? He was probably lying about possessing Bonesaw.

Lying like they were, Clay's hand on her mouth, his body against hers, Velvet was taken back to a memory. Thrust back into the shed, back into her body, still warm and scared. Back to Bonesaw's knives and his need.

"Love me?" Bonesaw pleaded, his waxy lips parted pitifully even as his knife slipped into the flesh of her leg, stabbing between muscle and bone. Velvet screamed into the oily rag in her mouth, the sound coming out less like a cry for help than a goose honking.

The killer backed away and looked down at her in genuine alarm. He reached out and tore the dirty cloth from her mouth.

"Please!" she panted. "Please don't. You don't have to."

He nodded his head hopefully. "You love me?"

Velvet thought she could do it, thought she could play his game, pretend for him. Days of starvation and torture had weakened her spirit, her will to survive, but not her spine.

"Not fucking likely!" she yelled, then spat at him.

Bonesaw quivered, and his expression changed to the one you get when you've just bitten into something rotten. His eyes closed solemnly and he nodded, as though responding to some silent question. Then he drove his knife into Velvet's chest and held it there.

It felt like he'd only punched her. She was numb and in shock, she guessed. Velvet glanced down at the handle protruding from her dirty shirt like a key in a lock. Bonesaw cocked his head and grinned.

Then twisted it.

A floodgate of pain tore open, and Velvet felt her body seizing, even as she was already outside of it, standing beside her killer, screaming obscenities and crying out for her body to stop spasming and jerking in the old-fashioned school chair. An inky puddle blossomed in the dust at her body's feet.

Too much.

Velvet slammed back into her present.

The memory exploded.

She was back in the Cellar and Clay was still muffling her, but pulled his hand away as Velvet heaved the first wave of squiggly glowing nerve endings against his palm. He glowered at the mess and looked back at her with disgust just in time for the second stream of puke to splatter his face. He gagged, sputtering the nerves from his open mouth. He recoiled and spat.

Velvet knew an opportunity when she saw one.

She angled her body just slightly and brought her knee up with the full force of her hate into Aloysius Clay's crotch. When it connected, the man howled, grabbed for his junk, and fell over on his side, moaning. Behind them, Pierre mimicked his master's pain with an empathetic groan.

Just then a loud commotion, shoe leather pounding gravel, scraped from nearby.

Rounding the corner of the broken cages, Manny screamed, "Velvet! Catch!" and launched a glimmering object into the air, a tail of ribbon streaming behind it.

Her interrogation key!

Velvet vaulted and snatched it out of the air, twisting as she landed in a feral crouch before Clay. She wasn't sure if the key could do more than simply incapacitate. She'd never used it that way, but on occasion, with the nastier convicts, she'd certainly had the urge.

After everything he'd done, if Clay truly believed he was being held back from dimming, she planned to help him out with that . . . a lot.

He pushed himself up to a seated position, back against the cell bars, his boy Pierre helping to steady him, pulling at his clothes.

"That's good," Velvet growled. "Hold him just like that."

Clay's eyes goggled, and his mouth dropped open as she lunged at him, stepping on his knee to get some height, and then slashing at him in a wide arc. Velvet kicked off the bars, spun, and landed a few feet away. White squiggles gleamed and dripped from the teeth of the key. She snapped her head back in the killer's direction to see him fumbling with his jaw. The flesh and muscle that kept it in place were severed clean. It flopped open like a Pez dispenser and rested on his chest. Clay's tongue twitched as he gurgled and mewled and glowered.

His eyes burned with hatred.

"It's not enough, is it, Clay? You'll find your way out of here and become their leader again, won't you? That's what they're expecting."

He cocked his head to the side, memories slipping from the wound into his tousled dark locks.

"Well, it's not going to happen. They'll have to find a new leader. You're otherwise engaged."

"Fuck you," Clay garbled.

Velvet screamed and stabbed the key into the soul's gaping maw. She worked at the back of his throat, sawing at his tongue until the hateful protuberance broke free in her fist.

She held it in front of his blinking eyes, a quickly dimming slug filleted over her palm, its pale white guts draining down her wrist in slithering wet streaks.

"You'll never utter another vile word, Clay. Your lies can rot in that insane head of yours."

Velvet tossed the tongue onto the man's lap and watched as he fumbled with it, tried futilely to put it back into his mouth, and finally went slack, his memories slithering out of his torn jaw in a plume of sparks.

He fell over on his side and seized. A blinding flash pulsed from the gaping hole of his jaw and spread beneath his flesh like oxygen feeding a fire, consuming him from the inside. His skin turned as black as creosote and he stilled suddenly.

Gone. Dimmed to hell, she hoped.

Behind him in the cage, his minion wept quietly.

Velvet crouched next to Clay's burned form and clutched a handful of the graying ashes, held them up to her lips, and blew them into the cell. She wiped the rest off on the cold Cellar ground.

She didn't want his ashes on her.

He didn't deserve that.

Manny approached with a robe and wrapped it around Velvet's shoulders. Velvet suddenly felt faint, as though the weight of the situation had finally occurred to her. The Latin Quarter was all but empty, the world as they knew it had changed in an instant, and for the first time, she'd been unable to control herself, as though she'd been on autopilot.

The violence had poured out of her, unbridled.

She glanced over Manny's shoulder and winced as she saw Nick in the distance. He wore a look of stunned horror that made her heart ache. Logan and Luisa flanked him, heads cocked, trying to figure out what they'd just witnessed.

They would all see her differently now that the violence was out on display.

That was probably for the best.

"Is it true?" Velvet stared into Manny's eyes.

"Is what true?" Manny stared back, her gaze steelier than Velvet had ever seen.

"Clay told me something . . . ," she began.

"Clay's gone. Nothing else matters."

"But . . ."

"Nothing. Else. Matters." Manny turned and disappeared into the depths of the Cellar.

Chapter 27

Velvet's team followed her out of the Cellar, chattering away eagerly.

"Oh, man," Nick said, covering his mouth as though he'd be sick. "That was harsh."

Luisa was stony-faced. Logan grinned wickedly.

"That was some ninja shit, Velvet." Logan threw some fake gang sign. "Respect."

The station was quiet and still. A handful of souls wandered amid the fallen glass and shattered columns; the walls were a web of cracks, as though silvered ivy had taken over and spread in their absence.

Velvet turned to Nick, held her hand out, and laced her fingers in his. "The crystal balls?" she asked.

"Shattered. All nine of them," he answered. "The Departurists made the mistake of being too curious. They carried them right to us when they came looking for Clay. *Bam!*" He slammed his fist into his other palm, but when he glanced back at her, his eyes squinted with something.

Sympathy, Velvet thought. She didn't want that.

"That's good. The souls are free." Were probably passing through the primary crack right then.

A calm washed over her as they passed through the wrought-iron gates into the Shattered Hall, and then after a few missteps found the crack that led them to the alley next to the Paper Aviary. She spilled through first and searched the shredded clothing for the keys she'd collected from Manny's desk and Miss Antonia.

Still there.

Nick brought her a long wool jacket. She didn't think to ask where he'd found it and didn't think she wanted to know, considering how close they were to the Paper Aviary. They wandered in silence back to the Retrieval dormitory. Kipper and Isadora stood at the door, as though guarding their home, their faces even more ashen than normal, devastated, broken. Kipper reached out and touched Velvet's arm.

"You stopped it," he said.

She shook her head. "Maybe. But there's a lot of work to be done."

"I'm sorry," Isadora mumbled as Velvet passed by.

Velvet turned and nodded politely at the girl, but said nothing. Isadora nodded in return.

The courtyard was in the same shambles they'd left it in, but the residents were busy cleaning, righting tables and chairs and sweeping up debris and ash. When they saw the team enter, they applauded meekly. Some cried.

"What now?" they asked.

"We pull our shit together and start planning," Velvet said.

"Yeah!" Kipper shouted as sternly as Miss Antonia ever had. "Starting with getting this place back to normal. Salon isn't going to happen until this place is spotless. Get to work!"

Several of the kids grinned, some grimaced, but everyone obeyed.

Velvet smiled at the boy and nodded. "Yeah. That's what this place needs. Normalcy. Kick 'em in the balls, Kipper!"

"Done!"

Nick wrapped his arms around her waist and nuzzled his cheek against hers. "You okay?"

"Yeah, just give me a second. I need to figure something out."

Velvet swept past the spot where she'd last seen Miss Antonia, up the stairs to the second floor, and into the Salvage mother's cell. Her movements were automatic; she knew what she was looking for. Velvet pulled out the stool and climbed atop it, reaching for the tiny black box where Miss Antonia had hidden it.

She held it in her palm for a moment and then slipped the first key inside the little metal opening. The hinge opened and a tiny origami bird fell out onto the floor.

She wasn't surprised. She wished she were.

Miss Antonia had been coming from a visit with Aloysius

Clay on that night they'd run into each other on the streets. She'd never lost contact with him. Velvet couldn't prove it, but she wanted to believe Miss Antonia was trying to talk the man out of his evil plan.

Only one person would know that for sure.

Velvet held out the other key in her palm and clamped her fist around it. She slipped it into her pocket and turned back toward the open door. Nick stood there, leaning as casually as ever, a half smile on his face, eyes sparkling like stars.

Manny would need to be confronted, but that was a discussion for another time.

"Sooooo," Nick said, scratching his head adorably. "Can we date now, or is it still against the rules?"

"I wouldn't call it dating." She shrugged as she circled him and passed into the hall.

"Would you say . . ." He cocked his head. "It's complicated?"

"There's no Facebook in purgatory."

Nick slapped his forehead. "Another thing! Jesus."

Velvet started up the stairs. "Let's say we're connected, in some strange way."

"By a twist of fate?"

"Sure."

"Say it, then." Nick jogged up the steps after her, catching her at the landing.

"Say what?"

"That you're my girl."

Velvet rolled her eyes and reached for the boy's hand, pulled him to her roughly, and caught his lips with hers.

The truth was, Velvet didn't know where she and Nick were going, whether they'd be together forever or a minute. All she knew was that if he stopped kissing her, pulled away, and tried to talk about their relationship or his feelings or something, she'd kill him.

ACKNOWLEDGMENTS

About five years ago, I asked my goddaughter, Delaney Hills, to read a middle-grade novella I'd written called *The Trouble with the Living*, about a spunky—but ultimately doomed—twelve-year-old detective named Luisa Albuquerque and a serial killer called the Green Man. The feedback she gave me was incredibly valuable; it boiled down to the fact that the story was too morbid for the age group. So I put the idea to bed and wrote really morbid stuff for adults for a few years.

But the idea of kids in purgatory clawed at the back of my skull, so, with the help of my always supportive wife, Caroline Henry, my critique group, the South Sound Algonquins, and amazingly talented author Tiffany Trent, I pieced together an even more morbid tale, which became *Velveteen*!

Thankfully, I have an agent, Jim McCarthy of Dystel and Goderich, who gets my weird brain and knew other folks who would as well. Namely, Krista Marino, my awesome editrix at Delacorte Press, who whipped my story into shape like I never believed was possible. A huge thanks to the cover-art ninjas who brought Velvet to grim life on the jacket, too!

Because a book doesn't sell itself, I'm so glad I've got a network of folks pulling for me, one that includes such intriguing and luminary groups as the Apocalypsies, the Harbingers of Doom, the Class of 2k12, the YA Rebels, and the League of Reluctant Adults. Looking at my choice of blogging partners, I am not surprised that people accuse me of being a supervillain.

Muahahaha!

Finally, I would be remiss not to tip my hat to the people who really have to put up with my fits and tangents while I'm writing a book: my friends and family. Caroline, of course, continues to be my reality check; my mother, Edna Henry, always has a book in her hand; the Friday-night dinner folks still hang out despite my moods; and my local writer friends (Synde, Amy, Richelle, to name a few) are always up for some commiseration. Thanks, guys.

And last but certainly not least, to all the online book geeks (booktubers, tweeps, and bloggers), my sincere gratitude, as always, for your support and encouragement!

Until next time . . .

ABOUT THE AUTHOR

When Daniel Marks isn't writing, he's vlogging his butt off at the YA Rebels and on his personal channel. He blogs regularly at the Class of 2k12, the Apocalypsies, and the League of Reluctant Adults, which he cofounded. Because he has no control over his incessant rambling, Daniel is forced to provide workshops on writing and social networking to scratch that itch. He's been unlucky enough to witness and survive a number of natural disasters and was a psychotherapist for twelve years (an entirely different kind of disaster). He lives in the Seattle area with his wife, Caroline, and three furry monsters with no regard for quality carpeting. None.